GOOD KING hARRY

GOOD KING HARRY

Denise Giardina

1817
HARPER & ROW, PUBLISHERS, New York

Cambridge, Philadelphia, San Francisco, London

Mexico City, São Paulo, Sydney

FIRST EDITION

Designer: C. Linda Dingler

Library of Congress Cataloging in Publication Data
Giardina, Denise, date
    Good King Harry.

    1. Henry V, King of England, 1387-1422—Fiction.
I. Title.
PS3557.I136G6 1984   813'.54   83-48813
ISBN 0-06-015277-X

84 85 86 87 88 10 9 8 7 6 5 4 3 2 1

For my mother and father,
and for Jim and Judy Lewis

PROLOGUE

I detest coronations. England has seen two such spectacles in my lifetime, and it has been my misfortune to attend both. The first was my father's, the second my own. Soon the crown shall be set upon the head of my young son. One compensation of my present condition is that I shall not have to suffer through it.

Coronations are especially fit subjects for deathbed musings. So pompous they are, so full of the pride of man's striving. Oh, they bespeak humility. The King is stripped of his clothing and entreated to selflessly serve God and his people. He bends his knee and pledges that this he shall do. Then he is weighted down with crown and scepter and sword; he is feted and serenaded and thrown to the wolves. It is needful, I suppose, for men to cloak the machinations and corruptions of their governing with ceremony. So it is that the poor victim of coronations, the King, must be miraculously transformed from frail man to God's chosen. The King receives upon his person the sacred oil and so is holy. The King is the father of his people. The King is God's servant, to work His will in the world. The King is England. Here then lies God's servant with the blood of thousands upon his hands. Here lies England, emaciated and staining his bedclothes with the foulness of the bloody flux.

My feverish mind skips like a startled hind at the hunt. Sleep brings no

1

respite, for my dreams are evil. Satan comes to me then (I know it is he, for his aspect is horrible) and points his finger. The dead flank him on either side and call mockingly to me. The dead I know well.

It is no surprise that I have been brought to such a sorry state, for it is the lot of kings. We are akin to Judas, who betrayed Our Lord. Someone had to do it, after all, just as someone must rule. Of course, our guilt is not lessened because we are so trapped. As Richard once told me, "Kings can choose other than to sin. They can choose death instead."

Richard, too, was a king. He was locked in the gilded cage and driven near madness. Many a time I saw him clutch his head and scream in rage at those who sought to serve him. He was very different from me, Richard, but still he was a king. He died young, as I do. He died in agony, no doubt, as I do. He brought about the deaths of others, as I have, though not so many. (I wonder if it matters, the number of dead?) What could we do, Richard and I? Two different roads we traveled, yet both proved disastrous. Why does God give His people governors at all, to stumble around searching for the right on behalf of others? Why not make each man a petty king in his own cage, and let each one play at being wise and just?

They prey over me like carrion: my advisers. My clerks. They live in fear of the impending death of the King. Oh, they care not for me, Harry, who faces the finger of Satan. Their care is for their positions. "Whose power shall be greatest when he is dead? Whose favor must I curry now?" So it was at my father's deathbed, when some of his attendants went at hazard over the hour of his passing. He was a great fool, my father, for he sought the crown when it was not his. Often did I curse him for it, but in the last year of his life I softened toward him. He had ordered Richard's death to protect the throne he usurped, and he suffered the punishment of God for it. I daresay he too dreamed of pointing fingers.

It is quieter now. Attendants and priests all have left me. I told them I would try to sleep, but it is only that I wish to be alone with my thoughts. I cannot long bear their solicitous questions, their pointless chatter. Our souls should pass from this world to the next in silence, as did Merryn's. A person dies only once, and nothing can be learned from the experience if there is constant clamor. But I am a king with affairs of state to conduct. I must plead drowsiness to be alone, to become acquainted with that death which is consummating its union with my body. It is amusingly like my wedding night to Katherine, when, it seemed, as the court fool said, "all present wished to know when England conquered France." We heard them roistering without our chamber door for hours.

Now, though, I have a precious time of solitude. It is late afternoon of

an August day, and the sun slanting through the slit of a window stamps a
golden rectangle upon my white bedclothes. I lie within the castle of Vincennes, east of Paris, but because I cannot see outside the window it is easy
to pretend that it is Welsh sun, Monmouth sun, which warms me. Could I
but raise my head, I would find the valley of the Monnow spreading greenly
before me, and the slow-flowing Wye in the distance. Ever have I cherished
Monmouth above any other place. Monmouth, the home of my childhood,
the place of gentle hills and green rivers. Monmouth, where I gave and
received love. Yet I have thought little enough of Monmouth these past
years, nor have I been there since I was crowned king. Once I took a vow
that I would never return to Monmouth, and even in death I shall lie at
Westminster.

As a child I left Monmouth only to visit my grandfather, old John of
Gaunt, at his stronghold of Kenilworth. My grandfather was the Duke of
Lancaster, adviser to the young King Richard and the most powerful man in
England, passing even the King, some said. I worshiped him, and likewise
he made a favorite of me, for he knew I was ill used by my father. Each year I
wintered with him, glad of his company, but just as glad to return to my
Monmouth hills. There, with my younger brothers, I ran wild and free. My
mother, Mary de Bohun, had died young upon the birth of my sister Philippa. My father, Henry Bolingbroke, was usually absent on some knightly
jaunt, searching for a war to hire himself to or, at the very least, a tournament where he might break a lance with the great champions of the continent. Father's exploits were widely sung across England, and he was
deemed a paragon of chivalry, a chevalier on the order of Lancelot. This was
foolishness, of course. In reality he hacked his way through brutal and
pointless battles in Lithuania and the Hanse so that he might return to
England laden with booty. Yet my father was a great believer in chivalry and
all its trappings. He detested King Richard, as did most of the nobility,
because Richard could come up with no war to engage his talents. Father
must take himself off to fight in Prussia and Estonia and God knows where
else. His lengthy absences were no source of sorrow to me, for he made my
life miserable with his presence.

I was quite sickly as a babe. I am told my father prayed for my death
because his second son, Tom, born a year later, was strong and healthy and
therefore a more fit heir for the future Duke of Lancaster. Contrary as
always, I refused to honor my father's prayerful entreaty and miraculously
survived three harrowing years of infant illnesses. I proved a continual thorn
in my father's flesh throughout my childhood, because I could never be as he
wished. His favorite insult was to name me "fit only for monks." I know now
this should have been taken as a compliment, but then it devastated me, as I
longed for his approval. Be that as it may, I saw little enough of him. My

brothers and I were entrusted to my grandfather in his absence. My grand-father, in turn, being much engaged at court, gave us over to a Welsh woman, Joan Waryn, and a bevy of tutors for raising.

As I grew older, provision was made for my training in the knightly arts of killing. I spent long hours with my grandfather's squires at the quintain, and I practiced the intricacies of swordplay. But when all this was done, I was Joan's. Joan Waryn was eighteen when I was born, a strapping woman with round pink cheeks and forearms like hams. She was wet nurse to all the children of Lancaster, and she was father and mother as well. Full-blooded Welsh she was, and as common as the good earth. Her low degree did not keep her from speaking her mind, and I have seen her put even my father to rout.

Joan did not forbid us the run of the village of Monmouth. My brothers and I frolicked with the sons of carpenters and cobblers, wild as bucks, in the summer tanned brown as chestnuts. We swam naked in the Wye, caught salmon with our hands, stole hot buns from stalls on market day. Of these escapades my father knew nothing for many years. My grandfather knew, for we spoke fondly of Monmouth on winter nights at Kenilworth. Grandfather did not neglect our education, for we were proficient in Latin and French and studied logic, history, and music. I daresay no children in England were so well versed in the ancient philosophers or the holy fathers of the Church as were we. But Grandfather was fond of saying there was more to learning than books, and more to ruling than knowing how to swing a sword.

"You shall learn as much of the world from the rude fellows of Mon-mouth as from Aristotle," he once said. John of Gaunt was the wisest man in England.

Grandfather was a great admirer of the common folk of the realm, deeming them greater of heart than those of higher rank. He came hard by this estimation, for time was when none was better hated by the yeomanry than he. Early in Richard's reign, when the King was but a boy, Grandfather had been Regent of England. It was a time of poor harvests and of turmoil, for the gentry were wont to turn out tenants from unprofitable land and set them wandering upon the high ways. John of Gaunt, being most visible of all the great men, was as well the most blamed. He further kindled their anger by imposing a stiff new poll tax, an act he ever after called the most foolish of his life. It took him not long to realize his folly and he quickly revoked the tax, but the fury of the people did not abate. The poor men of Kent rose under Wat Tyler and rampaged through London, where they beheaded the Archbishop of Canterbury and several other men of property. My grand-father and my father barely escaped to the north of England with their lives, and their grand palace of the Savoy was sacked and burned.

To his credit, Grandfather learned much from his errors, unlike many others of his station who were stiffened in their arrogance. He took note of the suffering of the people and went to great pains to deal justly with them. What wisdom he had gained he sought to pass on to me.

"These Welsh fellows of yours," he asked one day as we sat before the chessboard, "this Davy and Gwyllym and, oh, the other one—"

"Rhys."

"Aye, of course, Rhys. What have they been up to this year past?"

"We have built our own castle, Grandfather, on the brow of a hill above the Monnow, and we carry out sieges. Davy, Gwyllym, and John hold the castle, and Tom, Rhys, and I try to take them."

"Who are the captains of these splendid armies?"

"John commands the castle and I the siege. Rhys is my second-in-command."

"What, Rhys?" Grandfather feigned shock. "You give preference to the son of a herd over your brother of Lancaster?"

"But, my lord, he is more useful than Tom," I protested. "Tom is the strongest, it is true, and fierce for a fight, but Rhys has more cunning. Tom insists upon running straight at the castle even when the defenders hurl stones, and when they strike him upon the head, he stamps off all bloodied and angry. Rhys listens when I plot out tricks to take the castle."

Grandfather threw back his head and laughed. "Not only are you sly as Old Renard, Harry Monmouth, but you sound a regular John Ball," he said.

"Who is John Ball?"

"John Ball was a leader during Wat Tyler's revolt. The Mad Priest of Kent they named him, for he was a clerk. He preached to the mob at Blackheath before they pillaged London. His favorite saying was, 'When Adam delved and Eve span, who was then a gentleman?'"

I pondered this. "Who was, then?"

"None, John Ball would say."

I thought again. "Why, so then should I. It is but sensible, is it not, to think that we have made everything up as we went along?"

He raised his eyebrows. "Has not God set some to rule and others not?" he asked.

"Sure I am that God must ordain what is to be," I answered cautiously. "Yet do we not ever sin? Could it be that God has meant one thing and we have done another? It seems to me a sin to scorn Rhys for his birth alone."

"If birth be not reckoned with," he pressed me, "then why do you, a scion of Lancaster, lead the sieges of your Monnow castle?"

"It is not because of my birth. It is that they do as I say."

Old John of Gaunt roared at that. "A born leader are you, Harry? It is an arrogant rascal you are!"

I flushed hot, for I knew not how to take his words. Seeing my confusion, he tousled my dark brown hair and smiled.

"'Tis a leader you are," he said gently, "though your father will not see it. You are a sharp, gallant fellow, Harry Monmouth. I wager you shall be the best of us all."

"No, Grandfather," I said, "never better than John of Gaunt."

"Aye, better. But mind your tongue, boy. Your opinion of John Ball would be ill received by your peers. Society is well ordered, mind you, that turmoils and unbridled license may be held in check. Each man has his purpose, and each purpose is to be honored. Still, never hesitate to receive good service, from whichever quarter it may come."

Much good have I cast from my life, yet I have ever tried to live by these words of my grandfather. I profited not only from this advice but from the company he kept. His closest friend was a man of no title, the poet Geoffrey Chaucer. This Geoffrey came often to Kenilworth to recite his poems and discourse with Grandfather. Many a late night I nodded off to sleep before the hearth with the lilt of the English tongue for lullaby. And following the death of his first wife, my grandmother Blanche, John of Gaunt had fallen in love with the poet's sister-in-law, Katharine Swynford. Because Grandfather was a king's son, his second marriage was one of convenience, to a Castilian princess. But for twenty-five years his mistress, Katharine, was his true love, wife of his heart, and upon the death of the princess, Grandfather married Katharine, though her station was much below his. My father, the knightly champion of privilege, was appalled, but not I, for I loved Katharine, and that was enough.

Those days at Monmouth and Kenilworth run together now in my memory. Few details can I conjure, only a blur of contentment, save for my father's rare visits and a fever at age eight which near killed me. Those clear moments I can recapture are homely ones. The hearth at Kenilworth I can see, its flames populated by dragons and fairies which only a childish mind could fathom. My grandfather and his Katharine glide by as the minstrels play, dancing like young lovers while the torchlight glints upon their gray heads. Now again I am running like a deer through the green, green vales of Monmouth, or plunging wide-eyed into the waters of the Wye. There is Rhys, he of the wild red hair, bloodying the lip of a boy twice his size who dared suggest I was not true Welsh. And Joan, who clasps me tight to her ample bosom and fills my head with mystical tales of Arthur and Merlyn, of Madoc, and of the great kings Rhodri Mawr and Hywel Dda.

This was my world, secure and pierced with wonders. There is a gift of magic vision which children possess, and which we lose forever to age. When we are children, we think the gift to be eternal, and that manhood shall never come. Someday, I supposed, I would be Duke of Lancaster. But first John of Gaunt must die, and then my father, and how was such a thing possible?

Yet within the bounds of a year all was lost—my grandfather, my Monmouth, my childish fancies. On the eleventh anniversary of my birth, in 1398, my father of Bolingbroke was banished the realm as a traitor. By the next September he was preparing for his coronation as King of England, and I was heir to the throne. Had I now one wish, it would be to turn again to that year when all came apart and to become someone else, to view the treason of Bolingbroke and the fall of King Richard as an ostler or a fletcher. I would wager tuppence upon Bolingbroke's chances of holding the throne, and that alone would be my stake.

I

1398-1400

There is good men porn at Monmouth.

—*Henry V*, act IV, scene vii

1

I had been nine years in this world when my father put an end to his knightly ramblings. He was weary of the windswept plains of the east, so he told John of Gaunt, and longed for his green and pleasant England. He would tend for a while his own lands, perhaps marry again and father more sons.

"More sons?" John of Gaunt had chided. "The four you have are strangers to you."

Bolingbroke pledged it would no longer be so and rode to us at Monmouth with all his household. For a time my brothers and I took great pleasure from his visit. He was a gallant and exotic figure to us, with his splendid tales of travels in the storied lands of the east. Even to Jerusalem had he gone on pilgrimage, and he fired our imaginations with turbaned Turks and tumultuous bazaars. It was not long, though, ere I tired of him. More and more his attention turned to Tom, who had captured his heart long ago. Tom was his doughty crusader, the best of the four of us with sword and lance, and the strongest, though he was but second-born. I was Father's great disappointment.

I tried my best to please him, and prayed each night to Our Lady that he should love me. But he cared not that I had mastered Boethius' *Consolation*, nor that I had beaten the sons of the other peers at foot races.

What mattered was that I seemed to him ill fitted to be a knight and warrior. He made his scorn of me plain, and I was not sorry when he began to spend most of his time at court.

It was an unquiet time in King Richard's England, and a man of my father's mercurial temperament could not help but be caught up by intrigue. The King was loved by but few, while Bolingbroke the chevalier was the darling of both peers and peasants. My father possessed the auburn-blond handsomeness of English royalty, and his prowess in the lists made his reputation, especially when he unhorsed the famous champions of the French. When murmurings of treasonous plots came to the ear of the King, the name of Bolingbroke was whispered as well. Richard was not at his best when called upon to act decisively, and his fear of the people kept my father's head on his shoulders when others were losing theirs.

I knew few details of these matters of court, nor did I care. My concern in those days was all for my grandfather, whose health had begun to fail. So ill was he that my brothers and I were unable to pass our Christmas at Kenilworth but must bide with our father in his castle of Peterborough. It was a tedious time for all save Tom, who was ever following at Father's heels. Tom told Father much about our life at Monmouth—too much, it turned out, as Father did not care for what he heard. John was too dull for Father, Humphrey too flighty. As for me, there was no end to his discontent. John of Gaunt had failed, he decided. Gaunt was old, lax in his disciplining of us, perhaps even senile. He had left us too much in the care of a Welsh peasant woman, when it was past time for us to be educated in some noble household. Bolingbroke would have to take his sons in hand, else he would find himself shamed before his peers.

"You are all nearly grown to manhood. Harry, you are ten. Soon you shall be eligible for knighthood. Even little Humphrey is old enough to train with sword and lance."

We stood before him in a solemn row and awaited with dread the pronouncement of our fate. He paced back and forth, hands clasped behind his back, a picture of sternness.

"You have been too isolated, too undisciplined at Monmouth. You have learned too little of chivalry."

He looked most often at me as he spoke.

"You are too much in one another's company. You lead each other into mischief." This was of a certain meant for me. "I hear tales that you consort with the urchins of Monmouth. That is disgraceful, and it shall stop. You should be more with your peers, who shall some day be your comrades-in-arms."

He stopped his pacing and addressed Humphrey.

"My youngest, you go to Bolingbroke, the castle of my birth, where you shall be in the care of your uncle Thomas Beaufort."

"Must I go alone, Father?" Humphrey asked.

"Aye. You are old enough."

Humphrey was only six years old and he worshiped me, for I protected him from the bullying of Tom and John. He looked at me with quivering chin and ducked his curly head.

"John, you are for Framlingham. You shall serve in the household of the Duke of Norfolk and be companion to his eldest son."

John, ever stalwart and unimaginative, only nodded and answered, "Aye, my lord father."

"Tom, my warrior." Father paused to rub his red beard and smile. "You come with me to Berkhamsted, then to London. I must spend some time at court, and I would have your company. Sir Thomas Erpyngham, a great friend and knight whose name you bear, shall instruct you in the lists."

Tom flushed pink with pleasure. He dropped to one knee and rose quickly. "Thank you, my lord father. Shall Harry come too? I should like that."

Bolingbroke's smile vanished, and he stared at me. My stomach churned, but I forced myself to meet his gaze.

"Harry. My heir." He spoke softly. "Why should you come? You have no taste for the lists, do you?"

"No, my lord father."

"Why not?"

I swallowed. "You know it is because of the tournament at Pleshy. Why do you make me repeat it?"

"I wish to hear of it. Again."

The memory was excruciating. "I was unhorsed," I said, "by the son of the Earl of Warwick. My arm was broken, and I had a fever of the bone. I was abed for months." I watched his hands clench. "I shall not do it again," I said.

"You shall not do what again?" His voice was gentle.

"I shall not joust again. Ever."

He turned his back. "You are my great shame. You disgrace the name of Lancaster."

I fought the tears.

He whirled about, his face aflame. "What care I for your fears and your damnable illnesses? Do I not know you were ever a weakling and a coward? Do I not recall your mewling and crying, and that you hid behind your mother's skirt while she excused you with your sicknesses?"

"I could not help it that I was ill," I said. "I was often near to death. Joan says so."

"Joan!" he scoffed.

"I am stronger now," I pleaded. "I can run. I have never been beaten at a foot race. And William Bruer says I am the best at wrestling he has seen."

"You will roll in the mud with ragamuffins, but you will not joust."

"I will not joust," I echoed fiercely.

He came upon me suddenly, grasped my shoulders, pushed my back to the wall, and thrust his face in mine.

"Nor shall I force you," he said, "for the sight of it would no doubt be more humiliation. But I shall not have you with me. You are timid as a clerk, and a clerk you shall be. You shall go to your uncle Henry Beaufort, at Oxford, and say your prayers and study your lessons like a good boy. If you should find any manhood in you, come to me. Until then, I do not want you in my sight."

He pushed me roughly away. I heard Humphrey break into sobs as I left them. My own tears I mastered until I reached our bedchamber.

Despite my concern for my grandfather, despite my longing for Monmouth, I loved Oxford. I had ever cherished books, and now I found myself surrounded by them. My grandfather possessed more books than most men, some thirty volumes. But Oxford! Hundreds there were. What was to my father a shameful exile was for me a paradise of exotic ideas. This I know: there were many scholars at Oxford more learned than I, but none more serious. I read for hours on end of philosophy, of history, of poetry, and would raise my head from the page to stare out my window and lovingly stroke the rough leather bindings with my fingertips. Homer, Abelard, Bacon: all were my teachers and friends. I say friends for I was bereft of companionship that is flesh and blood, and the written words I thought were meant for me, Harry.

I was lodged in Queen's College, the poorest at Oxford. Only eight fellows could be supported there. It was a rougher life than the one to which I was accustomed. My tiny chamber held only a bed and a desk with its bench. There was no fireplace, and my first task upon rising was to crack the thin layer of ice which formed each night upon my washbasin, that I might splash the sleep from my eyes. We heard mass before dawn, studied in the gray morning light, attended lectures; then more study, save for those who were inclined to frequent the taverns. The food was plain, and the cold so fierce that I sucked upon my fingers to warm them while I read. At Queen's I acquired a simplicity of habit that would stand me in good stead in later years.

My father had placed me in the charge of my uncle Henry Beaufort, who was chancellor of the university. Beaufort's father was John of Gaunt, his mother Katharine Swynford. He was born a bastard, as was his brother Thomas, but when my grandfather was at last free to wed his beloved Katharine, King Richard had declared the Beauforts legitimate. My uncle was just ten years older than I, but like other churchmen of noble birth he was priested young and elevated at once to high office.

My grandfather had spoken well of me to Beaufort, and so I found him a congenial guardian. Father had ordered that I be instructed in swordmanship, and Beaufort was faithful to this charge. Yet he also granted me an hour each afternoon to run freely through the forests and fields along the Cherwell. Best of all, he did not hover about me. He watched me closely, I know now, yet at the time it seemed he kept his distance, and I reveled in this freedom.

Once a week I supped with him. It was not long ere he talked with me as a man, sometimes of theology but more often of statecraft. These discussions I considered another element of my education, for Beaufort held to ideas which I knew instinctively my father, and even my grandfather, would find revolting. One evening in February I recall most vividly.

"Tell me, Harry, what becomes of a man's body when he breathes his last?"

I was taken aback, for it seemed ill considered to speak so plainly of such things, especially at a meal. My answer was cautious.

"Why, sir, it rots or is eaten by worms if the man is buried in the ground, or perhaps shrivels and dries if the man has been hanged. I have seen such wizened corpses dangling by the wayside, though in truth I care not to look at them."

"Very good. And what happens to society, to order, to the body politic when it does die?"

"Good my lord uncle, how may the body politic die? Have order and society not ever been with us?"

He laughed. "Perhaps you speak truly. But what sort of society? What sort of order? Come, Harry, has your reading not yet taken you to the ancient world, to the Greeks and Romans?"

"Oh, aye, my lord," I said eagerly. "I do love to read of such times."

"Then you should know they were different times, alien times. We speak of Theseus and Ulysses as though they were knights, but read carefully, my boy. They were not. Yet your ordinary fool would have you believe that our society is an eternal one based upon eternal principles, that the ways of finance are unchanging, that chivalry was and is and ever shall be."

"And you say these things shall pass?"

"Shall pass! They have already passed. A society is not like a human body. When it dies it does not rot, save inwardly. Its outward appearance is uncorrupted, unchanged. So it shall remain for a time, until it collapses of a sudden to a foul heap of offal. Our chivalry, our nobility, are just such corpses."

"How do you know it?"

"I answer you with another question, as did the noble Socrates. What say you are the orders of society and their function?"

"Why, it is well known: the Church, which prays; the nobility, who rule and fight; and the peasantry, who work."

"So say your books?"

"Aye."

"And your father would say so?"

"Aye."

"What then of the great merchants? Where do they fit in your scheme?"

"They are not mentioned."

"As though they did not exist. Yet what king may rule without them? Indeed, what would your father do? They provide him with goods, aye, and coin. They are our destiny, Harry, and I tell you, they care not tuppence for chivalry, though they do acknowledge it from custom. Their code is not chivalry but power. Power governs the King and his nobles as well, yet they give not power its due. They live in their dream world of knights-errant and honor and family name."

He paused to drink of his wine, then said wryly, "I speak so because I am bastard born, and my mother was of a lower rank. I am one of these new men. Though King Richard has now declared me legitimate, to most I remain still a bastard. It matters not a whit, for I shall be a most powerful bastard."

There was much here to puzzle through. I studied him across the table as though to judge the truth of his words by his face. The firelight glinted on his raven-black hair, and his eyes were pits lost in the dancing shadows.

At last I said, "So then I am to be the Duke of Lancaster, one of these witless nobles you mock. God knows I am more fitted for the Church, but I cannot escape my birth."

"Fitted for the Church? You? No, you father says so, but more fool your father. You are no more fitted for the Church than I. Here I am, of course, but for one in my position it is the only way. I shall be no cloistered monk, that I vow. As for you, nephew, because you will not prance around tournaments with lance in hand, it does not make you a churchman."

He speared a hunk of fresh venison and gnawed it from his knife.

"You must play their game, Harry, but never believe in it. Pretend the corpse is still alive, clasp its hand, clap it upon the back. But take heed how it stinks and get no closer. Damn chivalry! You've a fine sharp mind, Harry Monmouth. Rely upon that alone."

"And upon God, surely?"

He smiled. "To be sure. Upon God."

The snows of winter melted into April, and with them passed my contentment with Oxford. Had I wintered at Kenilworth it would be time to go home, to Monmouth. More and more my thoughts strayed westward to the Monnow, to Rhys and Gwyllym, and to Joan. My solitude at Queen's seemed intolerable. I was not a student of theology, a clerk, as were the others, and I was younger than they. In addition I am possessed of a natural constraint of manner which has ever been a plague to me and which served to isolate me further.

The Cherwell was my only joy, save for my books. Daily I wandered the river's lush banks. I stopped often to fish, to read, or simply to let my thoughts drift downstream with the wild swans. My favorite haunt was a grassy knoll beneath a sagging willow. I named it my cathedral, for the newly green boughs of the willow arched downward, graceful as any nave, and when I lay flat upon my stomach in the tall grass, the sunlight dripped through the clumps of marigolds and cuckoo flowers as through the finest stained glass. My visits to the river took more and more of my day, until my uncle noticed and held me strictly to an hour.

One evening, after a dreary day when a thunderstorm had kept me from the river's solace, I sat in my chamber and listened to the clamor of the High Street beneath my window. The noise seemed a wound to my spirit, for twilight is a time of brooding silence in the Welsh hills.

"In truth," I muttered, "there is not so much tumult in Monmouth on market day."

I shut my eyes and conjured the square at Monmouth, where the good people of the countryside brought their wares. A boy would find companionship there, and plenty of mischief. Soon it would be Midsummer Eve. The bonfires would be lit, there would be dancing, and an abundance of ale would call forth quick laughter. This year I would know none of it. I blew out my candle and sat upon my bed. Without my window I heard voices raised in song. The scholars of Oxford were on their merry way to the taverns.

It came to me then that if I was indeed deprived of peace and quiet, why not seek fellowship at least? So it was that I found myself in the High. I nimbly dodged the mud puddles and picked my way carefully through Magpie Lane to Blue Boar Street and thence to Fish Street. I kept to the shadows, for night was falling, and night is the province of brigands who slit throats for a few pence. With relief I reached my goal in Fish Street, the Swindlestock Tavern. The pleasant sound of laughter and clinking glasses wafted through the open door. I held my breath and slipped inside as inconspicuously as I could.

None took notice of me. The large room was filled with men hunched upon benches drinking and talking or playing at dice or cards by lantern light. A few women there were as well, and lads of my own age, town lads by their dress. Summoning up my courage, I approached a porter and requested a tankard of ale.

He eyed me up and down.

"Aye, a tankard'll last 'e the night, won't it, lad? Let us see your coin."

I paid him, playing the man as well as I could, and swaggered off with my tankard clutched in both hands. I soon learned how to drink the bitter stuff without screwing up my face, then settled on a bench to watch a group of scholars playing at tables. Their gowns marked them as fellows of Oriel and Merton. They glanced at me and I smiled hopefully, but they went back to their gaming without a word. Slightly daunted, I sipped my ale and watched as they wagered, their coins in neat little stacks around the board.

Mind you, I was not used to strong drink, for my wine at meals was watered down. Before long I felt a strange and pleasing lightness of the head, and my surroundings assumed magical proportions. I listened enthralled to the snatches of conversation which came to me in a variety of dialects, and stared openmouthed at the bare cleavages of the women of the town who wandered in.

One lass with hair of fiery red paused in front of me, tickled me beneath the chin, and exclaimed, "Now, God's truth, here's a pretty boy. Your eyes, lad, are that lovely."

Her fingers ran lightly through my hair.

"Come to me in a few years. Name of Meg, in Ship Street."

She giggled and moved on. I sat transfixed. The world around me was a delightful blur. My recollection of what came to pass is a bit muddled, of course. I was aware of a great row, of overturned benches and voices raised in derision and anger.

"The Singers!" someone cried. "The filthy Singers are cheating again!"

I was drawn from my bench by the next outburst, for while the tone was strident, the words seemed music to me. Someone was speaking—aye, cursing—in Welsh. I moved toward the sound, which had become grunts as bodies locked together in combat. A table was smashed. I fell as others pushed past me to view the fray, and still I crawled forward between their legs.

The struggling bodies flew apart as one man was hurled beneath a table. He cried in Welsh, "Jesu, my nose!" Blood spurted dark red from his nostrils.

"Cheating, whoreson Taffy! I shall break your pate as well," the other cried in English. He moved toward the fallen Welshman.

It was someone in need of help who spoke with the painful lilt of home.

I scrambled up, yelled a Welsh curse of my own, wrapped myself around one leg of the charging Englishman, and sank my teeth into his thigh. He cried out in surprise and struck me a sharp blow to the neck. I loosed my hold and he sent me flying. As from a distance I heard, rather than felt, my forehead strike something hard.

I awoke to find a cold wet cloth pressed against my temple. Voices raised in contention floated above me.

"Leave the little Taffy be. Let one of his own wave a leek beneath his nose. That shall rouse him."

"How do you suppose a little Singer got here? He does not wear the gown of any college, and besides, he is too young. Perhaps we may make use of him."

A third voice answered, much closer and quieter. "Off with you. Go on about your drinking and let me see to the lad." This was the man who held me.

"'Tis not fair," someone said. "Why should you have claim to him?" But the voices moved away.

I tried to sit up, which worsened the throbbing of my forehead, and I moaned.

"Still, lad, still," the man said. "No harm shall come to you now."

I opened my eyes and saw that he was a youth of about sixteen years of age. He wore the gown of a fellow of Oriel.

"Can you see me clearly?" he asked anxiously.

"Aye," I whispered.

"That is good." He held a lantern close to my face. "You've a bad bump upon your forehead," he said, "and it is turning a wonderful shade of purple. Aye, as purple as a bishop's cope. But your pate seems to be in one piece. No cracks that I can find."

"Where am I?"

"In the pantry of the Swindlestock. Do you not recall? You were defending the honor of the Welsh."

"Oh, aye, they were beating a poor Welshman. And how does he fare?"

"Well enough, save for his nose, and that shall heal. The fight was broken up. But tell me, how comes it that you speak English now? Only a moment ago, you were a bellowing Celt. Whence come you?"

"I am Monmouth born. And I am Welsh," I added defiantly.

"And what are you named?"

"I am Henry, but all call me Harry."

"Well then, Harry it is. I am Richard, Richard Courtenay. And I am a Devon man."

I smiled despite my aching head. "Richard." It was a long time ere I had addressed anyone by his familiar name.

"Do you think you can stand?" he asked.

I nodded and, with his help, wobbled to my feet.

"My lodgings are close by, at Oriel," he said. "It shall be quiet there, and I can give you some hot spiced wine. Will you come with me?"

Nothing could have gladdened my heart so much as his gentle company. He guided me through the crowded rooms of the Swindlestock and out into Fish Street, his hand all the while resting protectively upon my shoulder. Slowly we made our way to Oriel, and when the throbbing of my head caused me to falter, Courtenay lifted me in his arms and bore me through an open doorway and up a long stone stairway to his tiny room. He wrapped me in a blanket and set me upon his bed. Soon there was a blazing fire and I sipped a warm spicy claret, much watered down. My head still pained me but my mind had cleared. I studied my new companion and liked what I saw. His eyes were deep-set and disappeared in the crinkles of his face when he smiled, which was often. His features were finely chiseled, his mouth generously long, his hair a tangled mat of brown curls.

He had come to Oxford, he said, from the village of Chudleigh.

"Never have I heard of Chudleigh," I said.

"Nor has anyone. There are more pigs than people in Chudleigh." His eyes disappeared.

"Yet Courtenay is a name known and honored in England."

"And what would a wild Welshman know of that?" he teased. When I hesitated, he said with a sudden understanding, "They say the Duke of Lancaster's grandson has become Beaufort's ward. Harry Monmouth. Faith, why did it not occur to me? I had thought Harry Monmouth older, but would you be he?"

"Aye," I said softly.

"Gaunt's heir," he mused. "Gaunt is the most powerful man in England, next the King."

I was unhappy with his discovery, for I feared in him that mixture of deference and distance with which the fellows of Queen's treated me.

I had determined to leave him as soon as I could, and made to put my blanket from me, when he asked, "Why was Harry Monmouth in the Swindlestock so late at night? What company sought you there?"

I shrugged, feigning nonchalance, but my misery must have shown in my face.

After a moment he continued, "It is perilous to be about alone at night. Yet I know the need for companionship may drive a man to take such a risk."

I nodded, not daring to look at him. The tears came quickly then, and soon after followed the tale of my father's scorn, of my loneliness and longing for Monmouth. It was a relief to weep out my hurts, but also an embarrassment. Had I been in my uncle's presence, he would have mocked me into a shamed silence. What then would this stranger do?

I smeared the tears over my cheek with the heel of my hand and waited for Courtenay to make light of my feelings, but he said nothing for a very long time. When at last he spoke, he only said, "I am glad you are here."

To my wonder, he seemed sincere.

I quieted myself and looked about the small chamber. In the shadows of the far corner I could just see the outline of a row of books that had earlier escaped my notice. It was a veritable library of at least twenty volumes. I craned my neck for a closer view.

"Go and look at them if you like."

I ran my hand appreciatively over the leather bindings and noted that no dust clung to them.

"You read Plato," I said. "He is out of fashion, yet I like him."

"So do I."

"Dante! I adore Dante. I weep with him over Beatrice."

One slender volume caught my eye, for it was written in English, in a strong plain hand.

"That one I copied out myself," Courtenay said proudly.

I turned to the first page and read, "'A Vision of William Concerning Piers the Plowman.'"

"A book about a plowman?" I asked, puzzled. "Never have I seen such a thing."

"No, you would not have. Your father would not approve, nor even your uncle of Beaufort, I should think."

"And why not?"

"It is not of knights and ladies. It is the cry of the poor people of England who ne'er were known to have a voice."

Courtenay took the book from me and turned its pages reverently.

"Hear this," he said, and read. "'So painful it is to read or to write verses upon the harsh lives of women who dwell in hovels, and of men who suffer likewise, ever hungry and thirsty, hiding their affliction, too proud to beg. I know this too well. The world teaches it.'"

I nodded. "It is so. I have as friends two such ones in Monmouth." I told him then of Rhys and Gwyllym.

"'Tis rare for a lad of your rank," he said.

"Aye. Father was angered by it. 'Tis one reason I am sent away."

"Our nobles are fools. Forgive me if I speak plainly, yet so I deem them. 'Twas not so many years ago the peasants rose up in Kent. We cannot ignore them forever, nor is it meet that we should. Only at our soul's peril do we misuse the poor."

"Yet do not all men give alms?"

"It is not enough." His pale face in the firelight was luminous as a sheepskin lamp.

"I would read this book," I said after a moment's thought, "and learn more of what you say."

"Then you must take it with you."

"I thank you for it. I shall guard it well and return it ere long."

"No. I give it to you. You must keep it."

"But—but—a book! Books are so precious. I could not take it! You said you copied it yourself."

"I copied it that it might be read. Come, I know it well. I would have you read it."

He gave me the book then, and I wrapped my arms about it, and smiled shyly at him.

"It is little enough," I said, "yet may I offer my friendship in return?"

"Well offered and gladly received. I think our paths shall cross often, Harry Monmouth. But now you should be in your bed, for it is well past Compline. I shall take you back to Queen's."

"Will it not be dangerous, since the hour is late?"

"I run fast."

I grinned. "So do I."

Two days after my escapade at the Swindlestock, Richard Courtenay came pounding upon my door.

"Harry! I am off to the Cherwell with a flask of wine and a book. Will you come?"

"I should love to."

"Good. I have with me burgundy and Boethius. Are both to your taste?"

"Oh, aye. And I know of a lovely place to go."

I led him to my cathedral and delighted in his enjoyment of it. We warmed ourselves in the sunshine and then settled beneath the musty boughs of the willow. Courtenay drank from the flask, then passed it to me. The rich Burgundy tickled its way down my throat, and I squeezed my eyelids together in appreciation. I nodded and handed back the flask, feeling very much a man.

Courtenay lay back upon his elbows. "This was well met, Harry. You have been much upon my mind these two days."

I blushed with surprise and pleasure. "I do not know why."

"No, do not say that. You hold yourself in too little esteem, I do vow. You have made a very great impression upon me, and that should not startle you. I see in you both courage and a sensitivity rare in one so young. You must know that I am honored to accept the friendship you have offered me.

Besides, there is some selfishness in my pursuit of you. I long for companionship even as you do."

"I should think you have many friends," I said. "You have an easy way about you."

He idly pulled at the tufts of new grass. "I have many friends of a sort," he said. "Friends with whom I drink and make merry. But when I grow serious they shake their heads at me. They study only what they must so that they may leave this place and make their way in the world. They never question, never." His voice rose in frustration. "Everyone who visits my chamber, I tell of Piers Plowman. Some find it tedious. Others think it a piece of foolishness. They tease me when I speak of the poor, and some of my fellows have named me St. Francis in jest. Oh, they mean no harm by it. But none respond as you did. Something alive I saw in your eyes, and my heart leaped at it. You want to do good in this world."

"Aye," I said, "though my father thinks I may do none."

"A duke may do much good," he mused. "Near as much as a king."

"Aye," I said eagerly. "I would learn how."

"Then shall we be seekers together," he said, his voice deep with satisfaction. "And may Our Lady bless this venture."

Boon companions we became, but for all too brief a time. We had not even the summer together ere I received bad tidings from my uncle. The King had named him Bishop of Lincoln. He would go at once to that city, and I with him. Once more I must bid farewell to friendship and journey even farther from my Monmouth hills. I begged my uncle to remain in Oxford. Few, I argued, would think ill of him for it. Most prelates were absent from their sees, busy with affairs of state, managing their estates, hunting or hawking. Such neglect is part of the sickness that afflicts the Holy Church, and I later felt shame that I had urged my uncle to avoid his duty. I was but a child, and all my care was for the unhappy prospect of going to Lincoln. It seemed to me then that my uncle displayed an uncharacteristically scrupulous sense of duty by taking up his charge personally. I soon learned it was nothing of the sort. My uncle went to Lincoln because our house of Lancaster had been brought to a precarious position by the intrigues of my father. It seemed prudent that Beaufort become the model of a conscientious prelate and an obedient subject of his King.

My father's folly had now overreached itself. With his past history of questionable loyalty, he should have settled down to an inconspicuous service of his sovereign. Instead, he continued to spread discontent across the land. Then he quarreled violently with his erstwhile confidant Thomas Mowbray, Duke of Norfolk, who, like Father, was mistrusted by the King. To this day, none know the reason for their quarrel, for neither would speak of it. Father took himself to the King and accused Norfolk of treason. Norfolk in his turn hurled a like charge at my father.

"And both guilty as sin," Beaufort grumbled. "Only fools seek such advantage one over the other."

"And what ought they have done?" I asked.

"Never to have quarreled at all. 'Tis death to a conspiracy when the plotters fall out. No doubt they argued over whose horse may run the fastest or some other matter of import. Still, if quarrel you must, there are more discreet methods of settlement. Well, it is too late. They are enjoined by the King to meet in the lists at Coventry, that each may seek to prove his charge upon the body of the other."

"No doubt Father deems himself the better jouster, and so he went to the King."

"No," said Beaufort. "There shall be no good outcome even if Norfolk is slain. King Richard has good enough reason to fear Bolingbroke, and now this charge of treason is openly laid upon your father. See if Richard does not punish him; Bolingbroke is a fool to think otherwise. So does he place us all in peril."

We rode side by side through the forest of Lincolnshire in company with my uncle's wary retainers. When we fell silent, nothing was heard save the clopping of our horses' hooves and the raucous cries of jays and tits. Our road fell away before us straight as an arrow, and upon either side the wood hung dense as a curtain. In vain my eyes did seek to penetrate that mass of green. It was a wood such as comes to us in our dreams, a place of fey wanderers, of demons and unicorns.

The approach to the city was aweful, for Lincoln is set upon a solitary hill. The cathedral appeared first, a great ship riding above the rolling forest. It was with relief that we passed through the Broad Gate even as the shadows of dusk fell about us.

My mood lightened when I found John and little Humphrey awaiting us at bishopshouse. Humphrey had been lodged at Bolingbroke castle, which is nigh to Lincoln, while John had been in the service of the Duke of Norfolk. After Father's quarrel with Norfolk, John was sent to Bolingbroke, and thence both brothers came to Lincoln. I learned that I had been far more fortunate than they. John had received a typical squire's education at Framlingham, serving at table and learning the lore of chivalry but seeing little of books. He had been immensely happy, of course, for he had not the imagination to be otherwise. An ideal subordinate I have ever judged him, content to be where he is and do as he is told. As much as he had enjoyed his servile existence, even so much would I have detested it. As for Humphrey, he had been locked away with nurses and a wearisome tutor, and none his age for companionship. He wept out of joy to see me again. I marked change in him. Ever skittish, he was now petulant, as well, and given to clamorous outbursts.

We were not long for Lincoln, as Father soon called us to Coventry. We lodged in our castle of Kenilworth, where my grandfather of Gaunt lay ill. I had not set eyes on him since he was stricken, and it affrighted me to see his weakness. He had ever seemed old to me, but also robust. Now he was perilously thin, cheekbones protruding and eyes sunk in bluish sockets, his skin stretched and peeling and splotched with red where he had been bled. He said little, but only lay breathing through his mouth while his faithful Katharine Swynford sat at his side and held his hand. The chamber stank of camphor and piss. After each visit I escaped his presence gladly, I am shamed to say.

The time of the joust drew nigh. My uncle Beaufort set the clerks of the household at their prayers, beseeching that God in His mercy might dispose the day to Lancaster's favor. All the household spoke in hushed tones, even the scullery maids, fearful of what the future might bring. We sat silent at our meals, much to my relief, for I had no wish to converse with Father. Only Tom seemed free of foreboding. His eyes glistened with excitement and he strutted about like a peacock, for he had been chosen to attend on Father in the lists. On the appointed day, he rode away to Coventry upon a white horse bridled with scarlet tassels and silver bells, his cap perched jauntily on the side of his head. I stood alone upon the battlement and watched him go, and despite myself I longed to be in his place.

Tom's return was something different. I had taken to my chamber and immersed myself in a book, that I might blot the joust from my mind, when I heard footsteps running up the stair. The door was flung open and there stood Tom, cap missing, his face stained with dirt and tears.

I leaped up with a thrill of fear. "What has happened? Is Father slain?"

"They did not fight!" Tom blurted.

I stared at him. "Then why do you weep?"

"Oh, Harry, he is banished the kingdom! The King has named him traitor and sent him away for ten years. What are we to do?"

I grasped his arm and guided him to the bed. "Sit here and calm yourself, then tell me the whole of it."

"They were in the lists and ready for the charge," he gulped. "Then the King flung up his hand and bade them forbear. He called both to him and declared them traitors together. Norfolk he sent away for life, and Father for ten years."

A strange lightness possessed me. I knew I should feel no joy, but I did.

"In truth," I said, "I have prayed day and night that his life should be spared. I do love him well and would serve him if he wished it. Yet he cares not for me. Afore God, I am not sorry to see him go."

Tom flushed crimson. "It is wicked, Harry, to say such a thing!"

"Is it? I care not. When he returns I shall be twenty-one. I shall be a man, and I shall achieve my manhood free of his heavy hand. God willing, I shall have some contentment."

"How can you say it? You are jealous, that is all. You are jealous, for he loves me best!"

"Indeed he does," I said quietly. "And should I weep then for a father I see but little of, one who has nothing for me save scorn?"

Tom sprawled across the bed and buried his face in the bedclothes.

"In truth, Tom, I am sorry for your sake," I said, and marveled at the coldness of my heart.

Father spoke tenderly with Tom ere he departed for France.

"It may not be so long, my son. The King may relent. If he does not, I shall have you with me in France. It would school you well, for the French nobility are the most chivalrous of Christendom."

Tom nodded. "Then would I become as fine a knight as Bolingbroke and gain revenge for the wrongs done to our house."

"No doubt you shall be such a knight. Yet speak not openly of revenge on my behalf. It may be I shall yet redress these wrongs myself."

I sat cross-legged before the fire and strummed my harp while I listened to their words.

"You shall mind your uncle Beaufort and have a care for your little brothers. I would have them look to you in my absence."

"Aye, my lord father," Tom replied proudly.

My hand froze upon the strings then, for Father was standing beside me.

"And you, Harry," he said sadly. "What shall become of you?"

I stared straight ahead.

"Your uncle speaks well of you and claims I neglect you. This trouble has caused me to repent of my hardness toward you. I had some hopes of taking you in hand myself. Perhaps, I said to myself, your heir is but stubborn and needs a firm hand to set him upon the right path. I fear it is not to be, at least for a while. What say you, though? If you stay at Kenilworth and work hard from this day on, I shall think better of you. I ask not that you best Tom in feats of arms, only that you try. What do you say? I shall send for you with Tom. Would it please you?"

My hands trembled. "My lord father, I should like to return to Monmouth, or at least to Oxford, and resume my studies. I beg you not to hate me for it. I would not part from you so cruelly."

He turned on his heel without a word and left the hall. Nor did he bid me farewell ere he sailed for France.

I pleaded with my uncle to send me to Monmouth.

"Your father would not wish it," he said. "I have pledged him that I would remain here. Kenilworth is the finest of Lancaster's holdings, and the safest. Your grandfather is here, and many retainers who are well suited to your training."

"I shall not submit to such training any more."

"Threats do not help you, Harry, nor shall you defy me."

"And shall you beat me? I care not! Only send me to Monmouth and I shall obey you. I shall do anything save joust. Only send me to Monmouth."

His eyes blazed with anger and he raised his hand to strike me, then thought better of it.

"Please," I whispered.

"Young fool," he said wearily. "I cannot leave your brothers. I must see to Tom's training, and this is the best place for it."

"Are you not my guardian as well as Tom's? Can you not say what is best for me? In truth, you think as little of Father's notion of learning as do I. That is why you do not beat me."

"It is no reason to send you to Monmouth on your own. The Welsh woman is no fit guardian."

"Yet she loves me well. And I know of a tutor, a young man of noble family and great learning. Will you not meet him and then decide?"

That is how I set out for Monmouth in the company of Richard Courtenay.

The harvest was plentiful that year. When Courtenay and I came to Monmouth, the fields beside the Wye and Monnow were shorn of their oats and barley, and the cows wandered far and wide chewing the stubble. Beans and peas had been carted away in round baskets, and apples gathered for drying into sweet leathery slivers, all awaiting the feast of Michaelmas. Then would we praise God for His bounty, and even the poorest cotter would fill his belly.

I sought out my friends of old, Gwyllym, Davy, and Rhys. Gwyllym, I learned to my sorrow, had died of the pox at Candlemas, as had two others in his family. Davy was now prenticed to a tinker and had no time for me. But Rhys ap Llewellyn was a swineherd upon my grandfather's land and glad as ever of my company. At Nones, when studies were finished and I had done practicing with sword and buckler, I went with Rhys into the woods along the Monnow. We clambered into the ponderous oak trees and shook the branches while the hairy swine trotted to and fro beneath the showers of acorns. Then we would search out the snares I had set for coneys. Poaching was forbidden Rhys, but I reasoned that none could complain if I caught my own grandfather's hares. Twice I brought down a deer with my bow, and Rhys and his family enjoyed venison often that winter.

There was a joyous reunion with Joan as well. "Harry, my babe," she called me as she crushed me to her bosom, then thrust me back at arm's length for inspection. "There's a foot you have grown since last I saw you. 'Tis a man you are becoming, and soon you shall break the lasses' hearts, so handsome you are. Whatever did your father think, to keep you from me so long?" She tutted and clucked over me for days ere she was satisfied that I was truly well.

She took to Courtenay at once, though she declared him too thin.

"It is what comes of keeping your nose in a book," she scolded. "You scholars, you think yourselves too good for food, and wary of women too, by my troth." She looked him up and down impudently. "'Tis a shame you are for the Church. Many a lass would be happy with you, though you be all bones." She laughed loudly and winked at Courtenay's embarrassed grin.

"Leave him be, Joan," I said. "I would not have him leave Monmouth when I have tried so hard to bring him here."

Richard Courtenay was the finest teacher I had known. He treasured knowledge above all else and for its own sake, asking no usefulness of it, but only joy. He often taught as we tramped along the riverbank. It was better, he said, to walk the Monnow than pace a narrow room, for when a thought had taken hold of him he could but move about with excitement. When yet I think of Plato's Republic, I see Courtenay explaining its precepts in the midst of a field strewn with hay, the stalks crunching beneath our feet, the Monnow rippling before us.

There were times of solitude as well. When Joan was spinning, and Courtenay reading, and Rhys tending to his family, I stole away to a magic place I had found years before. There was a high round hill beyond the Wye. The Kymin, it was named, and from its brow one might see the world, or at least all the world that mattered to me. I spent many peaceful hours there, and none ever came to disturb me. There was a rock upon the crest which had burst through the tight-packed sod. The Fairy Castle I named it, for its spires and turrets soared some five feet into the air. Never would I clamber upon it, for I deemed it enchanted, the entrance through which the wee folk passed on their way to midnight revels. I vowed that I would screw up my courage and pass a mild summer night at the Fairy Castle, but it was not to be. Nor would I know for many years the love and contentment of those months, for as Christmas approached King Richard sent for me.

2

Christmas has ever been my favorite of all the feast days. There is a sweetness about the carolings to Our Lady and the Holy Babe, and a richness to the steamed puddings and roast goose, which bespeak love and goodwill. Small wonder then that I wept to leave Monmouth, to part with Joan and Courtenay at such a time. My grief was compounded by fear, for I could guess why King Richard should send for me, the son of a man exiled for treason. Had not wicked King John murdered the boy Arthur of Brittany who threatened his throne? I thought to flee to Kenilworth, or even to follow my father into exile. (Such was my despair!) It was no use, for the King's men kept me ever in their sight. Moreover, they had come with such care that they knew beforehand of Courtenay's presence at Monmouth. They bore with them a parchment ordering him to Chichester, where he was to serve as subdeacon of the cathedral. He was bidden to seek no word of me after his departure.

It was a hard leavetaking. In the warmth of the great hall, I wept quietly into Joan's bosom while she tearfully implored me to dress warmly. She whispered in Welsh that I must send word to her if at all possible.

"What sort of king is this to send a child out in the winter cold? Go then, my lamb. I love you, Harry."

"I love you, Joan."

Then, as I stood in the bailey, wrapped against the falling snow, Courtenay pressed a parchment and a tiny bundle into my hand.

"Read this when you have need of it," he said. He forced me to meet his eyes. "You shall be brave. I know it."

"I am terribly afraid," I managed to say.

"Who would not be? But God goes with you. And who can tell these things? You may find in the King a friend. Old Gaunt has been the King's most devoted servant, and the King must bear him some goodwill. Think little upon your father's treacheries. You are Harry Monmouth. Make your own way, and judge the King for yourself. Peace, then. You shall be daily in my prayers."

He squeezed my shoulder with his gloved hand. The snowflakes burned my salty cheeks as I nodded and turned blindly toward the horse that waited to carry me to Windsor.

I held his letter until we were but a day from Windsor, when my despair was deepest. Then I broke the seal and read it by the flat winter light.

> Harry, take courage [he had written]. You are young and you do not yet know yourself. But I mark strength in you, a sharp mind and a good heart. England shall be glad to find such a one in her service.
>
> Your present unhappiness shall later strengthen you. When Piers Plowman sets to his task, he breaks the ground and turns it inside out. So Our Lord was broken, and this we must also expect. If all goes our way, we become like the hard-packed earth where no seed may take root. No crops but that the plow first cuts its furrow.
>
> Pray to Our Lady, the Blessed Virgin Mary. Ever she helps those who love.
>
> Richard Courtenay

Tenderly I unwrapped the tiny bundle that accompanied the letter. It was a statue of the madonna, carved of oak. Her coiffed head was slightly tilted back, that she might smile beatifically at the one who held her, and her face resembled that of my own dead mother, or so it seemed to me.

I slept that night in the manor house at Marlow, close by Windsor. The letter rested upon my breast beneath the bedclothes, and the rough parchment rubbed me comfortingly with each breath. The madonna I clutched tightly in my fist. Two Marys came to me in my dreams to give me solace, and never was I certain which was which.

I was presented to Richard of Bordeaux, King of England, on Christmas Day. It was a brief audience.

The King, I had been warned, cherished deference. I must kneel and bow as close to the floor as I was able. Under no circumstance should I raise my eyes to his. Trembling, I was led by a liveried attendant into his presence, my head bowed abjectly. I knelt at a signal from the attendant and stared at a pair of purple shoes with long toes which curved upward in a great arch. They were the most absurd shoes I had ever seen, and I gaped in amazement to think it was a king who wore them.

"Well, Harry Monmouth, I have heard much of you from your grand-father Gaunt." His voice was thin and refined.

"Aye, your grace." I answered as I had been instructed. This seemed a hopeful beginning, and I took heart.

The King spoke of a few trivial pleasantries then. I have ever loathed such conversation, preferring silence to pointless words. My answers were brief. He did not bid me rise, so I conversed with the purple shoes while my neck stiffened.

Then he said, "You had a pleasant journey."

It was not a question. He spoke in a tone which indicated I would shortly be dismissed. My fear now became fuel for an overriding anger. I had been torn from those I loved and dragged through winter storms to grovel like a whipped pup before a pair of ridiculous purple shoes. That he should so put upon me and then presume to dictate my feelings as well!

"No, your grace," I said. "The journey was not pleasant."

My voice rang like a bell through the hall. An astonished murmur rose from the assembled courtiers, then died away at once.

One shoe shifted. After a moment, the cool voice above my head said, "You were well tended."

"The winds were very bitter to ride in, and I was lonely. Nor did I wish to come to Windsor," I said. It seemed easier to speak boldly to purple shoes than to a king.

"I care not for these tedious complaints, nor for your manners. Let me hear no more from you."

The pointed toes turned then to reveal gold-embroidered heels. I glanced questioningly at the attendant, who nodded. I was dismissed. I do not care, I thought fiercely. I do not care what he does with me. I rose and had started shakily down the dais when Richard whirled around.

"Henry Lancaster!"

I halted, half turned, and willed myself to look at him. He was all purple and cloth of gold, his fair hair drifting in a cloud to his shoulders. He was very handsome after a sleepy-eyed fashion.

The attendant tugged frantically at my sleeve, and I retained just enough presence of mind to sink to my knees once more.

"Your grace?" I croaked.

"Do the lords of the Welsh marches never bathe?"

I stared at him, then reddened as understanding dawned. The courtiers behind me tittered.

"N-Not in winter, your grace," I stammered. "It is too—"

"Enough of your opinions," he interrupted. "Here you shall bathe once a week. Do not appear again in this company until you are less offensive to us."

From inside his gown he pulled a small cloth which he pressed with exaggerated anguish to his nose. The titters turned to guffaws. He turned away again with a pleased wave of his arm and left me to hurry the length of the hall, my cheeks burning with shame.

"You are lucky," the attendant said. "His mood is good."

The Christmas festivities at Windsor were both lavish and heartless. A host of mummers clad in gold and white entertained us with music of trumpet and clash of cymbal. It was a play of St. George and the Dragon they brought to us, and the noble saint wore a mask which resembled King Richard. I adored mummings, as do all children, but this jaded audience, having given only half an eye to the proceedings, stripped the foolery of all joy with its bored chatter. At Monmouth the floor would have been generously strewn with sweet hay, and the stableboys and kitchen maids would have crowded in at the doorways to giggle and point with glee at some jape.

Though only just arrived, I received a present from the King, as did all his household. My gift was a gown of green velvet embossed with silver swans, more elaborate than any I had owned. Fresh from the bath, I donned the gown and wandered shyly through Windsor Great Hall past the lolling courtiers. I had thought all would be laughing at me for the morning's audience, but none seemed to note my presence. None wished me Christmas cheer. They were richly caparisoned and bejeweled, both men and women. Their chattering was a continual roar which bounced raucously about the vaulted stone walls and set my stomach on edge. From the balcony over my head the minstrels bravely struck up a lilting air, barely audible above the din. I wandered first to the far side of the hall, then back again, and stood, at a loss as to what I should do with myself, unless it be to seek out some shadowy corner and hide.

Servants wound their graceful way between rows of tables bearing steaming flagons of wine upon their shoulders. Then I recalled my escapade in the Swindlestock. Nimbly I plucked a flagon from a nearby tray and momentarily studied the ruby wine. The aroma of cinnamon and cloves tickled its way up my nostrils. I leaned against a wall and drank. Waxen torches blazed in their sconces and flashed lightning at the bottom of my cup. I slid to the floor and settled into a warm haze.

The blaring trumpets summoned us to our food ere I was completely numb. Hastily I roused myself, hid the half-filled flagon behind a tapestry, and sought a place at table. I plopped down next a balding, heavy-cheeked young man who greeted me with false hilarity.

"Well met, cousin. The gown becomes you. You look and smell like Henry of Lancaster and not some marcher yeoman."

I cared not for him, and the wine had left me in no mood to suffer condescension.

"How do you come to name me cousin?" I asked coolly.

"I am Richard, youngest son of the Duke of York and nephew to your grandfather, the Duke of Lancaster. I was present this morning at your audience with the King. A most inauspicious meeting, my lord Henry. He thought you quite impertinent and said so when you had gone."

"I care not."

"Ah, a quarrelsome young pup as well as a rude one. Mark you, Henry, such insolence is to a point tolerated in one so young. At a riper age it would part you from your head."

A fanfare sounded, and an endless line of servants filed into the hall bearing with them food upon silver dishes. Each man was clad in a blue jerkin embossed with a white hart, the King's favorite emblem, and each was blank of face and walked with a short, rhythmic gait. The hall buzzed with expectation. A young page of about my age took his solemn place behind us, ready to serve.

"Were you not just arrived, no doubt you would be serving," said York. "Perhaps you may serve me. I shall speak to the lord chamberlain of it. What sort of pasties are these, boy?"

"Lark pasties, my lord," said the page.

York took one from the proffered dish and set it before me. Likewise roast venison, slippery oysters swimming in wine, and eel stuffed with walnuts and saffron all found their way onto my trencher, and I decided York must be done with harassing me. The food cleared my head and lightened my disposition most wonderfully. I eyed York cautiously and thought that perhaps it was not yet too late to make a friend of him.

"Are there games at court?" I asked hopefully.

"Oh, indeed. Idleness is a hallmark of this court."

"Chess is my favorite game," I said. "Perhaps you shall have a match with me. My grandfather taught me. You need not be bored, for he says that despite my youth I am very good."

"Are you, then," he said. "Why, so is King Richard. He has never lost. Though I know it for a fact that when things go ill for him, his opponent backs away."

"Do you mean they let him win?"

"Of course. He is no fighter, so he takes fanatical pride in his chess. God's blood, why anger the King over a game?"

"I should like to sit at the board with him. But I should not let him win."

"Would you not?" He was amused. "Would you take him, then?"

"I think I could. Has he bested my grandfather?"

"Old Gaunt?" York scoffed. "Gaunt never sat at board with him that I know. When one has the King by the nose as did Gaunt, one does not play games. England was Gaunt's chessboard."

"I should take offense at such words," I said, my temper rising again. "My grandfather did but seek to serve England and his king, as yet he does."

"He shall do no more service upon his deathbed," York said.

"It is a lie!" I whispered fiercely. "He is ill, but he does not die."

"As you will." He shrugged. "However it may be, he is out of the King's favor, that is God's truth. The King does think that he was too long under the authority of Lancaster. With Bolingbroke in exile and you in his grasp, he sleeps more soundly at night, I doubt me not."

"Will you have of the pears in syrup, my lord?" the page intoned.

I shook my head angrily and sat with fists clenched. I could well understand the King's enmity toward my father, but I had not known it extended to my grandfather as well. Were kings mere creatures of malice, then? I looked toward the dais where Richard sat and saw his eyes seemingly fixed upon me in a malevolent glare. Uneasily I shifted my gaze to the Queen, seated beside him, and near dropped my knife, so startled I was. She was only a child of about ten years, and she was very pretty.

"So the Queen has caught your eye, has she?" York said gleefully.

"And if she has?"

"She is the daughter of the French King Charles," he continued as though I had not spoken. "An exquisite child, Isabel. They say her hair is thick and black beneath her coif. How lickerish Richard must be as he waits for her to grow up. Or perhaps he does not wait."

I turned my head pointedly from him and sat in stony silence, but he would not be put off. He leaned forward and whispered in my ear.

"Have a care, Henry. They do say Richard prefers young boys even passing women. It may be your rosy cheeks shall entice him to your bed-chamber."

My patience was gone.

"In truth," I said, looking him in the eye, "my grandfather once told me his brother of York was a very great fool, and his sons no better. I have ever known him to be a man of keen judgment."

York reddened and gripped my shoulder tightly with thick fingers.

"Guard your tongue, young Lancaster. You are on dangerous ground here. You have no friends at court. None."

He released his hold on me and sat back.

"Commend yourself to the priests," he said. "If your father be as rash as I think him, even your tender years shall not save you."

I lay awake that night, haunted by his words.

On the day after Christmas, Richard and his court rode to the hunt in Windsor Great Park, but I was not allowed to go. I took to my chamber and there strummed upon my harp and sang to myself the melancholy lays of the Welsh until my hands slipped from the strings and my head nodded in sleep. I was roused by a horn sounding the return of the hunters and wandered groggily into the hall, that I might be near if the King should call for me. A rush of cold air followed the men inside, where they threw off their cloaks and called loudly for wine. Richard was in an expansive mood, for a large buck had fallen to his crossbow. He laughed heartily, blew upon his hands to warm them, and swaggered about clapping the backs of the courtiers. Then he spied me. All good cheer drained from his face.

"Here, then, is an impudent young ass!" he cried.

All eyes turned to me. I sank wearily to my knees and wondered what now my offense might be.

"You idly boast of your prowess at chess, Harry Monmouth, and claim you would trap my king. Is it not so?"

I stared at the floor in despair.

"Speak, boy! Did you claim to be a better gamesman than I?"

"Your grace," I replied in a small voice, "I made no such claim in general, only to say that I thought I might best you."

Under my breath I cursed Richard of York with every Welsh epithet that came to mind.

"It seems Lancaster breeds stiff necks and thick heads, but not respect," said the King. "This is not your first impertinence. Are you too dull to be aware of your position? Your father stands condemned an enemy of this realm."

"Your grace need not question my loyalty," I said hopelessly. "I am not of my father's mind. In truth, I am your faithful servant. I try only to be honest, as I have been taught."

"You are ill taught! None may belittle the King, not even Lancaster. I must teach you a lesson, as I did the arrogant Bolingbroke. What say you, my lords? What shall be his punishment? A proud back may profit from flogging, I'll wager."

"Your grace, if I may be so bold," said York with an unctuous smile, "it would be quite proper to flog the lad. Yet in addition, what more fitting punishment than a sound thrashing at the chessboard? 'Twould be quickly enough accomplished by your grace."

My dilemma was clear. If I lost, I would be chastened and mocked for my presumption. And if I won, far worse, for the King's chagrin would be great and his anger turned against me. Best perhaps to put up a good fight and lose, but I was stung by my treatment and my child's pride rebelled at it.

Richard, certain of his skill, was delighted by York's suggestion and called for the chessboard after he had supped. The board was most marvelously wrought of inlaid pearl and ebony, and the chessmen were of silver and gold. Richard seated himself and spread his robes delicately about him.

"You shall be flogged, Harry Monmouth, when our match is done. That I promise. Now take your place. You shall have the silver."

"Your grace," I said quickly, "I beg your permission to speak ere we begin." I had been thinking furiously and, believing that my situation could worsen but little, had hit upon one last gamble.

"It is too late to crave pardon," said Richard coldly.

"Yet upon one matter I must speak," I said. I turned upon him the innocent expression which so charmed Joan when she caught me at some mischief. "My cousin of York has told me that often your opponents seek to curry your favor and so throw the match to your benefit. I am sure it must anger you when they do it, for would it not take the edge off your enjoyment? I pledge you I shall try my best, no matter—"

I broke off, for the King had turned his attention from me to stare at my cousin York. As for York, he was so startled that he could but gape stupidly, making no protestation.

"Said you this, my lord?" Richard cried.

York dropped to his knees. "I—I—your grace, I do not remember."

"You do not remember," Richard said softly. "Could the boy make up such a thing?"

He glanced at me, and I looked properly bewildered.

"Pardon, your grace, what have I said to give offense? I can do nothing right, it seems." I cast my eyes down quite piteously.

"This is a lie!" Richard roared. "I am a student of the game. I win by my wits. Who dares discount my victories?"

"Your grace, do not believe this boy," York blustered.

"No! Your hesitation has convicted you. It is too late for denial. Get you from my court, I shall have none of you. Nor will I look favorably upon the petition you bear me concerning your Yorkshire lands."

"Pardon, your grace, pardon," York mumbled. He bowed low and stalked out, throwing me a venomous glance as he went. Among the remaining courtiers I noted some pleased smiles.

I bent my head again and said humbly, "Forgive me, your grace. I should have known that when York disparaged your victories he did lie. He has about him a look of deceit."

Richard had been pacing angrily. He stopped and looked at me suspiciously.

"Very well then," he mumbled. "You have much to learn, boy."

He sat abruptly at the board and shoved forward a pawn.

It was a lovely match which my lord of York missed. We sat at the board all that day and into the next morning, pausing only to eat and sleep. Richard was cunning, especially skillful in the use of his bishops. Patiently, cautiously, I probed his defenses while fending off his own lightning attacks. Often I would look up from the board to find him staring at me, his face tense.

"This is no idle challenge you present," he said once, his voice edged with iron.

"I but do my best," I said stoically.

At last, diverted by a feint from my queen, he overreached himself. I hung poised over the board while an urgent inner voice told me it was enough, that I had proved my mettle and affrighted him. Better now to back away and leave him be.

I leaned forward with a sigh, cradled my lone rook tenderly in my hand a moment, then set it opposite his king.

"I believe, your grace, you are caught," I said. I looked at him cautiously. He was staring at the board. The spectators who had attended us so long drew back in awed silence. Behind me a portion of the yule log fell popping and sizzling onto the hearth.

At last he looked up, his face ashen. "Have you sat at board with your father?" he asked in a strained voice.

I thought it an odd question. "I used to. But when I began to beat him badly, he would not sit down with me again."

He smiled, then laughed, long and loudly. The others laughed too, with great relief. I bowed my head and set my hands to my knees to stop my legs from shaking. The King came to me then and clapped me upon the shoulder.

"Well played, Harry Monmouth, cannily played. I have used all my tricks, and even invented some new ones. God's blood, I hope I shall remember them. I shall befuddle old Salisbury when next we meet. I near had your king once. You must show me again how you escaped."

"I shall try."

"And you must sit with me again soon. Afore God, I shall have my revenge."

"No doubt you shall, your grace." I stood shakily and bowed. "Now I will take my punishment."

"What mean you?"

"You promised me a flogging when our match was done."

"Indeed, I had quite forgotten it," he said lightly. "Never mind. I do forgive you, young cousin."

"No," I said gravely. "I have been judged impertinent. It is not meet that I should escape this reproof, for my tender years demand correction, and I would learn what it is to serve my King. By this submission shall you know my loyalty and my goodwill toward you."

"Hear you this, my lords?" he asked thoughtfully. "It seems I have been mistaken in this lad, for here is a model of courage and gentleness. I commend this young Lancaster to you all."

I took ten strokes from the belt of a servant without complaint and went sore to my bed. Yet did I count each welt upon my back as worthwhile for the respect it gained me. I was no longer friendless at the King's court.

I was with Richard as the moth that flits about the spider's web, drawn to its shimmering lace and unaware how fast its gossamer strands might hold. I watched the fawning of the courtiers with disdain and held to a course of cheerful frankness in the King's presence. I was rewarded with a position in the King's personal service, for Richard would have me ever about him. Harry Monmouth must serve him at table, Harry Monmouth must carry his falcon. He called me often to the chessboard, where we took turns at winning. He named me valiant, cunning, the most likely of all his nobles. Such praise was as fine wine to a boy more familiar with scorn. No ill could befall one who stood so high in the King's favor. I would but bide my time till that day, surely not far off, when the King would offer reward for service well rendered and grant me my fondest request. Then would I return, the King's liege man, to Monmouth.

In gaining the King's favor, I gained the young Queen's as well. Isabel, round of face and brown of eyes, was devoted to Richard, even though homesick for her France. The King had a gentle way with her, never raising his voice as he did with all others. She praised him to me as "beautiful, his eyes so blue, his smile so sweet. And he does not smell nasty, as did my father." Her father, the French king, was said to be mad and refused to bathe, claiming the water would burn him to death.

Isabel was far from home, as I was, and even more lonely because she spoke English poorly. At one time French was the language of the English court, but no more. Except for Richard, none bothered to speak French with Isabel save her ladies, and these were wrinkled old women who treated her with cold courtesy indeed. I made special effort to converse with her in my own halting version of the French tongue, and she rewarded me with laughter and kisses. But she loved best to hear my Welsh, though she knew not a word of it. I played for her upon my harp and sang the dark, pure songs of

Gwent. Richard listened as well, and it seemed to me there was a kinship between the desolate Celtic wailings and the brooding, terrified king.

For terrified he was. I came to see his fear in the fits of temper which empurpled his face and left him gasping for breath, in his nervous pacing as he guessed at some imaginary plot against his person. Some judged him mad as the French King. Perhaps, but who can say what madness is? None had called Richard's father mad, the Black Prince who had butchered the women and children of Limoges for a point of honor. And had Richard shown no fear, would he then be deemed sound of mind? I turned from those at court who disparaged Richard's sanity and thought them very great fools indeed. Foolish myself, for I began to think myself exempt from Richard's mistrust, secure in my role of King's favorite. This illusion was shattered one evening as I did harp for him a roundelay and he listened with chin in hand and eyes shut. A courtier idly likened us to Saul and David. Richard was so unsettled at this he bade me never play for him again, nor would he speak to me. A fortnight passed, and he called again for the harp as though nothing had happened. Still, a vision of a nightmarish future had been revealed to me. I shared this incident with the poet Chaucer, my grandfather's brother-in-law, who was often at court. He nodded gravely.

"I have survived two reigns by weaving illusions with words. You must create illusions of your own however you may. From what I have seen, you have a talent for it. Yet have a care you do not fall into your own trap. Expect nothing."

He bent close to my ear.

"I have seen Gaunt. He sends his love and bids you draw upon your wits and all your courage. His illness sits still more heavily upon him, and he fears he is not long for this world. He says that you are the hope of Lancaster."

A hand shook me roughly by the shoulder and pulled me from the depths of sleep. The stone floor was cold beneath my feet, the gown was drawn clumsily over my head, the candles wavered unsteadily.

"Come, my lord, to the King."

Richard sat like a golden ghost in the dimly lit chamber. The table before him held an untidy pile of open books.

"Here, boy," he said. I shuffled to him unsteadily. "I have word from France. Your father seeks to raise up rebellion against me."

"How so, your grace?" I asked, fully awake now.

"He is with the Duke of Brittany. The traitor Arundel has gone to join him, and others he calls to himself as well."

"E'en so, it is a long way across the Channel," I said timidly.

His fist crashed down upon the table, and a book fell to the floor.

"Do not seek to placate me!" he cried. "I see through your ruse, Harry. He has sent you here to lull me into carelessness."

"Your grace," I said, stunned, "'twas you who brought me here. Do you not recall?"

He buried his face in his hands. "Of course," he muttered. "Of course. I had forgotten for the moment. I am so tired."

"Your grace should sleep," I urged gently.

"Sleep! Who may sleep on such a night as this?"

"Your grace's manner alarms me. Has anything else happened this night?"

He ignored the question and stared hard at me. "You are sure you receive no word from your father? You swear it before God?"

"I swear before God I have no word from my father."

"It is just as well. I should have no taste for charging you with treason."

"Have I not demonstrated my loyalty?" I protested. "I had thought you fond of me."

"Indeed I am fond of you. It makes no difference. I brought you here, as you say. Do you know why?"

"I suppose I am a surety against my father's actions."

"You are my hostage," he said. "Should Bolingbroke threaten me, I have pledged to slay you. And if I have pledged it, I must be prepared to carry it out, must I not? After all, I am a king, and kings must do such things. Is it not damnable?"

"Your grace, I am true to you," I croaked through dry lips. "Lay not my father's misdeeds upon my head."

"'The fathers have eaten sour grapes and the sons' teeth are set on edge!'" Back and forth he paced, back and forth. "Do you hate me, Harry?"

"Hate you, your grace? No, yet now I fear you most dreadfully."

"Ah, it is good that you fear me. Kings are to be feared. Only then are we obeyed. Yet you do not hate me?"

"No."

"You lie."

"No, your grace."

"Since you do deny it, I shall test you. Harry, your grandfather Gaunt is dead."

I stepped back, stricken. "No!" I cried. "It must not be!"

"It is true. Word comes from Kenilworth this very night. John of Gaunt is dead."

I heard him numbly, the tears coursing down my cheeks.

"Now I must move against Bolingbroke once and for all," he continued coldly. "I cannot have him Duke of Lancaster, even in exile. There is too much danger in it. I shall enlarge his banishment to the duration of his life. I shall disinherit him. And, Harry, I shall disinherit you. It shall take a month or so, but when summer comes there shall be no Duchy of Lancaster. Bolingbroke shall remain abroad forever, and his holdings shall fall to the Crown."

"Monmouth as well?" I sobbed.

"Monmouth as well. Now do you hate me? Aye, I thought so. I see it in your eyes. Well, is it not the lot of kings? I must bear it, that is all."

"Why?" I asked. "You need not be so harsh. I have been ready to love you. It is as though you sought my hatred. Why?"

"I seek nothing. We kings are ever hated, ever abused. That is the way of it. Do you not know your history? The better man the King is, the more he is abused. That is the truth of it. Why else was the second Edward so ill used?"

"I have heard him named weak," I ventured.

"Then was his goodness mistaken for weakness." Richard snatched up a book from the floor. "I have read of him here, in this history. He was a peaceable man. He liked to work in the garden. Ah, the chroniclers laughed at that. Fat, sneering monks! And the nobles, thick-headed dolts as now. They wanted a warrior, and he was not one, and so they killed him."

I had heard other things of Edward: that he was capricious and cruel, that the kingdom had fallen into chaos because of his neglect. But I said nothing. Richard clutched his book to his chest and rocked to and fro on his heels. "So horrible it was. So horrible. His queen was a Frenchwoman. Evil she was, not like my Isabel, sweet child. This queen conspired with the nobles for Edward's death. They wanted no wound on his body to cry murder. Do you know how they slew him? They thrust a red hot poker up his arse into his bowels." He screwed his eyes shut. "They say the peasants of Berkeley heard the screams for miles around. Berkeley. I shall never go to Berkeley. So they treat kings."

I shook my head. "I am very sorry for you, your grace. Yet how am I to overlook your mistreatment of me? My grandfather would have me stand for my heritage."

"Harry, Harry. Can you not see it is best this way? John of Gaunt was once as a father to me, yet was he driven from my affections so that I cannot weep for his death now. It was his power that did it. None should have power save the King, else there is bitter rivalry. I have grown fond of you, as I have said, and I did dread the day you should come into your inheritance. Then would enmity have parted us. Now it shall not be. Think on it, Harry, and you shall see I am right. Never fear that I shall leave you to starve. You shall serve me well, I am sure of it, and I shall reward you for your service as a good sovereign should do. Perhaps you shall have Monmouth, since you love it so well. What say you to that?"

"Your grace, I may not speak more," I said painfully. "I have lost much this night, and I would be free to mourn."

"Get you gone then," he said with sudden irritation. "You keep me from my bed as it is."

I would have turned from him were it not for Isabel. I had grown to love her with all the passion a child of eleven can feel. I saw myself as her protector and confidant amid the lonely perils of the court, Lancelot to her Guinevere. I could not turn a deaf ear when she pleaded with me so prettily.

"It is not Richard who uses you so unjustly, but it is the crown which possesses him. Have I not seen my father's madness? I think it must take a strong man to be king, and my father is not strong. Nor, I fear, is Richard, but he does try. Will you not help him? Easy it was to love him when he heaped favors upon you. Yet it is now, when he mistreats you, that he needs you most. He spoke quite plainly with you and shared his fear. He would do so with few others, I think. He trusts you."

"He does not," I said stubbornly. "He accused me of plotting with my father."

"*Mon dieu.*" She sighed. "You are still in his favor. Is it not proof enough?"

When I made no reply, she touched my sleeve.

"Henri, would you be king?"

"Not for all the joys of heaven," I said forcefully.

"Then will you not have pity on him? The crown drives all friendship from him. He has me for companion, and you, if you will. Is it not sad that the King of England must depend upon two of such tender years?"

In the end I yielded to her entreaties. The hurt did not leave me, nor the desire for restitution. But I saw Richard's peril as well, and I could not abandon him to it. There was not a nobleman in England who did not shudder at his heavy-handed treatment of Lancaster and wonder who would be next. The air at court was fraught with anticipation of a rising, and Richard's face had a hunted expression. There was within me, born of my own experience, a cry of compassion for him in his isolation. I conquered my fear and anger and stayed by his side.

With summer came Richard's greatest folly. Rumor continued from abroad that my father meant to return from exile. Yet Richard, who in winter had been consumed with fear of Bolingbroke's intentions, now pretended to blithe unconcern.

"Where shall he go? To whom shall he turn?" he would ask airily. "I hold his castles, his wealth, his lands. I have his son, whose safety he must think on. The others of his peers will not act, lest they too suffer his fate. Let him come on! Would he dare invade this island? Does he fancy himself to be another William the Conqueror?"

In private he said to me, "In truth, I do not think I could bring myself to harm you. But Bolingbroke need not know it. You aid my defense, Harry, and I shall not forget it. Someday I shall reward you for that you forestall these rebels."

There was no accounting for such perversity save that Richard was governed by his moods and obsessions. My father having been dispossessed, the King's hatred seemed spent and he bent his energies in other directions. Yet this was a time when the King's fears would have served him well, for unrest was abroad in the land. I continually urged caution upon the King, as did others, but he would have none of it. He had made up his mind to go to Ireland, and no other subject could hold his attention.

Richard had long chafed under the charge of cowardice hurled at him by the barons of England because he was not a fighting man. He knew little and cared less of armies and battles. Still, when rebellion broke out in Ireland, he resolved to put it down himself. He judged it would be easy to win glory against the Irish; and besides, he had a personal quarrel with them, since the rebels had slain Roger Mortimer, the heir to the throne until Richard should have a son. No word of caution, no warning of danger would stay him. He would prove the power and majesty of the English king against the hapless Irish and thereby send a message to his own restive subjects. In June he set sail upon a glassy sea for Waterford with most of his supporters, and I among them. Those peers who stayed behind were no friends of the King, and the defense of the realm was left to the Duke of York, father to Richard of York, and an incompetent.

Richard at once sought a pitched battle with the Irish, but the fur-clad kerns only retreated to their forest hideouts. Richard's knights, clad in mail despite the summer heat, chased them vainly through the tangled undergrowth and often were lost in the pathless wood, where they would be set upon from behind and stabbed through their visors. They caught but a few of the Irish, and these must have been exceedingly slow. Mercifully I saw little of this for I was deemed too young for the fight. Instead I kept company in Dublin Castle with the King, who had quickly had his fill of such sport. Yet one day I did ride out a short way with Richard and in a fair meadow was knighted by him. This honor I received with high seriousness, for though I did see Richard's flaws, I pledged myself to him before God as my liege lord, and secretly to Isabel as my beloved lady. No longer did I lack a title but might style myself Sir Henry Monmouth.

We were sitting down to our supper in the gloomy hall at Dublin when a messenger arrived from England. This man, Sir William Bagot, was pale of face and trembling as he knelt.

"Tidings of peril I bring to your grace." His voice rattled through the silent hall. "Your realm has been invaded by Henry of Bolingbroke."

A score of voices cried out in alarm. Richard only squirmed in his chair, his eyes downcast.

"My lord of York rushes to oppose him?" he asked.

"The Duke of York heard of his sailing and moved south to meet him. Unhappily, Bolingbroke landed in the north, at Ravenspur."

All groaned.

"My people," Richard said plaintively, "my English people, do they rise to fight against him?"

"Your grace, forgive me that I must deliver such a blow. The people rise on behalf of Bolingbroke, and the barons as well, the Percies of Northumberland, Worcester, the Earl of Westmoreland. There are many strongholds of Lancaster in the north, and all have opened their doors to him."

"Lancaster's holdings are now mine," Richard fretted.

"Yet do they recall their former master," Bagot said.

"Your news seems overly late." This from the Earl of Aumerle, eldest son of the Duke of York. "When did he land?"

"The fourth day of July," said Bagot.

"And only now do I hear of it!" Richard cried. "What does this mean?"

"Pardon, your grace, we were delayed by bad weather. We could not make the crossing."

"'Tis time enough to lose the crown," Richard moaned.

"Where lies Bolingbroke now?" Aumerle asked.

"He was at Doncaster," said Bagot. "There he issued a statement to the people, saying that he came but for his own, and not for the crown. By now he is likely at Kenilworth or beyond, gathering support as he goes."

"He comes for his own! How dare he say it?" Richard dashed his wine-glass to the floor. "Does he think to use the King of England so? Jesu, why did I not behead him while I did have him in my grasp? This is poor reward for mercy shown. No mercy now for Bolingbroke. He shall die such a death that even the Turks shall speak of it."

Then his frantic eye rested upon me.

"Harry, come here," he commanded.

I rose shakily and stood before him. He placed his hands upon my shoulders and turned to Bagot.

"Here is his son. Does he not know I hold his son as hostage? Is he mad that he risks the boy's life?"

Bagot hesitated. "This is a hard matter to discuss before the boy, your grace."

"Speak on," Richard said.

"Bolingbroke sends you this message. He knows that the young lord Henry is with you. He asks you to recall he has three other sons, all healthy, promising lads, and these three are now with him. He bids you use young Henry as you will. He cares not. He will come on."

I stared stolidly at my toes. There were no words to speak.

"Is this how a father loves a son?" Richard whispered to me.

I shook my head mutely.

"What has your father done to us?" He dropped his head to my shoulder and wept in great, gasping sobs.

"Your grace, you must calm yourself," Bagot said after a while. "The time grows short."

"What of the Queen?" Richard asked through his tears.

"She is safe for the moment in the Tower. I doubt she shall come to harm whatever happens. But what of this boy? Shall you make an example of him? It may yet slow Bolingbroke and shake his followers if he receives the boy's head."

I lifted my eyes in prayer. "Mercy, Lord. Jesu, mercy," I breathed.

Richard's face was an agony of uncertainty.

"A soft heart will not save us, your grace," Bagot said sharply.

Richard shook his head. "I cannot slay the boy. I will not. He has done me nought but good service, though he has cause enough to hate me. I cannot do it." He sighed and shook himself, and a weight seemed to lift from him, so that he stood straight, his eyes clear and blue. He had so much the look of a king that I was drawn humbly to my knees.

"I pledge myself once more to you," I said. "Nor shall I forget your gentleness toward me. I stand with you against my father."

"Yet must you remain here," he said softly, "and I am for England."

"No, your grace! Take me with you."

"'Twould be too perilous for you," he said, looking pointedly at Bagot. "You shall stay in Dublin, under guard for your protection. Then I shall send for you when I have dealt with these rebels. You have my promise."

"Then I must be content," I said miserably.

As preparations were made for the return to England, Richard was calm as I had never seen him, seeming to call upon some inner store of courage. The tidings grew steadily worse. Father had reached the Severn and joined forces with the turncoat Duke of York, who had at least wits enough to recognize a winning cause. The place of their meeting was Berkeley Castle, where the second Edward had met his death. Richard seemed unmoved by this touch of bitter irony. He shook off all pleas to flee to France. Kings, he said, do not flee from rebellious subjects. He sailed for Wales, only to find there the last of his army had melted away into the hills. A fortnight later, nearly alone, he was forced to surrender at Flint. He was taken to Chester, still King of England but a prisoner of Henry Bolingbroke.

3

I did not know that Richard was truly fallen until a carrack came beating across the sea, the blue pennon of Lancaster flying from its mast. Sir Thomas Erpyngham, who had been one of my grandfather's most trusted knights, was sent to escort me to Chester. He had no trouble in securing the surrender of the Dublin garrison and greeted me in the hall with a bow and a smile.

"Good fortune, my lord Henry, for the honor of Lancaster is safely restored."

"I count it no honor to be set in opposition to the King I have sworn to serve," I said.

He looked surprised but said nothing, and I kept my own counsel throughout the rough crossing to England. Nor did I tarry in his company when we had landed, but made my way at once to the precinct of the castle where the servants of the King were lodged. I asked after Richard and learned that none had seen him, but he was thought to be well for he would soon ride to London with Bolingbroke. There were but few present of Richard's household, for most had deserted him ere he ever reached Flint. I wandered about, speaking with each one, and it was there that Erpyngham found me.

"Your father has been told that you went straightway to be with the

King's household," he warned. "He is furious with you. Have a care, then, what you say to him."

I found Father little changed since our parting the year before, a bit thicker about the belly perhaps, and heavier of cheek, but still a fine figure of a man. He had with him a purple-robed cleric who I knew from Richard's servants must be Thomas Arundel, the Archbishop of Canterbury. The younger son of a noble family, he had, like my father, been banished for treason despite his high office. He was a tall, bony old man with an unkempt thatch of white hair beneath his tonsure. His eyes were sharp and cruel as any falcon's, and I would not have been startled to see talons on his clawlike fingers, for so he did hover behind my father's shoulder.

Father spoke as soon as the door closed behind me.

"Why were you found among Richard's people?"

"Where should I have been?" I met his eyes defiantly.

"Most sons would have gone to their father."

"Richard has been more father to me than have you. He cares more for my safety than you. And besides, he is my liege lord, and I am his knight. I have not forgotten loyalty to my king as you have done. You come against your sovereign with sword in hand, and I cannot say aye to it."

"How dare you chide me so! Have I not rescued your heritage? I have done what I had to do, and if I have placed you in danger, well, no son worth his mettle would wish to live if his honor be stripped from him."

"It seems there is no appreciation here for the risks and hardships your father has suffered," Arundel said, wagging his head from side to side. "You are an impudent, ungrateful whelp."

"This is no affair of yours," I said.

Father struck me a blow across the face which dropped me stunned to my knees. Bright red blood dripped from my mouth onto the white hart embossed on my tunic.

"You will not speak so to the Archbishop or to me," he said. "Craven you may be, Harry, but I will not have you discourteous. Do you understand?"

I staggered to my feet and out of his reach.

"I understand well," I cried. "You have broken your oath of loyalty to the King, yet you speak of honor. Richard's servants tell me that your troops burn Welsh villages for their loyalty to the King, yet you speak of honor. You know nothing of honor! Nothing! You have proven you care nothing for me. By what right do you speak to me of anything?"

His next blow fetched me up against the door, and I slipped groggily to the floor.

"I have not done with you, Harry," I heard him say from a distance.

"The stakes are higher now, and I require a fit heir. I shall make of you such or, by all the saints, I shall break you. Now get you gone."

He gripped my arm, hauled me up, and dragged me out into the stairwell, where I leaned against the wall. Arundel was saying in his piercing voice, "I understand now why you sorrow over the boy, but this is not a hopeless situation. He does have spirit, after all. Perhaps he is as an untamed colt who has not yet felt the spur. If he can be disciplined, he may yet prove useful. Give him over to Harry Percy for a time. Percy shall put the fear of God into the lad."

The door slammed shut, and I was alone.

My uncle of Beaufort had taken my brothers to the Tower for safekeeping, and there I was reunited with them. Tom could scarce contain his joy at the sight of me.

"Harry!" he cried, and hugged me to his breast. "You are here at last. Is it not splendid? When Father is king, then all England shall be at our bidding."

"What do you mean?" I looked at Beaufort. "What does he mean? Richard is King."

"God's blood, you are slow-witted," Tom said. "Of course Richard is the King, but he must abdicate. Father would not be safe otherwise. And who is more fit to succeed to the throne than Father? He is the finest knight in the realm."

"Richard has a legal heir," I said. "He is Edmund Mortimer, next of kin to the King."

"Edmund Mortimer is a child, no older than Humphrey," said Beaufort. "England has seen enough of child kings. Richard was one, and see how we are now in disarray. These unsettled times require a firm hand."

"If the times are unsettled, then Father has made them so," I said. "At Pontefract he claimed that he came but for his own, and not for the crown. Is he now liar as well as traitor?"

"You shall not say that." Tom started toward me but was restrained by Beaufort. "He speaks as one of Lancaster's enemies."

"In truth, he speaks foolishly," said Beaufort. "Yet I am sure these past months have been a lonely and frightening time for your brother." To me he said, "Never repeat those charges, Harry. I had thought you possessed sharper wits than this. No one can rule save Bolingbroke, and that is the end of it."

"Richard is the anointed king," I persisted. "If he be set aside and the succession ignored, then any man may oppress another, and where does safety lie?"

"Safety lies in power," Beaufort said, his black eyes gleaming. "You must learn that lesson quickly, Harry, for your survival depends upon it. Though it pleases neither you nor Bolingbroke, you shall be king some day."

Little Humphrey clasped my hand. "I think you shall be a fine king," he said in a small voice.

I stared at him bleakly, only now fully understanding what had befallen me. Someday I would be King of England. Someday I would suffer the same torments which had plagued Richard—if I lived. It seemed to me then that heavy chains fell across me. No matter how dark the dungeon in which Richard should be cast, my own prison would be more foul.

Beaufort poured himself a glass of wine and raised it. "To the future King Henry who stands here before us, the fifth of that name, God willing. Long may he reign."

Humphrey cheered lustily. "Now, Harry, you must come see." He tugged at my sleeve. "They do keep lions penned in the Tower. Real lions! You must come see them."

I managed to speak with Richard once more. His cell in the Beauchamp Tower was guarded by a retainer of Lancaster who had often been at Kenilworth, and with the help of a gold noble I persuaded him to grant me a moment with the King. The man would not open the door of the cell, and so we were forced to whisper through the keyhole. Richard's voice was flat and lifeless. He asked after Isabel.

"I have not seen her," I said. "They have taken her to the manor at Sonning. It is said she shall be sent back to her father in France."

"Please seek after her and see that she is well treated," he begged.

"Aye, I shall. I love her as you do."

He shifted his weight against the door, and a stale odor wafted through the keyhole.

"So, Harry, you shall be king."

"It seems I must be," I said. "If my father does not first disinherit me."

"Or murder you in your bed."

I started. "Jesu! Do not say such a thing! Even he would not do that."

"Forgive me. It is not meet that I make your way more difficult than it shall be. I am told he shall make you a knight."

"Aye. He was angry that you had done so and claims that my allegiance must be with him."

"So it should, for your sake. I absolve you of your oath to me. I would have you serve him with clear conscience."

"I am not willingly absolved. I have taken blows on your behalf."

"Then take no more. I am past helping. Only pray for me. It is all I ask."

"Already I remember you to Our Lady each night."

"Ah, you are good, Harry. And, being good, you shall be either a very great king or a very great monster. Or perhaps you shall be both."

"I do not understand, but your words frighten me."

"Of course they do. Fear shall be your companion now."

The guard nudged me. "Only a little more, my lord," he said.

"I must go, Richard. Only hold fast, and when I am king you shall be freed and restored."

"No, I shall not live so long." His voice was fraught with emotion. "How do you suppose it shall be, my death? They say when William the Conqueror died, he was quite fat. His entombment was late, so that when they fit him in his sarcophagus, his guts exploded and did most horribly defile the church. Men laugh at this story over their cups in the taverns. Do you think they shall laugh when they tell of my death?"

Sickened, I bade him a hasty farewell and hurried away. He was sent next day under guard to the dungeon at Pontefract, there to be imprisoned for the remainder of his life.

On the thirteenth day of October in the year of Our Lord 1399, Henry Bolingbroke was crowned King of England. I have no pleasant memories of the day. The weather had turned passing warm for so late in the year, and the air inside the crowded abbey at Westminster was rank. Arundel's sermon was tedious. The good Archbishop attempted valiantly, if futilely, to give credence to the ceremony, as if my father were indeed rightful heir to the crown he now wore. Unfortunately it took some length of time to establish such a preposterous claim, and many fell asleep.

The banquet followed in the great hall of the palace, which had only recently been fitted by Richard with a magnificent roof of wooden beams. The King's champion, one Sir Thomas Dymock, rode into the hall on horseback, as is the custom, and offered to fight any who challenged the King's right to the crown. The gathered company lapsed into an uneasy silence. The iron-shod hooves of the horse rang upon the stone floor as Dymock circled the hall, hand resting upon the hilt of his sword.

Father rose at last with forced joviality and shouted, "Faith, Dymock, your services are not required, for I would gladly meet all challengers with my own right hand and prove my claim with my own body."

Ever the blustering paladin. He laughed heartily, and the company joined him uncertainly.

I exchanged a cynical glance with my uncle Beaufort across the table and went back to my wine.

Though none openly took up Dymock's challenge, there were those who plotted in secret and nearly ruined the house of Lancaster that Yuletide. The court had removed to Windsor for the hunt, and a great tournament was called for Twelfth Night to celebrate the new reign. Bolingbroke himself would enter the lists, and it was oft noted that in the glorious days of Edward the Third the king had been a jouster. This time I would be allowed to attend upon Father. After all, it would not be fitting to ignore the Prince of Wales. Indeed, Father now made much of me, at least when the eyes of the court were upon us, for the legitimacy of his rule depended upon a visible and praiseworthy heir. In private he was scornful as ever. I longed for the love of Joan Waryn and took little comfort from the nativity of our Lord.

We feasted well upon Christmas Day, though not so elaborately as Richard would have done. Nor was there so much of music as I had known before, and Geoffrey Chaucer was not called to read his poetry. The conversations of the courtiers were of a more sober sort, of the stability of the exchequer, of the Scottish borders, and especially the Twelfth Night tournament. My brothers were overawed by the splendor of Windsor, and I was able to impress them with my bored manner.

"At Christmas last year we had a sugar subtlety fashioned after the Tower of London," I informed them. "It was complete down to the last stone."

"How do you know it was complete?" Tom asked suspiciously.

"I was told it by Richard," I said. "And I was given a piece of the gatehouse to eat. The drawbridge was of honeyed almonds."

"I should have liked a piece of the drawbridge," Humphrey said, "but not now. I feel ill. My belly gripes me." He set his hands to his midsection and moaned.

"Mine gripes me as well," John complained. "Can it be we have eaten tainted meat?"

It was not long ere Tom and I felt ill as well. We looked at one another fearfully.

"This is strange," Tom said. "I shall tell Father. I feel—"

His words were lost as Humphrey screamed and fell from his bench. I had risen to go to him when a sharp pain tore through my belly. I staggered and bent double. A hand grasped my shoulder, and Beaufort's face loomed close.

"In God's name, Harry, what is it?"

"It hurts," I gasped. "Poison—"

I slipped to the floor, and the pain drove all from me save shrieks.

We lay near death for two days. When not convulsed in agony upon our beds, we retched long after there was nothing left to vomit. The royal physicians purged us with vile potions that were torture to swallow. Humphrey, the smallest, was most sorely afflicted and lay blind and speechless for three days. Yet God in His mercy spared us all.

Father had also been poisoned, but he did not suffer so severely. It was an inexperienced attempt, for only enough poison was administered to make a grown man ill, though it was nearly enough to kill a small child. Soon after, a squire who had been in Richard's service was found to be missing, and his guilt was assumed at once. In a fury, Father sent away all who had taken service with the former King. But he would not suspend the festivities of the season and declared he would yet be well enough to break a lance on Twelfth Night. It was not to be.

On the tenth night past Christmas I was roused from sleep by a rough voice.

"Come, your highness. We must be away. Rouse yourself. We must fly."

Strong arms raised me, bundled me into robe and cloak.

"What is it?" I whispered.

"No time for talk," the voice replied.

Behind his shoulder a torch flickered, and I heard Humphrey softly weeping. He was yet perilously weak. From the castle ward I heard the muffled sound of men calling and of horses' hooves on the hard ground. I grabbed the madonna which ever watched over my bed and thrust her inside my robe even as strong arms bore me up into the darkness.

It was bitterly cold. The ward was a maelstrom of armored men and their mounts, and the oaths flew thick and furious.

"What is it?" I asked again.

"There is rebellion abroad, your highness," said the man who carried me. "The earls of Huntingdon, Kent, and Salisbury even now ride upon Windsor with their armies. They may come upon us at any time."

"Do they seek to set Richard upon the throne?"

"So it seems," he said with a grunt. "Those three were ever favorites of his."

"Where are we for, then?"

"For London. For the Tower. The merchants of London are Bolingbroke's. You shall be safe enough in the Tower."

He handed me up to Sir Thomas Erpyngham, already mounted for the journey.

"I may be well enough to sit a horse," I said.

"No, you are not," said Erpyngham. "Even your father is hard put to it. Yet he must. He will ride for London, then out again to meet these treacherous earls."

Across the way I saw Beaufort astride his horse, Humphrey held close in his arms. Poor little one! I shut my eyes and tried to think. I was sworn to

Richard, yet he had absolved me. My heart raced to think he might be freed, yet had not these same earls tried to poison my brothers and me, and would they not slay us yet if they could? I had met Huntingdon and Kent at Richard's court and liked them not.

It was a rough, cold journey. My insides were jolted about and my nausea returned, compounded by fear. At any moment we might be set upon, and the men around me rode with weapons drawn. This, then, was what it meant to be a prince, to be sick with fear and torn between wrong and wrong, or between love and life. Never since have I faced a crisis that I did not recall that terrible night.

Father rode from London to meet the earls, and the rebellion was crushed. The leaders were harried through the countryside, set upon by angry mobs, and slain. Bolingbroke was for the moment the favorite of the people, and new heads were set to rot upon London Bridge.

In February came word that Richard was dead. How he should come to die so suddenly was not explained. It was rumored by the common folk that he yet lived, and so Bolingbroke had his body displayed in London for all to see. The casket was all enclosed in lead, so that only the King's white face was visible. All whispered at what wounds his body might bear.

I said not a word of this matter to my father, for I knew he had ordered Richard's death. I saw the horror of it in the bleakness of Bolingbroke's face, and I saw it torment him over the years. Still, it was wise, Beaufort said. There would be no more rebellions to restore Richard to the throne.

I did not weep for Richard, as I now hoarded my tears as closely as any miser did his gold. But often I would light a candle for him and pray before my madonna. I have ever hoped it was a swift death, and that there were no fiery pokers.

In April, though I was but twelve years of age, I moved from the court to my own manor of Kennington across the Thames from Westminster. Nor did I dwell in my father's house ever after.

II

1401-1403

I am not yet of Percy's mind, the Hotspur of the North; he that kills me some six or seven dozen of Scots at a breakfast, washes his hands, and says to his wife, "Fie upon this quiet life! I want work."

—*Henry IV, Part 1,* act II, scene iv

4

The people of Wales are as old as time itself. So Joan Waryn says. It cannot be true, of course, for was not Adam the first man, and did he not live in that Holy Land where Our Lord was born? Yet the Welsh cannot have come much later, perhaps after the scattering of the multitudes at Babel. Aye, an old people, the Welsh, and once familiar with sorcery. The stones of the ancient ones yet stand starkly upon the moors, the work of ancient magicians. Some say Merlyn himself fixed these stones in their circles, or piled them one upon the other. I cannot pass by such a place lest I cross myself against the Evil One, even though Merlyn must have been a Christian, for how else could he counsel good King Arthur?

The name of Arthur is revered in Wales. Arthur it was who fought against the hated Saxons, the yellow-haired English. The English peers have made Arthur one of their own, the founder of chivalry, but I know differently from Joan. Arthur was a Celt, a proud chieftain who gathered the clans to oppose the invader. He fought bravely but fell beneath the Saxon swords, and his people were driven westward into the mountain fastnesses. He was not all-conquering, Arthur, but more loved, I do believe, for that he faltered. He does but sleep, the Welsh say, hidden away in the mists of the folded hills, and he shall return to free his people. Even now he is awaited, and many have been mistaken for him. Rhodri Mawr, who drove the Norsemen from Wales and united the kingdoms. Lord Rhys ap Gruffydd, who won independence from Henry the Second. Llewellyn the Great, who wed the daughter of the English King John. Many tears were shed over Llewellyn the Last, who sought to expel the English once and for all but was slain by the warriors of Edward the First. Upon the death of this Llewellyn, King Edward placed many burdens upon the Welsh people. They were stripped of their ancient rights and heavily taxed. Thick-walled castles were raised to brood menacingly over the forests and heaths. Worst of all, the best land was seized and given over to followers of the English king. This was especially true in the rich borderland called the march, where proud English "marcher lords" held sway over the unfortunate Welsh. Of all the English nobility, these are the most arrogant. Such a marcher lord was my father, Henry of Bolingbroke, ere he became King of England.

I had long thought of myself as Welsh. I was Monmouth born, and as a babe I had sucked my milk at Joan Waryn's breast. Did I not love Joan better than my father, and Rhys as well as my brothers? Was I not dark of hair, and did I not speak the Welsh tongue as cannily as any Monmouth man? The pure lays of the ancient Celts had stirred my soul, and I had taken up the harp in emulation of the bards. It mattered not to me that the blood of Normandy, and Gascony and even of Spain flowed in my veins. Once born in the shadow of the Black Mountains, once having wandered in the dark woods of Gwent, a man could not be anything but Welsh. No wonder I was in agony when Wales rose in rebellion during the second year of my father's reign.

The new Arthur was one Owain Glyndwr, a landowner of modest means who had long been harassed by his neighbor Lord Grey of Ruthin, a marcher lord. For years, Lord Grey had cast covetous eyes upon Glyndwr's lands, and Bolingbroke's usurpation gave him a splendid opportunity to make a move. Glyndwr was loyal to Richard, as were most of the Welsh, while Lord Grey supported the new king, one of his own. Scarce had the crown settled upon my father's head when Grey seized Glyndwr's best fields and stole his sheep. For answer, Glyndwr raised the standard of revolt. Many were ready to join him. There were few in Wales who could not tell of some wrong suffered at the hands of the English, and with a marcher lord upon the throne there seemed no hope of redress. From green valleys to high heaths, men took up arms and left their cottages to seek out Owain Glyndwr. They would drive the English from their land and make mock of the king's son who dared style himself Prince of Wales.

It was unthinkable to me that I should be made the enemy of Wales. Not Harry Monmouth, who awaited the return of Arthur as eagerly as any. Unknown to my father I dispatched a letter to Owain Glyndwr. With youthful fervor, I proclaimed my love for Wales and vowed that he would have justice when I should become king.

We are not your people, but your enemy, was his reply. *We shall have none of you.*

Not even the loss of my grandfather had seemed so hard as this. I thought on the good folk of Monmouth, now my foes. Rhys and Joan—aye, even Joan—my enemies. I gazed westward from my window at Kennington toward the line of trees marking the Thames and tried to imagine where the swelling English forests would rear up abruptly into proud ranks of mountains cloaked in mist. My governor, Henry Percy, had been named by Father to quell the rebellion, and soon I must ride with him. Percy, I knew, would use Wales roughly. He had been my tutor for six months, upon the advice of Archbishop Arundel. Plato and St. Augustine were set aside for good, and my study was all of war. Percy was a soldier whose reputation surpassed even Bolingbroke's. The lands of his house lay in the far north of England, and his sword was often bloodied in skirmishes with the Scots. "Hotspur" he was nicknamed, after the frenzied way he pricked his horse's flanks when he rode into battle.

From my father, Percy learned that the Prince of Wales had no taste for a fight and no respect for his elders. He came to Kennington determined to break my spirit. I was shaken from sleep well before dawn each day and forced to drill for hours with the sword. Percy made me wait upon him as well, to serve him at dinner and clean his boots, that I might learn humility. Every day he heaped abuse upon me, and my slightest mistake brought a beating. I hated him as I had hated no other man and settled in to a test of wills. I would have died ere I complained to him, and I took my blows from him with as much arrogance as I could muster. As far as I could, I did his bidding only to keep his lash from my body, all the while priding myself that he had not altered me, nor ever would. I was wrong, of course, for I grew hard and reserved under his tutelage, brooding upon how he wronged me and sharing my hurts with no one.

It was intolerable that such a man should be set loose against the Welsh, but my father would hear none of my protests.

"The Scots fear Percy as the Devil himself," he said. "Now so shall the Welsh. This rebellion shall be ended soon enough. Perhaps it is a blessing in disguise. I have ever said that what you need is to see some fighting. If there is any mettle in you, this shall bring it out. By the way, I am pleased with Percy's handling of you, thus far, and shall tell him so. There is an iron look about you that I have not noted before."

"The first lesson," said Percy, "is to know your limitations. Conwy is near impregnable. To attack would cost us many men, and we would probably be beaten back. We could starve them out, but we are better served not to waste the time. We have a rebellion to put down. First, we shall negotiate."

We stood upon a promontory overlooking Conwy town. Beyond the castle, the brisk April wind stirred white foam in the estuary and ruffled the grass on the hump-backed hills. Deganwy, the place across the water was called, and long ago it had been the seat of King Maelgwn, who ruled all western Britain from Scotland to the Channel.

"When you negotiate," Percy was saying, "appeal to the self-interest of the other party. In this case, the expectations of the Twdors are modest. They have failed and now want only a pardon for their treasonous actions. We want the castle. So the Twdors shall have their pardon, we shall make an example of a few of their followers, and Conwy is ours. Everyone shall be happy."

"Everyone save the followers who are your example," I said.

He shrugged. "That is the lot of such rabble, to bear correction. Only then may we govern the rest of them."

"Would it not be more just to punish the Twdors?"

"You reason like a peasant," he said impatiently. "The Twdors are gentlemen even though they are Welsh. 'Twould be unchivalrous to handle them roughly if they submit to us. Yet do not fear, Harry, we shall prove our strength before these people."

The castle surrendered, the Twdors were escorted to the gates of the town and bade never to return, and nine hapless men-at-arms were set aside for trial. Percy pronounced their death sentences in the name of the Prince of Wales.

"I want nought to do with this," I protested.

"Shut up," he answered. "I shall have none of your whining. Your father gives me authority to act in your name. You cannot escape responsibility, nor should you wish to. It is time you learned what it means to be a prince."

The condemned men wore beards and were roughly dressed. They were Anglesey men, I heard tell. Their faces were contorted with terror, and most trembled so violently that they could not walk to the scaffold but must be borne there by their English guards. The assembled people of the town eyed the prisoners with resentment, and some taunted them, relieved there would be no sack of the town, glad that nine of the outsiders who had caused such turmoil would bear the brunt of English wrath. A noose was placed around each man's neck, and one by one they were shoved over the edge of the scaffold. Even as their bodies writhed, a black-hooded man plunged a long sword into their bellies, and their entrails spilled out to hang in a tangled gory mass against their thighs. Then they were cut down and their heads and limbs hacked off amid fountains of blood.

I watched it all. Often Percy's eye was upon me, and I struggled to hide my revulsion. I did not weep or retch. But as I stared, hands clenched at my sides, my eyesight blurred. The muscles of my neck were hard and my head jerked uncontrollably. The cheers of the crowd swelled above the roaring in my ears.

I could not speak until we had entered the castle ward. Then I dismounted and strode to where Percy laughed with his aides.

"Percy!" I shouted. He turned to me, the smile frozen upon his face. "Never would I submit any man to such torture as I have witnessed this day. Yet pray that my father lives a long life, for before God, Percy, when I am King you shall ne'er set foot in this realm. You may slay whom you will abroad, but the poor people of Wales shall be safe from you."

I turned upon my heel and stalked away.

I passed that evening tending the horses, having chased away the stable boys. I had no stomach for food, so I did not go in to sup. I knew I would be punished when I did appear. When I had cleaned the stalls and filled the troughs, I stood next to my own mare, Morgause, wrapped my arms about her neck, and took comfort in her familiar odor. When darkness fell, I walked slowly across the grass of the castle yard to my apartments.

Percy beat me so severely that the skin of my back did split in three places. Yet I sensed fear lay upon him like a cloak.

In Wales, the very earth recalls the sorrow of the people. The shaggy mountains brood, the wind cries out, the trees twist painfully toward the sky. Even on sunny days, when the air is thick with light, each blade of grass, each clump of heather stands illuminated, overwhelmed by its own dark shadow. When one has touched evil at its depth, such a land can drive one to despair. This was my mood when we rode with our men from Conwy. I carried my madonna inside my jerkin next to my heart and prayed often, that my soul might fend off the Devil.

By the next morning, a roof of dark clouds hung over us, and in the afternoon we left the Vale of Ruthin in a gray rainstorm. Percy knew of a village hard by the Dee, and there we thought to find shelter for the night.

"Over that hill, I'll wager," he cried above the splashing of the horses' hooves, and we followed him, heads bowed against the downpour. It was because my eyes were thus downturned that I saw the first body. I straightened with a shock, reined in my horse, and dismounted. It was an old woman. Her forehead had been smashed in, but the rain had washed away the blood. Her mouth was twisted in a toothless grin and her eyes hung from their sockets. I looked around helplessly. A score more of bodies were strewn awkwardly about in the mud, men, women, and children alike. Their huts had been burnt so that only the blackened walls remained.

"Come," said Percy behind me. "Let us see if there is a roof left in this place."

The tiny church had been plundered, but we found the priest cowering in the confessional. He wailed piteously at the sight of us, begging for mercy.

"Peace, old man," Percy said roughly. "We shall not harm you."

The priest continued, in Welsh, to beg us for his life.

"Will he not be quiet?" Percy said.

"He speaks no English," I said. I greeted the man in the Celtic manner. "You are safe with us," I said.

He calmed himself then and bowed slightly.

"When was the village destroyed?" I asked.

"Yesterday. They rode upon us at Vespers. Some escaped. I know not where they have gone. I am the only one left alive in the village. There is no one to help bury the dead."

"They shall have a Christian burial," I promised. "But know you who did this? Know you under which captain they rode?"

"I know not. There was no time to tell such a thing."

I cursed in frustration. "Afore God, it shall not be that English soldiers should slaughter the innocent and go unpunished. Somehow I shall seek out who has done this."

"Oh, no, my lord," he said. "This much I do know: they were not Englishmen but Welsh. Even as I ran from them, I heard them cursing us in the Welsh tongue for that we are tenants of Lord Grey of Ruthin."

I gaped at him in astonishment. Percy nudged my shoulder.

"What says he?"

I answered reluctantly. "He says that Welshmen did this vile work."

Percy laughed heartily. "Was it so? Well, Harry, where shall you take your ideals now? Welshmen! It is a fine joke, indeed. Perhaps you shall now be ready to fight."

"Leave me be," I said.

He smiled. "As you will. There is a large barn, I think, with the roof still intact. I shall lodge some of the men there and send the rest here to the church. You may do as you will." He sauntered out into the downpour.

I drew my cloak tightly about me. "How is it that Welshmen did this to their own people?" I said. "They are no better than the English."

The priest's head bobbed up and down. "All men are fallen. All are fallen."

"Then what may men do, father, whose souls are in peril?"

"They must confess their sin," he said as though by rote.

"And then?"

"Then they must do penance."

"And then?" I gripped his arm. "Then what must I do?"

He looked at me blankly. "That is all," he said.

I dropped his arm and wandered to the altar. It had been stripped of its finery by the looters, so that only the table remained, like a bare wooden tomb. I longed to pray but could think of no words to utter, so I went into the Lady Chapel, made my bed upon the hard floor, and slept.

Upon the fall of Conwy, Wales lapsed into an uneasy quiet. The English men-at-arms were disbanded at Chester, and Percy startled me by declaring that he would ride north to tend his own lands.

"Does my father know this?" I asked.

"I have sent him word that I resign as your governor."

"Resign?" Hope must have shown in my face, for he scowled.

"Aye, I have resigned. I have more important things to do than play nursemaid to you."

"No, that is not it. You are frightened of me."

"Frightened? Of you? Ha!"

"Aye, frightened. You have made an enemy of me, and I shall be king someday."

"King? My lad, you shall be fortunate to live so long. Mind you, I do not threaten you. I only give you fair warning."

We had no more words for one another, and I was glad to see the last of him. I lingered for a time at Chester and pondered where I should go next. Father would expect me to return to Kennington, but my heart was bursting with the horrors I had witnessed and I longed to unburden myself to someone dear to me. Much as I wished it, I dared not go to Monmouth. I feared to find Joan ranged against me, and that would be more than I could bear. Courtenay was far away in Devon. There was but one other person I might go to, and that was Isabel. Petite Isabel! My heart raced at the thought of her. She was still at Sonning manor with her household, for my father claimed her dowry, which had been Richard's, while her father, the French King Charles, wished it returned. Neither seemed to care for poor Isabel, only for the money, and so she lived a virtual prisoner until the dispute should be settled.

I came to her on a soft day in May as she sat in Sonning garden with her ladies.

"*Henri! Mon cher!*" she cried at the sight of me, and threw her arms about my neck. Her ladies made little noises of disapproval.

"*Ah, folles!*" Isabel tossed her head. "*Il est un garçon.*" She hugged me tightly.

I felt more man than boy at that moment and could say nothing, but only held her to me.

"*C'est le Prince de Galles?*" one of the ladies asked.

"*Oui,*" Isabel answered. "*C'est Henri, le plus beau prince du monde.*"
She stepped back and took my hand. The ladies curtsied and I bowed.
"*Enchanté,*" I said.

"But, Henri, how did you get in? I have a guard here."

"I merely pounded upon the gate and cried, 'Open up, it is the Prince of
Wales.' I am now a person of importance, and today for once I am glad of it.
Isabel, will you walk with me in the orchard?"

The ladies still eyed me suspiciously, but they had settled themselves
upon their pillows and taken up their sewing. We strolled hand in hand past
a green pond toward a copse of pear trees. A riot of daffodils and primroses
waved in the breeze, and a cuckoo sang above our heads.

"It is lovely here," I said dreamily, "and so unlike what I have seen. I
wish that I could stay here forever."

"It is very beautiful," Isabel said with a sigh, "yet it has been my
prison." She turned her heart-shaped face forlornly to me. "I would not wish
to stay here forever."

"Forgive me that I spoke so carelessly. It is only that this is a place to
match your own beauty. Yet if you are unhappy here, I shall carry you away
from here this very day."

"Henri!"

"Aye, and wed you as well," I said stoutly. "I care not what my father
would say."

"Oh, Henri, I would be so happy if you were my husband."

"You would be?" I blushed.

"*Mais oui.* I love you, Henri."

"I love you," I mumbled.

"Yet it will not do," she said sadly.

"Why not? My father was but fourteen when he wed my mother, and I
am nearly that. Besides, I think I may convince Father of the advantages of
this match."

"He knows of the advantages already. He has suggested it, but my
father will not hear of it. Father says Richard's blood stands between Lancaster and Valois, and a match with the son of a usurper would be cursed."

"Then defy him!"

She was shocked. "It cannot be done! He is the King."

And that was that. I sank dejectedly to the ground and watched an ant
drag an orange bit of butterfly wing. Isabel wept softly.

"I am sorry to hurt you," she said after a moment, "but it is all arranged.
I suppose you have not heard, since you have been in Wales. The dowry
dispute has been settled, and Father has sent for me. I am to sail for France
within the month. They have even made a match for me. I am to be wed to
the heir of the Duc d'Orléans."

I said nothing.

"Henri, I wish I did not have such hard news for you so soon after your victory."

I stared at her. "What do you mean? What victory?"

"Why, your victory at Conwy, of course. Everyone says the Welsh have given up the fight. As if such a backward people could stand against English chivalry! Did you wear my favor at the siege?"

"There was no victory, Isabel. Conwy was taken when the Welsh captains betrayed their own men, and there followed only torture and death. It is not a thing for boasting."

I told her then of all that made my heart ache so, all that I had longed to share. She listened in disbelief.

"But I do not understand. To fight as a knight is a noble thing."

"Is it? Is it noble to rip men apart, to slay the innocent?"

"You have not broken the code of chivalry," she said soothingly. "You must not dwell on it. You shall be a great soldier, I know it. As for the deaths you witnessed, you shall soon be used to it, will you not?"

"That is what I most fear." There was a sickness in my belly. She does not mean to be cruel, I thought. She is but a child and she knows only what she has been taught. I stood up. "I should go. I do not wish to cause you scandal."

"Henri, please kiss me ere you leave."

I hesitated.

"Please, Henri. It is the only chance we shall have."

Her brown eyes were wide with pleading. We were of a height, so I had but to lean slightly forward to set my mouth to hers. We pressed our lips hard together, neither moving nor taking breath. Then I stepped back and straightway left her, walking blindly past her ladies without speaking.

In June, Isabel took ship for France, and I never set eyes upon her again.

When a great lord rebels against his sovereign, it is simply a matter of meeting him in battle and vanquishing him. But the revolt of a people seeking justice is not put down so readily. Even as the breakers on a beach, the waters of rebellion rush in with great fury, then ebb. All seems peaceful, all rage spent. But the waves cannot be mastered, and they break again upon the sand. Just so the tide of Welsh wrath would not be stemmed and must run its course. No sooner had the people of Gwynedd retreated to their mountain strongholds, seemingly in defeat, when the south of Wales erupted and Glyndwr turned his attention there. Lancaster held many fine castles in the south, including Monmouth, and my father was determined to crush these impudent subjects himself. He ordered me to join him at Hereford, whence we were to cut a path to the sea.

From Hereford we rode to Hay and thence to Brecon, and as we went, we pillaged. Cottages and barns we put to the torch, and spared only churches. As we topped a hill near Bronllys, I turned to see our trail had been well marked behind us by gray coils of smoke rising toward the ceiling of clouds. Word spread through the valleys that the English brought with them fire and death, and the mountain folk fled before us, leaving their scrawny sheep and cattle to be slaughtered. What the sword could not do, famine might accomplish.

I stood that night upon the battlements of Bronllys Castle and stared into the black night. The acrid smell of smoke clung to my clothing and my hair. I yet heard the anguished cries of horses caught in the flames of one large barn and saw the dead faces of those few unfortunates who had not fled fast enough to escape English swords. Mindlessly I rubbed the rough-hewn stone of the battlement beneath my palm until the skin was raw. Then I hoisted myself onto the parapet and regarded the flat surface of the moat far below. The water would be quite shallow, for the season had been a dry one. I stared in fascination. Here was a way to avoid my own part in the subduing of Wales. Yet, I thought, it was a certain path to Hell. Besides, Father would rejoice, and I did not wish to give him such pleasure. I slid down in disgust and kicked the wall hard with my boot.

"It is a fine way to break a foot," said a nearby voice.

In my preoccupation I had not noticed the man's approach.

"They are making merry in the castle hall," he said. "I should have thought to find the Prince of Wales there."

"Do I know you?"

"There is no reason why you should. I am but a small landowner of no great family. John Oldcastle is my name."

"Well, John Oldcastle, now that you have introduced yourself, I should like to be left alone."

"Left alone so that you can throw yourself over the battlements?"

"I have no intention of doing such a thing," I said angrily. "And by what right do you spy on me?"

"I did not mean to spy. Like you, I sickened of the revelry below and thought to take a breath of air. That is all."

"And if you are so sickened by their roistering, why have you even come on this venture?"

"Why are you here?" he responded. "I am here because as a Herefordshire man of property I was requested by my king to defend the marches against the Welsh, and I had not the mettle to refuse. And you?"

I looked at him a moment in exasperation, and then away. At last I said, "It is the same with me. The same."

"A pair of reluctant warriors we are," he said. "If it is indeed warrior's work we have done this day. I think the meanest cutpurse in the London stews could have done as much as we have."

"What should we do, then?"

"As little as possible, by Our Lady." He laughed and clapped me upon the shoulder. "I am along for the ride, no more. What say you?"

"But who is your captain?"

"I ride under your brother, Thomas," he said.

"Then you must join my household to avoid his orders. Have you many men-at-arms?"

"Only three," Oldcastle said.

"It shall be simple then. Tom bears me no ill will. He will not begrudge me a poor country squire and three footmen if I plead nicely. I have managed to avoid the worst of this work, for the King ignores me in favor of Tom. By Our Lady, you shall hide beneath my cloak."

"It suits me well. It shall be an honor to serve under the Prince of Wales."

"It is a most indolent prince you serve," I said, laughing.

He bowed. "And I am a most insouciant servant."

"Shall we drink on it, then?"

We made our way to the wine cellar, where we sat beneath a flaming sconce and passed a bottle of claret between us. Oldcastle was ten years my senior, a short, sturdy man with auburn hair and a neatly trimmed beard which looked quite out of fashion. We spoke long into the night of horses and hunting, of music, and of alehouses. I had but little experience of the last, and Oldcastle swore he would accompany me to London, where he would show me the finest taverns in Eastcheap. And he told me of women. I listened wide-eyed as he recounted the pleasures of the bed.

"There is an excellent whorehouse in Botolph's Lane," he concluded. "No fleas in the bed, and no pox that I know of. Yet I do not relish whores as much as I was wont. I long to settle in with a woman I can talk to when we have done with rolling in the hay. How do you feel about it?"

"Oh," I said, and swallowed loudly, "I am sure you must be right."

Oldcastle looked at me quizzically. "Have you never had a woman, Harry?"

I shook my head.

"Jesu, it is time! You must be fourteen, are you not?"

"Aye."

"Then it is time. But you shall not want a tumble with some milkmaid.

When we are done with this sorry business, I shall go with you to London. Then you shall have a woman who will teach you the tricks of love."

His words echoed through the recesses of the wine cellar. Harry Percy had instructed me in the ways of war. Here would be a tutor of a different sort.

We gained the coast quickly, then turned east again by a different route. Certain lords in our company had heard it said that the abbey of Strata Florida on Afon Teifi was a center of rebel support. The Cistercian monks, they claimed, often provided shelter and arms for Glyndwr's men.

"It would be like a Welshman to make such use of a holy place," said Lord Grey of Ruthin. "They will not expect us to come upon them there."

My father agreed and set our course toward Strata Florida. We rode to the abbey on a night so dark that the buildings were not visible. Only the glowing of a few solitary windows, their glass lit by the flames of some hearth, warned us we had achieved our destination.

"Hi, Jack!" I cried. "The lights are like stars fallen to earth."

"It is a strange time to spout poetry," he muttered.

"Why? The bards found some perverse beauty in every routine massacre of the Welsh."

Suddenly the abbey wall loomed black before us, and I pulled Morgause up sharply. The gate was closed against the night, and so the bell was rung. The gate opened slowly, and the King's horsemen rushed in with swords drawn. I held back.

"Jesu!" I cried. "There can be no armed men here, or they would not open to us. Who do they rush to slaughter?"

"Fat, harmless monks," Oldcastle said. "Come on. We dare not linger here long."

We rode in to a scene of utter chaos. Scores of naked boys had been roused from their beds and ran screaming about the yard. Two lay broken upon the ground, trampled to death by the careless horsemen. The others were driven relentlessly at sword's point into the church. White-robed monks poured from the cloister to stand paralyzed with fear. One was run through with a sword; the rest turned and fled after the boys.

"Here are our armed rebels," Oldcastle said. "Bolingbroke should be proud of this night's work."

Torches flared all around us, and grotesque silhouettes played across the abbey walls, misshapen creatures whose arms flailed wildly. I spied Tom near the cloister, his horse rearing skittishly at the clamor. He was screaming at his men, but his boy's soprano could not be heard above the din. Behind him some soldiers had broken through the cloister gate, and the sack of the abbey was under way. Though supposedly searching for arms, the men would carry away from the servants' quarters and from the church itself anything of value. Any poor wretch of a kitchen maid unlucky enough to be found would be raped repeatedly. Well, I thought, I can do nothing about it, for none shall listen to me. Perhaps I might be of some use in the church.

Most of the soldiers had dispersed throughout the abbey in pursuit of booty and left only a handful of their fellows to guard the monks and boys. These Englishmen were standing bewildered before their captives, who were huddled in one transept and crying out for pity in a multitude of Welsh dialects.

"Listen to me!" I shouted in Welsh. "Listen to me! Quiet!"

One by one they fell silent and gaped at me.

"Now, in God's name, I am glad to see your highness," one soldier said as he knelt. "Will you speak to them some more?"

"Please remain calm," I continued in Welsh. "You shall be safer if you are quiet and offer no resistance. I am sorry for what has happened and I would have no more of you die. Settle yourselves and pray to Saint Dewi for strength."

They answered me with hate-filled eyes that shook me to my very soul.

I approached the monk closest to me, a quiet, dignified man, and asked, "Who are these boys? Whence do they come?"

"They study with us, some to join our order, others simply to learn," he replied. "They come from throughout the west of Wales. Most are of poor families, but all are clever lads."

"Are you their tutor?"

"I instruct them in Latin."

"Your name?"

"I am Brother Huw."

"I am Henry, Prince of Wales."

"Ah," he said. "Why do you come upon us so violently? This is a holy place, yet you loot it. You have slain children and a defenseless brother. Why?"

"You must direct your questions to my father," I said. "He has some notion that you harbor rebels here. A 'hornet's nest of treason' he named Strata Florida."

"It is not so. We are men of peace. There are no armed men here. Yet we serve our Welsh people well, as Our Lord bids us do. In times such as these, perhaps that service is enough to be named treason."

"Perhaps you are right," I said, uneasy beneath his disdainful scrutiny. "If that be so, then I must have a care myself. I am Welsh. I even know the history of this place. The Lord Rhys is buried here. The Brut y Tywysogion was compiled here as well, the tale of the great ones."

He seemed unimpressed with this recital.

"It is whispered that the Holy Grail itself lies at Strata Florida," I continued. "Is it true?"

He curled his lip. "You need not seek it," he said. "It was not meant for such as you to find the Holy Grail."

I stepped back as though struck. "Indeed, I would not dare seek it," I murmured. I thought him as pitiless as my father's soldiers. "Well," I said. "I shall trouble you no more."

I left after warning the guards to use their captives gently and went to look for Jack. I found him wandering beside a barn.

"Where have you been?" I asked.

"Walking," he said. "I wanted to have a look at this place. God's truth, you would not believe the size of it, nor how much treasure I have seen carried from it. I had thought that monks vowed to live in poverty. Harry! You do not listen to me."

"I heard you. I am weary, that is all. It is nearly dawn."

"There are empty stalls in this barn. Their horses have all been taken."

We curled up in the hay for a few restless hours of sleep, then woke and broke our fast with black bread and cheese. Afterward we tramped in silence through a meadow tinged with October frost to the river. A thick bank of fog rolled from the Teifi and engulfed the long buildings of the abbey.

"Shall we cast for fish?" Jack asked.

I shrugged. "As you will."

I wandered aimlessly while he threw out his line and drew it in again.

"They say all these lands belong to the abbey," Jack said. "If your father turns out the monks, they shall truly have to live out their vows of poverty. I should not weep to see that, I must admit."

The sound of a trumpet caused us both to raise our heads.

"The King calls his captains," I said. "Shall we go? I am sure there is some decision of strategic importance to be made and he is anxiously awaiting my advice."

We met together in the abbot's chamber. Father was weary and dispirited.

"There are no weapons, no soldiers here." He sighed. "And now my men have found the wine cellar and lie about in drunken sleep."

"Perhaps it is for the good," said Lord Talbot. "They marched a great distance last night. I am glad they have gained some plunder for their labor. My men have lately complained to me of the poverty of these mountain folk. A soldier without booty is often ill disposed to take orders."

"You speak truly," Father said. "As for these monks, they are an arrogant lot. I have no doubt their sympathies lie with Glyndwr, and likely they have given him aid at some time. They must be punished for it, else the Welsh shall not fear to defy us. I shall disperse them. What say you?"

"It is wise," said Lord Grey of Ruthin. "Lay waste the place as well, that none may shelter here after."

The others nodded their assent.

"It shall be done," Father said. "Another thought have I. There are several hundred able-bodied boys here, and this rebellion leaves our marcher estates lacking in laborers. Let us carry these boys back with us to work our fields as reparation for those peasants whom we have lost."

"Excellent," said Lord Talbot. "My fields at Goodrich could well use two score of strong lads, for so many have I lost either to Glyndwr or to my own muster."

Father clapped his hands together. "Then are we agreed?"

"No," I said.

All heads turned to me.

"Many of these boys are meant for the monastery, not the fields. Most of them have families. Would you tear them from their homes so young?"

"Aye," said Lord Talbot, "tear them from their cursed rebel roots."

"They are boys," I said. "Do we war against boys?"

"Enough, Harry!" Father said. I knew that my words did shame him.

"Perhaps Harry is right," a small voice said. Tom it was who spoke! "It does not seem quite right," he continued apologetically. "And how should we carry them all? If we are set upon they shall hamper us. I am one of your captains, Father. I am to think of such things, am I not?" His voice trailed off uncertainly. I longed to wrap my arms around him and hug him to me.

Lord Grey stood next to Tom, and he smiled and patted his shoulder. "Your sons are most astute, your grace. Fine, clever lads. Yet we must remember they are close in age to the urchins out there. If we are set upon, we simply abandon them, my lord Thomas. Nothing lost. To take them captive is a stroke of genius. It will show the whole west of Wales the price of rebellion far better than destroying a cache of weapons would do. Of course, my young lords, you would not be expected to think of this. Never fear, such knowledge shall come with years."

"I must disagree, my lord." This from Jack Oldcastle. "Do not judge the Prince and his brother by their tender years. They are canny lads, as you have said, and indeed I know some very old fools. Yet I am more of an age with you, if such you value, and I say that such an act will only breed more hatred. By such enmity are rebellions sustained. Further, I vow it is not the act of a Christian knight to bear these lads into servitude. God shall punish such a deed."

"Who are you to speak so boldly?" Grey demanded. "Under whom do you serve?"

"I am John Oldcastle of Hereford and I serve the Prince of Wales."

My father rolled his eyes heavenward.

"You are a marcher lord?" Grey asked.

"Of modest means."

"Yet you would endanger our holdings in the march by failing to deal sternly with this rebellion?"

"This rebellion," I said, "would not have occurred if you had not dealt so unjustly with Owain Glyndwr."

Lord Grey turned a most shocking shade of purple.

"You shall apologize, Harry," Father said through clenched teeth.

"No, I shall not."

"Then begone! You no longer stand in our counsel. And take your retinue with you."

I smiled grimly as I left with Jack. "We are like two dunderheaded knights who will not leave a joust, but crash into one another again and again," I said to my companion.

Neither compassion nor good sense prevailed. The abbey of Strata Florida was razed, the monks sent on their way, and the boys borne weeping away as prisoners. A few of the smallest were taken up on horseback. I carried upon Morgause one such lad of five. The rest were forced to walk and keep up as best they could.

Once these lads had been taken, capturing children became a sport. Most of the mountain folk still managed to avoid us, but Talbot and Grey twice sent out advance parties to fall upon villages unawares. Only children were taken, by the rules of this game, and their protesting mothers and fathers were struck down, for they would be too great a problem to deal with on our journey. After three days of slow marching we bore with us nearly three hundred children, girls as well as boys. In two more days, some dozen had died.

We came again to Hay, whence Lord Grey departed for the northern marches laden with booty and slaves. The next morning we labored up the Gospel Pass over Pen y Beacon. It was hard going, for the weather had turned bitterly cold and a stiff wind buffeted us into numbness. The children suffered terribly, too frozen to cry. We had no food to spare for so vast a throng, and so they went hungry. Jack and I shared of our provisions with Ianto and Morgan, whom we carried, and a few others.

"Mam," Morgan murmured as he chewed his crust. "Mam."

I wrapped the boy tightly against the wind in my spare jerkin. More I could not do.

The path over the mountain was narrow and perilous. I set Morgan and Ianto to cling upon Morgause's back while I dismounted and led her carefully over the treacherous ground. Morgause picked her footing gingerly as we wound our way downward. Then she set her hoof upon a loose stone and tripped. Her head swung out over the precipice and she blundered forward, knocking me against a small girl who had wobbled along in front of us. The child, weakened by fatigue and hunger, lost her balance and plunged head-long down the ravine, bouncing against boulders as she went. She came to rest against a gorse bush. I yelled for Jack, thrust Morgause's reins in his hands, and slipped my way down the gorge.

"Move on!" someone shouted.

I reached the girl in a shower of pebbles. Her face was scratched and bloodied. I raised her shoulders gently and her head rolled loosely back, her neck broken. Her gray eyes were open, and the freckles of her face stood out against the pale skin. I laid her down, prayed frantically to Our Lady, and made over her the sign of the cross.

"Harry." I heard Oldcastle from above. "They are leaving us. It is no good to tend to her here."

I shook my head angrily. Gathering her in my arms, I made my way slowly up the face of the chasm. When I reached the top, only Oldcastle waited.

"I sent the children and Morgause on with one of my men," Jack said. "Never mind. We can catch up when they stop."

I said nothing but walked ahead, the body of the girl clutched in my arms.

"Harry, do not blame yourself. Faith, man, you are pale as any ghost."

"I should have had more of a care for Morgause. I let her follow the child too closely."

"It was an accident."

"No. It was my fault. Now let it be."

We stopped that evening by Afon Honddu. I would have none with me and so sent Jack to his bed. When the priest had said his prayers over the body, I dug the grave myself near a solitary oak. In the distance, the high flat scarp of the Black Mountains smothered the last of the sunlight. When I had piled up a small mound of dirt, I sat down wearily and watched the moon rise, a white orb above the line of the mountains. There I remained until the cold drove me to the fire, yet I would not lie down to sleep for fear of what I might dream. After some time, a small figure loomed out of the darkness and sat on the ground next to me. It was Tom.

"Harry, I could not sleep," he said. "I am troubled and need to speak my mind."

"Go on, then."

"It concerns you," he said hesitantly.

"Well?"

"I have ever looked up to you, though you may not know it. I speak to you out of brotherly affection. And I speak to you the words Father should speak, only he cannot bring himself to it. He is stubborn, as you are."

"What is it?" I asked irritably.

"Harry, I fear for you. And so does Father. He fears what shall become of you when you are King. He has told me so. I vow he does not lack in love for you. He worries about you."

"It is no concern of his."

"How can you say it? He is your father. Ah, I know he slights you in my favor, and it pains me to see it. In truth, I fear you hate me because of it." His brow was furrowed, and he seemed near tears.

"Good old Tom," I said and tousled his hair. "Of course I do not hate you. You cannot help what he does."

"Yet I am often of a mind with him. And I am so in this. Harry, they detest you, Lord Grey and the other barons. They think you shall be another Richard. You and I know well that Lancaster's claim to the throne is slight, though we dare not speak it abroad. We hold the throne only because we are strong, and most of our strength lies with the goodwill of our peers. When they are unhappy with a king, that king comes to no good end. Do you not see it?"

I stared into the fire. "Of course I see it. And I fear it. Do you think I am blind? Yet it seems I must do what I loathe to survive. How can I make such a choice?"

"I know not what you mean. You speak as though our birthright is one of shame. You need do nothing horrid. Learn the arts of statecraft and war, then defend your throne, defend England. It is not loathsome. It is a manly calling, even a sacred one."

I knew there must be good answer for him, but I could find no words for it. How I envied his innocence, his easy acceptance of the way things were. Why must I fight the inevitable? Why should it tear at me that children died, that villages were burned and livelihoods destroyed? It should be for monks to ponder these things, locked safely away in their hermits' cells. Aye, monks could afford purity of conscience.

"Harry, it is not only yourself you must think on, but England as well. How shall England be served if you turn from your duty and if the barons turn against you? It will only bring the bloodshed you seem to dread. It is the way of the world to fight. Why else are we trained as warriors from birth? The Church does agree with me, you must admit. It is therefore given to you to strive mightily, to fight hardest and best. God shall bless your efforts if you stand bravely and for the right."

"Then I ask you, Tom, do we fight for the right here?"

"In Wales? Certainly. England cannot survive with a strong enemy to her west. With the Scots to the north and France to the south we should be encircled. The safety of England is at stake."

"And what of the safety of Wales?"

"It is the Welsh who have rebelled. We did not bid them to it. They should have taken more heed themselves of their well-being."

He stood, stretched, and patted my shoulder.

"Think on what I have said. As for me, now that I have unburdened myself, I am passing sleepy. Good night to you, brother."

I sat still after he had gone. I named myself a hypocrite. If you truly cared for the Welsh, you would never have come, I said. Yet here you are. Coward. You are in this as deeply as Tom, as deeply as Grey and Talbot. Indeed, you are worse than they are, for they have ease of mind while you do what you know to be wrong. If you have not the courage to resist, why then, do as Tom says. If you must sin, do it well, do it ably.

I brought my madonna from inside my jerkin. In the flickering firelight her smile mocked me. I tossed her suddenly into the midst of the flames, then watched in dull horror as she caught fire and burned into a blackened core of ash.

"Harry," I whispered, "you are dead."

Afon Honddu outs a deep, winding valley which is called the Vale of Ewyas, and it is a place of perilous beauty. Here monks had come long ago, as to Strata Florida, to seek God in isolation but had found wealth instead. All the land of the Honddu belonged to the monks of Llanthony, and these Augustinians had long been loyal to Lancaster, so near to the Monnow were they. Orders were given that no cottages were to be burned, though children and plunder could yet be taken.

"The monks are loyal, but their people are not," Father said. "The abbot wrote me that many of his tenants have gone to Glyndwr. He shall not mind, I think, if those who remain are disciplined."

There were no villages here, only the solitary stone huts of shepherds. At each one a few men-at-arms were sent to carry away small livestock and anything else of value and to search for children. Women were left unharmed but destitute and wailing for their babes. We found but one man, and he clearly was the only one who had not joined Glyndwr, yet he was beheaded before his screaming wife and children.

We halted at midday in a relatively broad bottomland to rest and eat. Farther downstream, where the Honddu curved slightly to the east, a thin curl of smoke betrayed the presence of another cottage. I had just dismounted when Tom rode up.

"Father says yon cottage belongs to your men," he said. "He wishes you to deal with it while we rest."

I groaned and ordered my men farther down the river but halted ere the cottage was in sight.

"Wait here, Jack," I said. "I shall deal with this myself."

He raised his eyebrows. "Is it not perilous?"

"What? Shall I be attacked by women and children?"

"The men shall grumble if they miss some booty."

"Then let them. Now do as I say."

The cottage was like all the others, rudely built and windowless. It was set back from the river, perched upon a steep slope in front of a thick wood. I tethered Morgause by the river that I might cause no one alarm and trudged up the hill. I was met by a scrawny brown hen who ceased her pecking long enough to blink a yellow eye at me. The door of the hut was slightly ajar and the wizened face of a peasant woman peered out at me.

"Good day to you," I greeted her in Welsh.

She stared at the sword that hung from my belt.

"Soldier?" she whispered.

"Aye, soldier."

"Welsh?"

I shook my head slowly.

She flinched and withdrew. I pushed back the heavy wooden door and stepped in. When my eyes had adjusted to the gloom I saw that the woman had retreated to the smoldering hearth and held a poker raised defensively before her. Her sharp elbows were thrust out defiantly and her thin chest rose and fell rapidly.

"I shall not harm you," I said. I dug into the pouch at my waist and laid a coin on top of a bench. "I only want your chickens. See, here is a crown to purchase more at market. I saw no other animals about, yet there were sheep droppings. Do they graze over the hill?"

"No sheep," she lied, her voice quavering.

"You needn't worry," I said. "I shan't look for them. I would not have you starve. Only you must keep them hidden when the soldiers pass by."

She glanced nervously at a small pallet in the corner, then at the door behind me.

"Do you have children here?" I asked. "The soldiers are kidnaping children, bearing them away to work the fields. Whatever you do, hide your children."

She stared at me, the poker forgotten.

"No!" she cried. "No children! I am old, you see. I have no man, no children."

"Very well. I shall trouble you no more, good woman. I shall take your chickens now. Soon the Englishmen shall pass by. Remember my warning."

I left her and shut the door firmly behind me. The pallet had been too small for the woman, of that I was certain. The child is tending the sheep, I thought, and pray God shall stay there until we are gone. I stunned the brown hen with a stick and wrung her neck, then thrust her under my arm and went round the side of the hut in search of more chickens.

Then it was I saw the lass in the wood.

She was slim and brown, and her hair streamed behind her as she skipped through a forest of waving ferns as high as her waist. I glanced quickly behind me and saw that a number of soldiers were gathering at the foot of the hill. Tom's banner, and Talbot's, fluttered in the wind. Thirty paces more and the girl would emerge in full view of them. I dropped the hen and dashed toward the wood. So caught up was she in her game of skipping that she did not see me tearing toward her until I crashed into the brake. She froze, then turned to run, but I was quickly upon her. She fell, the breath knocked from her, and I dragged her behind a fallen tree trunk. Her eyes rolled up at me, large gray saucers they were, and she gasped in terror. I clapped my hand roughly across her mouth to keep her from calling out and penned her arms to her side. She struggled against me and bit hard into the fleshy pad of my hand. I stifled a cry of pain and held fast to her. Brambles stung my face as I bore my full weight on top of her and forced my mouth next to her ear.

"Be still!" I whispered in Welsh. "The English are near. I shall not hurt you, only be still, be still!"

At last she relaxed, exhausted, her breath coming in short hard sobs. I sprawled unceremoniously atop her, afraid that my odd behavior had been noticed. Cautiously I raised my head and saw with relief that no one had appeared on the slope.

"They have not seen us," I said. "Listen to me. There are English soldiers just below your cottage. They are bearing children away with them, so you must hide here until they leave. Do you understand?"

She nodded. I took my hand from her mouth and looked ruefully at the wound on my palm.

"You have strong teeth," I said.

She sniffed. Her cheek bled from a bramble scratch and I dabbed at it gently with my thumb. She appeared to be nine or ten, a delicate little thing though she smelled of sheep. Tears cut crooked furrows through the dirt on her cheeks.

"Mam?" she sobbed.

"She is fine. She hides in the cottage. I am sorry to frighten you so, but I knew not how else to warn you. What is your name?"

"Merryn."

"It is a lovely name. I am Harry."

Her eyes narrowed suspiciously. "It is an English name. One of the monks is so named."

I hesitated. "Aye, I am with yon Englishmen."

"My da hates the English. He is away fighting them, and so are my brothers as well." She rubbed her nose emphatically.

"Oh." I rolled off her and peered through tattered brown leaves toward the hut. All was yet clear. I stretched out next to her.

"I must go or I shall be missed. Stay behind this log until it is dark, no matter what you hear. There may be stragglers."

"I have left my sheep alone."

"Never mind that. It is too dangerous to seek them now. Do you understand?"

"Aye, Harry."

She spoke my name in such a solemn, precise manner that I must needs smile. A little lady under the grime, she was.

"Good-bye, Merryn." I sat up on my haunches.

"Harry!"

"Aye?"

"I do not think I hate you, and when my da comes home I shall tell him so."

I reached down and gently tugged a lock of thick brown hair. "Stay down," I said, then walked out of the wood and back to the hut. There I retrieved the brown hen and quickly killed two more, but left a fourth hen and a cock behind. When I reached the bottom of the hill, Tom came to greet me.

"What are you doing here?" I asked.

"I thought to keep you company while we ate. Jesu, Harry, you took your time for such a small lot. And why did you take to the woods so suddenly? It startled me so I would have gone after, but that fellow of yours, Oldcastle, said I should not."

"I thought I saw a deer, but it was not so. Then I stayed to piss."

He shrugged good-naturedly. "Did you think to slay a deer with only a sword? What, would you run it down and stab it?"

"I could," I said. "I am fleet enough."

"And conceited enough to try." He laughed. "You are a puzzle to me, yet I do love you."

*   *   *

"The children do clamor this night," Jack said. We lay side by side before the fire and listened to the cries of misery around us.

"I know not how they have survived," I said. "Yet there is one child who shall not be so ill used." I told him then of Merryn.

"So that is what you did in the woods."

"Aye, and I thank you for restraining Tom. Ah, Jack, you should have seen her. Like an elf she was, a wood fairy."

He chortled. "'Tis a high-flown view of a peasant lass. Yet she would seem to have cast a spell on you."

"Her gentleness did cut me to the heart." I raised up on one elbow. "Someday, when I am king, I shall return to this Vale of Ewyas and I shall go to that cottage. I shall find the girl and she shall have babes of her own, and I shall say to her, 'I am Harry, who saved you from the English once upon a time.'"

"Will she remember you?"

"Of course. Perhaps she will have named a son Harry, after the lad who was her benefactor."

I dreamed of her that night, and in my dream I walked hand in hand with her through a fair meadow to the river. There I washed her tearstained face with the chill water. Her eyes were clear and gray as the pebbles of the river. She placed her hand on my cheek in silent blessing and smiled upon me in benediction.

5

In Wales, death and destruction reigned, but in London town, life was clearly the victor. Oh, the gravediggers of London are kept busy, to be sure. Pestilence carries off many people. Others die of broken crowns or dagger thrusts to the bowels, for there is much rioting. Yet to die in London is to die a lusty death. When the death bell tolls, all halt and cross themselves. But the cart bearing the body to the graveyard always sways through the rutted lanes and melts into a swirling, motley mass of Londoners, its clanging bell swallowed in the raucous din. Then it is off to buy a fat meat pie and fie upon death. The urchins of the city cry for want of food, yet they do not resign themselves to hunger but scrap and steal, living by their wits. Likewise the dogs are scrawny and vicious. They snarl defiantly and nip the legs of passing horses with joyful abandon. Some are crushed beneath the hooves, but most dance jauntily away to chase thin brown rats through piles of offal. Garbage and dung are everywhere, the reeking piles clogging the narrow passages of Watling Street and Budge Row. It is the stench of life.

I learned early to turn to London for solace. When Jack and I came at last to Kennington I had but one resolve, and that was to put from my mind all I had witnessed in Wales. There was no better way to forget, Jack declared, than to console oneself with women and strong ale, and he knew where to find both. We took with us to London one Henry Scrope, a young man of good family whom I had retained as steward of my household. He was a long-faced, solemn fellow, and Jack declared that a lark would do him good. We dressed ourselves in the shortest jerkins and tightest hose that we possessed and set plumed caps jauntily upon our heads.

"Do not forget to chew upon some mint leaves," Jack said. "That shall please the women. Well, lads, shall we swagger?"

Our barge was painted bright yellow and scarlet, and the bargemaster was a cheerful companion.

"Nick is my name," he said, "and glad I am to carry anyone who goes downstream. Do you look for tarts, young masters?"

"We should not weep to find a few," Jack replied.

"Then should you stay near Thames," Nick said. "Rivermen do know where to bed women who pitch and roll like a skiff."

The barge swept into the green Thames with a swoosh, and London spread her charms seductively before us.

"Yon is a sight," said Nick. "Never do I tire of it. Ah, 'tis fine upon the river."

As we drew closer, the bells of St. Paul's set up a giddy peal. My stomach leaped and I clutched my seat tightly. A most pleasant tingle traveled up from my toes and settled in my groin.

"Look at her, Harry," Jack said. "Someday she shall be yours."

We rode the swell of the river up to Paul's Wharf below Thames Street, climbed nimbly up the stone steps, and made our way toward West Chepe, a precinct known for its victuals. There were many wooden booths wedged against the leaning timbered houses and we wandered idly, looking to spend our coin. All London seemed packed into Chepeside. The steady roar of the throng was punctuated by the piercing cries of the most practiced hawkers. *Spices*, they cried, and *Apples, leeks and turnips, pies and yellow cheese, eels from Thames*. Pigeons, sparrows, and hens peered from wooden cages, their heads bobbing nervously upon soon-to-be-wrung necks. The sturdy goodwives of London town were about in their white kerchiefs, haggling profanely with the vendors, poking grimy fingers into the sides of fat geese, and kicking at the swine who rooted in the straw-littered street.

After much discussion we settled upon blood puddings for our meal, and ale to wash them down. We wandered as we ate, down the Chepe and past St. Mary le Bow, where we chanced upon a blind beggar. His eye sockets stared at us, gaping red holes. Jack tossed a groat into his cup.

"Who stole your eyes, old man?" he asked.

"The cursed Scots took them, they did, my Lord. May they rot in Hell ere they burn!"

He spat and barely missed my doeskin boots. I jumped back and crossed myself against the Evil One, for the man's face seemed to me a fleshed-out death's head. I was relieved when we moved on to a man clad in motley who juggled wooden balls.

We dallied thus in the crowded lanes until sunset, and then we hurried to a public house in East Chepe ere curfew should ring. The room we entered was a dark, warm haven after the tumult of the streets. Tankards brimful with ale and wine gleamed darkly, and the heartening aroma of a haunch of venison roasting on the open hearth overwhelmed even the dense smell of unwashed bodies. Jack craned his neck about the room until he spied the hostess.

"Mistress Brawley!" he cried out.

She peered at him for a moment, and then a smile cracked her face.

"'Tis a sorry sight!" she exclaimed. "It is more than a year since you darkened my door, young Jack. Did the fleas bite too hard last time?" She cackled and wiped her hands on her apron. With her round face and bright eyes she put me much in mind of a squirrel.

"These be hard times for a poor country squire," Jack said. "I have not had the means for London. Yet do fortunes rise like the tide on Thames. I have attached myself to the household of a gallant young gentleman, so you shall often feel the jingle of my coin in your pocket."

"I am as like to feel your fingers pinching my arse," she declared. "Now, who might these lads be?"

"Lord Henry Scrope of Masham, the steward of our household," Jack said.

Scrope bowed.

"And our master, his royal highness, Henry, Prince of Wales."

She sucked in her breath sharply and her eyes widened.

"Do not spread it about," Jack said softly. "We would not be pestered all the night."

"Not a word, not a word," she whispered and patted my arm. "I hope you shall be as comfortable here as in the palace."

"Pray do not trouble yourself," I said. "We wish only to enjoy your hospitality as any others would."

"Ah, you shall want more than my hospitality," she said and grinned. "Only sit yourselves here by the fire. You wish to sup? I've a fine roast near done. I shall have the best morsels for you."

We sat at a large wooden table. Beside us a towheaded boy turned the venison slowly on its spit while the fat dripped crackling and hissing into the fire. Scrope eyed it eagerly.

"I am famished," he said. "I cannot think on women until my belly is full. Where does this good woman keep her salt herrings? I would have—"

I turned my attention from him, for a movement across the way had caught my eye. Framed in a doorway was a woman—no, a lass—slender and clad in blue. Atop her head was an immaculate white coif. From the distance she appeared most comely. We watched one another warily; then she smiled and retreated from view, closing the door behind her. Reluctantly I turned back to my ale. Jack regarded me closely.

"You saw her?" I said.

"I did."

"Might I—might I spend the night with her?"

"Do not lose your heart so quickly. She is not a whore, Harry, she is Mistress Brawley's daughter. And while many a poor country lass is deflowered under this roof, no man may look askance at pretty Alison lest he be barred from the Boar's Head."

"That is her name then? Alison?"

"It is."

"How old is she?"

"I believe she is but thirteen."

"A ripe thirteen," Scrope said. "If Harry is taken with her, he should pursue her. She is ready for a man. Why should it not be Harry?"

"You speak so gently," Oldcastle said.

"Mock me if you will," said Scrope. "Yet Harry is the Prince of Wales. You saw how the hostess fawned over him. She would gladly give the lass to him, I'll wager."

I ducked my head. "I would not care for such terms," I said. "Yet if Alison did choose herself to love me I should be favored indeed."

"Love?" Scrope said. "What is love but a throbbing groin?"

"Leave the lad be," Jack said. "He needs no lessons from you. I daresay he shall find women to be the better teachers."

I could scarce eat the trencher of food Mistress Brawley set before me, so anxiously did I mark the door in hopes of glimpsing Alison once more. Jack shoved an elbow into my ribs.

"Eat up, lad," he said. "You cannot tussle a woman on an empty stomach. You shall have no staying power."

Scrope snickered as he gnawed a piece of gristle.

"You are skittish, well I know," Jack said. "Such was I the first time. Never fear. We shall find you a patient woman. Red Bess would be good with a youth, I am thinking."

"I do not want a whore," I said. "I have changed my mind. I want to make love, not roll in bed with a tart."

"You heed the minstrels too well," Scrope scoffed. "A woman is a woman. They are all the same between the legs."

"Then you could do as well with a cow," I retorted.

Oldcastle whooped and slapped the table so that others turned to look at him.

"He answers you well, Lord Scrope," he said. "Indeed, there is more to a woman than fucking. I like a woman to talk to when we are done with love."

"Men are for talking," Scrope said. "Women are for fucking."

"I have heard this from you before, Jack," I said, pointedly ignoring Scrope. "Do you not know then how I feel?"

"Why do you think you might share more than a bed with Alison?" Jack asked. "You know her not."

"She did seem—" I searched for a word to describe her.

"She stared at you," Jack said. "Her mother has told her who you are, and she gapes at the Prince of Wales. That is all."

"Shush!" Scrope whispered. "The hostess comes."

Mistress Brawley replenished our tankards. "Is the ale to your taste, your highness?" she asked.

"Splendid," I said. "I have seen your daughter," I added trying to sound nonchalant. "She was standing in the doorway a moment ago. She is very fair."

Mistress Brawley beamed. "Ah, she shall be most happy to hear of your good opinion." She patted my arm. "Alison is a dear child, a joy. You must speak with her."

"I should like that."

"She shares a bed with me above the pantry. Of course, I do not sleep till cock crow for I am busy with serving, as you may imagine. Now then, I hope you have found all here to your liking. Such an honor it is to have you under my roof. Since it is your highness's first visit, the food and ale are a present. I pray you shall enjoy the rest of the night here. All the Boar's Head is at your disposal. Well, I am off. These louts in the corner call for me."

When she had gone, Scrope leaned over the table. "It is an invitation, Harry, a clear invitation."

"Have a care," Jack warned. "I once saw her wield an ax after a prentice who sought to bed Alison."

"Harry is no prentice. He is the Prince of Wales," said Scrope.

I looked from one to the other. The ale was rich and full-bodied, and my head was light.

"I want no whore," I said.

Jack threw up his hands. "So be it. Only mark, if Mistress Brawley slays you, Tom shall be Prince of Wales and I shall be bootless once more."

Jack and Scrope went off with two tarts, Dolly and Red Bess, and I was left on my own. With thumping heart I found the chamber I judged to be Alison's. I had slipped through the pantry, startling a rat as I went, and crept up a rickety flight of stairs to a closed door. Through a crack I could see the flicker of a candle within. I tried to practice in my mind all that Jack had told me of lovemaking. The palms of my hands were hot and moist, my mouth was dry. Touch a woman gently, he had said, and murmur in her ear. I am clumsy, I thought, and now I am fretful. I would not please her. I would frighten her, hurt her. I backed away from the door, caught my heel upon the stair and tripped, clattering down three or four steps before I broke my fall by grabbing the railing.

The door creaked open and she stood looking down at me, a candle glowing in her hand. She wore a white shift and her golden hair fell loosely about her shoulders.

"'Tis a lot of noise you make," she said.

"I—I am sorry. I tripped upon the stair."

"Are you coming to see me, then?"

"Aye."

She stepped back and held the door open. I climbed the stair awkwardly and entered her chamber, a tiny room with a gabled roof and a rumpled feather bed. I stood beside the bed with my arms folded tightly across my chest. She shut the door firmly and turned to me. Her eyes were dark smudges and her face ghostly in the sputtering light of the candle.

"Are you truly the Prince of Wales?"

"Aye. Please call me Harry."

She smiled. "I am named Alison."

"I know." I looked nervously at the door. "Shall your mother come here soon?"

"No. She shall be serving all the night."

"So she said. Yet suppose she comes for some reason. She would be most angry to find me here, no doubt."

"You are wrong. She should be pleased to learn you were here. She does guard me from men, it is the truth. But you are different. It is not as it would have been had she caught Dickon the cooper in my bed."

"Dickon the cooper?"

"Aye. I am not a maiden as she supposes. After all, I am not a child. Dickon has been with me three times. But that is all. I did tire of him."

I shifted my feet and hugged myself more tightly. For a moment the spell was broken. She was quite common and she had no care for my yearning soul. I had made a mistake in seeking her out. Then she set down her candle, pulled her shift over her head, and stood naked before me, her skin glowing in the light. The flame flickered, and the shadows teased her full breasts.

I do not remember disrobing, only that I found myself naked beside her in the featherbed. All afterward was fire.

*   *   *

I woke with honeyed sun in my face and Alison's hair spread like a net over my chest. I saw her face clearly for the first time. She was indeed fair, I noted with relief.

I sat up abruptly and jostled her awake.

"Your mother!" I exclaimed. "It is late! She shall find us here."

"No." She pulled me down next to her. "She will have been drinking and will sleep it off below. She does not climb the stair when she is in her cups. Besides, she will have guessed that you are here. She shall be pleased, I tell you."

She traced my lips with her fingers as she spoke.

"You have lovely eyes," she said. Then she set her mouth to mine and teased me with the pointed tip of her tongue. Again I succumbed to her charms, and we made love with all the zest of youth.

I could have stayed with her in that bed for days had not Oldcastle and Scrope come pounding upon the door. I cursed them roundly but finally kissed Alison farewell, pulled on my clothes, and followed my fellows out into East Chepe.

"Well?" both said at once.

"Well. It was paradise. More I shall not say."

They chortled and slapped my back. I breathed deeply of the raw morning air and gazed contentedly about me. London was transformed. Urchins and old crones, fat merchants in their carriages, all had assumed mystical proportions. Harry Monmouth was now a man, and in love.

"She admires my eyes," I said. "What is there about them that should please her?"

Jack studied my face with mock seriousness. "Why, your eyes are quite large. They are most marvelously flecked with gray and brown and green. And when you raise your brows you have the look of a lost child. Surely such eyes would melt a woman's heart."

This recital pleased me no end, and I laughed delightedly.

"'Tis an occasion to mark with celebration," Scrope said. "Burgundy would be suitable."

"There is a house in the Vintry renowned for its Burgundy," Jack said. "Then it is home to Kennington and a well-deserved rest."

"Aye, I shall return to Kennington," I said. "Yet I vow I shall not linger there."

In London I was a student of both love and statecraft. Of these two, love is of course the pleasanter, yet I did not neglect more weighty matters. My uncle of Beaufort took it upon himself to instruct me, as my father showed no inclination to do so. With my uncle I sat in attendance upon the King's council and the meetings of parliament. I was seldom acknowledged at these sessions, being unpopular with the peers and youthful besides. Yet did I make good use of the time, for I had ever thought myself a keen observer and judge of men, and I honed these skills under Beaufort's tutelage. I soon learned which lord was a fool and which was not, who in parliament was bold and who unimaginative. I found out which of the King's advisers were most to be feared and I cultivated those whom Beaufort carefully marked as safe.

Sometimes my uncle returned with me to Kennington where, with Oldcastle and Scrope, we would talk over wine long into the night. Beaufort approved of Scrope, whom he deemed "levelheaded, though dull," yet he developed an aversion toward Jack. He thought Jack lazy and frivolous but, even more serious, Jack was impractical.

"Oldcastle is a dreamer. He has no sense of the way things are," he said to me once. "Such men are dangerous companions for a prince."

"Why is that?"

"Because they speak too much of how things should be, and take too little account of the present. They prate of their ideals straight until the time their heads fall upon the block. And they will drag with them any king foolish enough to rule by virtue rather than might."

"Should a king not seek the right?"

"That search is a luxury for monks. It is not for you, Harry. When you rule by ideals you shall be lost."

"And what of my soul?"

"God's blood, you shall be King! You may establish chantries all over England to pray for your soul when you are dead: a chantry in every town, if you like. That should be sufficient to pray the Devil himself into paradise."

Often he urged me to send Jack away to Hereford. Always I refused. Jack was of a world ruled by laughter and wine. It was a world I clung to desperately when the cold of the council chamber gripped me. At Westminster I did learn to sit silent and impassive, implacably judging others. With Jack I shouted and sang, drank and loved. I feared what I should become without him.

I found my way to Alison's bed several times a week. Jack and Scrope often accompanied me to the Boar's Head, for Jack had been smitten by Dolly, who was fresh from Kent. Scrope cared not whom he lay with so long as she was free of the pox.

Alison now spoke boastfully to others of our trysts. This discomfited me, but I said nothing lest she turn against me. Her mother, too, proclaimed our lovemaking round and about so that she was the envy of that district. Thus did I become well known about the city, yet my worst fears of being specially marked were not realized. A drunken shoemaker cares not that his compan-

ion is a prince, so long as he is a jolly fellow. Soon I was held in no awe but
sat easily with the Londoners who crowded the taverns of the city. I came to
know many of the taverns, from Aldgate to the Fleet, but when curfew rang I
ever sought the shelter of the Boar's Head.

In London town the night belongs to brigands and cutthroats. Prudent
men tarry indoors until dawn, or travel with armed escorts if they must break
curfew. In truth, when a man has a woman and a warm bed, he is foolish to
stray. Still, my companions and I, being young and headstrong, ventured into
the dark streets from time to time to brawl with prentices or play some prank,
and I lost much of my fear of the night. These adventures began when Jack
found a new bawdyhouse where he drank cheap wine until sated and was
relieved of his purse. A doxy there, after having him in her bed, demanded
payment. When poor Jack had searched in vain for his coin, she consigned
him to a ruffian who would beat the fee from Jack's hide ere he would set him
free. In desperation Jack sent to the Boar's Head after Scrope and me.

We went grumpily into the cold, trudging through the mud of Lombard
Street and cursing Jack mightily.

"I was ready to have another go at Meg," Scrope muttered through
clenched teeth, "and now I must needs traipse to Catte Street after Jack
Oldcastle and pay for his wenching besides."

"Alison did pout when I left her," I moaned.

I forgot my own misery when I set eyes upon Jack. He was slumped
astraddle a bench with a rude knave towering over him. His drunken relief
at the sight of us gave us much merriment. I tossed his captor half a crown
and we headed back toward the Boar's Head with a wobbly Jack in tow.

"'S'cold," he said and blew upon his hands as he stumbled along.

"'Twas warm in Alison's bed," I said.

"Aye, you will be angry with me. 'Tis not a fit time to be in the streets.
Our throats shall be slit. Jesu! My head is splitting open! The wine there was
like piss."

"Soft!" I whispered and halted. "I hear horses."

We did panic and slipped through the mud to a narrow lane, where we
huddled in the shadows expecting a band of cutthroats to ride down upon us.

Instead, the horsemen were clad in mail and wore the King's livery.
They clattered proudly by on their way to Westminster.

"They come from the Tower," I whispered.

On an impulse I picked up a hunk of loose paving stone and flung it at
the retreating backs of the horsemen. It struck one man upon his helmet
with a clang and he fell forward, nearly unseated. The horse started and
pranced. I let fly again and caught a horse upon the rump. The frightened
animal reared, dumped his rider into the mud, and dashed off down the
Chepe. The men cursed and fought to control their mounts. One drew his

sword and cast wildly about for his attacker. I saw nothing more, for Scrope
was tugging at my sleeve and I turned and ran after him down the lane. Jack
followed, limping and laughing uproariously, and fell into a dungheap alongside a wall.

"You shall smell like a Hereford pigsty," I taunted.

"Quiet, or I shall throttle you!" He struggled to his feet and made as
though to hug me.

I danced merrily away and called, "Try to get a woman now, Jack. It
shall cost you a king's ransom."

"You are both mad," Scrope said.

"And you are a spoilsport," I retorted.

"You have assaulted officers of the King."

"So? The King is only my father."

"It is yet a serious offense."

I stopped and faced him, angry now. "Then charge me for it! Hale me
before the magistrate."

"Don't be foolish," he muttered. "I did not mean that. But why in God's
name did you do it?"

I shrugged. "They were too proud, too clean. I wanted to muddy them
up a bit."

"By 'r Lady," Jack swore, "you did cast those stones splendidly. It calls
for a drink."

"I shall not drink with one who stinks so," I said, with a laugh. "'Tis
Mistress Brawley's pantry for you, Alison's bed for me, and a tankard of ale
on the morrow."

Alas, it was not so simple. Alison was petulant and would not open her
door to me despite my pleading.

"God's name, Alison. I could not leave Jack to be beaten."

"It was his own silly fault," she said from within.

"He would have done the same for me."

"You spent a gold crown on him, I have no doubt. You do not think so
much of me."

I leaned against the door in exasperation. "What am I to do? Is it that
you wish to be rid of me?"

There was a silence on the other side of the door. Then she said, "No,
Harry. It is only that you should have more of a care for my feelings."

"Have I truly been unkind to you?"

"You have been unthoughtful." The door opened a crack. "Yet do I
forgive you."

I slipped gratefully into the chamber and soon had her in bed. When we
were done with our lovemaking we lay with our limbs entwined.

"Harry, am I your mistress?"

I thought a moment. "I had ever thought that only old men have mistresses. Yet I suppose that is what you are."

It seemed to me a fine thing to say, Aye, there is this bond between us. I cupped her breasts in my hands and tenderly kissed the wisps of yellow hair that strayed across her forehead. She sighed with pleasure and spoke so softly that I bent my head to catch her words.

"Then am I a member of the court?"

"I had not thought of such a thing. Why do you ask?"

"I should like very much to be at court," she said dreamily, "to wear a dress of velvet and lovely rings upon my fingers. And to see you wearing my favor at a tournament, as knights do for their ladies."

"I do not joust," I said shortly.

"Why ever not?"

"Because I fear it."

She looked at me incredulously. Of course she will not understand, I thought miserably.

"I am very tired," I said and turned abruptly on my side. "I shall sleep until cock crow."

She said nothing more, nor did she touch me. I left her still abed at dawn and returned to Kennington with my companions.

A fortnight passed without my seeking her bed. I was as sick with longing as any lover in a troubador's roundelay, but my wounded pride held me aloof from her. I moped about Kennington while I thought in vain of ways that I might prove my courage and my devotion to her. My uncle Beaufort grew impatient with me and took me to task one morning as we cast for salmon upon the Thames.

"It is unseemly for a prince of the blood to take on so over a tavern wench. Of course she does not love you. If you were not Prince of Wales she would say 'fie on it' and never think on you again."

I stared bleakly at the white shroud of fog which hung upon the gray water. "I cannot believe that," I said at last.

"Why not? What do you expect? It is a rare woman who would have no care for your station. You shall be hard put to find one who shall, as you put it, love you for yourself."

"Am I unlovable then?"

"Fool. You do not listen to me. People at bottom are selfish and cruel. Princes should know this better than any. You shall hear many sweet words of flattery and love. Heed them not. Behind every honeyed word is ever a motive. This strumpet does not want you. She does not even know you. She only desires your jewels and a place at court. No, do not expect love from women. Only expect a good lay, and perhaps you shall not be disappointed."

"And you would say this of my friends as well, that they care not for me?"

He shrugged. "Oldcastle you have rescued from obscurity and penury in Herefordshire. Scrope shall be treasurer of the realm some day."

"And you, uncle?"

"Ah, you cut to the bone, do you not?" He smiled and stroked his black beard. "You shall be king. I freely admit I prefer your company to Tom's because of it. Yet do not think I feel no fondness toward you. Remember, I was drawn to you ere you were Prince of Wales. You are a fighter, and you are more hardheaded than you will admit to yourself. I like that. Unlike my stupid brother, I think you are just the man to hold the crown for Lancaster."

A lone swallow sliced the veil of mist. My uncle's reasons for loving me gave me no comfort. At last I said, "I do welcome whatever measure of affection I might receive from you or from Alison, and for whatever reason. If I must be realistic, as you say, then perhaps it would not be unwarranted to give Alison what she craves. If that is the way a prince must gain love, well then, I must be resigned to it."

"Spend your coin as you will, only never forget what you are doing. Old King Edward gave many jewels to Alice Perrers, his mistress. And when he lay dying, she stripped the very rings from his fingers and left him."

These cold words rang in my ears as I made my way once more to the Boar's Head. I had thought through carefully all that my uncle had said and finally found it unacceptable. Either Alison loved me or she did not, and one way or the other I must know it for sure. I found her downstairs washing tankards. Her mother spied me first.

"Alison!" she cried. "See who is here!" She bustled up to me and planted a kiss upon my cheek. "My dear prince, we have been most fearful of your safety. It is back to Wales we thought you were, and in God knows what peril!"

There was fear in her bright eyes right enough. Alison, too, seemed eased to see me and smiled shyly.

"I have missed you," she said.

"You two shall wish to be together," Mistress Brawley said. "Upstairs, the pair of you, upstairs." She thrust a brimming tankard at me. "Here is ale to warm you, your highness. No, do not show me your coin."

I thanked her and followed Alison through the pantry to her chamber. No sooner had the door shut than she threw her arms around me so that I sloshed ale upon the floor.

"Oh, it has been forever!" she exclaimed. "I was frightened to death."

"Were you? Why?"

"Why? I knew not what had become of you, of course." She took the ale from me and tugged eagerly at my hose. "You must help me, Harry. Why do you stand so?"

"I have brought you a present," I said.

I brought a ring from the pouch at my belt. Its stone was a ruby, a drop of blood clinging to the slender gold band.

"O-o-oh," she breathed. She plucked it at once from my outstretched hand and retreated to the window, where she examined it closely in the waning light. "It is a fair ring," she crooned, "a lady's ring. Oh, Harry, it must have cost you dear. Yet you are a prince. I am sure it is nought to you, the merest bauble."

She slipped the ring on her finger and held her hand this way and that. "Does it not become me?" she asked.

"Aye," I said. "It suits you well."

"I shall be the envy of East Chepe. Bess shall not speak to me, she shall be so jealous."

"It is a farewell present," I said.

Her smile froze.

"I shall not be seeing you again."

"You cannot mean that!"

"But I do. You have the ring. It is plain that you care more for it than for me. You should be content."

I turned to go. She clutched at my arm. "No, Harry! It is not enough! I pray you, do not leave me."

"Very well. Return the ring to me and I shall stay," I said quietly.

"Return the ring?" She looked at it. "But why? Whyever would you give it to me and then take it again? It is cruel to tease me so."

I flung out of the chamber, slammed the door behind me, and clattered down the stair. Behind me she threw the door open and screamed, "No, come back. You cannot be so cruel!" She was sobbing. "Bastard! Whoreson bastard!"

Her mother appeared in the pantry door. "God's blood, whatever—"

I brushed past her and ran out into the street.

Oft did we ply the Thames to London, yet had the pestilence struck down the denizens of the Boar's Head, we could not have given them wider berth. We dallied now in Billingsgate, and I was more often in my cups and less in the bed. Many a time I drank myself into a stupor and Jack to protect me would lug me abovestairs to huddle in a corner of the chamber while he did romp in bed. Later, though, when Alison's face became blurred by time, I tumbled many a whore myself.

One wild bout with drink and women laid me up in bed for three days, my head splitting and my stomach churning. Jack went to London alone and returned in a strange subdued mood such as I had not seen upon him before.

"How now, Jack," I said. "Has Nan thrown you over, then?"

"I did not see Nan," he said. He stood looking out the window, his head illuminated in the golden sunlight.

"Where did you go? To the Dancing Bear?"

He rubbed his head. "I was with a man of God," he said abruptly.

"What? Do you mean the whole time? Faith, did he have good wine?"

"Have a care, Harry," he said. "You would do well to be more reverent. He spoke words to shake the soul."

"He did shake you indeed. What said he to so affect you?"

"That I am responsible for my own soul, and the Church cannot save it for me. That I must work out my own salvation by reading the scriptures. He said the Church is evil and we do not need it. He called the Church the 'Whore of Babylon.'"

"Archbishop Arundel would name this heresy."

"No doubt the truth of God would sound heresy to one such as Arundel. The Church does stink with corruption, that you know, Harry."

"I know it well. Yet does this man have the answer? 'Tis rash to say we do not need the Church."

"And if you decide this is heresy, what shall you do? I have purchased a book of scripture from this man. The Church would condemn me for it. Shall you report me?"

"Report you? God's blood! What do you take me for?"

"I take you for a prince."

His words stung like a lash. I whispered painfully, "Afore God, I know not the value of what this man said to you. Yet if it does turn you so quickly against your boon companion, there must be some harm in it. I had thought to find more trust in you."

He passed his hand over his eyes. "I meant you no hurt, Harry. It is a grave charge, heresy. Well you know the penalty. It frights me. I have walked many miles this day to put this from my mind, yet I cannot. It was by great chance that I met this man, and in faith I do believe God was in it. I have been wallowing in debauchery, and I want something better. This thing draws me, Harry."

"For my part I detest Arundel and his party. They are vultures who prey on the poor. Aye, I have a care for the reform of the Church, for England's sake and for my own soul's health. But I must sort this out slowly, for though I need no reminding of it, I am a prince, and many poor souls might I bear to perdition if I err."

We sat for a time in uneasy silence. Then I said, "Is it an end then to our merrymaking?"

He smiled crookedly. "I am not yet a saint. I am shaken and discontented, that is all."

"Where did you meet this man?"

"He is a limner. His shop is in Paternoster Street."

"I should like to go there."

"Very well. I shall take you on the morrow."

Of all months, March is the most detestable. The rain and cold eat through to the bone, and one's thoughts leap ahead in vain to fair May. In March it is difficult to believe in the renewal of the earth, for there is a raw, rotting smell that is more akin to death. Jack and I trudged through septic puddles to Paternoster Street, our cloaks wrapped about our thighs to keep them from the mud.

We found the limner, one William Parcheminer, at work in the tiny room behind his shop. He greeted Jack warmly, cast a wary eye upon me, and went back to his illuminating. We watched as he sprinkled gold leaf around the head of a scowling John the Baptist.

"Who is the lad?" he asked presently.

"His name is Harry," Jack said. "He is a cousin from Hereford. I told him how we spoke together of the religious men of the march, and he wished to meet you."

"Oh, aye," said Parcheminer. "The spirit of the Lord is working mightily in Hereford."

"So my cousin tells me," I said. "Yet I must confess I know little of it, as I have not been in Hereford for some time. I would learn more of you."

The limner fixed a sharp eye upon me. "Forgive me if I am reticent. One must be careful how one speaks of these things, and with whom. Your cousin and I spoke together for the better part of a day. Only after much questioning was I satisfied of his sincerity and his hunger for the truth. What then should I make of you?"

"I vouch for him," Jack said.

"Does he also serve the Prince of Wales?"

"Aye."

"I like it not," said Parcheminer. "This is too close to the heart of things."

"Our master is not to be feared," I said. "He is not cruel, and he likewise seeks after truth."

"Perhaps," said Parcheminer. "It may be there is some of his grandfather in him. John o' Gaunt was a friend of the faithful. He saved the life of the great Wyclyf. Aye, that is why the monks revile Gaunt. Though I must say I ever questioned Gaunt's motives. He was shrewd, that one. He wanted Church land for the crown, that is my wager. Sure it is I have heard none name him pious."

"John of Gaunt was a good man," I said.

"You knew him then? I pray for his soul's sake that you are right. For myself, I weary of these lukewarm John o' Gaunts. I look for a ruler who shall wield the sword of righteousness, aye, and cut deep with it."

"How so?" I asked. "What would such a ruler do?"

"He would reject the authority of the pope, that false shepherd who leads men to perdition, and turn out the priests as well. Strip the Church of its wealth and purge it of these unholy monks. Cleanse the churches of their idolatrous images. Aye, and he would stop this veneration of Mary, who was but a woman and so was a weak vessel."

"How would a king do all this?" I asked in astonishment.

"He would simply do it," the limner said.

"Even should he wish to bring about such drastic changes, he would be fiercely opposed," I persisted. "The whole of the realm would be out of joint."

"Did not Our Lord say, 'I do not come to bring peace, but a sword'?" He wagged a gold-girt finger under my nose. "If you read your scripture you would know that. Without such knowledge you shall be lost."

"Tell him of the scriptures," Jack said.

"We have the scriptures in English from Wyclyf." Parcheminer was warming to his subject, his reticence forgotten. "They contain all things necessary for salvation. We do not need priests. The true believer is his own priest."

"What of the host?" I asked. "The Church teaches that Our Lord's body is—"

"Sorcery!" Parcheminer interrupted. "It is not the Lord's body, but only bread. Why would God play such games with us? No, God gives us His Word, plain and true."

I asked no more questions, for I was much shaken. It did seem to me that the man assaulted all that had sustained me in my doubts and fears. I tried to recall what my grandfather had said about Wyclyf and his followers. "Lollards" he had called them, which means "mutterer," for thus they were commonly known by the people. I seemed to remember that he had judged Wyclyf a good man, courageous and sincere.

"I do not hold with much of his teaching," Gaunt had said, "yet I would not burn him for it. I've enough to mind my own soul. I shall leave Wyclyf's to God."

Jack and I were wrapped each in his own thoughts until we sat huddled close together in our barge.

"Well?" Jack whispered. "What do you think?"

"I was drawn by some of this teaching," I said cautiously, "yet frightened by some of it as well. I must have time to sort it out. I promise I shall study these matters as seriously as you do. More I cannot say."

He sat back and sighed. "I am content," he said.

I was in attendance upon the King's council when word came from Wales that Owain Glyndwr had attacked Ruthin and taken Lord Grey prisoner. The peers sat in shocked silence to hear that one of their own had been captured by knaves. My thoughts were upon the poor children Lord Grey had borne off, and I snickered softly at the tidings. The sound carried more loudly than I had expected in the quiet chamber, and several pairs of eyes turned to me in astonished fury. My uncle kicked me beneath the table. No word was spoken against me that day, for my father was absent, but he lost no time in sending for me upon his return.

I was left cooling my heels for two hours in the Painted Chamber as though I were a fishmonger from Dover come to plead my case. The King's retainers stood idly about and whispered behind their hands. At last, Father swept into the room without looking at me. I knelt before him and kissed his ring. He did not bid me rise. Nor did he mince words.

"I hear that you have shamefully mocked the misfortune of Lord Grey."

"Lord Grey's misfortune did seem justice to me."

"What do you know of justice, impudent whelp? Lord Grey's ransom shall break his treasury. A man is ruined for loyally serving his King, and you find justice in it? Why do you not follow the Welsh?"

When he saw I had no words for him, he leaned back in his chair and groaned.

"My son, my son. You are the great sorrow of my life. A man should lean upon his heir, yet you are a frail crutch. I hear you spend your hours in the taverns."

"You hear much of me, it seems."

"How may I avoid it? Indeed, I would know of more pleasant things than your wenching and drinking. When I tire of your antics I cheer myself with reports from Wales and France. The French threaten us as in the days of old, though I doubt you care to hear about it. I have just returned myself from the Channel. The French have attacked Swanage and slain many people. They set upon our fishermen in the Channel. Why should they not? England is torn with dissension, and the King has no one upon whom he may depend—no, not even his heir. I will not have it! You are for Wales at once, Harry, and London shall not see you again until you have put these rebels down. Of course, I cannot trust you to go alone, and I need your uncle Beaufort at Westminster. You shall again have a governor."

"Percy," I said with dread.

"No, Percy is in the north. I am sending you to Lord Despenser. You are for Powys, and you shall leave two days hence. God's blood, Harry, remember your station and do not shame me again. I need you to bear a man's burden."

6

From Whitsuntide to All Hallows we chased Owain Glyndwr up and down the labyrinthine valleys of south Wales. It was a fool's errand, for we could not even catch sight of him, much less bring him to bay. We rode for endless hours, and burned lonely cottages, and then laid ourselves upon the stony ground to sleep, only to rise in the wet dawn and ride again. It was whispered among our soldiers that Owain practiced black magic, that he could change himself into a wolf or a hawk and so would never be caught. I had fashioned my own explanation for our lack of success, and that was the ignorance of my father and my governor, Lord Despenser. Caught up as they were in their knightly charges and pitched battles, they were no match for the elusive Welsh, who carried the burden of neither armor nor chivalry. I laughed inwardly at English ineptness, yet I did not share my thoughts, for the whole business repelled me. I listened impassively to Lord Despenser's tedious advice, sent terse dispatches to my father of our pillaging, and attended to my prayers more fervently than ever. I touched no women. There were opportunities for rape, but, God as my witness, never did I force myself upon a woman. Of that, at least, I am proud.

In December the gentle snows blanketed the mountains and Owain's men returned to their hearths to wait out the cold. Our Englishmen we likewise sent to their homes. Jack Oldcastle, who had stayed by me through the privations of the campaign, went to his manor in Hereford. He offered me his hospitality, but I had other plans. I had not set eyes upon my Monmouth since that day four years earlier when Richard's messengers had carried me away to the court. My longing for the place overwhelmed my fear of the rejection I might find there. With my weary band of retainers I set my course down the Monnow toward my heart's desire. We made our approach at dusk as the bells of St. Thomas pealed a welcome. Castle and town hovered on the rise of land even as they had in my dreams. I set an eager spur to Morgause's flanks and we surged forward, pursued by the ghosts of happier times.

Joan Waryn was plumper, her toothless grin was wide as ever, and her embrace still could crush the breath from a body. She wept loudly to see me again.

"'Tis a man's height you have, Harry, and a man's voice. Where is the boy I tended?"

"Gone forever, I fear."

"It is so long, so long. Why did you not come to me?"

"My time is seldom my own. Besides, I feared that I had lost your love."

"What! Lost my love? No, Harry, never!"

"I am fighting your people, Joan."

"Aye, I know it. And did I not wipe the dung from your wee bottom when you were but a babe, and take you to my breast, and are you not my boy? Never say such things." She hugged me again. "Will you bide through Christmas?"

"Aye, and until the snows melt."

"My poor Harry. 'Tis little enough love you have had these years, with that cold fish of a father. Yet I do hear you are a great one with the lasses."

I grinned. "How do you hear such a thing?"

"Ah, William Bruer has been to London on Lancaster's business. He heard it said that the Prince of Wales is no stranger to the bawdyhouses."

"And if it is true?"

"Why, then, my kitchen maids shall not be safe," she crowed.

"Never mind," I teased. "I shall not fuck them while they are cooking your supper. I would not have you go hungry."

"Fie on you!" she cried and boxed my ears.

The bedchamber I had shared with my brothers was unchanged. The same tapestry hung upon the wall, a summer scene of jolly huntsmen and their ladies pursuing a hart through a leafy wood. I curled up contentedly in the great feather bed. Lost in its soft mounds I dreamed of unremembered bliss, and when I awoke it was as if I had never been a prince, but only Harry.

Joan and I celebrated our Lord's nativity in a simple manner. In the morning we heard mass and afterward feasted upon a roast goose, puddings, and sweetmeats. Then I harped and we sang carols with the simple folk of the castle. The servants scraped and blew upon their instruments, and we danced a clumsy estampie until Joan did sink panting and laughing onto a bench. A vat of steaming wassail was carried into the hall and set upon the hearth, and we drank before the blazing fireplace until all were nodding with sleep.

I often spent my days afterward in hunting. I ranged far and wide, up Monnow and Wye and throughout the Forest of Dean, where boars and hinds were thick as any herd of sheep. It is fearsome to hunt the wild boar, for many a man who had missed with the first bolt of the crossbow has been gored by the creature's knife-sharp tusks. I have seen this myself, and it is a horrible way to die. Yet have I ever been a sure hand with the bow, and I brought down five boars while at Monmouth. One I had dressed, and I took the meat myself to the family of Rhys ap Llewellyn. Rhys and his father were gone with Glyndwr this last year, even as I had feared, and they had not dared return for the winter because they were tenants of Lancaster. Rhys's mother and brother were left to fend for five younger children, all bony and hungry. They cried after the boar's meat, and I saw to it that Joan would provide for them regularly from the castle larder. Small time I spent with them, for I was now their enemy. Many a cottage such as theirs I had seen burned to the ground, and they well knew it. Suspicion and unease filled their hollow eyes during my rare visits, despite the food I provided. Each time I left them, I prayed for Rhys's safety, and that we might never meet in battle.

Relentlessly the spring pushed winter aside, the snows melted and swelled the mountain streams, and my father sent word to me that Glyndwr had left his hiding place and did range freely across the north. With heavy heart I made ready to join the pursuit once more. Joan and I sat glumly at table my last night at Monmouth.

"Shall it again be four years ere I lay eyes upon you?" She was near tears.

I shrugged, not wanting to speak, and crumbled the crust of my kidney pie with my knife.

"Soon it shall be sixteen years since first I gave you suck," she said. She swayed and spoke rhythmically as though telling her beads. "Now you are a man. Aye, and you have old eyes. Old eyes. I wonder what they have done to you. You are not so merry as once you were. When you sit and think, and the shadow passes over your face, then I fear for you. At such times I want to hold you upon my lap. Yet you are too big for that!"

"Indeed I am." I smiled weakly. "Though it should be quite a sight."

"You shall be a fine king, if that is what you fear."

"Aye, it is the crown I fear, and what I must do to wear it."

"I am a poor, unlearned woman and I know nothing of such matters. Yet I know my Harry well. You have a good heart. It was so when you were a child, and I see that has not changed. Is it not enough?"

It was long ere I answered. "God knows," I said.

I rode first to Hereford, where Jack Oldcastle awaited me with a company of archers. We greeted one another as brothers and shared what had passed since last we met. Jack's talk was of country matters, of harvests and sheep. Then he leaned to my ear and whispered, "I have studied the scriptures most diligently."

I watched him warily. "Oh?"

"This fighting the Welsh, it is not as we thought."

"What mean you by that?"

"In my district, there reside many good knights who also read the scriptures, and I have opened my heart to them. They say we worry for naught. God blesses our striving against the Welsh, they do say, and the scripture I have studied does seem to agree. God often sent the men of Israel into battle against a heathen foe. The heathen are to be smitten, man, woman, and child, so the Word of God says. When King Saul did spare the Amalekites out of unmanly pity, God was angered. God withdrew His blessing from Saul, and so Saul fell. You must not fear to use the sword, Harry. Only fear disobedience."

"Yet even were it so," I said doubtfully, "the Welsh are Christian folk."

"No. It is a soiled gospel they proclaim, and that is worse than no gospel at all. They cling to the old heathen ways, casting spells and calling upon sorcerers such as Merlyn. It is the Devil, and yet it masquerades as the true faith. Our mission is to defend Christendom against false doctrine."

"So say the knights of Herefordshire?"

"Aye, many of them."

"They are marcher lords. They would have much to gain by such a mission."

"To be sure! They preach that God does reward the faithful, either in this life or the next."

I knew not how to answer him, for I knew little of scripture save what the Church taught. I tossed upon my bed that night. Here was a new Jack. No, not so new, for he embraced his new faith as lustily as ever he did a woman. What if he were right? Then everything should be easy. He was himself content, at peace as I had not seen him before. Now he could ride cheerfully against Glyndwr. I longed to be as he was, to go blithely with sword in hand to slay the enemies of God, but I could not. I pondered and wrestled until I thought my soul itself must be a battleground.

Lord Despenser had taken a fever and died that winter, and so the Earl of Worcester was placed in charge of the Welsh expedition. I was ill pleased to have him as governor, for he was a Percy, uncle to that Henry Percy who had misused me. We rode to him at Shrewsbury and thence into the mountains in pursuit of the rebels. Once more we searched in vain while Glyndwr pillaged at will the lands of the marcher lords. Ever he struck where we were not, causing the hot-tempered Worcester to rant and curse at each setback.

Worcester was a man of high spirits, yet he was not inclined to mistreat me as had his nephew, and I grew to tolerate him. For his part, he seemed intrigued by me and often probed me with questions. At first I resisted, clutching my thoughts close about me like a cloak. In the end I was worn down by his persistence and shared with him my disgust for our task.

"What irks you most?" he asked.

"That we destroy the livelihood of many poor people, and set them to starve, because of the defiance of one man, who has himself some cause to oppose us. And all our plundering does not stop him but only drives more desperate folk into his camp."

"I shall speak roundly. It is said that the Prince of Wales is a coward and that he does not wish to fight Glyndwr at all."

"I care not for what is said." I answered him angrily. "Perhaps I do not wish to fight him, and I have my reasons for it. Yet if I did choose to do so, I would make a better job of it than these proud marcher knights who prance about with their helms on backward."

His eyes narrowed. "Is it so? And what would you do?"

"It is Glyndwr who leads the rebellion. Why not strike at him instead of some poor peasant who wishes only to milk his cow in peace? Nor do I mean that we should continue to chase Glyndwr all over Wales. He has a large estate. Burn that, not the cottages of poor men."

"And then?"

"He holds many castles. I would take them. Castles do not move. They do not hide in the mountains. I would leave him not a fortress in Wales. I would guard the marches well. I would issue a pardon to his followers. And then I would let him roam the valleys until he is ninety, if he so desires."

Worcester said nothing, only rubbed his chin reflectively. My throat was dry, and a cold chill ran up my spine. I wondered what it was in me that could plot so clearly the downfall of another. No, I thought then, it is right to have spoken to Worcester, for this plan is far better than the wanton destruction of the present.

The next day we turned west, at Worcester's command, and made for Glyndwr's estate of Cynllaith Owain.

Glyndwr's was a rambling half-timbered manor with frosted-glass windows and many outbuildings. We burned it and razed it to the ground so that not one stone stood upon the other. It was Maytime, and the lush green water meadows were awash with marigolds. A grove of plum trees in full blossom was hacked down, thatched beehives were smashed, a field of matted flax was trampled beneath English hooves. The rebel's family and retainers had escaped, so our soldiers fell upon the livestock. The death screams of cattle and swine are as unnerving as any human cry. The long grass was soon sticky with their dark blood.

It is one thing to plot out such devastation and quite another to witness it. I sat upon Morgause beneath a twisting ash tree and bowed my head before the carnage. I had set Jack in charge of my men, and he went about his task with grim determination.

"All goes well," he reported to me. "Will you yet hold back?"

"I am not of a mind for this," I said. "I am young enough to plead my age as an excuse. Besides, I have done enough. The blame for this rests upon me."

"Call it not blame," he said. "We do what we must do."

Mountains floated like blue smoke beyond the verdant sweep of grassland.

"It was a fair place, this," I said.

"Aye. This Glyndwr is no rude yeoman to possess such holdings. The house was richly furnished, and our men fill their packs with many costly baubles."

"Is that not theft? Do your scriptures not condemn it?"

"Not if God gives the enemy into our hands. The children of Israel took a land of milk and honey from the Canaanites."

Our men feasted that night upon freshly slaughtered meat, but I would have none of it. I wandered afield and snared a coney for roasting upon the campfire. I gnawed the tender meat from the bones with a stubborn relish, until Jack pointed out with a grin that I had likely poached Glyndwr's game. He danced nimbly to duck the boot I hurled at his head.

By late June the coin for our expedition was spent and no more was sent us from London, despite Worcester's pleas to my father. After enduring a fortnight with no pay, the soldiers drifted away home. The force under my command fell to a paltry forty men-at-arms. Worcester fared better, for he had with him several hundred of his own northern troops. He was forced to pay them from his own pocket, and he spoke scathingly of my father.

"Was ever a servant so ill used?" he raged one night as we lay camped beside Afon Vyrnwy. "'Tis the same with my nephew Harry Percy. Our house is bankrupted by its service to the crown. The King thinks little enough of those who placed him upon the throne."

"I cannot speak for him," I said.

"God's blood! What can he be thinking? He even confiscates what is rightfully ours to pay his debts. Know you that my nephew took prisoners among the Scots, and Bolingbroke kept their ransom for himself? A rich ransom! As if Bolingbroke and not brave Hotspur had risked his life's blood in England's behalf."

"I did not know it."

"He informs you as little as he does me, and you his own son. Is he a tyrant who guards his power, or is he merely inept?"

"I know not. I do know he is yet King of England."

Worcester stared at me, his face ashen, and I met his gaze coolly. His eyes dropped.

"So he is. I forget myself, and I beg your highness's pardon."

"Pardon is granted."

Strange it was to me to feel defensive upon my father's behalf, yet I sensed peril in Worcester's mood. I took careful note of him for several days afterward. He was plainly uneasy and often stood lost in thought, his head cocked to one side.

We were moving slowly toward Shrewsbury, where we would make an empty show of protecting the march. Worcester often sent out messengers to prepare for our arrival in Shrewsbury, or so he said. There seemed over-many of them to me. I sought out Jack as we broke our fast and I shared my fears with him.

"Aye, something there is in the air I do not fancy," he said. "It bears watching."

"Perchance it bears more than that. I know what sort of man Harry Percy is. If he indeed bears a heavy grievance against Lancaster, he shall act upon it. He is passing proud."

"You think he seeks to overthrow the King? It would be extreme."

"My father has set him a good example."

"And Worcester would join him?"

"Worcester is his kinsman. He sends to Percy, I am sure of it. And I like not the odds here. Worcester has three hundred men to my two score."

"What do you propose?"

"That we flee at once."

"If you are wrong you shall appear very foolish, and Worcester shall have good cause for insult."

"And if I am right, our lives are not worth tuppence here."

"If you are right, we may even now be prisoners."

We regarded one another soberly.

"Your father must suspect something," Jack said. "Why has he not sent to you?"

"If he knows aught of this, he shall have packed Tom safe away to the Tower with no thought for me. If I am indeed in danger, I must save myself. And save England as well, for Percy on the throne should be a disaster."

"Is this Harry Monmouth speaking? I had thought you would gladly thrust the crown away from you for the sake of your soul."

"There is much for me to think on here," I said irritably, "yet in truth it is not the time for reflection. We must act."

"What shall we do?"

"We must leave soon. Tonight. We shall ride straightway for Shrewsbury. The castle there is a strong one. The town is well guarded by its rivers and, I believe, loyal to Lancaster. Perhaps we may hold it for a time with a small garrison. Aye, we flee tonight. If we are pursued, we shall know I am right. If I am proven wrong, I shall beg pardon of Worcester for some boyish whim."

"Speak highly to him of Shrewsbury bawdyhouses."

"Exactly. Yet I'll wager you he shall be after us."

We dared not flee with our footmen, for they would travel far too slowly. Our day's march would leave us twelve miles from Shrewsbury, and we thought to make a dash of it that night. I was unwilling to desert my men for I feared they would suffer Worcester's wrath when he found me missing. I called them to me and bade them ask no questions, but to make ready to depart the camp that same morning. This they did with admirable discretion. I sought out Worcester as they made their preparations and told him of their leaving.

"I cannot pay them as you do your men," I said. "They are grumbling, and I would not hold them in so disaffected a state. I hope to call upon them in future, and so desire their goodwill. I have bidden them return to their homes, and they do so this morning."

He raised his eyebrows. "It is sudden."

"There is no reason for them to delay. They may travel far ere the sun sets."

"Is it wise for you to be so unprotected?"

"Good cousin Worcester! I am here guarded by three hundred of your stout north countrymen. Is that not safety enough? I place myself under your protection."

He smiled thinly and said, "As you wish."

Two men I sent toward London and my father to bear word of peril to the crown. Two others I sent to Shrewsbury to warn the garrison of my arrival. One of these, William Bruer, was an old servant of Lancaster. He went on foot but with gold crowns in his purse to purchase a horse as soon as he might to bolt for Shrewsbury. By midmorning all my household had departed save John Oldcastle and my esquire, Raulyn de Brayllesford, a youth of sixteen. Raulyn I had apprised of my plight, and he was eager to stand by me. We plotted as we ambled along the banks of the Severn, holding ourselves apart from the others and laughing occasionally as though whispering of young men's pranks.

"We should go separately," Jack said. "Raulyn shall cross the Severn and ride to the northeast, I to the southwest, and you, Harry, straight to Shrewsbury."

"Aye," Raulyn said, "and Jack and I should take pains to be seen so that your highness may slip away unmarked."

"No, I shall not have it," I protested. "You bear too much danger upon yourselves. If you are seen that quickly you shall be captured. We should leave together, and quietly."

"It is you Worcester wants, Harry," said Jack. "We must take risks to get you safe away from here. That is what matters."

"I am loath to leave your highness alone," said Raulyn, "yet I fear it must be. If we can slip away together, well and good. But I think we shall be watched. The only escape would be by some diversion."

I knew them to be right and offered no more objections.

We agreed that there would be no time to saddle horses, so that we must plan to ride bareback. I had not done this since childhood, and I prayed that I might stick to my mount. The horses were herded together that night in a field apart from our encampment and a watch set upon them. Worcester had set guards around the camp as well. We laid ourselves on the edge of the camp and waited for our companions to wrap themselves in their blankets and sleep. Then we crept away from our dying fire, keeping a sharp eye out as we went.

Jack, who was in the lead, held his hand up suddenly and whispered, "There he is!"

The shadowy figure of the watch loomed at the edge of a thick copse.

"In truth," said Raulyn, "he does not guard against Welsh raiders, for he turns his attention to his own camp."

"I was right," I said, "and it is prisoners we are."

Raulyn crept away from us, then walked boldly and noisily toward the guard. Jack and I dropped into the tall grass and crawled into the wood. Raulyn's pleasant voice faded as we scrambled on hands and knees over brambles and fallen branches. We came scratched and sore to the edge of the pasture where the horses grazed. Raulyn was to speak to the guards of tending the Prince's horse, which he would claim had been favoring one of its legs. He had already emerged from the wood some fifty yards from us and walked slowly across the meadow, his right hand upraised in greeting to the guards.

Only two of them there were, and both hearkened to Raulyn, their backs toward us.

"Thanks be to Christ," whispered Jack, and then we raced silently over the turf. We stopped downwind of the horses and approached cautiously so as not to startle them. I first made for a gray gelding but thought better of it, for fear the light color would be too visible. I settled upon a bay mare, whispering sweetly to her and stroking her neck. She shuddered and was still.

From the wood came the blast of a horn. We had been missed. The two men talking to Raulyn turned then and spied Jack and me.

"Who goes?" one called.

"Fly!" Jack cried.

He leaped upon the back of his mount and rode with sword drawn toward the two footmen. As the confused fellows turned to meet this challenge, Raulyn vaulted onto Morgause and was gone. The wood was alive with the noise of pursuit. It seemed an eternity ere I clambered onto the mare's sleek back, clutched her mane with sweating hands, and dug my spurs into her flanks, expecting at any moment to take a bolt between the shoulders. As I galloped for the far wood, I saw from the corner of my eye that Jack was away, following the line of trees to the south.

We had crossed the meadow and skirted the forest ere I conquered my panic and came to my senses. I pulled the mare up short and tried to get my bearings. God in His mercy had cleared the sky, and I looked to the stars. My horse had veered to the west when I should have held to the east. In any case it was sure that the forest lay between me and Shrewsbury road. I must find a way through, and quickly. If I retraced my path I might run into my pursuers. There was nothing for it but to push on westward. I had gone nearly a mile out of my way when I came upon a rough track into the wood. I turned the mare's head and plunged into the sheltering darkness of the trees, certain I had not yet been seen.

"Holy Mary, save me," I prayed to the rhythm of the hooves.

It was a fine mare I had chosen, sure of foot and swift, yet to stay on her back was no easy task. I crouched to avoid low branches that were invisible in the dark, my arms wrapped tightly about the horse's neck and my knees gripping her flanks. The muscles of my back and thighs burned from the strain. In a blessedly short time we burst from the wood onto Shrewsbury road. I paused to listen. All was silence. I prayed that Worcester's men had not found a way through to the road ahead of me. If they had, they would surely be lying in wait for me. In an agony of uncertainty I decided to stay upon the high way, for I would go more straightly and easily upon it. I turned east and set off at a brisk clip.

Fear and weariness told on me as we covered the miles. The rough gait of the mare jolted me; her hooves pounded into my brain. My head swung left and right as I searched for the expected ambush. Cool judgment had flown from me. I stopped often, foolishly, to listen. I heard nothing but the sounds of a summer night, of owls and crickets mocking me with their hootings and scrapings. My mind was peopled with Worcester's horsemen just out of earshot topping the rise behind me, swords drawn, ready to cut me down in the dust. Evil thoughts came unbidden to me of Jack and Raulyn taken and slain, of William Bruer arrived at Shrewsbury to find Percy already established, his standard waving from the battlements. A tiny, insistent voice whispered that I was too weary to ride farther, that I should stop and sleep.

I knew Shrewsbury road well enough to judge that I was yet four miles from the town when the mare threw a shoe. I slipped from her back and rested my cheek against the moist, prickly hair of her neck. Then I slapped her rump and cried "Hi!" to send her out of sight. She hobbled off through a field in search of water.

To find another mount might take hours. I stood in the road and swayed with weariness. It would be folly to go on. Besides, they would have given up the pursuit. They had followed Jack, not me. I had lost them in the wood. Sleep would be so good. There was a thick hedge beside the road. I was thirsty.

Then I heard the horn.

I could not have sworn to the sound, so faint it was.

There it was again. A horn, to be sure. Thus did the huntsmen blow when they had picked up the trail of their prey. Then would they ride down their quarry and slay it.

A royal quarry these huntsmen sought.

I ran then, bolted like a hare down Shrewsbury road. I had ever prided myself upon my running, for never in my life had I been bested in a foot race. Often I hunted deer on foot. Never had I vied against horses.

I ran steadily, trying not to wind myself too quickly. The road rose and fell over undulating hills so that I labored up the one side and flew down the other, the wind whistling in my ears. I tossed my sword into a ditch, pulled my tunic and my undershirt over my head as I ran, and threw them away as well, caring not if my pursuers found them. The sweat dried cold upon me in the night air. I knew nothing save for my feet, heart, and head all pounding as one.

I was less than a mile from Shrewsbury when I saw them. Only a glimpse it was, when I turned my head as I ran, of torches flickering through the trees at the top of the hill.

I drove myself on. My hands clawed at the air, my lungs were consumed with fire. The walls of Shrewsbury loomed gray in the dawn, beckoning me to safety. There were Welshgate and the wooden bridge before it which would carry me across the Severn.

Five hundred yards more.

I twisted my head again and saw the knot of pursuing horsemen, their torches held high.

I stumbled and sprawled headlong in the dirt. The breath left me. The ground shook with the thunder of hooves. I writhed, breathed at last with a kind of sob. I dragged myself, raised myself, limped, gasped, somehow ran again, across the bridge to the gate. I pounded, kicked.

"Open!" I screamed. "Open!"

The wood moved beneath my splayed fingers even as an arrow whistled and buried itself where my arm had been. The gateway swallowed me. Voices and torches danced about me.

"It is the Prince himself! Praised be Our Lady!"

"Bar the gate," I gasped.

"It has been done, your highness," said William Bruer.

I sank to my knees and fought for breath. "The Percys have risen," I sobbed.

"So it would seem," Bruer said. "No doubt Hotspur marches for Shrewsbury thinking to find his uncle of Worcester settled in. You have played them a fine trick, Harry Monmouth."

He stretched me out with my back against a wall and put a dipper of water to my mouth.

"Bring a blanket," he called over his shoulder. "The lad is shivering."

"My father?" I asked when I had regained my breath.

"We must pray that he is on the march as well. Yet we have heard nothing."

"And if Hotspur should come to Shrewsbury before the King, my tricks are for naught, for our garrison here is tiny, I'll wager."

"Some two score men, no more. Yet your highness's courage has roused all our hearts. We are safe enough for a while. You must sleep, and when you are rested we are yours to command."

"If John Oldcastle and Raulyn de Brayllesford reach these gates, they are to be admitted at once. Instruct the watch to keep a sharp eye out for them."

Worcester came against us that day with the rest of his three hundred. I slept until Nones and awoke to see the familiar Percy colors fluttering across the Severn. From Shrewsbury wall I could just make out the stocky form of my governor stalking about as he positioned his men for the siege. Poor siege it was, with so small a force. I could imagine the cursing of the volatile Worcester when he found the city shut against him and the alarm spread far and wide. By Vespers he had sent to seek terms for our surrender. We refused to treat with him. This would be expected, for all knew that both sides waited, Worcester for Hotspur, I for the King.

Jack Oldcastle slipped into Shrewsbury when darkness fell. He clasped me to his chest when we met in the castle ward. He smelled of dung, and I guessed he had spent the day hidden in some barn.

"I feared to find you were dead," he said.

"So shall I be if you crush the life out of me."

He released me. "They followed me less than a mile," he said, "then the horn called them away eastward. I knew they sought you."

Raulyn arrived before cock crow, still on Morgause, to my great joy. Jack and I brought him to the hall and toasted one another with claret. Raulyn bore a tale similar to Jack's, and foul tidings which chilled the marrow of our bones. North of Shrewsbury he had chanced upon three men in the livery of Lancaster come from Pontefract.

"They claimed Percy is even now moving upon Shrewsbury, and with great speed," he said. "They think he shall be here in a day or two."

"Why are these men not here?" I asked.

"They say they are awaiting the King. I believe they fear to be trapped in this town."

Jack threw up his hands. "Then why do we sit here? We few cannot hold Shrewsbury against Percy. He shall overrun us. Can we not slip by Worcester in the dark?"

"No," I said. "Shrewsbury is the most vital stronghold in the northwest. Why do you think Percy wants Shrewsbury? He wants the marches. He wants to use Welsh discontent for his own purposes. No, he may take Shrewsbury, but I shall not give it to him."

"Are you truly so concerned about strategy?" Jack asked. "Or do you fear your father would name you coward if you leave?"

"You speak too roundly," Raulyn said.

I waved my hand. "Jack may say what he likes. My reasons are my own. I shall not leave Shrewsbury. You are both free to go if you like."

"Do not think I would desert you," Jack said. "But you must know that if Percy takes Shrewsbury ere your father arrives, your head will be on a pike. Percy shall not repeat Richard's mistake of holding you hostage."

"And if I forsake Shrewsbury, and my father arrives before Percy and finds the gates shut against him, then Lancaster may be lost. Percy shall not be King! I shall not have it!"

Jack sighed. "What ever happens, we are like to die."

"It is a question of honor," Raulyn said. "It is honorable to stay."

"It is," I said, "what will be. And that is all."

I was weary of this wrangling and went off to bed.

*   *   *

After passing two tedious days we stood upon the battlements and watched a
billowing cloud of dust to the east. Here and there a tiny figure of a man
appeared in the cloud, but we could see no colors.

"From the east," Jack muttered. "It could be either one."

"Thousands there are for sure," said Raulyn.

The white July sun glinted upon burnished armor so that the dust cloud
seemed afire.

"They must be thirsty," I said. "Glad they shall be to see the river."
Colors floated in the dust.

"The banners!" Jack cried. "I see red—and blue!"

Wisps of dust blew over the emerald forests and meadows.

"Red and blue!" Jack said. "It is the King! God's blood, Harry, we are
saved!"

On they came, the gleaming swords hanging from their belts like
lighted tapers.

The Earl of Worcester prudently withdrew his little band, and the royal
army marched unhindered into Shrewsbury town. Many lords were present:
Talbot, Roos, Stafford, and hundreds of knights. Most though were poor
men, and miserable ones at that. I surveyed them all as I awaited my father
at the castle gate. They had no taste for this fight, that much was plain, and
little wonder. Englishmen to fight Englishmen. Sturdy country fellow to slay
his own kind for the sake of his master's quarrels. They shuffled into Castle
Street, their faces long dusty masks, gnarled hands gripping bows and
cudgels. Thousands there were, and more thousands would Percy bring to
engage these little ones in combat.

My father brought with him the despicable Arundel, the unholy Archbishop of Canterbury, to lend spiritual aid to his cause. Arundel was making
his reputation as the most powerful man in England next the King. He was
hated by clerks and yeomen alike for his arrogance and greed. No poor man's
land was safe from his grasping. My father tolerated Arundel's highanded-
ness because the Archbishop gave generously of his wealth to the Crown.

I ushered king and archbishop into the castle hall, where meat and wine
were set before them. Father looked far older than his thirty-seven years as
he bent preoccupied over his meal. When he took note of me it was to
remark, "Poor tutors I have seen fit to give you, is it not so, Harry?" He
spoke into his cup.

"So it would seem, your grace."

"Hmmm. It is a wonder to me that Worcester did not take Shrewsbury.
I had thought to be at a great disadvantage when I met Percy. How came you
to be in the town without Worcester?"

"Through no help from you, that is certain," I said.

He set down his cup. "What mean you?"

I ignored his question. "Where is Tom?"

"All your brothers are in the Tower. 'Tis the safest place in such unset-tled times."

"Indeed. And yet you did leave me unwarned in the hands of a man who has taken up arms against you."

"I knew not for certain Worcester would rebel."

"What thought you, that he would betray Percy?"

"You speak as though I wished you harm." His voice rose. "Have you so little regard for your father? I was caught unawares, that is all."

"Your grace, if I might say a word."

It was Raulyn de Brayllesford, on his knees.

"Go on, then."

"The Prince speaks sharply to you, yet I ask that you pardon him. It is his weariness which speaks for him. He has done you good service these few days, and this you should know."

Raulyn told then of what had passed, while I stood staring at the floor. A murmur of appreciation filled the hall when he had finished, and cries of "Well done!"

Even Arundel nodded his approval. "In truth, it was boldly and wisely done," he said.

"Aye, so it was," said Father. "I am often hard on you, Harry, yet this warrants praise."

"I seek no praise," I mumbled. "That is not what I seek."

"You stand with me against Percy?"

"Against Percy, aye."

Arundel folded his hands upon his sunken chest. "Such faithfulness deserves a reward," he said, his thin head bobbing up and down.

"Indeed, I would have Harry know my pleasure in him. What do you suggest?"

Arundel smiled at me. "The Prince has attained a man's estate. Your highness is near sixteen, are you not?"

"Aye."

"The Prince has served an apprenticeship on the marches," he contin-ued, "under the tutelage of fine soldiers. I may charitably name them so, even though they stand against us. The Prince has shown his courage, and it seems he keeps a cool head in time of danger. It does appear to me he is ready for greater responsibility. Perhaps it is responsibility he has lacked all along to steady and subdue his high spirits. I suggest you set him in com-mand of one wing of your army."

I stared at him.

Father stroked his beard. "It is a heavy burden for one so young. And Harry—"

"The Black Prince was of the same age at Crécy," said Arundel, "and he did acquit himself most admirably. His conduct made his reputation for life."

I am not the Black Prince, I thought, he who slaughtered the innocents of Limoges, men, women, and children.

"What say you, Harry? It would be perilous." Father spoke as though adding figures in a ledger.

"Indeed it should be," Jack said behind me. The tone of his voice urged me to caution. "When an attack is called, Harry would lead it. Perilous indeed for a lad who has never known hand-to-hand combat save in training."

"What say you, Harry?" Father repeated.

"I shall accept your decision," I said. "I shall lead them if you wish it."

"So be it."

Jack cornered me later and whispered, "The good archbishop would honor you by slaying you. Loathsome old crow! He wants you out of the way because he fears your strength and knows you shall oppose him in the future. If Worcester could not finish you, Arundel shall see that the battle does."

"I knew not what to do. How could I refuse? I am sick to death of scorn and derision. I have been so confused these last days. I am weary of struggling, Jack, weary of seeking what is right. I want only to survive. I want to live. And, God in heaven, somehow I shall. I shall not be beaten, not by Father, not by Arundel, and no, not by Percy either. Damn them all! I shall survive!"

Percy came to Shrewsbury that very night. When he found the town held against him, he retired to a nearby field and made ready to do battle.

"I shall drown inside my armor," I moaned. The day was warm, and the sweat dribbled down my back even as the armorers worked.

"Your highness shall be glad for armor when the arrows fly," said Raulyn.

"I shall be too frightened to be glad of anything," I replied.

My jupon was pulled over my head and draped across my burnished shoulders. Jack Oldcastle eyed the three white plumes that stood out boldly against the dark blue cloth.

"It is a most distinctive jupon," he said. "You shall be a target."

"What do you suggest?" I asked. "Shall I disguise myself as an archer?"

"All the lords wear their colors," said Raulyn. "The Prince must be recognized by his own men. How else shall he lead them?"

"Let me tell you what I hear," Jack said. "The King does require four of his esquires to wear a jupon like his own. Then when Percy's men seek to slay the King, they are likely to strike down a counterfeit."

"It is not so!" I exclaimed.

"It is what I hear," said Jack.

I chortled. "The glorious, chivalrous Bolingbroke! What would King Arthur say of such deceit? It is not exactly the stuff of ballads, is it?"

"Nor is it a time for foolery," said Jack. "Percy shall strive mightily to slay the King, and you. If he can accomplish it, all that we others may do shall be worthless."

"Oldcastle speaks truly," Raulyn added. "I could wear your highness's colors, and surely there are others who would do the same."

"And let you and other poor fellows die simply because you are mistaken for me? No, I shall not have that blood on my hands."

"It would be counted a great honor," he said.

I swung my arms to test my cuisses. "Honor!" I mocked. "It is no honor to die. It is done every day."

Even Jack was shocked. "In truth, Harry, the honor lies in the justice of the cause, and well you should know it. Have done with this strange mocking. It bodes ill."

Chastened as I was by the nearness of the impending battle, my earlier vows to survive did seem presumptuous. I had lain awake all the previous night and made my peace with death, and I was in no mood to glorify it. Jack and Raulyn had shared my bed, and neither slept, I knew, but not a word passed between us. I listened to their soft breathing, and my own, and saw us all lying senseless corpses upon the field. Well, then, why not? Death must come sooner or later, so why not upon the morrow? 'Twould be a quick death, no doubt, and if it kept me from love and good wine, why, it would also keep me from the crown. By the time dawn's shadows crept across the ceiling my breathing had become slow and shallow, as though my lungs prepared to empty themselves once and for all.

Percy had ranged his army over a hill north of Shrewsbury, and the King's knights rode there to oppose him, the archers and men-at-arms following on foot with trumpeters, drummers, and standard-bearers. To the eye, all was as bright and gay as a country fair amid the fluttering pennons of scarlet and azure. The horses were most pleasing, with their manes and tails plaited and the colors of their noble riders entwined in the braids. When fear lies heavy in the air, horses will sense it. These coursers sidled and shook their heads furiously as they pranced along. I held tight rein upon my own mount, a raven charger whose back was nearly too broad for me to sit. Morgause had been left in Shrewsbury to save her from the slaughter.

As I rode to the obligatory parley, I studied the footmen who would fight for Lancaster. They stood listless and silent and thrust out their tongues to receive the Host from the chanting priests. Whatever might entice such woebegone fellows to run screaming up a hill at my bidding into a hail of arrows? No, there would be no fight. If I ordered a charge they would only laugh and wander back to Shrewsbury in search of some tavern.

The parley was a formality called to fulfill the requirements of chivalry. Worcester came with his heralds to represent Percy, and we stared at one another but said nothing. When he left us after haughtily rejecting all offers of clemency, my father called his captains together.

"My lords, we cannot avoid this fight, nor should we seek to, our cause being just."

The noblemen listened eagerly. There was upon their faces a look of dazed agitation. For most it was their first battle. All their lives had been a rehearsal for this one joust with death.

"There is no change in our disposition," Father continued. "I shall command the right, the Earl of Stafford has the vanguard, and the Prince of Wales shall lead the left, as was settled last night. Percy is in the defensive position, and a strong one it is. He shall await us. It is up to us to take the fight to him." He looked at me. "The honor of the first charge lies with the Prince. You shall attack the hill, Harry, and force them down toward us. We shall catch them in our own charge and squeeze the life from them between our two forces."

I stared out at the field that lay before our army. It was sown with summer beans, a tangled mat to impede our progress. Beyond the field the hill reared up, its crown bristling with Percy's knights and archers.

"It is a perilous ascent," I said, my tongue thick.

"Aye, yet more perilous for us all if Percy's attention is not diverted. Do you understand then the importance of your task?"

He watched me closely, as did the others, their mistrust plain on their faces.

I nodded and rode back to my position with Jack and an old nemesis, Lord Talbot. The men on the hill cheered, a thin, eerie sound from that distance.

"Percy is haranguing them," said Talbot. He looked at me doubtfully. "You are clear on how to proceed?"

I licked my lips and repeated my instructions. "I am to lead my knights and footmen up the hill. The archers follow to cover us. When we are within range, Percy's archers shall doubtless fire upon us, and our archers shall stop and fire upon Percy. Our charge shall carry us through the arrows onto their position and we shall join battle with them, if all goes according to plan. . . ." My voice trailed off.

"And if not, their archers shall cut us to pieces ere we reach the crest," growled Jack. "It is a harebrained scheme."

"Enough of that!" barked Talbot.

A horn sounded to our right. I was to attack as soon as I was able.

Jack clutched my arm. "God with you, Harry. You have been dealt a rough hand, yet I know your mettle."

For the first time, I panicked. "Jack, what shall it be like? They are men, flesh and blood. What shall we do to one another?"

"You must not think of them as flesh and blood, not now. Pray for them later. Now they are the enemy and they mean to slay you. But you will not let them. You shall survive, as you said."

"Your highness's knights grow impatient," Talbot called.

I set the visor of my basinet over my face. The world was a slit of light.

"Forward!" I ordered, and the command was passed behind me.

I rode slowly through the beans that my horse might not trip. The other knights trailed closely, their standard-bearers at their sides, then the foot-men armed with swords and pikes, and lastly the archers. Ten yards we went, fifty, faster now, that our momentum might carry us up the hill.

In manus tuas, domine, I whispered.

Then came the hissing.

Terror forced me to look up. Through my visor I saw the arrows leap up like an angry swarm of insects, rising as one, buzzing, whining, plunging around us. Men and horses screamed. One arrow glanced off my shield, which I nearly dropped, so frightened I was. My mount reared in terror. As I reigned him in I saw behind me the lightly armored footmen strewn about like mown hay, heads and bellies split open by the bloodied shafts.

"Keep on!" Talbot screamed. "Keep on! Your highness must not falter!"

My horse lurched forward again. Sweat ran down my face, stung my eyes, tickled my nose. I could not breathe inside the basinet. The field blurred and spun before me. I gripped the saddle to keep from falling, thrust up my visor, and gulped. The air whistled and exploded with pain. I slumped forward clutching the wooden shaft which protruded from the in-side of my helmet. The bright red blood flowed across my mailed fingers and ran into my mouth.

"Jesu!" someone cried. "The Prince is slain."

An arm went round my chest as I slipped forward.

"Back! Back! Out of their range!"

"I am not dead," I murmured. Then I fainted.

I came to myself in a patch of beans, basinet off, head cradled in Raulyn's arms. With his right hand he pressed a bloody cloth against my head.

"What is it?" I mumbled. "It hurts fearfully."

"The arrow did not pierce your skull, Mary be praised. Half an inch and you would have taken it in the eye."

I shivered. "Like King Harold?"

"Like King Harold. It is bad enough. The flesh hangs in a flap from ear to cheekbone, and you have lost much blood. You are finished for the day."

"And what of the battle?"

"We have sent to the King to explain the delay. We shall attack again shortly."

"Who shall lead?"

"My lord Talbot."

"And I am to be safe while Talbot slaughters more wretches with these wild charges? No, it shall not be. I am yet in command. Help me to stand."

He did so reluctantly, and I leaned against him while I surveyed the field. Nearly a hundred dead or wounded men were scattered about, all victims of Percy's archers. Talbot and Jack came to me with water, and I drank gratefully.

"It was a Cheshire arrow that struck you," Jack said. "The Cheshire men are the best. You are fortunate you can stand."

"My hurt is mild compared to those others. How many of our archers were lost?"

"None that I know of," said Talbot. "They ignore our archers, of course."

I looked at him in surprise. "What do you mean?"

"They placed their arrows in the front ranks," he said impatiently. "They sought to stop our charge by striking our horses, and here and there they hit a knight. The footmen were in the way as well."

"But why? Why would Percy ignore our archers?"

"Archers are not fighting men," Talbot said. "They are of little account."

"That is absurd!"

Talbot could scarcely bridle his temper. "Percy is a chivalrous knight, traitor though he be, and his quarrel is with princes and knights, not yeomen."

"No knight loosed the arrow that struck me."

"I shall be blunt. Your highness was foolish to raise your visor. You delay us now. You know little of the ways of battle, and you are not yet ready to conduct yourself properly."

"No, it is you who are the fool. Yet Percy is as great a one, and perhaps that shall save us."

"What mean you, Harry?" Jack asked while Talbot sputtered.

I pointed shakily to the hill. "See, he sets his archers apart as we do. He expects us to take our fight to him and his knights, as indeed we had planned. Our honor demands that we face such danger. Is it not so, Lord Talbot?"

He glared at me.

"Well," I continued, "we shall not oblige him. It is the archers who have done hurt to us. We take our fight to them."

"It is unheard of!" Talbot protested. "It is shameful!"

"I am in command!" I barked. I turned to Jack. "Take charge of our archers. They shall stay behind us for protection. We shall advance as before, but we shall stop and loose our arrows as soon as we are within range. Loose them upon Percy's archers, not his knights."

"They wear no protection," he said. "It shall be a terrible slaughter."

I looked at the dead in the field, at those around me yet living. "If I were to avoid this," I said softly, "I should have done so long ago. The blood is upon my head, and I shall answer for it. Now do as I say. Be sure we loose the first shafts."

He went to the archers to explain my plan, and I watched their faces brighten with approval. I turned to Raulyn. "The wound is painful, but I have regained some strength. Bind my head. I shall not leave the field."

He was plainly troubled by my decision, and he would not meet my eyes as he wrapped a cloth about my head and tied it.

"I am sorry, Raulyn," I said. "I am sorry I cannot be your Lancelot. It is not worth the lives of my men."

It was comforting to close my visor once more, to hide away in the dark and block out the carnage around me. I was calmer when we resumed our charge. Once more we advanced and drew within range of their archers, only now we halted when I threw up my arm. The hiss of death came from the rear and waned as the dark cloud lifted above our heads and flew toward the hilltop. Percy's archers were making ready to bend their bows. Now they stood frozen, faces upturned, then ran as the deadly hail fell into their midst. Their distant screams were as the cries of birds. Again our archers bent their bows, and once again. Percy's knights milled about in helpless chaos.

Only later did I understand fully what happened next. Only later did I realize how our charge up the hill carried us unhindered into Percy's confused ranks, driving them down into the path of my father's now advancing troops; how thus confined and unprotected Percy's crazed men fought more to escape than to win; how Percy himself was slain, Worcester taken prisoner, the rebellion crushed. This was not what I knew of the battle. For me, there was the jolting ride up the hill, armor clattering and head throbbing. Then we were upon them, amid much screaming and grunting. Faces were distorted with pain and raw fear. Arms flailed, swords and pikes battered my shield.

"The Prince! Death to the Prince!"

Holy Mary, mercy.

A pike was thrust toward my vulnerable armpit. I lashed out desperately with my sword and the man's arm fell from his body, the jagged end of bone protruding from his shoulder. Another reached to drag me from my horse. A long blade, I knew not whose, split open his face.

Dizziness returned and threatened to overwhelm me. In the summer heat, to wear armor was to be in an oven, slowly baking. My head pounded. I feared I should faint again, and if I fell from my mount I would not rise again for the weight of my armor. Then I would be slain. I must find shelter ere my strength waned.

I slid from the horse and warded off a blow with my shield. My left arm was numb from the constant beating, my breath came in great sobs. I fell. A man lay dead beside me, his guts pouring in frothy coils from a gash in his belly. Someone dragged me to my feet. It was Jack.

I screamed, for a man had appeared behind him, cudgel raised above his head. Jack wheeled and slashed his throat. I screamed again. Jack shook me.

Two more men set upon us. Reluctantly I faced one. He wore no armor. He attacked me with a long knife such as the Welsh carry, and I tried to fend him off, yet he came on.

"Jesu, leave me!" I sobbed.

His yellow teeth were bared in my face. He thrust the knife at the slit of my visor. His aim was wild and I pushed him away.

"Do not make me slay you!"

Again he came, a fiend, a madman, and I ran him through the heart. His eyes bulged at me as he hung upon my blade. My sword arm felt as though it were set afire.

The fiercest fighting passed me, moved down the hill. I slipped to my knees, head spinning. I must keep going, must defend myself, for my jupon still marked me for death. I clutched at the blue cloth, ripped at it, tugged it with great effort over my head, pitched forward on top of it. It lay crumpled and rent, the plumes no longer white but stained with blood. Jack found me again and dragged me beneath a clump of bushes. He turned me upon my back and raised my visor so that I might breathe.

"I shall stand by you," he said.

I slipped gratefully into oblivion.

My servants found me at day's end with Jack's help. Gently they removed my basinet, cushioned my head, gave me water, bathed my wound. I gazed unspeaking at Jack, trying in vain to focus my eyes.

"The day is ours," he said as from a great distance. "Percy is dead, he who tormented you so, slain by an arrow. Worcester is our prisoner and shall go to the block. The King left the field early and is unharmed, though two of his impersonators were slain. The Earl of Stafford is killed."

"Raulyn?" I whispered.

"Wounded in the thigh, but likely to survive. As is Harry Monmouth."
He smiled at me.

"At great cost," I said.

"Ah, Harry, the yeomen sing your praises. They say the Prince of Wales
saved the lives of many poor men this day."

"I have bartered lives for lives," I said. "Who has dared to grant me
such power?"

They lifted me then and bore me down the hill. Across the wide sweep
of land to the river, men were strewn about, tangled in heaps. As we passed
by I saw many were dead or dying, but others only rested. They huddled
with arms entwined, heads resting upon heaving bellies, King's men and
rebels together, seeking some human solace. Their weapons seemed to rust
in the orange sunset. I longed to weep for them all, for myself, for our folly,
yet something hard within me had driven away all such tears.

I was borne to a makeshift tent where the royal armorers were at work. I
leaned against Jack while one brawny man removed my breastplate. As the
piece came away from my damp body, I smelled a foul odor. I dropped my
eyes in shame.

"I fear I have soiled myself inside my armor," I said.

The armorer smiled toothlessly. "Aye, and so have all the other knights.
When a man is locked away in armor and fighting for his very life, there is
nothing else for it, is there, young prince?"

"The old men do not speak of this when they tell their tales of knightly
glory," I said.

"No," he said. "Who would wish to hear it?"

III

1404-1412

Where is his son,
The nimble-footed madcap Prince of Wales,
And his comrades that daff'd the world aside
And bid it pass?

—Henry IV, Part 1, act IV, scene i

7

I was one month abed with the wound to my temple, and ever after bore a thin scar from the top of my cheek into the hair above my ear. It was a tedious recovery, for Jack was called to his lands in Hereford. I passed my time in strumming my harp, staring at the ceiling, and refusing to think upon the Battle of Shrewsbury. This last was no mean feat, for after an exhausting time of success I would fall asleep and dream of headless men and screaming horses. In the end, Monmouth came to my rescue, for I learned to train my thoughts toward her peaceful rivers, and at last even my dreams followed to that place. When I was able to ride I traveled there myself, to be mothered and spoiled by Joan. Then, my health restored, I went to London at my father's bidding.

I found that the London folk had made me their hero. Whenever I rode about with my retainers or walked the crooked lanes to some alehouse, the people would crowd about me and hail me as "Good Prince Hal." I learned to smile and wave, to answer their plaudits with a bow and a sweep of my cap. I knew the reason for my fame, but I would not acknowledge it. As their adulation swelled, it overwhelmed my reticence, and I would stop and exchange pleasantries with this one or that, raise a cup with Ned in the White Horse or tweak the nose of Moll's babe. Soon I could call many by name. I was adored even more that I took notice of them, and for myself, I drank in their praise like one dying of thirst. It was easy to forget that King Richard had once been London's darling, and Bolingbroke as well.

For the first time in my memory I had my father's affection and I basked in it, having despaired of it for so long. "My gallant lad" he named me, and I was invited to share with my brothers in hunting parties at Windsor and Christmas festivities at Eltham. Tom, a simple creature, showed no jealousy at my good fortune, but stood in awe of me and pestered me rather more than I would have liked for stories of Shrewsbury field.

The young ones, John and Humphrey, had grown as strangers to me. Fearful of my influence upon them, Father had taken pains that they should avoid contact with me. They had been at old Gaunt's castle of Kenilworth or at Windsor. They were quiet with me at first, especially Humphrey, yet soon the years did melt away and we harked back to the frolicsome days of our boyhood at Monmouth. John was fourteen, broad of face and sturdy, and Humphrey was thin and intense at thirteen. Both were mere apprentices at love, and I, judging myself now a master of the secrets of the bed, took them in hand. They soon were swaggering about Windsor with knowing smirks upon their faces.

I engaged in a new dalliance of my own. Practiced though I was, never had I slept with a highborn lady. In my state of disgrace such dainty creatures had ignored me, despite my inheritance, and indeed I had scorned them as well, preferring the forthright lustiness of London's wenches. My days at court, however, pricked my interest in lace-covered bosoms, for it was whispered that the noble ladies of England now spoke passionately of the Prince of Wales. After much teasing from my brothers, I determined to seduce the most beautiful woman at court.

With cool deliberation I stood before a mirror and appraised my own gifts. My tavern wanderings had taught me that women were drawn to me and went away purring with contentment at my lovemaking. I was taller than many men, my body was slender but well knit, and I was skilled in the use of my long brown fingers and my manhood. I was blessed with large hazel eyes, a straight nose, rosy cheeks, a cap of dark brown hair, and a cleft in my chin which women loved to kiss. I was the Prince of Wales. Might I not have any woman I desired?

The woman I desired was Lady Anne Mortimer. I saw her first at Westminster, where she sat in attendance upon the new queen, as was the custom for women of her station. My father had recently been remarried to the Duke of Brittany's widow, a pretty but silly woman he had met during his exile. I endured the tedious company of my stepmother only that I might cast a hopeful eye upon her ladies-in-waiting. No doubt, the fairest of all was Anne Mortimer. She sat straight upon her bench, her head bowed, seemingly absorbed with embroidering gold leaves upon linen. Yet while I spoke pleasantly with the Queen, I felt the gaze of Anne Mortimer upon me. Thrice I caught her at it, and the last time I winked. She flushed prettily as she bent to her work. Hers was a round delicate face of the type artists adore to paint on Madonnas. Her eyebrows and forehead were plucked smooth according to the fashion of the day, to emphasize her flawless white skin. Her eyes were sparkling blue, and her little mouth puckered into an inviting pout. She was indeed fair, and she had about her the added spice of danger, for she was the sister of young Edmund Mortimer, who by right should have sat upon the throne in my father's place. Much reason she had to despise me, yet her sideways glances told me it was not so.

Still more I should have been cautioned by her married state, for her husband was Richard of York, that same York whose disgrace I had brought about at the court of King Richard. The troubadors sing that the most sublime love is that of a man for a married woman. Certainly the spice of adventure is an aphrodisiac when a man beds the wife of another. The possibility of cuckolding Richard of York only whetted my desire. The Lady Anne was fifteen, a fresh flower, and York an old man of near thirty years. It was my youthful duty to rescue her from the gropings of such a churl and bestow upon her the rewards of my own lively ardor.

I set about this conquest with that singleness of purpose which has ever been part of my nature. The court removed to Eltham for the Yuletide, York was tending his lands in the north, and I did resolve to have the Lady Anne in my bed ere Twelfth Night. I had not even that long to wait, as it turned out. Upon the eve of the new year I danced an estampie with her, and the Queen's ladies were aflutter at the burning looks which passed between us. I had broken through her defenses earlier with many little favors. With the tickle of my finger in the palm of her hand as we were introduced, her walls were battered. I rode close by her when the court went hawking and helped her from her horse when we returned. She stood against me for a moment, and our eyes met when the arm with which I steadied her tightened about her slender waist. The battlements were crumbling. With the gentle pressure of my leg against hers as we sat that night at table, little remained save the storming of the breach.

"Come to my chamber tonight," I whispered as she danced gracefully beneath my upraised arm.

She nodded, her lips slightly parted from anticipation and the exertions of the dance. The blue velvet bodice of her dress was smudged where my eager fingers had pressed into her back.

Henry Scrope, who often shared my chamber, took himself away to find his own bedmate. Alone, I paced before the hearth. She slipped silently into the chamber when my back was turned and placed a hand upon my shoulder. I took her in my arms and kissed her full upon the mouth. Neither of us spoke, as though our words would chase away the delicious mischief that had inflamed our tryst.

She was of course no maid, having been wed nearly two years. Yet York was a dreary lover, and I taught her much she did not know, delighting in her surprised gasps. She giggled, as we lay together afterward, and said, "My lord husband does climb atop me, and that is that."

I laughed. "In truth?"

"Aye. It is nothing like this. Oh, Harry, you only need look at me and I am rent asunder. I could scarce breathe when we danced."

I rubbed her shoulder and smiled to myself. I remembered Richard of York for a foul bully, and this seemed a fine trick to play him. Still, I was not anxious for him to find us out. I spoke of this to Lady Anne as we dressed beside the fire.

"He shall not know," she assured me. "I would not be banished the court and thus torn from you."

"What of the Queen's ladies? Do you not share a bed with them? They shall have missed you."

"Fie! They shall say nothing. They do all have lovers of their own at court and are not anxious to carry tales. No, they shall think nothing of it. In truth, they have guessed already what lies between us and no doubt wait eagerly to know how I did spend my night."

"And what shall you tell them?" I was suddenly self-conscious.

She smiled and said, "Only those things which shall turn them green with envy."

I knew then that I had not been alone in coolly planning this seduction. Lady Anne had longed for a noble lover to boast of to her companions, and the Prince of Wales would be a catch indeed. I could well imagine the ladies giggling together as they appraised my various parts. I was chastened, but not for long. I had outgrown all childish illusions of being loved for Harry alone. No woman could be expected to ignore my rank, to forget that she lay with the future King of England. Best then to shrug and cheerfully accept the favors bestowed upon me, basking in any reputation gained along the way. Would not most men long to be in my place?

We parted in the sweetness of springtime, Anne and I, she to her husband at Stamford, I to Wales. She shed many a tear at our parting. I was not so deeply moved, for at last I had tired of her. She had grown practiced in the ways of love but bestowed her favors with more concern for performance than passion. Besides this, we did not like to talk of the same things. I never failed to be aroused at the sight of her, yet when all was said and done she did not touch me. When I departed London, my heart was heavy only because I must pick up the sword again.

Lord Talbot now led the English in wild chases after Glyndwr. My father's newfound trust in me persuaded him to grant me more responsibility, and even Talbot did grudgingly heed my advice. I was weary of the rebellion and still mindful of the sufferings of the Welsh, yet Shrewsbury field had refined in me some metal of obduracy. The strife would not end if I withdrew from it, I reasoned, but only if I defeated Glyndwr once and for all. That I was capable of vanquishing him I now had no doubt. Carefully I laid my plans. I would work my way west, seizing strongholds and ignoring Glyndwr. I would treat the captured lands firmly but not harshly, and I would administer them myself, not trusting them to the oppressive whims of the marcher lords. I would entice the rebels to lay down their arms not by fierce reprisal but by liberal pardons, thus robbing Glyndwr of poor hill men heartsick for the sight of home.

Excellent plans, these, but they were thwarted from the start by a lack of money. In May I had penetrated to Carmarthen, but no wages were forthcoming from London for my men, and by late June I had been forced by desertions to leave behind a small garrison and withdraw to Worcester. In Worcester I sat with a dwindling force while Glyndwr pillaged. Even Herefordshire was not spared, and English villages felt the sharp edge of war with which we had formerly lashed the Welsh. Jack Oldcastle raged, for his small holdings were overrun and a score of his tenants massacred. The oppression of the marcher lords had called forth a hatred in the Welsh which, in turn, drove them to commit outrages against poor English peasants, and so it went in a never-ending litany of enmity.

We sought Glyndwr in the valley of the Wye, but he proved as elusive as the shattered peace. We withdrew again to Worcester, our spirits as diminished as our army. I wrote to Scrope at Kennington and begged him to seek audience with the King in hopes that his presence might move Father to our aid more forcefully than any letter of mine had done. Then Jack, Raulyn, and I settled in to commiserate over our problems.

We greeted Scrope a week later at Worcester castle. The dust of midsummer clung lightly to his clothing, and he called for ale ere he was unhorsed.

"Damn your ale, where are our wages?" Jack bellowed. "You did not ride this far to tell us Bolingbroke has refused us."

"Indeed not," he replied. "You shall be displeased nonetheless. I shall not be denied my ale because of it. I have swallowed half the dust on the road."

I noted his baggage was light. "You have brought no coin," I said.

"The King's messengers have it," Scrope said. "They are delayed upon the road. They are a demon-plagued company, I tell you. Two fell ill at Oxford, and we left them behind. One was thrown from his horse soon after and broke his leg. Now one of the sumpter horses has gone lame. They have put the coin in a cart and come slowly on."

"Why did you not lend them your mount?" Jack demanded.

"And walk to Worcester?"

"When may we expect them?" I asked.

"They say they shall come on straightway and are likely to arrive after darkness falls."

"'Tis perilous," Jack fumed. "They risk losing our wages to thieves by traveling at night."

"Indeed, 'twould be small loss," Scrope said.

I sighed. "I have expected such tidings. What do they bring?"

"Two thousand pounds."

"Two thousand pounds!" Jack exploded. "'Tis but a pittance."

"Bolingbroke says he can spare no more."

"It is not so," I said. "In truth, the crown is not wealthy, yet he does find coin for what pleases him best."

"He believes the amount to be sufficient," Scrope said.

"Sufficient for pillaging with a small force," I said. "To hold castles and govern here does require more. What does he expect of me? God's blood, it was this which drove the Percys into rebellion!"

"Then to arms, Harry," Jack said. "Let's ride to London and strip Bolingbroke of his jewels."

"First I require ale," pleaded Scrope.

I ran my fingers through my hair. "Two thousand pounds shall not long hold even those troops we have in Worcester. Scrope is right. 'Twould be small loss if highwaymen did set upon them."

I kicked up a cloud of dust and watched it settle on the toe of my boot. Then I looked up with a smile.

"Though if the King's messengers are so foolish as to be robbed of the gold entrusted to them, the King should be obliged to make good the loss, should he not?"

Scrope shrugged, but Jack watched me closely. "I do not like that gleam in your eye," he said.

"How many couriers are left?" I asked Scrope.

"Only three." He read my purpose then. "You do not intend to rob them?"

"Ha!" said Jack. "Ha!"

"Why not?" I was caught up now in the mischief of it. "If Father makes good our loss we shall have double. We can pay the troops we have and even have enough left to save the garrison at Carmarthen."

"It is stealing!" Jack pointed a thick finger at me and grinned.

"It is taking what is due my soldiers."

"There are but three of us," Scrope cautioned. "They are armed. Would you shed blood over this?"

"No," I said. "Surprise shall disarm them. And Raulyn shall join us, so we shall be four."

"Raulyn." Jack sniffed. "Will he stain his honor in such a venture?"

"Aye, he shall or I will send him from me."

"And if we are caught?" asked the ever-cautious Scrope.

"Then shall I be disgraced," I said cheerfully, "and all shall be as before. Well, are you for it?"

They were, and we slipped out of Worcester at dusk with a most reluctant Raulyn in our company. With us were two sumpter horses to bear our treasure. We had stripped ourselves of all rings and badges and wore the rough plaincloth of yeomen. If the guards at St. Martin's Gate were surprised to see their prince thus attired and quitting Worcester at such an hour, they gave no sign of it. When we were well past them, we left the high way and pulled black hoods over our heads. These precautions were well taken, for the night was as day. The moon was full, and the few clouds blowing smoke across its face could not dim its light. The trees which crept to the edge of the road glittered with drops of silver and cast the shadows of their trunks across our path like the bars of a dungeon. The hooded figure riding alongside me crossed himself.

"Fairies are about at such times, and goblins or worse. This wood seems bewitched to me, and our errand as well." It was Raulyn's voice beneath the mask.

I shuddered in spite of myself and said nothing. It is best not to speak of such things, best to banish them from one's thoughts. Joan Waryn did say this broke any spell such fey folk might cast. We ventured but a mile into the wood to a place where the road narrowed and dipped into the bed of a small brook. Here the ruts were deeper than usual where carts had carved their way with wet wheels into the soft bank of the stream. Raulyn secured our horses well out of sight in a stand of birch. We squatted together in the stream's bed beneath an overhang of greensward. The tangy scent of rich earth and rushes enlivened all my senses. I thrust my hand into the cold water, and my entire body seemed cleansed and refreshed.

It was not long ere we heard the clatter of wheels. I peered cautiously over the bank. The cart lumbered toward us like a great awkward beast. Two men sat behind the carthorses, and a third was perched upon the bags of treasure. All three swayed and gripped their seats as the cart rolled tipsily into the stream. The water churned, the horses climbed the far bank, and the front wheels of the cart were poised upon a high ridge when I cried, "Stand!"

We rose together, swords drawn and flashing in the moonlight. Scrope seized the reins while we each placed the point of our swords at the throat of a startled courier. The cart sank forward with a sigh into a muddy furrow.

"Throw down your weapons and you shall not be harmed," I said.

They did my bidding quite nimbly. I smiled inside my mask, for these good fellows clearly had no intention of laying down their lives to protect the King's property. Common folk do know that too much honor makes good meat for worms.

When swords and daggers had been tossed into the weeds, we led the men to a nearby oak, sat them down, and trussed them to the trunk. Then we strolled back to the cart to examine the King's gold.

"There are more sacks than I had thought," I said.

"Aye, and these sacks shall not escape the notice of the guards," said Jack. "They shall puzzle over where we have been, and when they hear of the robbery their thoughts shall turn to us. Your high station shall not allay their suspicions, Harry, for the circumstances are too bald."

"Why did you not say this before?" Scrope asked.

"I was caught up in the foolery of it all."

"Yet was I not," I said. "Leave the guards to me."

It was well before cock crow when we returned to Worcester, our horses weighted down with bulging sacks of gold coin. Two men opened the gates to us and stared as we rode jingling under the portcullis. I slid from my horse and strode up to one of them. The man knelt before me at once and I bade him rise.

"Know you what is in those sacks?"

He shook his head.

"It is gold from the King's court, sent for your wages. Only it is not enough to pay you properly."

His face brightened, then fell at these tidings. I looked him over carefully. He was a sturdy fellow with a pockmarked face. I had seen him about Worcester, a swaggering sort with the voice of a frog.

"Now," I said, "I want you to ride a mile or so hence, and you shall find three men trussed to a tree. They are messengers of the King sent hither with gold, and they have fallen among thieves. Tell them the Prince was worried by their tardiness and sent after them. Then bring them to me. I wish to hear of their troubles. As for your wages which were taken, the King shall no doubt make good his loss."

He looked from me to the sacks and back again. He was clever, as I had judged. His eyes gleamed and he croaked, "'Tis foolish to travel so late upon the 'igh way, your 'ighness."

"Indeed." I smiled. "That is why I do not wish it known that I was abroad this night. I would not be thought foolish."

"Aye." He grinned broadly. "I shall breathe no word of it, nor shall this other fellow, or 'e will answer to me for it."

"Good. What is your name?"

"John Wotten, an' it please your 'ighness."

"I shall remember you, John Wotten. You have a good head about you." He nodded, pleased. I strolled over to my companions.

"Your brashness shall be your downfall, Harry Monmouth," said Jack. "Yet this should make a fine tale for a London alehouse."

"If it were to be told," I said.

Father was furious at the news of his financial loss and would have dismissed his foolhardy couriers had I not intervened. I wrote him an impassioned plea reminding him that the unfortunate men had faced a dozen fierce cutthroats, by their own accounting, and that their own numbers had been diminished by a series of misfortunes. They had fought valiantly, I wrote, but were at last overborne by force of numbers. Grudgingly he relented, and the men were retained. Just as reluctantly he dispatched more gold for the payment of my troops.

Even with the additional wages my plan for defeating Glyndwr lay in ruins, for my force was not sufficient to besiege Welsh strongholds. Stubbornly I held to the remnant of my strategy and tried to wait out Glyndwr, to my father's chagrin. He wrote to me bitterly of my inactivity and accused me of squandering his money, of turning again to my former ways. He sent to my chaplain and asked if I was often found in the brothels of Worcester.

His impatience grew to alarm with the news that Owain Glyndwr had signed a treaty with France, ancient enemy of England. I myself was shaken at these tidings. The French had threatened invasion during Richard's reign, and I remembered well my childish nightmares in which howling French soldiers chased me about the garden of Monmouth castle. That fear had matured now into the knowledge that as heir to the throne I would most surely be murdered or imprisoned for life if the French were to mount a successful invasion.

Father thought the French would establish a base in Wales from which England would be attacked. This seemed preposterous to me, for the French would handle the Welsh terrain no better than we had, they being even more pigheaded about the proper form of chivalrous combat. My fear was of a Welsh diversion and a French invasion of our southern coast. Even so had King Harold been occupied by the Danes when William the Bastard landed in Sussex. I was less inclined than ever to yield to Father's wishes for a wild foray into the mountains. But at last he ordered it, threatening to relieve me of my command and lead an expedition himself if I refused. The sure knowledge of the devastation he would visit upon the Welsh led me to obey. For three weeks we rode up the Wye and across Mynydd Eppynt to Llandovery, thence to our garrison at Carmarthen and back, passing through the misty Brecon Beacons to Caerphilly. With great difficulty I managed to keep my impoverished soldiers in check, and, God be praised, the usual excesses of such ventures were avoided. All was for naught, of course, Glyndwr having flown to the north. I sent my men home to the harvest and settled myself in at Monmouth to brood. October was wet and chill, robbing the golden brown land of its beauty, but the weather did suit my mood.

I had now turned seventeen. I was a man, and heir to the throne. I had survived two attempts upon my life and been blooded in combat. I had commanded men and seen them respond, seen them turn desperate eyes upon me, begging for protection and guidance. Someday the well-being of an entire people would rest just as securely upon my shoulders. How could anyone bear such a burden? With enemies lying in wait and old enmities between English, Welsh, and French setting snares across my path, how could I be both governor and good man? One thing was clear: the fighting must stop. If it did not, it would consume me and all I hoped to accomplish. War was a wolf that preyed upon the innocent. Somehow I must learn why men fought, and I must stop them.

I turned this puzzle over and over in my head during many a sleepless night. Why should a Frenchman fight an Englishman, or an Englishman a Welshman, when the two had never met? Perhaps because they were strangers one to another, and men ever hate and fear what is strange. Or perhaps because men are sinful, and the evil of violence is rooted within each one. So taught the Church. I beat my pillow in frustration at such explanations, for they were no help to me. Here was nothing I could change, yet as king I must bear the burden. Would a just God expect it? No, there must be more, something I could do.

Why had poor men met their deaths upon Shrewsbury field? I sat up in my bed.

Because I had ordered them up the hill, and they knew no better than to go.

Because Percy had rebelled and called his followers into the field.

Because there were too many contenders for the throne, too many powerful ones to order poor men about that they might achieve their own ends.

Too many princes.

I pored over my grandfather's volumes of history which I ever kept with me. I studied Crécy and Poitiers, where Edward of England had taken the measure of the French nobles. I read of the squabbles of the various lords of France: Angevins, Normans, Poitevins, all jealous for territory. Then there

were the princes of the Empire, a horde of petty tyrants slitting one another's throats. Back and back I went to Salamis, Thermopylae, Troy. Had
there never been a time of peace?

With beating heart and bated breath I was drawn to the great empire of
Rome. To be sure, Rome fought many wars upon her borders, yet within her
provinces there was relative quiet. Egyptians, Provençals, Greeks, Syrians,
all living in peace. All ruled by one man.

I was somewhat daunted by the decadence of the emperors. They had
gone mad, persecuting the Church and drinking the blood of their own kin.
Was power their downfall? An uneasy question, this. But then, they had not
been Christians, the evil ones. Had they been God's standard-bearers, they
might have persevered. Perhaps a true son of the Church might command
the allegiance of so many peoples and defend his own soul as well.

I turned finally to Charlemagne, the wise one crowned Holy Roman
Emperor by the pope himself. He had ruled the diverse lands of Christendom in peace, fighting only against the perilous heathen. There were no
jealous knights to lead reluctant vassals to bloody deaths for power or land,
since Charlemagne alone held the power and he ruled justly. My hands
trembled as I traced upon parchment my lineage through my father to his
grandfather King Edward, thence backward to the second Henry's wife,
Eleanor of Aquitaine, a direct descendant of Charlemagne. The blood of the
unifier of Christendom coursed through my veins.

I tramped the hills of Monmouth in a trance. By all that was right, I
should never have been heir to the throne of England. I should have been
dead long ago from poison or sword. Yet here I was. Could it be that God
called me to pick up the crown of Christendom, to heal her warring factions
and establish His justice? Such a vision breeds both arrogance and the most
abject humility; it is both blessing and curse. There seemed some reason
now why soldiers hung upon my words when I spoke, why the wretched of
London flocked to my horse. God had Himself coupled in me an aversion to
pillage with an uncanny prowess in the leading of men. I burned therefore
with noble purpose, with longing to serve God and His people, and could
think of none better fitted to accomplish such great deeds. Yet my doubts
were more agonizing as well. If the crown of England alone was a peril to the
soul and a heavy load to bear, how much more this! What if I should fail?
Would I cease to be a man and become that monster King Richard had
warned me of? I fortified myself against such doubts with the assurance that
the Devil seeks diligently to dissuade those whom God has marked.

God willing, many years would there yet be ere I wore the crown of
England. I resolved that they should be years of seeking and testing. I must
pursue this vision, for I had none other.

In my eagerness I tarried not for the springtime but left Monmouth in

January for Hereford. Wales would be the first test. I had no doubt now that Owain Glyndwr and I were met in a contest for the hearts of the Welsh people. Glyndwr must be vanquished if Welsh and English were to cease their contention, and his defeat would be a further sign of God's call to me. Wales was weary of war, her husbandry ravaged by the assaults of rival bands of brigands. Once the Welsh had tasted of the justice I would establish as their Prince, they would accept me gladly. As yet I had no coin for an army but it was of little consequence, for I would not be a conqueror but a ruler. From Hereford I must set about restoring what order I could.

I called Jack Oldcastle to me, and Henry Scrope from London. Together we went about the governing of those Welsh lands that were then in our hands. Justices I sent out to hear grievances, men I chose especially for their fairness. I set forth many judgments myself with great care that the Welsh should not be abused. There were grumblings from the marcher lords when I relieved one man of an unjust debt or ordered payment to another for services rendered. I cared not, for I was accomplishing my own purposes. Word spread throughout the valleys of the southeast that the Prince of Wales freely offered pardon to the rebel and redress to the abused. By March, Glyndwr's hold upon the people had melted as surely as the snows. Hundreds in south Wales came forward to receive their pardon.

Glyndwr must have received word of his people's disaffection, for he came down early from the north. This time the rebels were not well received, and Glyndwr retaliated by plundering as rapaciously as any marcher lord. He was used to gathering strength as he came south, drawing the ragged men and boys from their hillside huts to his colors. Now they did flee him, taking with them their meager provisions. Hungry and desperate, it was Glyndwr's army that wandered aimlessly about in search of an enemy, hoping to rouse Celtic spirits with a victory over the English. I had begun to gather my own men-at-arms in Hereford. Glyndwr sent roving bands up the Wye to entice me, but I would not be drawn out in force. I did send small parties of my own men to harass Glyndwr on his way. They often struck at night, throwing the Welsh into a panic. In dire straits, Glyndwr committed his gravest blunder. Leaving the cover of the mountains, he attacked the castle of Grosmont with his dispirited force. Grosmont, long a stronghold of Lancaster, is nigh to Hereford and likewise perilously close to Lord Talbot's castle of Goodrich, where that gentleman had assembled a force of goodly size for the protection of his lands. Talbot rode at once for Grosmont, and Jack Oldcastle led my troops from Hereford. Between them they caught the desperate Welsh in the open upon the banks of the Monnow and cut them to pieces.

I stayed behind, for I could not bear to face the slaughter for which I was responsible. I knelt all day in Hereford cathedral, fasting and praying for pardon. I received upon my knees the messenger who arrived breathless and exultant with word of an English victory. I returned then to the castle, where I shakily wrote a letter to my father, set my seal upon it, and sent Raulyn to bear it to the court.

Jack returned the next morning, grimly triumphant, his red beard streaked with mud. He broke his fast with slabs of brown bread and yellow cheese.

"It is the beginning of the end for Glyndwr," he said. "Everyone says it, even Talbot, and he sings your praises, Harry, if you can believe it. He promises he shall write to your father and to the parliament, and the credit for this victory shall be yours."

"With the credit goes the guilt."

He sighed. "Harry, Harry. Are you still about it, this breast-beating? At times it does weary me."

"Then leave me! I have slept ill and I am in no mood for you."

He sat where he was and chewed his food. "What said you to me not three days ago? 'I must defeat Glyndwr ere Wales knows peace,' you said. Did you not mean it? How would you defeat him then, with wishes and prayers? Look you, he shall soon be finished in the south."

I traced patterns in the wooden table with the tip of my knife. "What were they like, the Welsh? What was their condition?"

"Wild and half starved," he said. "Lean and ragged, many little more than boys. Never have I seen faces so full of fear. They did not stand to fight but threw down their weapons at the sight of us. It was like riding to the hunt." He stopped eating. "God's blood, Harry, do you think me bloodthirsty? Think you I enjoyed it? I tell you, my stomach turned. 'Twas worse than Shrewsbury. But what else was there for it? I did not ask them to follow that rebel, to take up arms against the Crown. You may call them your people, yet they came against you, remember that."

Three weeks later, Lord Grey of Codnor caught the remnant of Glyndwr's army at Usk. Hundreds of Welshmen were slain, including Owain's brother, and his son Gryffyd was captured and sent in chains to the Tower. Glyndwr fled to the north.

The success of my schemings now acquainted me with the cost. To bring peace in the way I had chosen, men first must die. I saw my life set upon a heavenly scale and wondered if the good I might achieve would be weighty enough to prevent the pile of bodies from tipping my soul into the fiery pit. I became yet more scrupulous as I went about governing south Wales, for I wished to do no more wrong than was absolutely necessary. Men remarked upon my fairness, and upon the gravity of my demeanor, unusual in one so young.

*   *   *

In June, England was troubled once more with rebellion. I called to me Henry Scrope and reluctantly gave him the dispatch from my father.

"Your uncle, the Archbishop of York, has taken up arms against Lancaster," I said.

The blood drained from his face. "My uncle!" he said. "It is not possible. He is a clerk."

"As is Arundel, and yet he rose against Richard."

"My uncle is not rash, but a man of good temper, and honorable," he protested, his voice rising. "I was often with him as a child. The man I recall is not a rebel."

"Yet did he gather an army and join with several knights of the north, including the father of Hotspur. They are dispersed already, for they have surrendered."

"Without a fight?"

"Aye, 'deeming their cause hopeless,' as my father puts it in his letter."

"Only a burdensome grievance could lead my uncle to these desperate straits," Scrope said.

"My father writes that he sought redress for the ills done to King Richard."

"Indeed, Lancaster must bear great guilt for that."

"Do not reproach me with it." My voice rose in turn. "Well you know I counted Richard my friend and liege lord, and I have been estranged from my father over this matter."

He fell silent and would not look at me.

"My father intends to execute him," I said.

"Execute him? An archbishop? It is unheard of! He is a holy man, consecrated by the Church."

"Already I have written most urgently and said as much to my father. I am pleading for your uncle's life, Scrope. I know not what else to do."

"Aye." He spoke as though he had forgotten my presence. "A man who would murder an anointed king is not above this."

His anger was justified, uncomfortable though it made me. It seemed plain enough that God Himself would have vengeance if my father took such a rash step. I judged him to have taken leave of his senses. Twice I wrote impassioned pleas for the life of Archbishop Scrope. Even Arundel rode to my father to beg for clemency. All was for naught. The Archbishop was beheaded at York as a sullen crowd looked on. Within the month people did flock to his tomb as to that of a martyr, and many miracles were wrought, both signs and healings. Thereafter, a series of calamities struck my father which were commonly counted as the work of an angry God.

First, the French invaded Wales. It was a foolish gesture and I could not rouse myself to great concern over it. This was but a small force by all reports, mostly knights in heavy armor seeking plunder. They thrashed about for weeks, lost in the maze of mountains. Poor Wales, ravaged by years of cruel civil war, had little plunder to offer. I did not seek out the invaders, for I knew they would soon be sent bootless back to their ships. Still their presence did hearten Glyndwr, and he gathered about him a small force for one more desperate foray into the south.

All this activity proved too much for my father's pride. The presence of French knights in his realm seemed as clear a challenge as any gauntlet which, tossed at his feet, would draw him into the lists. The code of chivalry and the expectations of his peers required him to move at once against these intruders. He rode to Hereford with a great host of the flower of English chivalry. These mighty lords were impatient, for, once blooded, they had seen no battle since Shrewsbury and longed to test themselves against the French. They came eagerly to Hereford with much pomp, their hands often straying to their sword hilts in anticipation.

There was merriment in Hereford town, both drinking and wenching, while the army was provisioned for its march into the wilds of Wales. When knights gather there is much backslapping and rough, humorous talk late into the night, a conjuring of foes and women long ago conquered. The abundance of hot wine refines the impurities from such memories, so that the women are ever lovely and the battles bloodless. I was not a popular companion at these times, for though Shrewsbury and Wales had burnished my reputation I would not speak blithely of them. I grew used to the uneasy stares when I entered a room, looks of scorn chastened by a fearful respect. If none cared enough to penetrate my reserve, neither were they anxious to cross one who so successfully displayed little regard for the niceties of chivalry by which they ordered their lives. I went my solitary way, untroubled by my father's nobles.

I was most disturbed when I learned of my father's plans, for his intention was to march up the Honddu. I had not forgotten the lass with the gray eyes I had met in the woods some four years earlier. Even now she did haunt my dreams with her gentleness, and I would wake entranced to wonder what had become of her. It was yet in my mind to seek her out when Wales should finally know peace. To come upon her now in the company of this ravaging host of warriors would be to destroy not only my dreams but quite possibly the lass of flesh and blood as well. I argued vehemently with Father. Nothing there was upon the Honddu, I said, save a handful of wattle huts and the priory of Llanthony. We should travel more swiftly and directly through the Wye valley. He would not hear of it. Ever had he followed the Wye, never had he found Glyndwr upon it, and the poor folk living upon its banks had no plunder left to give. He believed the more isolated Honddu to be a natural hiding place from which Welsh brigands could launch raids upon both Hay

and the Usk valley. I asked what all this had to do with Owain Glyndwr and
the French, who were reported to be marching together toward Carmarthen. He grew impatient, saying that his purpose was to let every whoreson rebel in the south of Wales know that he was on his way to take the
measure of the French. I gave up wrangling with him, for I knew of none
more stubborn than he. Indeed I was loath to push him, for I was disquieted
by his thin and haggard appearance. Though not yet forty, he had the
bearing of an old man. Dark smudges encircled his eyes, which darted here
and there as though seeking out enemies in the shadows of the chamber.

I need not have been so anxious of the girl's safety, for the hand of God
smote us ere we reached Llanthony. The heavens opened and released a
torrent of rain. The Honddu, fed by countless mountain rills, swelled and
spilled over its banks, sweeping away horses and carts. The royal regalia
which ever accompanied the King on his travels were lost, as well as most of
our food and weapons. Men screamed to be heard above the rushing torrent,
and some fell into the foaming river. We recovered their bruised and
swollen bodies far downstream as we turned back, chastened, to Hereford.
There was no coin to mount another expedition, nor were any particularly
anxious to continue. Men blamed this extraordinary misfortune upon the
dark power of Glyndwr, who was named a sorcerer, and upon a king facing
divine wrath for the execution of an archbishop. In York, white roses
bloomed about Scrope's tomb. The nobility of England went meekly home
to ponder the signs.

As for the French, they made a show of taking Carmarthen, which I had
quietly ordered evacuated. Then, finding little there save stones, and these
unsuitable to eat, they burned a portion of the deserted town and set sail for
France. Glyndwr retreated north to await the winter.

Misfortune had not yet done with my father. With the smothering snows of
December came a hideous disease that laid him upon what many named his
deathbed. It was a strange malady and most foul, for it left him unable to
walk and covered his skin with running pustules which were noxious to
behold and to smell. The royal physicians knew no name to set to this
affliction, but all England went hazard that Archbishop Scrope and good
King Richard had struck him from the grave. The King did not die, but pain
became his constant companion, twisting his limbs and blighting his skin.
The once handsome Bolingbroke, the bold knight of the red-gold hair, England's champion, was an unsightly invalid.

At the age of eighteen I began to bear upon my shoulders much of the
burden of governing England, and to confront face to face those demons
which devoured the body and soul of my father.

In the summer of 1406, my sister Philippa was betrothed to King Eric of

Denmark. The royal family and all its entourage gathered at Lynn to send the Princess to her new home beyond the sea. I had not seen her in many years, this sister of mine, for at the age of three she had been sent to our aunt Elizabeth, my father's sister, Father deeming it proper for her to be educated by a great lady. Philippa it was whose birth had sent our mother to an early grave, and when I saw her it seemed to me as though the soul of the dead woman had settled upon her daughter. To look upon her, to speak with her, was to be a child again in the presence of the mother I recalled so tenderly. Likewise Philippa was drawn to me, and I was put in mind of the babe learning to walk who would totter after me until I did pick her up and swing her around to much delighted shrieking. I lamented our long separation and mourned the parting to come, for when she set sail for Denmark it would be as though she had died.

"Dearest Harry," she said once as we walked in a green garden, "you alone of our house have I not seen these many years, yet I think now it has been a very great loss."

"I have not often been at court, and I was discouraged from seeking you out elsewhere," I said. "I was kept from John and Humphrey as well. Father thought me a bad influence."

Her dark eyes were grave. "You say it blithely, yet I think that is to hide the pain. Is it better now with Father?"

"Oh, aye, somewhat. Though my duties in Wales have yet kept me from the rest of you. In truth, I knew not that you would even wish to see me."

"You must never believe it, Harry. I have thought of you often, and worried about you. I was so small when I was sent away that I could not remember what you looked like. Yet I cared for you more than the others, and prayed for you. Is it not strange?"

I squeezed her hand gratefully.

"I think it was what they said about you which caused me to take your part," she continued.

"They?"

"Oh, everyone. But especially our aunt Elizabeth and her husband of Cornwaille, and Father, of course. Uncle named you a dissipated coward and said you would be the ruination of England. I suppose I believed it for a time. Then three years ago a priest came to call upon Uncle, to transact some business. This priest said he had known you well. He spoke quite highly of you, even in opposition to Uncle."

"God's blood! Who was this priest?"

"Why, Richard Courtenay of Exeter. A kinder man I have never met."

"Courtenay!"

"Aye. He called upon us thrice afterward, and each time we spoke of you. I must say this plainly to you, Harry. He was sorely hurt that he received no word from you. He claimed that he wrote to you but was never answered. He thought there must be some good reason, yet he grieved for lost friendship."

I flushed with shame. "No," I said, "there was no good reason save fear."

"Fear, brother? What would you find to fear in this good priest?"

"It is no flaw of his, I assure you. I cannot speak easily of it."

"Perhaps you may speak of it to him, for Richard Courtenay shall soon join us here at Lynn."

"Courtenay is coming here?"

"Aye. I must have an escort on my journey to Denmark, and a clerk to preside over my chapel until my husband provides such a one for me. I have chosen Richard Courtenay, for I know of none other with whom I am at such ease."

"How long should he be abroad, then?"

"But a few months, I should think. Much to my distress."

She smiled tightly and I saw that she was near tears. With one hand she rubbed the sleeve of her blue velvet gown so that the nap stood up roughly. She was no self-assured princess but a frightened child of twelve about to leave her home forever to go and live among strangers. I pulled her awkwardly to me and stroked her chestnut hair as the tears flowed.

"Sad it is to lose love," she said as she wept, "but sadder still to lose what has only just been found."

Richard Courtenay drifted serenely among the chattering courtiers, his black clerk's robe drawn tightly about him. He was slim, taller than most of the men, and many paused to take note of him. His wavy hair was prematurely streaked with gray, and his long face still shone with gentleness and intelligence. We greeted one another quietly, but strong feeling leaped in our eyes. When we went in to the banquet, I seated Courtenay at my right hand and served him myself from a flask of Burgundy.

"You do me too much honor," he said.

"Not too much for an old friend," I replied.

"It is good to see your father here."

The King was a piteous sight, the scabrous skin hanging in yellow folds at his neck, his hands raw and peeling. His courtiers either refused to look at him or stared like idiots. Father, to his credit, stolidly ignored them all. He sat perched high upon the dais, a scarecrow in ermine robes, and vigorously chewed his venison.

"He has some relief from his illness and is determined to carry out his duties," I said.

"Is it not strange, the changes the years bring?"

"They have not changed you, Richard, though it is near eight years since we parted."

This was no empty compliment, for at twenty-five his face was as smooth and lively as ever, his hair still thick despite the gray.

"You had not taken holy orders when I knew you before," I added, "yet sanctity has not quenched the twinkle in your eye."

"Nor were you a prince, Harry Monmouth; rather, a frightened boy carried off hostage to King Richard. And you are greatly altered."

"Strange it would be if I were not. I soon shall be nineteen."

He sipped his wine. "More it is than age. There is a hardness which was not there before."

"Nor should that surprise you. Even in faraway Devon you must have heard much of what has befallen me."

"Indeed I have, though tidings come late to us. I must admit it was with difficulty that I imagined the boy I once knew taking the field against Percy or roistering in the brothels of London." He paused at my look of surprise. "Aye, the lowliest shepherd in Devon knows his prince to be a rascally fellow, a lover of wine and women. The doings of royalty are noted by all."

"I have been a carouser, it is true," I agreed. "Yet there is more to me than that."

"There must be, for in truth, Harry, your manner is that of a man who has lived many, many years and borne many burdens."

I shrugged and said nothing.

"Have you still the madonna?" he asked.

"No. I lost her," I lied.

"Oh." He lapsed into an uneasy silence.

"You must forgive me that I have not written to you," I said. "It was not for want of affection, you must believe that. I did not write you when I was with Richard, for I feared to bring you trouble. And since then, I have had another fear." I gathered my courage to meet his eyes. "It is simply this. The boy you knew was slain long ago with other poor wretches at Shrewsbury and in Wales. These other souls have some hope of resurrection. But the boy is dead. He shall never live again. And being dead, he could not write to you. Do you understand?"

"I understand, but I do not believe it."

"You must believe, for you have yourself noted the change in me."

"I do not deny it. But I have seen the boy as well. He looks out at me from your eyes. He is in the pain that haunts them."

I turned from him in confusion and began to eat the cold meat upon my trencher.

"Do you still harp?" he asked.

"Aye."

"And do you yet love Monmouth above any place in the realm?"

I smiled and nodded. "Aye. And Joan Waryn still does rule there with a heavy hand and a sharp tongue."

He laughed. "I should be happy to set eyes upon Joan Waryn's great bulk again."

"Then you must accompany me when next I go. Better still, when you return from Denmark, I should be very pleased if you accepted a position in my household."

"I fear your offer is too late. I have been elected chancellor of Oxford, and I have accepted."

"Ah. It is just as well, I suppose. I know you love Oxford. And it is a great honor for you."

"Aye. And my new post shall send me often to London. Nor would it be inappropriate for me to cultivate the friendship of the Prince of Wales. After all, the Prince should be a patron of Oxford."

"I shall look to see you often, or else my favor shall be bestowed upon Cambridge."

"God forbid," he said cheerfully and bit into a jellied eel. I studied him through narrowed eyes. By my sister's influence, no doubt, he was no longer an obscure Devonshire clerk. As chancellor of Oxford he would have the ear of king, prince, and archbishop. Did he calculate, even now, how best to wield his newly acquired power?

"Do you know," I said, "that I shall someday make you a bishop?"

He stopped chewing and regarded me with astonishment.

"Perhaps," I added, "you shall even sit at Canterbury. Arundel shall not live forever. What say you to that?"

He frowned. "It would not be wise, Harry."

"And why not?"

He hesitated. "I bear you too much affection," he said with difficulty. "It would be dangerous for us both, since I fear my goodwill toward you might blind me to your shortcomings. You shall want a good man for Canterbury, one who supports Lancaster and loves the Church, but most of all a man who will not fear to reproach you when you are wrong."

I raised my eyebrows. "There are few such men about."

"You need but one Archbishop of Canterbury."

I laughed with relief, for there was no ambition here save to serve. I returned to my food with renewed appetite.

"Tell me," Courtenay said as we ate, "who is that lady with the Queen's party, the pretty one who stares at us constantly?"

"That," I said, "is Lady Anne Mortimer."

"Surely I do not interest her."

"Perhaps you do."

"Is she your mistress?"

"Upon occasion."

"The lady is wed to Richard of York, I do believe?"

"Ummm. Have you turned friar and shall you now preach a sermon upon the evils of adultery?"

"No. You will know your own mind in this. I only would say to you that you have named this affair correctly, for adultery it is."

"Gently but bravely spoken, and I accept your chastisement. Perhaps you are direct enough for Canterbury after all."

"But still you shall see her?"

"I have promised her tonight."

"Do you love her, Harry?"

"Love her? My dear Courtenay, love is a luxury princes cannot afford. Lady Anne collects me like a precious bauble to dangle upon her wrist before the other ladies. For my part, she is fair and lusty, and that is that."

When the feasting was done, there was music and wine aplenty. At Philippa's behest I played upon my harp and sang. It was an old lay I chose, and at the familiar words little Philippa wept.

"I have a little sister
Far beyond the sea
And many love tokens
Has she sent to me.

"She sent me a cherry
Without any stone.
She sent me a dove
Without any bone.

"She sent me a briar
Without branch or leaf.
She bade me love my lover
Without any grief."

My voice was fine, if I may so compliment myself, and women especially took pleasure in it. They sat rapt before me like a bouquet of flowers in their gowns of yellow and green silk, their coifs perched like white birds upon their heads. Idly I wondered what it should be like to sleep with each of them on successive nights. I decided I should become bored by the third or fourth evening, and dreamed wistfully of rolling upon a mattress of straw with Alison. When one is jaded by lust, the innocent love of youth teases the heart with a special sweetness.

I made love to Anne that night as though from a great distance. It was a steaming August night, and I rolled away from her when we were done so that I might cool my sweating body. She complained that I had not spoken to her, that I would not hold her. I replied sharply, and when her voice took on a high whine I ordered her from my bed. She slipped out of the chamber, weeping bitterly.

Philippa set sail the next day for Denmark, a brave little figure clad in green who stood upon the deck of her ship looking back at an England she would never see again. Courtenay stood by her side, and I prayed to Our Lady for their safe passage. Long after all others were gone I remained at the harbor, until the tiny white speck fell over the green line of the horizon. Then I wandered heartsick with loneliness to my quarters and set my retainers packing, for I resolved to return at once to London that I might seek solace in the taverns. I was delayed by a summons from my father, who was lodged at Greyfriars so he would be close to those who prayed hourly for his health. I found him before a blazing hearth in the refectory, wrapped in a coverlet despite the summer heat. The ever-present Arundel hovered at the King's shoulder as a vulture guards a carcass. I acknowledged him but coldly.

"I have not spoken with you in some time," Father said, "and there is a matter, small perhaps, which I should like to discuss."

"Your grace, with all due respect, I should prefer such an audience in private."

I turned pointedly to Arundel, and he stared back with a look of pure venom.

"My lord of Canterbury is ever with me these days," Father fretted. "He is a great comfort to me."

"No doubt he is," I replied, "yet you need no assistance in talking with your son."

"On the contrary," said Arundel, "such conversations have in the past been most trying for his grace."

"There shall be no conversation unless we are left alone," I said. Father's pockmarked face collapsed in pain at the tone of my voice, and I repented at once of my anger. For the first time in my life, I pitied him. It was a pity born of my own fear, of a sure knowledge that we were bound together, he and I, by something stronger than even blood. He was my destiny, his torment would be mine, and all the anger of the past seemed as nothing compared to this.

"Forgive me," I said, "for I am concerned for your health and eager to speak with you, despite my harsh words. It is only that I cannot share with you as son to father with someone else present."

He picked at a scab on his earlobe and stared into the fire. "Would you leave us then, Arundel," he said at last. The Archbishop bowed and left the room.

"Father, may I sit?"

He nodded, still studying the fire, and I pulled a bench next to him, trying to ignore the heat.

"Why do you hate him so?" he asked. "He is true friend, and there are but few of those."

"It is mutual," I replied. "He has detested me from the first."

"Because he deems you impudent and irresponsible. You have given him cause."

"This is old ground, Father, and you have not summoned me here to replow it, I pray."

"You do not know. You sit there in your youth and you know nothing of pain."

"Father—"

"I am hated the length and breadth of England. Men have sought my life, yet have I crushed them. Now has God afflicted me, and I am helpless before Him. Do not begrudge me my few loyal friends, Harry. You have no right. You have been poor enough son to me."

I sat in miserable silence.

"You wait for me to die. I know it," he said.

"It is not true," I said wearily.

"You shall be king, and all England shall be at your feet. Or so you now suppose. But you shall dream of poison, or the assassin's knife, and who shall be your friend then, eh? That fellow Oldcastle? I like not his looks. He is not to be trusted. What of your uncle of Beaufort? He cares not for you, Harry, no more than for me. He is my half brother. I know him well to be a heartless knave—"

"Is it this for which you summoned me?" His words had struck me all unprotected.

"No. It is the woman I would speak with you about."

"The woman?"

"The Mortimer woman, York's wife. I do not preach to you, Harry. I but wish to warn you. You are indiscreet."

"I do not know what you mean."

"Indeed you do. How would I know of your affair if my courtiers were not chattering about it? York is bound to find out, and he is said to be exceedingly jealous. It is rumored he bears Lancaster ill will. We have enough enemies as it is."

"I had not known we were found out. In truth, she is not so dear to me to take such a risk."

"Good. Then you shall not see her again?"

"I shall not. Indeed, I did cast her out of my bed last night, she berated me so. She is peevish as a tired donkey."

Father chuckled, and I joined in. A joy I had seldom known stirred within me and I wondered at it, not quite trusting and yet longing to with all my heart.

"I hear you are quite a one for the women. Of course a son of mine would be, for such was I when I was young. Yet I stayed away from the whorehouses, for I feared the pox. One fool of a physician dared suggest that the pox afflicts me now. It is nonsense, for I have avoided the baser sort of women. That has worried me about you, my son, for I would not see your youth wasted by foul disease."

"Your concern touches me. I shall be very careful." I tried to sound the dutiful son, though I was unpracticed in that role. "Had you many mistresses?"

"A few." He smiled at the recollection. "The fairest women of the kingdom."

"After Mother died?"

"Even before. The finest was a Venetian woman I met upon my travels."

I cursed myself that I was startled, that I took this news as a child. Of course he had mistresses, all gentlemen did. The romantic love of which the minstrels sang was said to be impossible between wife and husband.

"The pleasures of love are not to be denied a vigorous young knight," Father said. "I was often away from your mother. Ah, and she was herself practiced in lovemaking, no doubt. She was a beautiful woman."

My throat was dry. "Are you saying my mother was unfaithful?"

"Well, I do not know with whom, but I am sure she must have been. All women are unfaithful at one time or another. It is their nature. Indeed, at times I did attribute your paternity to some other, for I did not see how a son of mine could be such as you."

I stiffened and stared straight ahead, my vision cloudy.

"But I have no such thoughts since Shrewsbury," he went on. "I saw your mettle there, though I yet have many concerns for you. You do not mix well with your peers, and that could be fatal for a king."

I said nothing. Uneasy moments passed.

"I am very tired," he said at last in a strained voice, "and you seem to have turned sulky. In truth, Harry, I know of none so cold and moody as you can be."

I stood up. "Then I must take my leave."

I fled the oven heat of the hall.

8

I wintered that year in London, where I sat for the first time as a full member of the King's council. I now held considerable power, for Father's illness continued to keep him abed, and my own reputation had grown as the situation in Wales improved. Men who once scorned me now scurried to gain my favor, the honeyed words heavy upon their tongues, and I learned to take advantage of their fawning and greed for my own purposes. Upon such foolishness is the realm built.

With the spring thaw, Father returned to his royal duties. The warm sunshine of Maytime dried his sores once again, and, though weak, he was free of pain for the first time in months. Arundel now served as his chancellor. Chafing at my presence, he complained to the King that I was far too idle and required a useful diversion. Once more I was packed off to Wales. Of Owain Glyndwr's revolt, nothing remained save the rebel occupation of the castles of Aberystwyth and Harlech. Lord Talbot was sent to besiege Harlech, and I was given the task of recovering Aberystwyth for the Crown. I took with me Jack Oldcastle, now a sheriff of Herefordshire, and Richard Courtenay.

Our progress toward Aberystwyth was slow, for many Welshmen sought me out along the way, suing for pardon or seeking redress of grievances. I received them gladly, for I remained anxious to rule justly and thereby gain the loyalty of the people. We reached Aberystwyth a fortnight past Midsummer Eve. The fortress towered over a lofty headland, its walls melting into sheer cliffs, the sea clawing at the rocks upon three sides.

"She looks as though she should topple into Cardigan Bay," I said as we sat our horses some distance away.

"Indeed I have heard that when the sea is wild, the very walls tremble," said Jack.

"The view from the keep must be incredibly lovely," said Courtenay.

"Not for the poor wretches inside," said Jack. "We shall soon have them starving, and they cannot eat the view."

Methodically I set about the siege. The townspeople were impoverished and in no mood to be starved. After promises of fair treatment, the gates were opened to us and supplies taken in to feed both English and Welsh. The castle with its garrison remained closed to us. We settled in for the tedious task of waiting them out.

Jack and Courtenay, though newly met, had become fast friends, to my relief. Jack had not given up his interest in Lollardy. He had assaulted Courtenay on our first night from Hereford with his views on the corruption of the Church, and to his surprise the gentle clerk had agreed.

"I read the works of John Wyclyf while I was a student at Oxford," Courtenay told us, "and I admired his thought. While I cannot agree with all his conclusions, I have no doubt that the Church should take to heart much of his teaching. It is repugnant to me that prelates live in splendor while many poor folk, and even the clerks who serve them, go hungry."

"Exactly!" cried Jack. "Arundel's treasury would feed the whole of London town, yet he takes it upon himself to bring charges against those who rebuke him. It is not what Our Lord taught. And one thing more. We could finance the putting down of this rebellion from the coffers of the Church."

"No!" I cried. "I would not have it. The Church must be above such things."

Jack spread his hands. "The Church blesses our warmaking. Why should she not pay for it?"

"If the Church sinks to such a level, how can she save us?"

"Sinks to such a level? It is your damnable conscience again, Harry! I had thought to be done with this. Why are you here, then, if this undertaking be so foul?"

I clenched and unclenched my hands. "Do not mock me, Jack, for God's sake!"

Courtenay had been listening intently. "There are times when force may be necessary, Harry. As a prince you are called to take up the sword if greater good may come of it."

"Exactly!" Jack cried again. "This is a good man, Harry. Listen to him. Tell me, Courtenay, what think you, is the Body of Christ present in the Host?"

They proceeded to argue far into the night, Jack forcefully presenting views perilously near to heresy, Courtenay listening patiently and asking occasional questions. I said nothing and finally drifted off to sleep. I cared little enough then what the Host was, only that it should comfort me.

We returned to Aberystwyth one July day after an afternoon of hawking to discover a great commotion. A company of knights had arrived, some fifty of the unruly young lords of the realm, and had proceeded to mill about the town in disorder, alarming the townspeople, who had retreated behind barred doors and hidden their daughters beneath mattresses. Till Vespers it took to restore order, and it was with thinly veiled impatience that I sought out the leader of this brave expedition, the young Earl of Warwick. This was the same Warwick who had unhorsed me years before in my first and only joust. Jack and I found him in the mud of Darkgate breaking out a keg of ale plundered from a nearby tavern.

"Well met, your highness," he cried when he saw me. "We have only just arrived, the lustiest bachelors in Christendom, to render service to our Prince."

"What are you doing here?"

"Why, soon the Welsh wars shall be at an end. Everyone says so. These marcher lords should not have all the glory, eh? We are eager to wield our swords and perform deeds of chivalry while there is yet time, so that we may take our rightful places among English heroes."

I glanced sideways at Jack and saw that he bit his lip in amusement. I looked Warwick up and down. He was of an age with me and possessed a thick shock of hair the color of straw and an open, cheerful face. I folded my arms and said, "You stay here only if you accept my orders."

"Why, of course," he said, somewhat offended. "Did I not say we came to join in your service?"

"Then know this," I said coolly. "I forbid plundering." I looked pointedly at the ale.

He laughed good-naturedly. "I have ridden all afternoon in the warm sun. I do but slake my thirst."

"Good," I said and smiled. "Then you shall be happy to reimburse the innkeeper."

I clapped him upon the shoulder and walked away, then turned back and said, "Bring your men to me tonight that I may impress upon them the seriousness of this enterprise."

We left him standing in the street while the rich brown ale spilled untended into the mire.

"Must I indeed suffer such fools?" I moaned.

"You have been waiting for God to punish you," said Jack. "Now should you be satisfied."

*   *   *

Richard Beauchamp, Earl of Warwick, and his gallant followers were a hair shirt to me those next months. They soon tired of the inactivity which ever attends a siege and beleaguered me daily to mount an assault upon the castle walls. My refusals brought much grumbling, and I knew they did deem me craven. Unbeknownst to me, Warwick issued a challenge to the garrison that he and four of his knights should meet five rebels in the lists, the outcome to determine who should hold the castle. There was, of course, no reply, and my comrades and I enjoyed much merriment when we heard of it, for most of the garrison would be ragged and barefoot hillmen who had never witnessed a joust, much less broken a lance. Warwick was disheartened to find himself ranged against so unchivalrous a foe. To keep up his own spirits and those of his men, he took to reading aloud to them from the books he had brought over the mountains, tales from the writings of the French and Angevin chroniclers, the *Chanson de Roland* and *Gesta Dei per Francos*. Incessantly he lectured upon honor, courage, and chastity and read of chevachees and jousts, of pitched battles in which knights fought head to head and then retired (those who survived) to speak courteously of their foes and drink to their health.

"Surely such valor in war, such gentilesse, is the glory of mankind," he was fond of saying. "Such deeds shall be renowned until the end of time."

Fortunately, it was not hard to avoid him, for we were encamped in many small tents about Aberystwyth and I could escape to my own billet when Warwick's eloquence offended my sensibilities.

In early August, two chaste and honorable young knights in Warwick's entourage brutally raped a girl of the town and left her half dead upon a pile of offal next the town walls, where she was found naked and babbling by her distraught father. The young gallants returned swaggering to our encampment and boasted to their fellows of the outrage. In as cold a fury as I have ever known I called them out before the others and gave them a choice— either they should pay retribution to the girl and her family, and thereafter turn one third of their revenues each year into alms for the poor, or else I would have them hanged as miscreants from the town wall. They chose to part with their coin, and I thereupon ordered them from Wales. When they had gone, a shocked quiet settled over the encampment. No others would have deemed it an offense to ravish a baseborn Welsh girl. Indeed, if there were to be no assaults upon castle walls or Welsh bitches, of what value was this venture? The brave knights grew increasingly restless, and well before Michaelmas they prevailed upon Warwick to return with them to England.

I, too, thought to leave the siege. Winter would soon make the mountains impassable, and I did not wish to spend Christmastide shivering in a tent. I sent Richard Courtenay to the garrison to discover if the time was ripe to negotiate a surrender. Free passage to their homes I offered to all who would lay down their arms.

They were a stubborn lot, this remnant of rebellion, and they clung to the hope that their beloved Glyndwr would somehow rescue them and restore Aberystwyth. They were thin and ill-dressed, Courtenay reported, and their food supply was nearly depleted.

"Still they wait for Owain," he said. "But they do know their time is short. They say that if Owain has not relieved them by February, they shall surrender."

"And we should be forced to winter here," I complained. "Besides that, my funds do run low."

"They shall not be moved before that time," Courtenay replied, "unless you order an assault."

I thought a moment. "No, I'll lose no lives here. Tell them this. I shall appoint Sir John Bromley governor of Aberystwyth until the summer next. If Glyndwr has not relieved them by the day they have set, they shall surrender to him. Have them swear to it upon the Host."

Jack shook his head. "I do not like it. Sir John is not so capable as you are."

"What? Shall I leave you here instead? I am going, Jack. There are times when I must depend upon my captains. I shall leave Sir John with fifty men. Those few can be lodged in the town, where they shall be more comfortable. After all, I can pay only fifty men. The rest would stay under duress. How many inside, Courtenay?"

"I saw but a score."

"There may be more," Jack warned.

"And if there are?" I said. "I have offered them free passage, so they would have little to gain from attacking Bromley. Even if they did try, their strength is not sufficient to destroy him. They could only escape, and the castle would be ours, and that is what they do not want."

"What of Glyndwr?"

"What indeed? Glyndwr is finished. He has enough to do to keep himself alive, no doubt. I am for Monmouth, then London. I would spend Christmas beside the Thames with a woman in my arms."

At Hay I dreamed again of the gray-eyed girl. I do not recall the substance of my dream save that her face was tense with fear. I woke certain that I must seek her out now that my task in Wales was done.

Jack sighed when I revealed my intentions. "You would take us through the Black Mountains because of a dream about a lass you chanced upon six years past?"

"Aye, I would. It sounds foolish, I know, yet I must search for her. I must. Had you seen her face—"

"Perhaps the girl is in trouble," Courtenay said. "God sometimes speaks to us through dreams."

"As does the Devil," Jack said.

"I know not why she haunts my dreams. I only know that I must find her. Let us be gone this very morning."

A gray rain drenched us as we wound our way down the Gospel Pass with our small escort. The mountains swelled as we descended and pulled us into their foggy crevices, until there was nothing of the world save the Honddu's roar. I watched the river warily, remembering the floods of my father's ill-fated expedition, but though the waters were swollen, they did not leave their banks.

I was soaked through to the skin, though I wore a cloak and several layers of clothing. My bones ached from the cold. I rode with head bent and watched the brown grass pass beneath my horse. My memory had not served me so well as I had expected. Thrice I spied stone huts which put me in mind of the one I sought. The first housed a bedraggled family of ten who knew nothing of the girl. The next two proved to be abandoned and roofless. I was in an agony of uncertainty, for it seemed either could have been the one.

"Harry!" Jack cried and pointed.

The hut was nearly invisible against the rocky hillside, for though the rain had now ceased, the mist rose like a dream from the river.

"This is it!" I exclaimed. "I am sure of it this time. There is the wood where I found her."

"Indeed it does seem familiar, though it was long ago," Jack agreed.

Courtenay smiled from the recesses of his hooded cloak. "I have been praying," he said.

I studied the hut, and my belly tightened. "There is a great hole in the roof," I whispered. "It cannot be."

Jack peered through the mist. "So there is. They must have gone, then."

"They cannot have gone," I said. I was near to weeping.

"Harry," Courtenay said, his hand upon my shoulder, "all Wales lies in desolation. This can be no great surprise."

I shrugged away from him. "Speak not to me of the desolation of Wales. Do I not bear it upon my soul?"

"Perhaps they shall know at Llanthony what has happened here. It is the monks' land, I'll wager," said Jack.

"First I must see for myself," I said. "Stay with the others."

I slid from my horse and trudged up the hillside. As I drew near I saw that the door was ajar. It was one more sign that the hut must stand empty. I forced myself to continue on but then stood frozen. The sweet mustiness of the damp earth had been overcome by the stench of decaying flesh. I crossed myself, waved for Jack and Courtenay to join me, and stood with head bowed and fists clenched while they clambered up the hill.

"I cannot go in," I said as they came closer. They halted. "Someone inside is dead."

Courtenay walked past me, his cloak drawn over his nose and his crucifix in his left hand, pushed the door open and disappeared inside. I swallowed the bitter stuff which rose in my throat.

"Harry! Jack! Come here!"

I rushed inside. A shaft of light from the damaged ceiling fell upon a pallet near the hearth. There lay the putrefying corpse of a woman.

"Jesu!" I whispered and crossed myself again.

"Harry! Over here!"

I saw Courtenay then standing by the wall. Cowering in the corner, face contorted and eyes wild, was the girl.

"You must speak to her, Harry. She does not respond to English."

"Merryn?" I said softly.

She whimpered, her eyes never leaving Courtenay. One filthy clawlike hand grabbed at the wattled stone of the wall as though she sought to scratch a hole through which to escape.

"Go to her, Harry," Courtenay said, "else she shall die of fright."

I knelt beside her and placed a hand upon each of her arms. So thin they were, I thought I might have snapped the bones had I squeezed too hard. She froze at my touch and gasped.

"Merryn," I said again.

She sought to pull away, her back sliding up against the rough wall. Her head rolled from side to side and her tangled mat of brown hair fell across her face.

"No!" she screamed. "No!"

I grasped her chin, forced her to look at me. "Merryn! Merryn! I am a friend."

Her eyes found me then. They were just as I remembered, large and gray, and they dominated her thin, bony face.

"How do you know my name?" she whispered.

"I met you once before, a very long time ago. In the wood. I am Harry. Do you not recall it?"

Still she stared.

"My mam is dead," she said.

"Aye."

"The monks would not bury her. They would not bury her. English monks."

I translated for Courtenay. He grimaced.

"I will do it then."

"Here is a priest," I said to the girl. "He shall give your mother a proper Christian burial."

She slumped against the wall. Gently I pushed the hair back from her face.

"When did you last eat?"

She only moaned.

"Merryn?"

"They gave me cheese," she mumbled.

"Who? When?"

"The monks. Very long ago. Very, very—"

"Get some food," I called to Jack, who stood in the doorway. "Where are the animals? Once there were sheep here, and chickens."

"Gone. Stolen," she said. "Will you dig the hole? I could not dig it very deep. I dreamed the wolves found her. I screamed at them and they saw me. They came for me."

"We shall dig it very deep."

"I feared to put her into the hole. The monks would not come. The Devil is waiting to snatch her soul. I have kept watch over her. I will not let him have her. The wolves are outside."

Jack had returned. "I shall have some hard words for the good monks of Llanthony," he said.

"Leave them to me," I replied. "There is much they shall account for." I put my arms around the trembling girl. "We have food," I said to her. "I shall carry you outside where the air is fresh and you shall eat."

"My mam." She wept.

"Sh-h. The Devil shall not have her, for a man of God is with us."

"I shall pray over her all the while you eat," Courtenay said.

I smiled at him and lifted the girl. There was little enough of her beneath the rags she wore. I bore her outside, wrapped her in the warmth of my cloak, and set her upon the sodden turf. Jack had found some salted beef and a slab of brown bread. These she gnawed upon weakly.

"Better if we had some broth," said Jack in English. "Her belly shall gripe her after such rough fare."

"Better belly gripes than starvation," I said.

Jack rubbed his red beard. "Well, Harry, you have found your Welsh lass. Now what shall you do with her?"

Merryn was chewing stubbornly upon a crust of bread, determined despite her lack of strength to force this unexpected feast into her belly.

"What has become of your father and brothers?" I asked her.

Her face darkened. "Dead! Killed by the whoreson English. At a place called Grosmont it was."

I looked at Oldcastle.

"My father and Davy were run through with swords. The English horsemen ran them through. Gwyllym saw it. He was sorely wounded by an arrow. He made his way back to Honddu and died in my arms. We buried him by the wood, my mam and I. The monks would not come for him either."

Her face was all sharp edges as she mulled over these wrongs, the anger narrowing her eyes and thrusting out her chin.

"I hate the English," she said. "I have seen Englishmen but once and if ever again—"

She broke off so abruptly that I knew she remembered. I waited in dread, as does a condemned man who anticipates the fall of the ax.

"You are English!"

"No," I said. "I am Welsh. I was born in Wales."

"Harry!" Jack said. "You shall only make it worse."

Never in the heat of battle had I seen so fierce a hatred as that which contorted her features. Her thin chest heaved. "Murderer!" she screamed. "Bastard! Murderer!"

"It is not so! Do you not recall? I saved you from the soldiers."

She struggled to her feet, thrusting the cloak from her, and covered her ears with her hands.

"They are all dead," she wailed. "Da and Mam and Davy, aye, and little Gwyllym, did I not hear his death rattle? You killed them!"

"No, it was not I!" I grasped her arms and shook her. "You said once you did not hate me. You must say it again! You must!"

She fought to escape my hold on her, though she had little enough strength for it.

"You are hurting my arms! Shall you murder me as well?" she sobbed. "Murderer!"

"No! I am no common brigand. I am the Prince of Wales."

She grew quite still. "Owain Glyndwr is Prince of Wales," she whispered.

When I replied, it was without hope. "I am Henry of Lancaster," I said. "I am the Prince of Wales by this conquest of mine."

She stepped backward, her face pale as death save for a spot of pink upon each cheek. She turned and fled to the hut. I found her there in the shadows, cowering behind the robes of a startled Courtenay.

"Keep him from me," she pleaded.

"She flees me," I said. "She knows who I am."

"I would slay you if I could," she said. "I would slay you for what you have done. And I care not what you do to me."

I left her to Courtenay. That he too was English did not seem to concern her. He was a holy man and would bury her mother. The unlikely pair bore the rotting corpse upon its pallet from the cottage while Jack and I watched from a distance. They stumbled up the hill to a twisted yew, where Gwyllym likely was buried, and Courtenay finished digging the grave. The girl stood with head bowed and from time to time flung a suspicious glance over her shoulder to assure herself that I had not drawn nigh.

"You look like to swoon," Jack said.

I started at his voice. "It is only that I am weary."

"What, Harry? Did you seek absolution from her?"

Courtenay shoveled clods of dirt into the hole.

"What shall you do?" Jack asked.

"She would die here."

"Aye, most likely."

"There is only one thing to be done, though I know you shall try to dissuade me. I shall take her to Monmouth. It may be that Joan Waryn can tend to her."

"And what then?"

"Perhaps marriage to a tradesman or a bailiff of our lands there. If it is her desire, of course."

He nodded.

"You do not think me foolish?" I asked.

He smiled. "I think you the greatest fool I have ever known."

I returned his smile.

"Yon lass shall ill repay your kindness," he said. "Stay away from her or she shall sink her claws into you. And well I know how easily you do bleed."

She did not go with us gladly. She had never been from the Honddu, and she wished to keep vigil over the graves of her mother and brother. She wanted nothing to do with me. Courtenay reasoned with her and Jack served as translator while I wandered along the bank of the churning river. At last Courtenay hailed me.

"She has agreed to join us," he said, "but only if you swear a sacred oath that you shall neither speak with her nor seek her company."

"I do not accept such a condition," I said in Welsh.

She glared at me. "Then leave me to die. I shall not go with Glyndwr's great enemy and the murderer of my people."

"My patience is at an end," I replied. "I had hoped you would come with us freely, but now I give you no choice. If you do not agree to come with us, I shall have you bound."

She turned to flee but I caught her ere she had taken three steps.

"Rope, Jack!"

Soon we had her ankles and wrists bound, despite her screams and sobs.

"It is hard to watch this," Courtenay said.

"What of it? Have you a better idea? Most would rape her and leave her here to perish."

"No," he said. "I do not chastise you. Yet is there irony here. When she was a child, 'twas this very fate from which you spared her."

"Much has changed since then."

"Aye."

We rode then for Llanthony, tucked away in its bowl of hills. Courtenay carried the girl upon his horse, for only he was able to calm her, though he could not speak with her. She did seem to sleep. When we halted at the priory gate, Courtenay said, "I fear she is ill. She burns with fever."

I dismounted and went to him. "Think you her mother died of such a fever?"

"It is likely. That and lack of food."

"Give her to me," I said.

Now she did not protest as Courtenay handed her down. Her eyes were bright and did pierce me to the heart.

"I am cold," she said.

I wrapped Courtenay's blanket more tightly about her. "We shall soon have you before a fire," I said.

"No, we have no wood for a fire. I have not the strength to gather it. Forgive me, I did try. It was so heavy."

The gates were opened to us and I strode inside, shouting orders to startled monks as I went. They scattered like a flock of black crows. The abbot came scurrying from his quarters at the commotion.

"You know this girl?" I said to him as he bowed before me.

He studied the bundle in my arms. "I have seen her," he acknowledged.

"She recently sought your help, did she not?"

"Aye, she came begging."

"And you refused her?"

He was a very fat man with two chins which grew to three as he sullenly ducked his head.

"We fed her," he said.

"It was little enough from what I can see. And her mother? Did you feed her?"

"I don't know."

"Did you refuse to bury her?"

"With respect, your highness, this girl is from a family of notorious rebels. The father was a supporter of Glyndwr and thus your sworn enemy. We would not be treasonable, your highness."

"Nor would you be compassionate, it seems. Is the girl your tenant?"

"The land she lives upon belongs to our order, aye."

Jack's anger boiled over. "You sack of flesh! Do you suck the life's blood

from your people and then kneel at your prayers while they starve? Hell is
plagued with fat monks."

"Enough for now," I said. "We shall require your most comfortable
quarters for this lass. Your own quarters, no doubt, abbot? Good. Show
them to us at once. And send me your physician."

While Jack saw to the comfort of our men, I laid Merryn upon the abbot's
fine featherbed before the blazing hearth. She shivered and brought her
hands, still bound together, to her chest as though she sought to clutch a bit
of the warmth to her. I had forgotten the ropes and the harshness with which
I had bound her. The shame of it sickened me.

"Jesu," I whispered, "what have I done?"

I pulled a dagger from my belt and cut her bonds. I stroked one of her
slender hands which fell across my own.

"See," I said to no one in particular, "how thin her hands are, and yet
how rough."

Courtenay stood beside the bed. "You had best cover her," he said.

I pulled the bedclothes up to her chin and felt her forehead.

"It is like fire," I said.

Her eyes fluttered open then and I withdrew my hand for fear of her
anger. But she said nothing, only breathed slowly with lips slightly parted.

"I am thirsty," she croaked.

I propped her head against my arm and gave her to drink from the
abbot's own dipper. Her lips moved and I bent close to catch her words.

"You cannot be the Prince of Wales," she said.

Then it was I wept, seated upon the floor next to her bed, my face
buried in the covers. The sobs racked my body until my chest did ache from
them and I leaned back spent and wet from my tears. Courtenay placed his
hand upon my shoulder.

"Never have I wept since my grandfather's death," I managed to say.

"It was time," he answered.

Beside me, Merryn slept.

For three days she lay near death while the fever raged within her body. A
woman servant of the monks kept the bedclothes piled high upon her,
tended the fire, and poured hot coltsfoot tea and honey down her throat. For
my part I kept the hours with the monks, humbling myself in prayer in the
hope that God in His mercy would thus spare Merryn's life. Those moments
when I was not upon my knees in supplication I spent at her bedside. Most
often she lay still and fought for breath, but at times she would babble
incoherently, conversing deep within herself in an exotic tongue. Once only
did she speak clearly.

"Not the knife," she said in a flat voice.

I shuddered at this utterance, for it seemed a shadow passed over us when she spoke. I told myself it was but the guttering of the candle by the bed.

When it did seem that heat from her body would ignite the very bed-clothes, her fever broke. At my command the monks grudgingly sang a Te Deum and distributed from my own treasure alms for the relief of the poor of that district. Merryn slept peacefully now, her breathing no longer tortured, and I felt free to enjoy a time of hunting in the mountains with Jack. After days of anxious confinement, the chill autumn air was as a draft of fine claret. The brown fastness of Waun Fach beckoned us up into the clouds. We spurred our horses like madmen, our spirits exulting more in the ride than in the hunt, but toward day's end we did manage to bring down a hart with the bolts from our crossbows.

I went back to Merryn that night and sat beside the bed. She lay upon her back, the bedclothes pulled up to her chin, and stared at the ceiling.

"I have prayed for you these three days," I said.

She did not move, nor did she speak. I tried again.

"Were you able to take some of the venison stew for supper?"

Still she ignored me. I felt my face burning with chagrin.

"I brought down the hart myself, this very day," I said, and thought myself a great fool for trying so hard. "I might as well be a tree stump," I muttered, and stood to leave.

"It was very good." She spoke so softly I was uncertain I had heard.

"Thank you."

"I dreamt of you."

"Oh?" I sat down again. "What did you dream?"

"I cannot tell you."

"I trust it was no nightmare."

"I dreamt of my mam as well." Tears welled up in her eyes. "I thought her to be alive again."

"I am sorry." I wondered what I might say to ease her pain. "Shall I harp for you?"

She sniffled. "Davy did play the harp. It is a long time since I heard one."

"Then you certainly shall this night!" I called for my harp to be found. While we awaited it I cast about for more to say to her.

"You shall go to Monmouth when you are better?"

"You say I have no choice."

"Yet do I wish you to go gladly. I have suffered much anguish that I was so harsh as to have bound you. I want you to be well fed and warm, and so you shall be at Monmouth. There is a woman there, Joan Waryn. She nursed me when I was a babe. I think she would love you very much, and perhaps you might learn to love her as well. And there is more if you wish it. You could learn to ride a horse, to play upon the recorder, even to read."

I watched with satisfaction the wonder growing upon her face, though she did try to hide it.

"Would you like to learn to read, Merryn?"

She turned her face to the wall. "Why are you doing this? Why should you wish to do this for me? I am nothing to you."

"I do not understand it well myself," I admitted. "But this I know. I thought of you often since that day in the wood years ago. Do you recall it now that the fever has passed?"

She squeezed her eyes shut and nodded.

"I thought you would," I continued. "For some reason I knew you would not forget me, just as I could not forget you. You were very brave then, as you are now. You were gentle and—" I broke off and went to stir the fire upon the hearth. "As you have so pointedly told me, I am responsible for the evil which has befallen you. I want to make amends."

"There must be hundreds who suffered as I did at your hands," she said. "How shall you make amends to them?"

Her words cut to the bone. "I shall try to govern them as justly as I may."

I am not so bad as Percy, not so bad as Talbot or Grey, I longed to cry out to her.

"The woman who tends me, she tells me that Henry of Monmouth is known to have his way with women. Is it true?"

I quivered with indignation. "Why do you ask such a thing?"

"Because she says your kindness is but a ploy to lure me into your bed. It shall not work. If that is why you speak prettily to me of music and books—"

I threw down the bellows with a clatter. "That bitch! How dare she put such ideas into your head! God's blood! I am the Prince of Wales. Any highborn lady in England would gladly be my lover. I need not kidnap a half-starved, filthy Welsh waif when I want to share my bed with a woman."

She jerked the bedclothes over her head.

"Pout if you like," I said. "I'll not bear such charges."

"You are too proud of yourself!" Her muffled voice betrayed her hurt and anger.

"And you shall suffocate yourself with your stubbornness."

My own ire was quickly turning to amusement. I went to the bed and pulled the covers from her head.

"Merryn," I coaxed, "soon you shall be well enough to have a bath and your hair shall be combed, and you shall be as fair as any lady."

"I care not!" she cried. "I do not need to look like a lady, and I do not need to please you. I have never had a bath save in the Honddu, and I shall not have one at your bidding."

"If you live at Monmouth, you shall bathe once a week. I have done so myself since I was a child at King Richard's court, and so shall you."

"Why should I bathe once a week simply because you do?"

"Because I wish you to."

"Indeed, I have known no one so arrogant as you. I loathe you!"

"I do not believe it."

A squire appeared with my harp. It did seem a most inauspicious time for music, yet I was exhilarated by this clash of wills.

"What shall I play?"

"Nothing. Leave me to rest."

"No. My music shall soothe you. Do you like tales of Merlyn the Great?"

I plunged ahead with a Celtic lay of the deeds of King Arthur's mighty sorcerer, and how he slept in a cave in Gwent until Wales should call upon him again. Merryn closed her eyes and feigned sleep.

When I had done, I set my instrument aside and said, "Well then, what think you of my harping?"

Her mouth tightened. "How is it that you sing and speak in Welsh?" she asked, ignoring my question.

"You are not the only one who loves Wales. I was born in Gwent, at Monmouth, and there I grew to manhood."

I awaited another outburst but she was silent, seeming to sleep again. Then she said, "A weed which grows among violets is yet a weed."

"Do not forget," I said, "there are many lovely weeds."

She smiled in spite of herself.

"I have been waiting for that," I said.

Flustered, she turned upon her side.

"Good night," I said.

She did not reply.

The next day a messenger arrived from the court. Parliament now sat at Gloucester, and the King had once more been stricken with his illness while en route. He lay at Reading and would return to London as soon as he was able to travel. Since my dispatches proved me to be no longer engaged in Wales, I was to ride at once for Gloucester, there to represent the King, and then on to London to report upon the proceedings.

I received these tidings with keen disappointment. I had thought to spend Christmas at Monmouth in Merryn's company, to take her training in hand myself ere we went our separate ways. I knew well that once I returned to London, with Father ill and affairs of state depending to some extent upon me, it might be months, even years, ere I saw Monmouth again. I spoke of this to Jack and Courtenay.

"I had hoped to win her friendship," I said. "Now I do fear she shall be discontented. Perhaps she shall even run away."

"Surely you may trust Joan in this," said Courtenay. "She shall be a fit guardian for the lass."

"Aye," I admitted, "but what of Merryn's lessons? I would have her learn to read and to play upon the recorder, and would wish to be informed of her progress. Joan herself cannot read and write, so how shall I know if Merryn fares well?"

"There I may be of help," said Jack. "My lands in Herefordshire are not so far from Monmouth. I shall escort the lass to Monmouth as soon as she is strong enough to travel, and I shall explain everything to Joan. I shall engage a good old priest to teach her her letters, and if you like I shall ride over the hills to visit her from time to time."

"And you could send me tidings of her?"

"Aye. Though your interest in this does baffle me. One would think you in love."

"Don't be absurd. She is my ward. My concern is that of a father or a brother."

I went to speak with Merryn, to tell her I must depart that very day. To my surprise and pleasure she was upset.

"But you cannot leave ere I am well!"

"Merryn! Shall you miss me then?"

She looked confused and shook her head. "I do not know," she said.

"I shall be very sorry not to go to Monmouth. I had hoped to enjoy the Christmas festivities with you and to hear the first words you read from a book. But it shall not be. You shall be in Joan's care, and Jack shall visit you."

"When shall you come to Monmouth?" she asked in a small voice.

"I cannot say. Perhaps this summer, if Father is better. Would you like that?"

"Aye," she said. "I would have you return as soon as you may."

I took her hand. "Then shall I try very hard. I daresay I shall not recognize you. No, that is not true, for I would know you anywhere by your eyes. Now I must go. Promise me you shall write to me as soon as you have some words."

"I promise."

Richard Courtenay rode with me from Llanthony, for he planned to return to Oxford. I twisted in my saddle and looked back as the priory melted into the hills.

"Strange it was," I said. "She was distraught to see me go, yet she would not look at me. And when I held her hand, it was as limp as though she were asleep."

"She has many moods, and there is much she thinks which she does not say. Still, she speaks with you now, Harry. Considering her ordeal, I think she does remarkably well."

I looked back again. Only a wisp of smoke against the gray sky betrayed the location of the priory. I said little the rest of the day. By Sixte a cold sleet had begun to pelt us. Above our heads, ice glittered upon bony chestnut trees. Puddles laced with white formed in our path, framing the blood-red leaves that were scattered about. I pulled the hood of my cloak tight about me and carried Merryn's one smile close for warmth.

Never was London so dreary as that winter of my twentieth year. The rain was relentless, with not a snowflake for relief, so that had the entire city been submerged in the Thames it would have been no more sodden. I passed my days in the damp state chambers of Westminster Palace amid flickering candles and scurrying clerks. Father's illness laid him flat upon his back with running bowels and excruciating headaches which at times caused his screams to carom through the gloomy passageways. Seldom did he send for me, nor did I seek him out, but went for advice upon affairs of state to my uncle Beaufort at his house in Holborn. My uncle was resented at court, especially among Arundel's coterie, for ambition so great as Beaufort's could not be hidden. Often in council meetings he clashed with Arundel, and the Archbishop in turn had once humiliated him by marking publicly upon his bastardy. Beaufort was most pleased to act as my counselor, and on several occasions we were able to successfully oppose the machinations of the Archbishop. Arundel was furious at our interference, but given the gravity of my father's condition he had no recourse.

Jack wrote in December to say that Merryn was safe at Monmouth, that Joan had taken to her like a mother hen to a chick, and that a certain Brother Llewellyn from the Grace Dieu Abbey at Troddi had been engaged as a tutor.

"She refuses to learn to dance or to speak English," Jack wrote. "Indeed she is stubborn as any stiff-necked Lancastrian. But she studies Welsh and Latin and can already read the catechism. There is nothing wrong with her mind, to be sure. She forever asks questions about you. Of course Joan never tires of answering her, and I am ill with hearing how at age nine you did save your brother John from drowning in the Wye."

A month later I received a parchment covered with an awkward scrawl.

I read now. I walk with Joan to the river. There is a cat here. Kittens too. Four. When will you come?

I pulled her letter from my shirt that afternoon and showed it to Scrope as we sat drinking at the White Swan in Catte Street. He turned it over in his hands, a puzzled expression upon his face.

"In truth, Harry, is it not a waste of time to teach a wench to read and write? Surely you do not need books when you take her to bed."

I snatched the letter from him. "You misunderstand. She is my ward. I do not force my attentions upon her. As for her lessons, why should she not learn to read? She has a good mind. Jack says so. She wants to learn. You should have seen her eyes light up when I offered her a tutor."

"This much I do understand," Scrope replied. "It is not proper for peasants to be raised above their station. Are you mindful that it is but a few years since rude fellows were pillaging and murdering throughout England?"

"Of course. My grandfather spoke often of the revolt of the peasants. He held some sympathy for them."

"Forgive me, then, but it is such misguided softheartedness which does encourage them to oppose their betters. To teach this wench—"

"Do not speak of her thus."

"—to teach her as though she were a lady is like dressing a jackass in a fine gown and introducing it at court. Even many ladies do not bother with learning. Why do they need it?"

I fought to curb my temper. "To force her into my bed would be a different matter, of course. She is not too base for that."

"Such ones"—he nodded at a buxom whore lolling next to the hearth— "were placed upon this earth to relieve us of our desires. They are good for nothing else save to bring more of their kind into the world."

I pushed away my mug and stood to leave. He grabbed my arm.

"Harry, I speak out of friendship, out of concern for you. If it is known that you thus give airs to a Welsh peasant girl it shall seem a slap in the face to your peers. It can do you no good."

I left him for the bitter cold of a London winter and the solace of my own thoughts.

I was roused one night from a deep sleep by an urgent summons to attend my father. I slipped into a robe.

"Is his sickness worse?" I asked the servant who had summoned me.

"No, your highness, I know nothing save that he is distressed over some news from the west."

"Jesu," I moaned, and followed him to the King's quarters.

I found Tom waiting in the antechamber.

"What is it?" I asked.

"I know no more than you," he replied.

"It must be grave indeed to summon us both."

"Not these days. His judgment is not as it was. Shall we find out?"

Father sat propped against scarlet pillows, his golden hair lank upon his shoulders. His eyes smoldered with contempt at the sight of me, and I knelt before him with a sinking heart.

"Was ever a sovereign so ill served by his own heir?" he lashed out.

"Your grace, I do not know how I have given offense."

"You know not! Glyndwr has relieved Aberystwyth, thanks to your negligence."

"But, it—it is impossible," I stammered. "They were near to surrender."

"Near! But they had not surrendered, had they? And you left your post early, did you not?"

"My lord father, you saw no fault in it at the time."

He waved a twisted hand. "I knew nothing of it. I thought you capable of judging the situation correctly, more fool I. Now Glyndwr has slipped in and provisioned the garrison, and they have driven our troops away. The siege must begin again."

"Father," Tom said, "had I been in Harry's place, I might have done the same thing. We all thought to have heard the last of Glyndwr."

"No!" he cried. "No! Harry has ever been irresponsible. I have borne it too long."

"Your grace," I said, my cheeks burning, "I have tried to serve you. I have done battle for you."

"Enough!" he screamed. His scarred face was contorted and his eyes cold with hatred. "I suffer enough without you here to torment me."

"My father—"

"I want you out of London, Harry. You shall not return until Aberystwyth is mine. Do you hear?"

"I have no gold to raise an army," I protested. "It is the middle of the winter. Perhaps in April—"

"You shall quit London upon the morrow or I shall have you thrown into the Tower. Do you understand?"

I stiffened with shame and nodded. Tom gave me a sideways glance of sympathy.

Father sank back into the pillows. "Tom, you shall send at once to Canterbury for the good Archbishop. I require his services, and yours, until I am able to do more myself."

"It shall be done," Tom said.

Father nodded as though to say, *I knew I might depend upon you*. Without a word of farewell he closed his eyes to sleep. Tom plucked at my sleeve and motioned toward the door. I slipped from the chamber after him. When the door had closed behind us he draped his arm around my shoulders.

"You must not take it to heart," he said.

"How can I not?"

"He is ill. He is not himself."

"Not himself? He is indeed. He has ever hated me."

"It is not so. I know him, Harry, better than you. He mourns that you are not close to him. But this disease, it eats at him. He trusts no one, at times not even me. He is often in pain, and his reason sometimes leaves him. Indeed, you see how it is. This siege at Aberystwyth, it is but a delay. Glyndwr is beaten, thanks to you, and we all know it. Yet he acts as though Glyndwr had laid siege to Westminster itself."

"In the meantime I am banished London and I have no army. What am I to do?"

"Go to Monmouth and wait there. I shall raise some treasure as soon as I can, and then you may proceed."

"There is nothing else for it, I suppose. You have been good in this matter. I am grateful."

"I have feared to lose your love, Harry, for Father does set us one against the other. But this you must know, I would never oppose you or seek to supplant you. I have admired you since we were children, and I pledge you my loyalty now."

He towered over me, three inches taller and broader in the shoulders. We embraced.

"Good my brother," I whispered. "I shall have need of you, for I fear it is not disease which torments our father but the crown that sits beside his bed. You must stand with me when I take it up."

"So I shall. Now get you gone ere morning finds you here."

"Holy Mother of God!" Joan spread her arms wide. "Where have you come from?"

"I wanted to surprise you."

"That you have done," she said as she embraced me. "Let me look at you. Aye, as handsome as ever. Did the London lasses weep to see you go?"

"They were disconsolate." I looked about the hall. "Where is the girl?"

"Up in the solar studying her letters. Brother Llewellyn has just left."

"She does well, then?"

"Aye, so he says. There is a canny one, that girl. And a sweet disposition as well, but only when she takes a mind. She has her moods."

"Has she been a burden for you?"

"No. There is company she is. She wanted taming when first she came. She would not bathe, she gobbled her food, and she stood no correction. But she has been better since Jack Oldcastle left. And she does love her lessons, though I know not why she shall need them."

I climbed the stair to the solar, Joan at my heels. Merryn was so absorbed in her studies that she took no notice of me. My spirits rose at the sight of her. Here was no half-starved urchin. She was still thin, but not gaunt with hunger. Her frock was plain but clean, as was her person, and her brown hair was combed neatly back from her face. She chewed upon her lower lip, intent upon the book before her.

"Hello, Merryn," I said.

She started, then sprang up as though she might flee. No welcome was in her face, but only fear. I smiled to hide my disappointment.

"It pleases me to find you well and at your studies," I said.

She ducked her head and did not reply.

"Have you no greeting for the Prince?" Joan asked. "'Twould be respectful to curtsy to him."

"No, Joan," I said. "I shall not have forced deference from her."

Merryn still stood wary as a cornered doe. I tried again.

"You wrote to me, did you not, and asked when I should come to Monmouth. Well, here I am."

She folded her arms across her chest as though for protection.

"I did not know it would be so soon," she said.

"Nor did I. I left London rather unexpectedly, and in disgrace."

"Oh, Harry, no!" Joan exclaimed.

"Aye." I turned sheepishly to her. "Glyndwr has relieved Aberystwyth and I am held responsible. Now I am threatened with the Tower and banished London until I do take the castle."

Merryn marked this exchange, but I could not tell what she thought of it.

"Shall you be off again?" Joan asked.

"Aye, but not soon. Tom must first raise money for an army. Until then, I am here."

"We shall have a merry time of it then," she said. "But that father of yours, what can he be thinking? If I had him here—"

"You would make him more miserable than does his illness," I said.

I tried to converse further with Merryn, but she persisted in her coldness. I soon gave up and returned to the hall to drink of cup of hot wine.

"I do not understand," I complained. "I thought she would welcome me. Jack wrote that she often asks after me."

"Aye, 'tis true." Joan's heavy brows were knit together. "She has had many questions about you."

"What sort of questions?"

"Angry ones at first. She knew me to be Welsh and wondered how I could serve you. I told how I nursed you as a sickly babe and loved you as my own son. She did seem to soften then. She wondered what sort of child you had been. Were you cruel? What kindnesses had you done others? How did you pass your time? Who were your friends? By my faith, I did think the lass in love with you, so avid was she." She shrugged. "Who can know? At times she wanders far away behind those gray eyes of hers, and the roof might fall

in and she would not know it. Do not let it trouble you. Soon she shall be
wed, and that will be that. Though I shall miss her then. She is good to help
me with my spinning."

We supped that night in near silence. Joan asked after my brothers and
I answered briefly. Merryn sat with eyes downcast and ate little. At times
she did seem to pray, so still she was. I escaped to my bedchamber as soon as
I could, weary from my long journey and Merryn's aloofness. Tired though I
was, I could not sleep but lay rigid upon my back and stared at the canopy
above my bed. Her ingratitude was maddening. She would be dead if not for
me. Certainly she would not be learning to read. How then could she—

I started at the creaking of the door as it slowly opened. Then I relaxed,
for the slight form of a woman was framed by the doorway. Merryn. I closed
my eyes and breathed deeply, feigning sleep. Why had she come? Could
Joan have guessed rightly? Perhaps Merryn's silence was but shyness, perhaps she did indeed love me, and at last had steeled herself to come and tell
me so.

The thought stirred me with unexpected desire. And what was I to
make of that? It had been simple enough to roll a London whore in my bed,
or even a noble mistress like Lady Anne Mortimer. Yet I knew I could not
take this girl save out of love, and I wondered why she should be different.

She stood beside the bed, and her breath came in short gasps as though
she had been running. Her gown rustled as she leaned forward. I waited for
the touch of her hand upon my shoulder and wondered what I would say to
her. But she did not touch me. Several moments passed and I fought the
temptation to open my eyes. Then I heard her move away from the bed and
cross to the hearth. I sat up. Her form was outlined in the glow of the dying
fire. I sprang from the bed and went naked to her. At my approach a long
object slipped from her hand and clattered among the glowing embers. We
stood together and watched as tongues of flame lapped at the long kitchen
knife, blackening its handle.

A spasm of weakness washed over me and I braced my arm against the
warm stone of the hearth to steady myself.

"Were you standing over me with that?"

She nodded slowly, as though dreaming. Still she watched the knife.

"You were anxious for me to return to Monmouth because you wished
to kill me?"

"Aye," she said. The tears upon her cheeks glittered in the firelight as
the knife handle caught and burned.

"Had you plunged the knife in, you could not have wounded me more
deeply," I said. "After all I have done for you—"

"I asked for none of it," she broke in. "You did it to ease your concern
for your soul."

"Enough! You dare seek to slay me and then to judge me?"

She pushed a stray lock of hair from her forehead. "I suppose I shall be executed," she said.

"What mean you?"

"I have tried to slay the Prince of Wales. Is it not an offense punishable by death? I am ready to die. It is what I have expected these many months."

I shivered, for the room was chill. I found a gown and draped it round my shoulders. "Don't be a fool," I said. "Never could I put you to death."

"What does your father, the King, when someone tries to kill him?"

"The person is beheaded."

"And other kings, what have they done in such cases?"

"Why these questions?"

"Because I wish to know why you will not kill me."

"Merryn, it is very late, and I have not slept. After what has passed this night, I know not if I can have you about me. It is time to seek a husband for you, but we shall speak of it on the morrow. I believe Joan has someone in mind. Perhaps you could go at once."

"No!" She stamped her foot. "You have not answered me."

I ran my fingers through my hair. "Merryn—"

"No! If you will not speak then I have something to say. I, too, have refused to shed blood. I could have stabbed you where you lay, but I did not. Do you not wonder why? It was because I do not hate you any more. I yet mourn for my people, and I despise what you have done in Wales. But I do not hate you. 'Twas easy to loathe you when you were away. But when I held the knife ready I recalled your kindness to me, and your laughter. I remembered how you did harp for me. And so it was only the hatred which died. I do pray it is gone forever."

More than anything in this world I longed to kneel beside her, to lay my head in her lap and to weep. But I found myself shaking my head and saying, "I cannot trust you, Merryn. Not now."

"And you will not answer my question?"

"There is no answer."

She walked to the door, then stopped.

"Do you know what Joan says of you? She says you are too good to be a king. She fears your goodness shall be the death of you. And she says you mistrust your own goodness for that very reason. I am trying to understand. Perhaps she is right. It is no wonder. Joan and Brother Llewellyn have taught me a little about the ways of kings. I know not how you bear it."

Then she was gone.

The last cinder grew cold upon the hearth. I bent and felt through the ashes for the knife. The charred handle came away easily in my hand and I tossed it aside. I ran my finger along the blade and sought to hone my spirit as keen as the metal.

*   *   *

I avoided Merryn for two days by rising early and riding to the hunt, and I supped alone in my chamber upon my return. I left to Joan the inquiries after a suitable husband. On the second night she carried my food to me and told me of her success.

"I spoke with Lloyd ap Lloyd at market this day," she reported. "He is bailiff of your lands over Monnow, a sturdy fellow."

"Aye, I know the man."

"He is but four and twenty, and he has lost his wife to a fever, poor lass. She left him two babes with none to mother them. He would be most happy to come speak to you of Merryn."

She saw that I hesitated.

"William Bruer speaks highly of him," she said. "He shall keep a roof over her head and food in her belly."

"Will he beat her, do you think?"

"No more than most would. A box of the ears might do her good when she pouts. I would not see her go, Harry. I have taken to her. But if go she must, he is a good man."

"I shall speak with her tomorrow."

When we sat down to break our fast the following morning, Merryn did not appear, nor could Joan find her about the keep.

"I've a mind to seek her in the loft above the stable," she said. "She often goes there to fondle the kittens. Shall I fetch her to you?"

"No. I had thought to go hawking this morning. I shall speak to her on my way."

I climbed the rickety ladder to the loft and found Merryn sprawled upon her belly in the sweet hay, teasing a gray kitten with a straw. She sat up at once and brushed the front of her dress.

"You were not at breakfast," I said.

"You were not at breakfast for two days past," she replied.

"That is no concern of yours. I ask after you because I am responsible for you."

I hoisted myself through the opening, sat with my legs dangling and surveyed the loft.

"I have not been here since I was a boy," I said, "yet I used to play here often."

"It is strange to see you here. I know not what to make of you. Sometimes you do not seem like a prince at all. But then you can also be so arrogant I think you a very tyrant."

"Do you? Well, you need not puzzle over me much longer. Joan has found you a husband."

She blanched.

"He is a good man," I continued. "I know him, a bailiff over Monnow. He is Welsh. That should please you well."

She clutched the kitten to her breast. "It is sudden," she whispered.

"Aye, but not unexpected. We have spoken of it."

"I do not know him," she said.

"He is well spoken of. 'Tis all you need to know. Many wives do not know their husbands until they are betrothed. It was so with my own father and mother."

She began to weep.

"God's blood," I muttered. "You need not take on so. If you dread to cease with your lessons you need not fear. I shall still send Brother Llewellyn to you."

"If I do not wish to wed this man, will you force me?" she sobbed.

I studied my fingernails.

"No," I said at last. "I have not the heart for such a thing. But I urge you not to refuse. 'Twould be foolish."

"Then one thing more I would know. Do you want me to marry him?"

"Merryn, I shall not play games with you. Have I not said it already? It would be best—"

"Not what is best, Harry, but what you want!"

She had not called me by name since that day in the forest long ago.

"You were so gentle before," she continued tearfully. "It was I who was filled with hate. Now you are cold, and it is because of what I have done to you. Oh, Harry, I would not leave until it is made right. You cannot wish me to leave, can you?"

I saw the future then, saw what must be, and I was strangely content with it.

"No. No, I do not wish you to leave."

"Then I shall not go."

We regarded one another across the loft for a very long time.

"I am off to hawk," I said, bestirring myself at last.

"Oh."

"Would you care to come with me?"

"I cannot ride."

"Of course. It had slipped my mind."

I walked to the slit in the wall which served for a window. The March day had dawned warm and clear, a harbinger of spring, and wind ruffled the surface of the green Monnow below us.

"It is a glorious day," I said, "far too fine for studies. Would you like to learn to ride?"

Her mouth formed a tiny o. "Would you teach me? What of your hawking?"

"I can hawk another day. Come, you must choose a mount."

She nearly fell down the ladder, so excited she was.

"Here are two mares and a gelding. Any would be gentle enough. Which do you like?"

She rubbed the neck of a small gray mare. "I have ever liked this one. She does seem glad to see me when I come here."

"Ah, so you are no stranger to the stable?"

"I come here whenever I have something to ponder." She smiled. "'Tis an old habit of mine. I used to talk to my sheep upon the Honddu."

"My confidant was a horse named Morgause."

"I know it. Joan told me."

"Has Joan told you all the secrets of my life?"

"Nearly all of them." She ducked her head shyly. "What is this horse named?"

"Your horse is named Fille."

"My horse! My very own?"

"Your very own."

"Harry, how shall I thank you? Fille! What a funny name."

"'Tis French for 'girl.'"

"And do you speak French?"

"Un peu, mais je ne parle pas bien."

"It sounds lovely. I should like to learn it."

"Someday, perhaps, but first you must learn English."

She made a wry face.

"No pouting," I said. "If you are to stay here you will want to know what is going on around you. English is spoken often here, for many who visit do not have Welsh."

"They should learn."

I pulled her hair and grinned. "Finally I have met someone more stubborn than myself. Run to Joan and ask for some food to carry with us into the hills. I shall see to the horses."

She skipped away.

"And dress warmly," I called after her. "The wind has a bite."

I went to rouse the stable boy.

We forded the Wye and rode toward the foot of the Kymin. Merryn was perched upon a pillion behind me, her arms wrapped tightly about my waist. Fille followed after us, her reins tied to my saddle. It was one of those days when the air is as glass and the wind tousles the grass and rouses the land to new life.

"Soon the daffodils shall be out," I said.

"Oh, I do love them, and the columbine as well."

"Spring is my favorite time of the year. After the cold and damp of winter, the warm sun is that much more pleasant."

"It is a fine time for lambs as well. They are still on the teat and ever so much fun."

We stopped in a wide meadow which had lain fallow and was free of stubble.

"You shall have a soft landing here," I said.

"Do you expect me to fall?"

"You may. Are you afraid?"

"Only a little."

I helped her onto Fille's broad back. She had refused to use a sidesaddle and so her coarse woolen skirt was drawn up above her knees to reveal crimson stockings.

"Your legs shall keep the crows away."

"Harry! Do not mock me."

"Here. Keep your heels down as I have told you. I shall walk beside you."

The ground oozed as we paced the thawing meadow. Fille broke into a trot and Merryn slid sideways upon the saddle.

"It hurts my bottom," she cried as Fille's uneven gait jolted her.

"Grip with your knees and move with her," I said.

She managed to right herself, though she yet clutched the saddle as if her life depended upon it.

"Good! Good!" I had been running alongside but now I stopped and watched Fille weave her awkward way across the meadow. Merryn slipped again and threw her arms around Fille's neck. The horse slowed to a walk.

"Good horse," I called. "She is helping you."

Merryn sat up again.

"Use the reins to turn her. Bring her back."

Fille came round and lumbered back toward me. Merryn bobbed up and down, her elbows flailing and her hair streaming behind her.

"I am riding her!"

"So you are!" I caught the reins as they passed me.

"Oh, Harry, do not stop us now. I have just got the trick of it."

I slapped Fille's rump and sent them off again. Round and round they went for well over an hour while I sat upon a flat stone and admired them. At last I stopped them.

"You shall be too sore to walk if you ride much longer," I said. "Besides, I am famished. Let us tie the horses here, climb to the top of the Kymin, and eat our dinner."

"Help me down then. Slowly!"

Gingerly she slid from Fille's back, a grimace upon her face.

"Are you able to climb or must I carry you?"

"Of course I can climb. I am not one of your delicate ladies to moan at the least exertion."

We found my old path, which wound its way up the Kymin's slope past a stand of ash and birch that rubbed their branches together and creaked in the wind.

"The Kymin is enchanted," I told Merryn as we climbed. "Joan says that when the moon is full and the night is as clear as day, the fairies dance upon the top of the Kymin."

"Do they live here?"

"Oh, I am sure of it. When I was a boy, I found a rock of bewitching shape which I thought must guard the entrance to a fairy lair. When I sought to move it, it was too heavy, of course."

"Perhaps you might move it now."

"I doubt it. And I would rather not try. Such matters are best left to dream upon, else they lose their magic."

The hill seemed to breathe, to sigh as we clambered higher. Beneath last summer's mat of withered grass, new seeds of flower and herb would be bursting unseen with that commotion which would impel them to seek the sunlight. The hill smelled ripe with new life. The crest of the Kymin commanded an unsurpassed view. The silver rivers, Wye and Monnow, draped themselves over patches of meadowland and wrapped tiny Monmouth in their comforting arms. Past Monmouth the little hills swelled, brown bowls turned upside down. And far beyond, at the edge of the earth, a wall of mountains reared up, brooding, impenetrable. Massive banks of clouds sat upon the peaks, and pink-tinged mist melted into stone. The Black Mountains of Wales.

"I do love this land," I said, "far beyond any other."

"You love Wales so much? Better than England?"

"Aye. Though I do love England well. But this land, it is in my blood. It is a part of me." I turned from the view. "Well, shall we see what bounty Joan has provided?"

It was bounty indeed—cold venison pies, yellow cheese, dried apples, and a suet pudding. We sat upon the ground to enjoy our feast with Monmouth and her valley spread before us. Merryn broke off a bit of cheese and popped it into her mouth.

"Why did you bring me here?" she asked.

"More questions," I moaned.

"I ask only because it seems a special place to you. I daresay you do not share it with many."

"With no one," I conceded. "I only come here alone."

"Then am I honored."

"I only wished to coax some smiles from you. If you are to remain at

Monmouth, we two must learn to get along. We cannot ever be at one another's throats."

"We shall get along now, I am sure of it. Now I can be happy here. I hated Monmouth when first I came. I was frightened and overborne with grief. I still grieve, yet I am happy. Is it not strange? Perhaps it is because we have forgiven one another."

I chewed my pie in uneasy silence and wondered why she must ever dwell upon the wrongs done her. Merryn gazed at the valley.

"Which way is the Honddu?" she asked.

I pointed toward the northwest.

"Far beyond where the Monnow bends into the mist," I said.

"So very far." She looked at me. "Harry, I must tell you how it was that I sought to slay you."

"It is an unpleasant subject. I would as soon put it from my mind."

"No. It yet lies between us and must be dealt with. It was because of a dream I had when I was ill. A nightmare. My mam came to me. A ghost she was. She named Harry Monmouth the murderer of my father and brothers. She said I must slay you. In her hands she held a long curved knife, and she bade me take it. I did try to refuse it. I told her you had once saved my life, that I could not slay you. But she would not hear it, and she forced the knife into my hands. She said my father would not know eternal rest until he had been avenged. Then she vanished. When I awoke, I realized she was truly dead, that all I had loved was lost to me. And then I hated you and I determined to do her bidding, and afterward to join my loved ones in death."

She pushed the windswept brown hair from her face.

"Strange it was," she said. "When I stood by your bed ready to strike, it was not my mam's shade which came to me. It was a boy I saw, a boy I met in the forest who warned me of soldiers. I did not forget you, Harry, not even your name. 'Twas my illness and grief which kept me from knowing you. I dreamt of you often while I tended my sheep. I did not then know you for a prince, but a prince I named you. You were so handsome, so gallant. I liked to imagine that the soldiers had come upon us there in the wood, and you had fought them off and swept me away to safety upon your charger."

"'Twould have been quite a feat, since I was but fourteen."

"Indeed. Yet I was but a child, and such dreams do children have."

She blushed then, her eyes downcast.

"Am I too forward in this?" she murmured. "You must tell me if it is so."

"No, you are not." I rushed to assure her. "I had dreams of my own. When the weight of my rank did threaten to overwhelm me, I remembered what you had said, that you did not hate me. That alone gave me hope."

"Hope of what?"

"Hope that I was not yet beyond gentleness, not yet beyond love," I said painfully. "Two nights ago, in my chamber, you said again that you did not hate me, yet you despised what I had done. Well, so do I despise it. It does seem to me that princes are loathsome creatures who deal only in pain and death. Yet I am a prince, may God save me."

"Why must it be that way for you? Can you not be different?"

"I do try. I am different in some ways and they detest me for it, my father and the others of our rank. Yet I am not different enough, for you see what I have wrought in Wales. More and more, I fear it is beyond me. My choices shrivel. It is the way of the world, the way of power, and I cannot fight it."

"It is the way of the world to hate," she said, "yet we two do not. It is the way of the world to behead any who would kill a prince. Yet is my head upon my shoulders. You must keep trying, Harry; you must not give in. God shall honor your struggle. And even should you fail, God is good. God shall not turn from you."

"Good, aye, but also just. How do you know He shall not damn me?"

"I know, that is all. Now you must show me the fairy stone."

She stood and brushed the crumbs from her cloak. Her words still held me spellbound.

"You did not learn such sentiments from the monks of Llanthony, by my faith. If only you speak truly—"

She laughed and tugged at my arm to pull me up. "'Tis past time for serious matters. I must know where the fairies live."

We wound our way around the crown of the hill to the outcropping of stone that thrust its turrets skyward. Merryn clapped her hands in delight.

"The stone is itself a castle!"

"Aye, and here is the gate, and here the keep," I pointed out. "And beneath is a secret passage, an enchanted passage. If a mere mortal were able to thrust even a finger beneath this stone, he would be a slave of the fairies forever."

"And did the fairies themselves carve this castle?"

"They did, and they chose this stone because better than any it does match the gray in Merryn's eyes."

Far below us tolled the Angelus of St. Mary's.

"I love you, Merryn."

She stood quite still. "I love you, Harry."

I leaned forward and kissed her ever so briefly, our lips clinging gently as a butterfly greets a blossom. Then I took her in my arms and set my mouth firmly on hers. Her lips parted and I tasted upon her tongue the piquant spices of Cathay. Her fingers caressed the nape of my neck. Our cloaks billowed in the wind and enveloped us, the earth rose and fell beneath our feet. I showered kisses upon her hair, her forehead, her neck. Reaching inside her cloak I cupped my hand over one small breast and felt the warmth of her skin through the wool of her dress. I kissed her again, harder now as my passion rose. Her breath came in gasps.

"Harry," she murmured, "I have never felt this. Never."

"Have you known a man before?"

"No. I am a maid."

I knew that her longing matched my own, that I could take her if I wished, there beside the enchanted castle. Yet was I constrained. I wrapped her in my arms, held her tightly to my chest, and stroked her hair.

"Merryn, my desire for you does torment me," I managed to say. "Yet stronger still is my fear of hurting you. I am afraid you are not yet ready."

"My longing tells me that I am. And I trust you would be gentle."

"'Tis more than that." I recalled Scrope's rebuke in London. "Our love shall be opposed. It shall not be understood. We will be scorned and mocked. You must see, for a prince to love a shepherdess—"

She searched my face. "Does it matter to you?"

"It matters not to me. But you must know this as well. It is unlawful for English and Welsh to intermarry, even if our station did permit it. As a king, I must be wed some day, to get an heir for England. I could never marry you, else we would both lose our lives. On the other hand, I could not take you as my lover now with thoughts of casting you off later. I have done so with other women, yet I could never treat you so. I have loved no woman as I love you, and I would bind myself to you for as long as we both may live. But that binding can never be marriage. You must accept that ere you give yourself to me."

When she did not answer, the fear mounted in me.

"It may be you cannot accept such conditions," I said. "I pray it does not alter your love for me. I would be plainspoken with you. I have caused you much pain, and I would not willingly do so again. You have forgiven me once. Can you do it again and again?"

She touched my cheek. "I love you still, Harry Monmouth, and even more that you do curb your passion out of concern for me. Yet are you right, for I must think on this. I must consider what it is to love a king. I, too, would pledge myself in faithfulness. This is all so sudden; it blazes too hotly for clearness of judgment. Our love promises to be perilous and hurtful, and we must both think on it."

Reluctantly we parted.

"When it is time," she said, "we shall know."

Our progress down the Kymin was slow, for Merryn's backside had grown stiff and sore from her ride upon Fille. When we reached the horses, she held back.

"I fear I cannot straddle a horse," she said. "I shall walk beside you."

"'Tis well we did not make love," I said. "You could not have borne it."

She swatted me in feigned anger. "Fie on you, Harry!"

I laughed and mounted my horse. "Come sit sidesaddle before me and you shall be comfortable as may be."

She did as I bade and was soon snuggled warmly in my arms.

"I could ride across the world in this manner," she said against my chest.

As we traversed the golden meadows which bounded the Wye I burst into song.

"Summer is a-coming in,
Loud sing cuckoo!
Bloweth seed and groweth weed
and springs the wood anew.
Sing cuckoo!"

The cuckoos chanted back in gay profusion.

Merryn ate her supper that night perched upon a plump purple pillow. Merrily she described to Joan our outing, while Joan watched me shrewdly with a glint in her eyes. Once I winked at her, but she would not be put off.

"Well," she said, "it would seem there shall be no match with Lloyd ap Lloyd. Are you lovers?"

Merryn's face flushed crimson. I took her hand protectively.

"We should not expect to keep such a thing from Joan," I said. "It is not possible."

"Not possible where you are concerned, young Harry!" Joan exclaimed. "Never could you keep a secret from me. So then, you are lovers."

"We have declared our love," I said, "but we are not yet lovers. We do not wish to act rashly, so we shall remain continent until we can give ourselves without reserve."

"Continent!" Joan scoffed. "You've not been continent since boyhood. Indeed, I told the girl of it, did I not, Merryn?"

Merryn nodded miserably.

"Your bed was not empty in London this winter past, was it?" Joan continued. "'Twas too cold to sleep alone, with every wench in London, highborn and baseborn, clamoring for your bed."

"It is true," I admitted. "Yet do I now pledge continence."

"Humph!" Joan sopped her bread in rich brown gravy and shoved the morsel into her mouth. "Do you believe that, my lass?"

"Aye," Merryn said.

Joan pointed a greasy finger at me. "You see how she trusts you, Harry? She is not a tavern wench to be used, nor a high-born Lady Anne lusting for a pleasant dalliance." Her fat cheeks puffed out even farther. "I have no daughter, Harry, and I have grown fond of this lass. I shall not have her hurt, not even by you, though the Holy Mother knows I would give you sun and moon if I might."

"I love him, Joan," Merryn protested. "It is small risk to me that he might hurt me."

"And you, Harry?" Joan demanded. "Do you love the girl?"

"I love her. It is different than with the others, you must see that. I love her."

Joan sat back, her big hands upon the table. "And what shall your father say?"

"He shall be furious," I acknowledged.

"And you, Merryn, will you follow Harry to London town, far from the green hills, to face the scorn of the English? Will you make Harry's way more difficult by bringing upon him the censure of his peers?"

Merryn turned an anguished face to me.

"Upon such must we deliberate," I said. "It is why we wait."

"It is much to think upon," said Joan.

"Indeed. Yet despite your warnings I think you are not displeased with us."

A tear coursed its way down her cheek. "I have prayed for this," she said. "Yet now that it is come, I fear this is not the last tear I shall shed over the pair of you."

Merryn went to her, but Joan shooed her away.

"Off with you. I am a silly old woman. You and Harry should be together now. Up to the solar with you, there is a fire all ready. I shall send you some hot wine."

We climbed the stair as quickly as Merryn's aching legs allowed and fell into one another's arms.

"Did her words frighten you?" I asked.

"Aye. I would not put you in danger, my Harry."

"Nor would I take you from your Wales. Yet such must we face."

I kissed her and buried my face in her hair. The tang of the outdoors clung to her.

"Love without fear does seem to be impossible," I said, "for when two people love, there is everything to lose."

Joan came with a sparkling claret and left at once.

"Will you sit before the fire?" I asked as I poured the wine.

"I think I must stand."

"You should ride again tomorrow." I laughed at her pained expression. "It is the only way to become used to it."

She raised her glass. "Perhaps if I am well fortified with this I shall not feel the pain."

"A toast then to our next riding lesson."

"What is a toast?"

"Ah, I forget much is new to you. A toast is a gesture of goodwill made over a full cup." I lifted my glass. "To Fille, that she may run smoothly, and to us. God be with us, and may Our Lady guard our love."

We drank and then we kissed, and I savored the wine upon her lips. We drank again. Merryn, being unused to strong drink, was soon lightheaded.

"Harry," she said, "you have not named me beautiful. Am I beautiful?"

I observed her for a moment. She did not wear her hair upon her head as did ladies, and even tradesmen's wives, but let it fall loose and tangled about her shoulders. She was pretty, no doubt. But somehow her features were irregular and did not admit to beauty. The large oval eyes were too wide-set, perhaps, or the shape of the nose not just right.

"No," I said. "You are not beautiful."

She was crestfallen.

"You are pretty," I assured her, "but not beautiful. You are the most desirable woman I have ever known."

I tried to kiss her again but she would have none of it.

"This Lady Anne of whom Joan spoke, is she beautiful?"

"Aye. She is one of the most beautiful women in England. She is petite and fair and full of figure. Her skin is like cream."

"I am thin and my skin is brown as a deer's hide," she said ruefully.

"So it is."

"How can you desire me then, when you have known such beauty? Be patient with me, Harry, for when Joan speaks of ladies and how they admire you, my heart does turn over. I could not face them unless I know what you favor in me."

"Had I a looking glass, I would hold it before you and show you gray eyes that have haunted my sleep. I would show you a generous mouth which I love to kiss, and a chin fit for raising in proud defiance. I would show you a face both strong and gentle, and intelligent as well. It is a face to grow old with, a face I shall love when your hair is white and your skin worn and wrinkled. Is that enough?"

"Aye."

"Indeed, as Joan says, I have bedded many women. Long have I searched for love. Never did I find it until now. You must believe that."

"I do believe it, with all my heart."

We rode together the next day and every day thereafter until Merryn could handle Fille with ease. Blissful hours we spent casting for salmon in the Wye, or lying in the tall rushes while flotillas of imperious swans sailed by. Often we would carry with us a flask of wine and a book, the love poems of Dafydd ap Gwilym perhaps, or something in the English tongue, which Merryn had finally consented to learn. For more than a month we spent each afternoon in this fashion, drunk with wine and wildflowers, lying upon our backs, smothered by the scents of spring, of new grass and blossoms, while the white puffs of clouds twirled in the sky. At night we went each to our own beds, where I would toss and turn and pound my pillow for want of her.

Late in April came the call I had come to dread. Raulyn arrived from London with word from Tom: an army was assembling at Hereford for the taking of Aberystwyth. Father wished me to join it at once and proceed with all haste to the siege. The castle must be mine by winter.

I heard these tidings in the morning while Merryn was with her tutor. Anxiously I paced the hall until she came bouncing down the stair from the solar. Her footfalls echoed as she ran to me and flung her arms around my neck.

"I love you," she said in English, then lapsed into excited Welsh. "You must hear what Brother Llewellyn says. He says soon I shall not need him for Welsh, for I can read 'most anything in it. If only my Latin and English improve I shall be a scholar, shall I not? Am I not clever?"

"You are indeed." I smiled with great effort.

"What is wrong, Harry? Have I displeased you?"

"No. I have received bad tidings, though they are not unexpected."

"What tidings?"

"Orders from the King my father to proceed with the siege of Aberystwyth."

She stepped back as though I had struck her. "You shall not go?"

"Merryn, I must. Defiance would send me to the Tower. This parting is as hard for me as for you. Perhaps it shall not be so long."

"You cannot go! You cannot! Not if you love me!"

"Merryn—" I touched her shoulder.

"No!" She pulled away. "Do not tell me you go against my people."

"It is nearly over! Only this castle and there shall be peace in Wales."

"More Welshmen shall die. How can you feign love for me and do this thing?"

Her words cut to my heart. "My love is not feigned," I whispered. "I have no choice in this."

"No choice? How can you say it? You have every choice. No one forces the sword into your hand; you take it up yourself. You sing like an angel, and harp most prettily, and shower me with kisses, and woo me with gentle caresses. Why must you also war? Harry, it shall destroy you."

"Why do you berate me now? You have known what part I played in Wales. You forgave me. Or so you said."

"I thought you to be sorry. I thought you would not do it again. I dared to think you had changed out of love for me. But you have not changed! You are the same!"

I fell back before her onslaught. "You must understand," I said. "I have tried to change. There is only so much I can do. It is the way of the world."

"That is no excuse. It is a coward's reason."

Bitter gall choked me until I near retched. "It is as I feared," I said. "How could I have been such a fool as to trust you? I did flatter myself that you loved me. Now I see you have played me false, as has every woman. You care not for me, but only teased me with your withheld charms that you might keep me from Aberystwyth. Well, it did not work. You shall be sorry now you did not use the knife."

She slapped me hard upon the cheek.

"You are vile," she said. "I hope you never return."

Then she was gone.

I journeyed to Aberystwyth in cold silence, speaking to no one save to give orders. Once there I lost myself in the details of the siege, the setting of the machines, the digging of trenches, the provisioning of my men, and the governing of the countryside. Glyndwr, I learned to my relief, had slipped out of the castle at word of my approach, probably bound for the fastness of Snowden. There may he rot, I thought.

After some weeks had passed I conquered my anger, swallowed my pride, and wrote to Merryn, asking forgiveness for my harsh words and declaring anew my love for her. Anxiously I awaited the reply that never came.

In July I received a letter from Joan, dictated to Brother Llewellyn. Merryn had left Monmouth castle and attached herself to Brother Llewellyn's abbey of Grace Dieu, where she served with hard labor, laundering habits and cooking meals. Brother Llewellyn thought her inclined to take orders herself in some nunnery, for when not working she could ever be found in prayer.

> My Harry, I am so sorry [wrote Joan]. I pleaded with her, but she would not stay, nor would she write to you. She has been terribly hurt, and so, I'll warrant, have you. I beg you, when you have made a finish at Aberystwyth, go not straight to London but first come here. Perhaps the sight of you shall sway her, and wounds be healed. I shed many tears for you both, my dear ones, my children. Perhaps it did blossom too quickly, this love of yours, like the flowers that bloom too early in spring and are taken by frost.

I ripped the letter in half. Indeed I shall go to London, I thought, and I went about removing from my mind all memories of the gray-eyed girl. No more did she visit my dreams.

Late in September, not long past my twenty-first birthday, the Welsh garrison at Aberystwyth surrendered. Each Welshman was pardoned and sent to his home. Only Harlech remained to the rebels, and it was soon to fall to

Lord Talbot. I might have felt some satisfaction. After years of being dragged along on the pointless chevachees of Henry Percy and my father, I had pursued Glyndwr in my own way and I had been proved right. The English had had no success until I gained the command; were it not for me, marcher lord and rebel would yet be spilling blood. So I told myself. These self-congratulations did not raise my spirits. I felt instead a vast emptiness. The task in Wales was complete, aye, but the land I loved lay in ruins. Before me stretched years in London, years spent in dreary council chambers watching my father die and waiting for the crown to pass to me. Lonely years. Jack Oldcastle was now wed to a Lady Joan Cobham, a wealthy widow, and settled in to manage her Herefordshire estates. Richard Courtenay was occupied with his duties in Oxford. Raulyn would soon return to his home in Cumberland. Scrope I depended upon, but I had not found the heart to love him. Merryn—

The thought of her came to me unbidden, unwelcome. It was nearly a year since I found her starving beside the Honddu, six months since I had last set eyes on her. With what harsh words had she dismissed me then? "I hope you never return!" Rebellion rose within me. Why should I let her keep me from Monmouth, from Joan's company? I would not go yet to London but would seek the girl and wish her well in her search for a nunnery, that she would know I cared not tuppence for her.

My soldiers I gave leave to return to their homes, and they slipped away in small bands when we had crossed the mountainous backbone of Powys. By the time I reached the Troddi, I had with me Raulyn de Brayllesford and eight men-at-arms. I judged any danger to be slight, and we rode lightly armed, clad only in mail shirts beneath our tunics. Darkness caught us when we were yet a few miles from Monmouth. Grace Dieu Abbey was hard by upon Troddi, and Raulyn urged me to stop there the night. The men would be uneasy, he said, for night is the province of the Devil and of brigands. I would have none of it, for I feared to come upon Merryn so suddenly. We pressed on.

No sooner were we past Grace Dieu than I regretted my decision. The knowledge that Merryn was so close, perhaps preparing for bed at that very moment, left me trembling. Had I thought myself done with her? No, it was but a ruse to ease our separation. Now I yearned with sweet pain to behold her once more. Send her blithely to a nunnery? Rather would I beg her to return to Monmouth and hope that the sight of me might move her even as the merest hint of her had humbled me. Too late now to turn back, but on the morrow I would ride straightway to Grace Dieu and confront her. I knew myself to be persuasive. Might I not melt her heart as before, woo her with bright passion and ardent kisses?

Suppose she were already a nun? The thought of it caused me to sit

straight upon my horse. Suppose she had been taken ill? Perhaps her hatred
of me was unsurmountable. At first I did not understand when the man
riding ahead of me screamed and pitched forward in his saddle. His frightened horse balked in the midst of the narrow track through a black wood.
The stricken man slipped to the ground. A shaft of moonlight glittered upon
the arrow which protruded from between his shoulder blades.

"To cover!" Raulyn cried. "Into the trees!"

I had just pulled my horse's head around when a figure hurtled toward
me from behind a tree trunk. A dagger flashed. I thrust out my arm and
twisted in the saddle. The man clutched at me, clung to my waist, and flailed
with his knife. The blade struck my mailed left shoulder, glanced off, and
sliced deep into the unprotected flesh of my upper arm. I grasped my
assailant by the throat with my good right arm ere he could strike again. I
squeezed. He loosened his hold upon me, and I pushed him away. My horse
whinnied and reared up, throwing me sideways. The surprise attack had
already loosened my grip upon the saddle. Now, as I sought to steady
myself, my weight was thrown upon my left arm. I nearly swooned from the
pain. My left hand, wet with blood, slipped upon the saddle. The stallion
reared again upon his hindquarters. Somehow I disengaged my boots from
the stirrups as I fell. The weight of my mail shirt carried me headlong; I
heard the dull thud as my head struck the ground.

I opened my eyes to darkness and quiet. In vain I tried to recall where I was.
White pain ran across my arm. I attempted to raise my head, but the agony
of the effort brought a low moan which seemed to come from somewhere
outside me.

"God save your highness, as He seems to have done," said a faraway
voice.

"Who is it?"

"It is Raulyn, your highness."

"Raulyn? What has happened?"

"We came under surprise attack. I have sent Alain spurring to Monmouth in search of aid, but it shall not be necessary, I think. We have driven
them off. There were not so many as first it seemed."

"Alain? What did you say of him?"

"He has gone to Monmouth," Raulyn repeated. "We lost Dickon, taken
by an arrow. Of all others, only your highness was wounded. You lay senseless for a time, and we feared you beyond help. You know not what relief it is
to hear you speak."

"Help me to sit up."

They raised me cautiously. My head seemed to weigh a great deal more
than it should, and the ground whirled beneath me. My mouth tasted of
metal.

"Give me a drink," I said.

I sipped water, then a bit of wine.

"Does rebellion yet live in Wales?" I asked.

"I think not," Raulyn answered. "These were but brigands, and desperate for food from what I could see. I believe they misjudged our strength."

"What are my wounds?"

"You have a cut on your head, but I do not think your skull is cracked. There are no broken bones. You took a dagger in the arm, and we have dressed the wound. We shall take you to Monmouth as soon as it is light. Until then you should rest."

I needed no persuasion, for I could scarce keep my eyes open. I lay upon my back and was soon asleep.

Ten men of the garrison of Monmouth came to us before dawn. The commotion of their arrival woke me, and with Raulyn's help I rose to receive them.

"This is a welcome sight!" Their captain, William Bruer, greeted me. "That fool of an Alain has frightened us all, for he named you dead."

"Dead!"

"Aye. 'The Prince is sore wounded unto death.' Those were his very words. We could scarcely learn your whereabouts, so wrought up he was. The ninny! He has all Monmouth in mourning and the bells tolling. For myself, I would not send to your father until I knew the truth."

"Then Joan does fear me dead?"

"Aye, she has been weeping and wailing. But it is the girl who is most distraught."

"The girl?"

"Aye. The Welsh lass. She had come from Troddi to stay the night with Joan. When Alain came with the news she ran straight to me, for I was ever a favorite of hers, I know not why. Grabbed me, she did, tore at my cloak. 'William!' she cried, 'he cannot be dead! Promise you shall bring him back safely.' 'I know not how it stands, lass.' So I said to her. I cannot stand to see a woman take on."

I was lightheaded again, but now with joy. She loves me, I sang to myself. She loves me.

"Took to calling upon our Lord, she did. 'Please, Jesu, don't let him be dead!' At last Joan takes hold of her and smacks her and carts her off into the hall. Broke my heart, it did. Oh, but when they see you! Though you do look a sight, all bruised and bloody."

He spread his lips over bare gums and I smiled back.

"Your words renew my strength," I said, "more than you know. Even now morning breaks upon us. Shall we be gone?"

"Are you fit to ride?" asked Raulyn.

"Indeed, I am weak, yet I believe I can sit a horse if we go slowly. Help me up."

We reached Monmouth well after Sixte, for we stopped often that I might husband my strength. When we clattered across the Monnow bridge, the bells of the town leaped in a tumult of thanksgiving. The narrow street had filled with good folk who cheered and raised their caps as I passed. Their faces, familiar since childhood, floated before me: Clyd, the cobbler, Ianto, the weaver of warm woolen caps, and old Angharad, who had plied me with oat cakes as thanks for carrying her firewood. Near the smithy I spied the mother of Rhys, he of the red hair who had disappeared with Glyndwr long ago. She waved her kerchief, and I blew her a kiss.

We topped the hill and there was the castle, its gateway yawning a welcome. Joan I saw at once, bouncing up and down, tears coursing down her cheeks despite her broad smile. I slid from my horse with the steadying aid of Raulyn, and then she had me in her ample embrace.

"Mind my arm!" I both laughed and winced.

"Oh!" was all she could say at first. "Oh!" Then, "It is a fool's trick to travel at night, Harry, a fool's trick."

"Can you do naught but scold me? I had thought to be spoiled instead."

"Do not mock me, Harry Monmouth, for you have frighted twenty years from my life. That fool Alain! I shall flay him alive when next I see him."

"Poor Alain!" I looked around the castle ward, but Merryn was nowhere to be seen. My heart sank.

"She is not here," Joan said, reading my thoughts.

"So I see."

"Harry, heed me well. She has been out of her mind with grief. No words of mine could comfort her. She loves you still."

"Where is she then? Why does she not greet me?"

"When she heard you were yet alive, she rejoiced, as did we all. But she feared to face you. Before you went to Aberystwyth, she called down evil upon you, and she blames herself for what has happened. She thinks you cannot love her now, after all the hurt that is between you. She waits secluded for word that you are safely arrived, and then she shall doubtless slip away."

"She must not leave again!"

"Then tell her so."

"Where shall I find her?"

"I know not where she is. You must think which place would give her solace."

The chapel? I wondered. The loft? Perhaps. But first I would try Fille's stall. Slowly I walked across the ward, swaying once or twice. The stable was bustling with activity as the garrison tended their mounts. I passed on to the far end where Fille stood. She snickered as I came closer. Next to her, arms wrapped around her neck, face buried in her gray mane, was Merryn.

She did not note my approach because of the commotion around us. I slipped into the stall beside her and touched her tousled hair.

"Hello, Merryn."

She raised her head. Even in the stable's darkness I could see the anguish upon her face. Her wide eyes took in the bloodied bandages upon my arm and head, my garments stained and torn.

"When I said I wished you would never return, I did not mean it." Her voice caught. "Truly I did not."

"When you did not answer my letter, when Joan wrote to say you were gone . . ." I searched for words. "I thought I had lost all I ever knew of love."

"And when I thought you dead, I thought my own life ended."

I put my arm around her and she nestled against me.

"Oh, Harry, can we two truly love one another? We do rend each other's very souls. I cannot banish my care of Wales for your sake, nor you relinquish your duties for mine, it seems. 'Twould be easiest if we did part."

"Easiest? No, 'twould be impossible. Merryn, there is a coldness which grows within me, which clutches at me more and more as the throne beckons. Never has it threatened me so much as in these last months. In you had I thought to find the remedy. We must not part! It is the very Devil I fight, and you must help me. This is selfish pleading, I know. Yet I believe you need me as well. Say you shall not leave me, I beg you. Promise me you shall never leave me."

She placed her slender hand in mine. "I do promise," she said. "I swear it before God. I shall stand with you and fight. Never shall I leave you. Never."

"For my part, I love you beyond knowing. I have asked you to bear much for my sake. I know not what I may vouchsafe in return save my love, and it be small compensation for the path down which I shall lead you."

"Your love is more than sufficient, my Harry." She stood upon tiptoe to kiss my lips. "And you are too uncharitable toward yourself. Do you think I could love you if there were not great good in you?" Then she gasped. "Your arm! It bleeds again." She pointed to a circle of bright red upon my dressing.

"So it does. It must be cleaned as well. And I fear I am dizzy again. I need food and some wine—"

"—and a hot bath, and then to bed."

I ate of a hot savory pot of mutton, endured Joan's cleansing of my wound, soaked in a steaming tub, and fell into bed. I slept without waking through the afternoon and night, and most of the day after. When I arose toward evening it was with a clear head and renewed vigor. There followed a pleasant time before the hearth with Joan and Merryn catching up with the goings-on at Monmouth. The harvest, I learned, would be a fine one; the wife of Gruffyd the fletcher had given birth to a daughter; the loft was home to a new litter of kittens. We did not talk of Aberystwyth. Merryn, indeed, spoke little but sat preoccupied while Joan chattered on. I watched her thoughtfully, for I could guess what it was that held her thus spellbound. After we had supped, I bade them both an early good night and retired to my chamber. I washed my face and had stripped to my hose when there came a tapping at my door.

"Come in."

She slipped in quietly as a wisp of smoke. "I am ready," she said. "I am ready to leave my bed and come to yours."

"Aye. It is time."

"Have you healed enough? I would not hurt your arm."

"It yet pains me, but in a few moments I shall have forgotten it."

She stood before me. I removed her robe and laid it upon a bench. Beneath it she wore a plain white shift. This I untied at the neck—fumbling with unexpected clumsiness—and raised over her shoulders so that it fell in a heap at her feet. She cast her eyes down. I caressed one milk-white breast, bent and kissed it. She trembled.

"Indeed you are lovely," I whispered.

She lifted her face to me. "Please hold me."

I took her in my arms, and she buried her face in the thick hair of my chest. My hands worshiped her, praised her neck, her breasts, her loins. I bore her to my bed. We were beyond speech, beyond thought.

She cried out when I took her. I raised my head. Her fingers twined about my neck and forced me down again, my mouth murmuring wordlessly against hers. My passion I gave to her and gave yet again until emptied of all save an abiding tenderness.

In the womb of the great bed, in the darkness, we clung together.

"Now are we truly one," she said. "One in body and one in spirit."

"Aye. Nor ever parted."

The tip of her finger traced a pattern upon my cheek, lingered at the cleft of my chin.

"You were passing gentle," she said.

"I feared I had hurt you. When you cried out."

"Aye, it did hurt a bit. But it was a necessary wound, was it not? And 'twas pain borne freely out of love, and so no pain at all."

I held her tightly.

"I have much to learn of this lovemaking," she said. "I think I must have been very clumsy. Yet you did seem to me a most skillful lover, Harry. Perhaps it is because I do care for you so."

"Perhaps." I smiled in the dark. "Or perhaps it is simply that I am a skillful lover."

She pinched me upon the buttock.

"And an arrogant rascal. A lovely rascal."

Long into the night we spoke thus of our love, now teasing, now ardent. We slept with limbs entwined and woke at cock crow to love again. We rose at morning's light and stood naked beside the window. Upon the bedclothes was a single red-brown stain. Of all the women I had taken to my bed, only Merryn had shed her blood out of love for me. Now, I thought, I am clean.

9

I was invited, along with many other marcher lords, to mark the feast of All Saints at Ewyas Lacy, the Duke of York's castle in Herefordshire. I was reluctant to accept the invitation, for I knew Duke Edward's brother, Richard of York, would be present with Lady Anne Mortimer. I feared to place Merryn so soon into such company and was likewise loath to leave her behind, for I thought, in my ardor, it would be torment to be parted from her even for a night. On the other hand, with the Welsh rebellion quelled and the King's health precarious, it did seem wise to cultivate at least a semblance of friendship with the powerful men of the realm. Merryn it was who finally convinced me to go. She was ready, she said, to face Lady Anne or any other who might sneer at her; ready, too, to be shunted aside when propriety demanded she not be in my company, so long as she could share my bed at night.

On the morning of All Hallows we set out through the little hills with a splendid retinue clad in the royal blue and wearing upon their tunics the white plumes of the Prince of Wales. Merryn rode at my side, perched proudly upon her Fille. They were a handsome sight, Merryn wearing a cloak of plain Welsh wool as gray as was the mare. Her dress was likewise of a rough green wool, it being unlawful for her to wear the velvet and other sumptuous stuff reserved for noble ladies. Nor did she care to wear such finery for, as she said, she could not go traipsing about the Kymin or casting in the Wye with me if she must worry about ruining such garments.

As we approached Ewyas Lacy she left me to fade back into the anonymity of my retinue.

"I shall tend to Fille when we arrive, to see how she is stabled," she said. "I trust no one to care for her as well as I do. That way none shall notice me when you make your grand entrance."

"Do not be long, though."

"I shall find your bedchamber as soon as Fille has been fed."

I blew her a kiss as we parted and held her close in my thoughts, even as I dismounted in the castle ward to receive the acclaim of the Duke of York and his company. From the corner of my eye I glimpsed her poised by the stable door watching as the richly caparisoned Duke and his followers knelt in homage before me.

Edward of Aumerle, Duke of York, was a portly man, and it was with some heaving and puffing that he rose from his knees.

"Welcome, fair highness and good cousin," he proclaimed and ushered me with fanfare of horns into the great hall, where many lords and knights idled with glasses of wine dangling in their hands. Among their number was Jack Oldcastle, now Lord Cobham.

I waited impatiently for the formal greetings to be done and went straightway to Jack. It was a merry meeting with much hugging and back-slapping.

"The life of a country squire does suit you," I said and poked his belly. "What do you do save survey your estate and eat?"

"I roll in bed with my wife!"

"Your wife? Is it not out of fashion to love one's wife?"

"Fie upon fashion! Harry, this is a woman! She is no skinny girl but a widow, five years my senior. A strong will she has, lad, and thighs to grip a man the whole night long. You shall meet her, for she has come here with me."

"And how shall I judge the truth of your description?"

We laughed as though we were met in a tavern, oblivious to the stares from the other lords.

"Good fortune it is to be relieved of both poverty and passion at one swoop," Jack said. "You should be wed, Harry. Yet you may not be so lucky. Some sausage-faced German princess doubtless awaits you, poor prince."

"Do not weep for me, you great oaf. I am content, though not wed."

"Indeed? Indeed?" He rocked back and forth upon his heels. "Aye, there is a twinkle in your eye I have not seen for a time. You come from Monmouth, do you not? Who might there be in such a wasteland to entice you? It cannot be Joan Waryn."

I chortled. "Guess again."

"It could not be—" His mouth dropped open at a sudden thought. "It is not the Welsh lass?"

"It is, and do not name me a fool. Never have I known such happiness, Jack, never. She does not love me because I am a prince, but in spite of it. She loves Harry Monmouth. And I do adore her. Her gentleness, her kindness—"

"Enough!" He raised his hand. "You need not woo me as well as the lass. Is she here?"

"Aye. She shares my bed now and we are pledged to one another."

"It is one thing to have a mistress. Many men do. But a peasant lass, Harry? Most men would ravish her and then discard her. It shall not endear you to these—" His hand swept the hall.

"You disapprove then? I care not if you do."

"Disapprove? Harry, I do not begrudge you your happiness. I worry about you out of love, that is all, and for the lass as well. I grew fond of her when she was in my charge, though I saw her claws more often than the gentleness you describe."

"She is stubborn," I said with a smile. "She possesses a strength few could match. She knows what lies ahead and she accepts it, as I do. We do not come to this blithely." I told him of what had passed between us. "Now we shall not be denied our love. She is all I have in this world, and I shall not renounce her, whatever happens."

"Well then, know me as yet a true friend."

"I know it. And now I must find Merryn and change my travel-stained garments, so that I may present myself this evening as a prince worthy of this exquisite company."

Merryn had not yet found our bedchamber. I walked to the window and threw open the shutter. The window looked onto the ward, but Merryn was nowhere to be seen. I heard a soft step behind me.

Lady Anne Mortimer stood in the doorway, an angel in pink and gold. She held the folds of her skirt before her, lifted and pressed to her waist in the dainty manner of gentle ladies.

"Harry. It has been a long time. Over two years."

"Aye."

"I saw you leave the hall and followed you here. I have been so sad since we quarreled at Lynn. I have never forgotten you."

She placed a white hand upon my arm, promised me secret delights with her eyes. She smelled of violets.

"Richard is as boring as ever. I have taken another lover, the Earl of Salisbury. He is away on a jousting tour on the continent. Besides, I had begun to tire of him as well. I never tired of you, Harry. I cannot even recall why we quarreled. Richard has his own mistress, that horrible Beatrice of

Arundel. He shall not miss me tonight. May I come to your bed after the dancing is over? It shall be as before."

Merryn burst into the chamber, hair flying, a squalling white kitten clutched against her breast.

"Harry, they have the most wonderful—"

She stopped short. Lady Anne eyed her with distaste, looking her up and down from her tangled hair to her rough leather shoes.

"Merryn," I said and held out my hand to her. She came to me, ducking her head shyly. I put my arm around her thin shoulders.

"You see how it is, Anne," I said. "What you suggest is quite impossible."

Lady Anne's tall headdress quivered. "This—this is beyond belief! You dare to bring a common whore here and flaunt her before me?"

Merryn stiffened.

"Get out of here!" I said. "Get out!"

"You are mad! You are a libertine, as everyone says, and you drag England into the gutter with you. I shall see to it that Richard knows of this."

She flounced out past a startled servant bearing a pitcher of steaming water for our toilet.

I whistled softly.

"Now there shall be trouble," Merryn said.

"Don't worry, she cannot say much. I am sure York knows of our dalliance, but I doubt she cares to remind him of it." I kissed her forehead. "A whore and a libertine. We are well matched, are we not? Now sit here on my lap and tell me what wonders you have discovered in this horrid castle."

"It is this kitten. Poor dear, I nearly squashed her, I was so flustered." She sat upon my knee and pried the frightened animal from her cloak. "Look at her eyes. Never have I seen blue eyes in a cat. They are blue as the sky."

"So they are. Now tell me, have you been climbing about the loft?"

"Aye, and I shall go back tomorrow while you are drinking with your fine lords and ladies. It is the proper place for my sort of person."

I laughed. "And you shall pass the day more pleasantly than I shall."

"Poor Harry." She kissed me on the nose, then let me taste her lips.

"Now," I said, "we must change our clothes and wash ourselves. Even the servants shall not eat with you if you smell of the stable."

Most of the company had entered the hall to be seated when we made our way downstairs. I pointed Merryn toward a table near the door where the retainers would be fed, and strolled toward the dais where I would have the seat of honor. Jack met me in the middle of the hall with his bride. She was sturdy and buxom as he had implied, with large mouth and ready smile and hair the color of straw. Her storied thighs I could not see, for they were hidden beneath a gown of azure velvet. I liked her at once and told her so, while Jack stood by beaming behind his red bush of a beard.

I had just bade them a pleasant good evening when a commotion drew my attention to the rear of the hall where the various retainers had gathered to eat in their particolored surcoats of bright crimsons and royal blue. Richard of York was there, pointing toward the door, and in the midst of the agitated knot of servants stood Merryn. I shook off Jack's warning hand and hurried back, only to see Merryn flee from the hall.

"What has happened here?" I demanded of York.

"There is no great cause for concern, your highness. I have tossed out a camp follower, that is all."

"The lass who just left is no camp follower, if that is what you mean. She is a member of my retinue, one of my servants."

"Exactly. We all know how it is she serves you, your highness. Certainly I have no desire to dictate the personal behavior of the Prince of Wales. But I will not have my brother's guests insulted by the presence of that doxy. She has been sent to the pantry to eat with the stable hands. I trust you understand."

Every head in the hall had turned toward us. Here was Lady Anne's revenge. It was to me as though York had ravished Merryn before the host of lords and ladies.

"At Monmouth," I said, "even the stable hands eat in hall."

"A quaint old custom. The house of York has not observed it for years."

I saw that further protest on my part would only expose Merryn to greater insult.

"I shall not forget this, my lord of York."

I turned upon my heel and strode toward the dais, the hum of the crowd following me. I plopped down in my seat and glared as the guests took their places, gossiping and smirking behind their hands. Richard of York, his face bloated with his little triumph, and his brother Edward mounted the dais and sat upon either side of me. Lady Anne passed by me with a malicious smile. In the gallery a band of musicians began to scrape their viols and blow upon their recorders. A page who bore the white rose of York upon his tunic filled my cup with ruby red wine. I set the glass to my lips, but the taste was bitter as gall.

I pushed my glass away, stood up, and said to Edward, Duke of York, "Forgive me, cousin, but I cannot eat with you this evening." I looked pointedly at his startled brother. "I fear I have been taken ill. I beg your pardon."

I bowed and left.

A deathly silence fell as I quit the hall. A scandal would follow, I well knew, but I cared not. I found the pantry down a narrow passageway. There sat ten or twelve of the rougher sort of servants and some scullery maids as well, eating and making merry. At the far end of the table, alone, was Merryn, picking at a trencher of food, her face wet with tears. All fell silent at my entrance. I must have been quite a sight in my long gown of brown velvet embossed with gold leaf. I went to the hearth where a pot of cabbage still boiled and heaped some upon a trencher alongside a slab of salt pork. I strolled over to Merryn.

"May I join you?"

"Harry! You cannot eat here!"

I sat down opposite her.

"Why not? Am I not good enough for you?"

"They shall be furious, the Yorks, or whatever you call them."

"I am already furious with them. There was never love between us to begin with. They are a foul, treacherous lot. They likely would have poisoned me anyway."

"Harry, do not joke at such a terrible thing. And do not speak so loudly, the others shall hear."

"I have said nothing they do not already know. And now, if you do not mind, I am famished. If you are done with scolding me, I shall eat my supper." I stuffed my mouth full of cabbage.

"I see now why Joan does wring her hands over you," she said with a sigh. "Yet I do love you."

"You'd better."

I reached across the table and twined my fingers with hers. The others watched us with elbows propped upon the table. After a while, one man approached me shyly.

"Pardon, your highness, but I see you have had nothing to drink. Would you share our ale?"

"That would be splendid."

He soon returned with two brimming tankards and a loaf of brown bread. The ale was rich, heady stuff. Before long we were laughing and joking with the others, and the pantry was cozy as any tavern in East Chepe. There were mince puddings sent back from the hall, and we ate to near bursting. Then the tables were pushed back, a recorder appeared from under a peasant's blouse, and the dancing began.

Merryn and I watched for a while and then slipped away to our chamber. The great hall where now there was dancing and revelry was directly below us across the way. When we opened our windows the laughter and the singing of lutes floated up to us on the cold night air. The movement of the dancers was reflected in the waving of ghostly shadows upon the castle ward.

"Shall we dance?" I asked.

"I have not yet learned how. Will you teach me?"

I smiled for answer and put my arm about her waist. I led her through the steps of a swaying estampie that wafted from below. Never once did I take my eyes off her. Whether the music ceased I do not know, only that we danced no longer but only stood.

She ran her fingers along my temple.

"Yours are the most beautiful eyes I have ever seen in a man," she said. "I am lost in them."

"Do you seek to seduce me, woman?"

"Aye." She set her lips to mine and the world retreated for the rest of that night.

I heard mass the next morning, the feast of All Hallows. Merryn stayed away for fear of a repeat of the previous day's humiliation. Afterward the Duke of York had proposed a morning of hawking and I strolled with Jack and his Joan from the chapel to the mews.

"You gave us an interesting evening," Jack said.

"I could not abide the company of that whoreson Richard of York."

"It was deemed a terrible insult."

"Good. It was meant to be."

"Then must you deal with Richard, and here he comes now."

He was striding toward us, his face grim. With him was a party of jaunty young knights and several ladies, among them Anne. I saw the gauntlet in his hand.

"Harry of Monmouth," he said, "last night you heaped insult upon my brother and myself. Prince or no, our house shall not bear such mocks. I challenge you to meet me in the lists this very afternoon. The honor of York demands it."

He tossed the gauntlet in the dust at my feet.

I thought my limbs had turned to water. A joust. Childhood memories flooded over me—the lance bearing down upon me, myself falling, the sickening crash, the pain in my arm, my father's insults. York knew I had not jousted since then. All knew it, and none had ever challenged me, out of courtesy and deference to my position. It was not spoken of, this fear of mine. I looked down at the gauntlet. To leave it there in the dust would be an admission of cowardice, a dangerous liability for a prince.

Richard was smirking. He was powerfully built and experienced with the lance. I licked my lips and looked at Jack. He shook his head almost imperceptibly. He will kill you, his eyes said.

"No," I said.

Richard's smile broadened. He glanced around at the others as though to say, Do you see?

"My lord," I said, "you know that I do not joust. Why then do you trouble me? What feat of bravery would it be for you to defeat one so inexperienced? Besides, the situation does not warrant combat. I was but ill and left your table. That is all. Had I done worse, for example made you a cuckold, then I might understand your anger."

This last was a blow well placed. His smile froze. Everyone knew of my dalliance with Lady Anne, but Richard dared not admit to it for his honor's sake. Anne herself pushed forward to answer me.

"I told you he would not fight. He is a craven, a coward. You lords, will you have such a one to be king over you? He is not even the rightful heir, for my brother, Edmund Mortimer, was meant to succeed King Richard. It is Edmund Mortimer who should even now sit upon the throne."

"My lord of York," I said, "is your wife used to speaking treason?"

York was on perilous ground, and he knew it. "Silence, woman," he muttered, his bald pate flushing pink.

"For your sake," I said, "I shall forget what I have just heard. And for England's sake, I shall not joust with you."

"For England's sake?"

"Aye. I would not deprive her of my rule." I turned away.

"King Richard feared to joust, or so I have heard." The speaker was Sir Thomas Grey, a rash knight of York's entourage.

"Sir Thomas," I said, looking him in the eye, "do not be so foolish as to underestimate me. That was Percy's mistake, and his head now rots upon London Bridge."

I walked back to the keep, Jack and his lady in my wake. When we were out of sight, I held up my hand that they might see how it trembled.

"It was the best of a bad situation, Harry. 'Twas all you could do and, Jesu, you shut them up nicely," Jack said.

"I like it not. They shall spread this about the realm. Nor do I feel safe here. Lady Anne dares speak openly what many of them say behind closed doors. I mean to be away from here this very day, as soon as I may be ready, else York may arrange a convenient hunting accident."

"I am with you then. My escort shall strengthen yours until our way does part."

"Good my friend." I clapped him upon the shoulder.

Merryn was frightened when I told her what had passed, but calm.

"I am proud of you," she said.

"Proud? Why?"

"That you did not try to fight him. It called for more courage than taking up the lance."

"It did not feel like courage. I was terrified. He had me at bay, and I knew not where to turn."

I sat upon the floor beside her and grumbled on for a time, but I quieted as she rubbed my temples.

"Harry?"

"Mmm?"

"May I take the kitten back to Monmouth? The blue-eyed kitten? She is yet in our chamber. I fed her with scraps from the kitchen."

"You would insult the honor of York by stealing one of their cats?"

"It is not stealing. I asked a groom. He said I could have her, that they've more cats than they need."

"And so do we."

"But none with blue eyes. Please, Harry."

"Oh, aye then, but you must bear her with you. I'll have none other troubled on the journey."

"Of course." She flung her arms about my neck. "I have named her Anne."

We left within the hour, not even staying to eat. None of York's guests seemed surprised at our going, but rode sullenly to the hunt. So we quit Ewyas Lacy, and never was I more glad at the leaving of a place.

The fiasco at Ewyas Lacy set me to mulling over the precariousness of my position. I was heir to the throne while a man with better claim yet lived, Edmund Mortimer, the childless King Richard's chosen successor. I was disliked by the King my father, mistrusted by the peers, and in particular hated by one of the most powerful families in the realm. I had no friend in the Archbishop of Canterbury. Yet did I refuse to surrender to despair. Even as I took stock of my enemies I laughed at myself. A formidable list it was indeed, an honor roll of chivalry, with the illustrious Bolingbroke ranged at the top against me. Only a man of distinction might claim such notable foes. No matter, I would defeat them all. Capable of compassion I was, of gentleness and gaiety. But when I was pushed to the wall there was roused in me the fiery spirit of the wild boar run to ground, the will to fight for my life and even to enjoy that fight. I would be king despite them all, despite that part of me which was loath to put on the crown. I would be more than a king. I would be the greatest king England had ever known.

Into the midst of these musings came word that my father was once more taken ill, and this time likely to die. I must ride for London at once.

These grave tidings turned my thoughts again from greatness to survival. I had been foolish, whiling away my hours at Monmouth as though I would be prince forever. I longed with a sweet pain to spend my days roaming the Monmouth hills with Merryn, but it could not be. For both our sakes I must stand and fight.

I shared not a thought of this with Merryn, for I feared she would dislike this calculating, ambitious Harry. She in turn had grown quieter, and I often caught her eyes fixed gravely upon me. But she said nothing. She did not even protest when I rode on to London before her, though it meant we must sleep apart for the first time since we became lovers. Haste was essential. She understood this well, and so traveled with the ponderous main body of my household. She would not hear of staying at Monmouth.

"You shall have need of me," she said, "and I should be miserable without you."

I bade her a grateful farewell and set out to ride day and night over winter's muddy roads to Londontown. I took with me a troop of well-armed retainers, for word of my father's condition would have ranged across England. For any man bold enough to challenge my claim to the throne, this would be a splendid opportunity.

We clattered into Westminster on a dark midnight, exhausted and spattered with mud, but unscathed. I was shown at once to my father's sickroom and noted uneasily the stares of all I encountered on the way, as though they envisioned the crown already upon my head and wondered how it would sit. Many courtiers were about, though the hour was late. They spoke in whispers and walked with muted step as if the noise of their comings and goings might fright the life from the King. I followed a servant with a guttering candle through shadowy passages, my own heavy riding boots ringing upon the stone floor.

I thought him already dead when first I saw him. He lay with the bedclothes heaped about him, a shriveled figure lost in the great pillows. The pox upon his face had broken out anew, so that yellow pustules seeped atop brown scabs. His closed eyelids were blue as the skim of milk, his lips were cracked and parted to reveal a thick brown tongue. My stomach turned at the stink. I fell to my knees beside him and crossed myself in prayer.

Above the crackling of the fire I heard the slow rasp of his breathing. Behind me there was a rustle of robes, a low cough. I knew the room to be filled with people, but I sought not their identities. Physicians they would be, confessors, and peers. My brothers were likely present as well, and my uncle of Beaufort. For the moment I cared not. Somehow I must come to terms with the ghastly figure in the bed. Father. King. The crown, which sat beside his bed upon a pillow of purple velvet, glittered in the firelight, an exquisitely wrought circlet for such a wretched head. In vain I searched my heart for the tears a son owes to a father dying. There was but the crown between us, a golden bond, his legacy to me.

A hand rested cold upon my shoulder. I rose to face the Archbishop of Canterbury, Arundel, arrayed in all his purple splendor, a gold mitre upon his skull-like head.

"A word with you, your highness," he said.

I nodded and walked past a dozen men to a far corner of the chamber. There was my uncle Beaufort. His black eyes caught mine as I passed by, but he did not acknowledge me.

"The King has been shriven," Arundel said. "His physicians fear each breath may be his last."

"It does seem likely," I said.

"Your latest escapade was no aid to his health." Arundel's voice was a dagger. "The whole court heard of it, and the King was deeply shamed. He wept for your cowardice and your wanton lechery, which so offended the House of York."

"Afore God, Arundel, you shall not blame me for this my father's illness, nor will you prate at me of morality—"

"Hear me out, you young fool! Do you not perceive the gravity of your situation? You were near to King Richard in the last days of his reign, yet you seem to have learned nothing from the experience. Your enemies are many and powerful."

"Indeed, you should know my enemies well, being the chief of them."

He raised his head and his eyes became slits. "In truth, I love you not, good prince. Yet have I sworn an oath to your father that I will not turn from you. Aye, he thinks of you despite your folly. I have ever been a servant of Lancaster, a servant of Bolingbroke and old John of Gaunt before him. I say to you plainly, you disgrace them both. Yet do I stand by you out of care for them. I have doubled the guard about the palace and likewise have set guards to follow you at all times. King Richard has friends yet living, and few there are who would weep if you fell to an assassin's knife. You are beloved in the alehouses, but no farther."

To my chagrin, I had no answer for him. He moved away and left me alone, stung to my very soul. I hoped my uncle, Arundel's enemy, would come to me with a word of solace, but he did not. I joined my brothers at the bedside.

For two days my father clung to life. I slept but little and spoke with no one. When I did retire for rest, two armed men followed me and posted themselves without my door. It was with unspeakable joy, then, that I took myself wearily to bed upon the third night to find my household and baggage arrived and, with them, Merryn.

She had made her way unchallenged to my chamber with the aid of my loyal retainers from Monmouth. I had no words for her but could only clutch her to my breast. At last I was able to whisper, "You were right. I have need of you here, very great need."

"Dearest Harry." She led me to a large oak chair carved like a throne, where she sat while I knelt beside her and rested my head in her lap.

"I do know now," she said, as she stroked my hair. "I know something of what it means for you to be a king. I beheld this palace, grander than anything I could ever imagine and yet so forbidding, and I wondered what should become of you here. The people I have seen, they have faces which bear no touch of love or hope upon them. They are clad in lovely gowns but are so pale in appearance, comely and yet sad. I fear for you among them."

"Courtiers thrive by sucking the very life's blood from the King. They seek their own gain, nothing more. With such ones must I make common cause if I am to survive."

"But not all are such creatures," she replied, "for more have I observed.

I wandered about outside while your goods were unpacked. There was a company of men gathered before the chapel, poor men I took them for. I judged they had been doing some work about the palace and would soon wend their way home. They took no heed of me, a poor lass myself, and I have now enough English to mark their words. They spoke of rumors about Westminster, rumors that if the King were to die, your enemies would seek to overthrow you. I was frightened near to despair for you. But I took heart from those good men, Harry, for they spoke plainly of the affection they bear you. They have seen you in the streets of London and praised your open way with the people. They said you have a care for the common folk, that you deal justly with them, unlike many who trample upon the poor. They named you the best prince in Christendom and vowed that not a hair upon your head would be touched. All London stands behind the Prince of Wales, they said.

"Yet are the people fickle," I said. "One day you are their darling, the next day they scream for your head. So it has been with many kings."

"It shall not be so with you, Harry. It is not only in London that you are loved. In every village, as we traveled across England, people rushed to us at the sight of your standard and called out to us in praise of you. 'Long life to good Prince Hal,' they cried. How shall their love then abate?"

She was so vehement in holding this opinion that I would not disabuse her of it, for it did give her comfort. I was more cynical than she. Still, I might learn from the information she brought. What if I did not have the peers with me? No longer did they hold all power as in days of old, even as uncle Beaufort had taught me in my childhood. *All London stands behind the Prince of Wales*. I chewed upon my lower lip and thought this over. Then I smiled, for I knew what I must do.

"Arundel may burn in Hell," I said, "and the House of York with him."

I stood up and stretched. Merryn still sat, her expression troubled.

"What shall it do to you, this scheming and worrying?" she asked. "You do not share your thoughts with me. Would it not be best if I helped you bear this burden? Is that not what you want?"

"I am very tired."

"Always you say that." She stood to face me. "What do you fear? Do you fear to lose my love? It was possible once, but no longer. If I can forgive you Wales, I can forgive you anything. I see more than you may know. I see the ambition which gnaws at you even as you lament that you must wear the crown. I see the hatred burn in your eyes when you speak of Arundel. But you should tell me of these things yourself."

"Merryn, I have slept but little these three nights, and before that I rode without rest the width of England. The very floor spins beneath me. We shall speak of this when I have rested."

She folded her arms across her chest.

"I give you my word," I said. "I shall speak to you of this."

I lay for hours in an exhaustion so deep that sleep would not come. Beside me Merryn tossed fitfully and mumbled beneath her breath. Toward morning I must have dozed at last, for I started awake to hear her crying, "No! No!"

"Merryn!" I shook her awake. "Merryn, you are dreaming."

She clung to me in the darkness.

"Were your dreams evil this night?" I asked.

"Aye, and I would tell them to you, though they may fright you. There were many men in armor. I could not see their faces. You stood in the midst of them, in chains, and they heaped abuse upon you. They named you a traitor and a coward. And then—and then they forced you to your knees and they cut off your head. Oh, Harry, it seemed so real, and I am so frightened for you. I want to leave this place."

I listened tensely. "I cannot leave. You may, if you wish, and I shall think none the less of you. You may return to Monmouth."

"You know I do not mean that. Forgive me for waking you."

She fell silent so that I thought she slept again. But then she asked, "Why can you not leave? What would happen if you renounced the crown in Tom's favor and went back to Monmouth to live out your days?"

"It is not so simple. King Richard walked away from the crown by his abdication and in the end it did not save his life. Ever would there be men ready to rise up in my name, and so I would pose a threat."

"Even to your own brother who loves you?"

"Even so, and to any who might come after him."

"You shall wear the crown then. What must you do to hold it? Must you threaten your enemies? Slay them? Go to war?"

"Perhaps. Perhaps all of those things."

"And if you do not?"

"Then shall your dream come to pass."

"And if you do these things, if you destroy others with your power, what then?"

"Jesu, Merryn, you torment me!"

"You torment yourself anyway, Harry. What shall happen?"

I put my hands to my face. "I fear I shall lose my soul. Indeed, I fear it is already lost. There is no good a king may do, none, for when the King raises his little finger, someone is crushed by it. Yet I cannot step back from it, God help me. I fear to die. And I want to rule."

The words tumbled from me then. I told her more of Wales, of Shrewsbury, of the good I had sought to do, of the pillaging and the men I had slain with my own hand. I spoke of Richard and his downfall, and of the history of the endings of kings he had recited to me. Of the enmity between myself and Arundel, the estrangement from my father, the cold desire to stand above them all. Of the plan I carried in my head to unite all Christendom by diplomacy or by conquest, if necessary, that the warrings of the many sovereigns might cease.

"Suppose that I war," I said. "It would quiet my enemies, bring support from the peers. It might save my own life, though it cost the lives of many other poor wretches. But suppose again that I do not. Imagine then that the peers grow more restless, that they chafe as they did under Richard's peace. They have been trained all their lives for one purpose, and one purpose only, and that is to fight. They yearn for a king who shall lead them to glorious military victories in France, as did the third Edward. Suppose I will not fight. It is sure that they will slay me and set Tom, or worse, in my place. Then they should have their war. But Tom would fight as did the Black Prince, pillaging, burning, and raping, with no care for the well-being of the people. I know him well. He is not evil, but simple and pliable. He would fight for no purpose save for the sake of fighting and the wealth gained from plunder, as would all the nobility. So it was in Wales until I made an end there. What then? Still there is war but it drags on, is more capricious and devastating, without me to guide it. Am I not still responsible? May I wash my hands of this power and preserve the purity of my soul at the cost of even more lives? I fear not. I think it is wicked to care so much for one's own soul. I must carry this burden myself though it bear me down to perdition."

Outside our window, a cock crowed.

"Another dawn," I said, "and it seems I am not yet King. That is something to be grateful for, I suppose."

"And one thing more, Harry, this our love. It is no answer, yet take some solace from it."

I wept in her arms then, wept like a child while she tenderly brushed away my tears.

With the stubbornness which does characterize our House of Lancaster, my father clung to life. Christmas came and went, and Twelfth Night, and still he breathed. By some miracle of God his condition improved, and by February death had been cheated and must wait longer to carry away his soul. But renewed life did not bring with it strength. His body was left twisted and festering, and the headaches continued to torment him. Affairs of state passed into the rapacious hands of Arundel, now chancellor of the realm. I moved with my household across the Thames to my manor at Kennington. Though I judged myself safe enough for the moment, it was unthinkable to return to Monmouth, for I had been shaken into a realization that I must soon consolidate my power. Nor could I rest as Arundel filled his purse while the people cried out for justice. I rode into the city to call upon my uncle Beaufort at Holborn. My uncle was now Bishop of Winchester but he seldom visited his see, preferring instead the pleasures of London. His house was one of the fairest in the city, with many half-timbered peaks and windows of bright stained glass. Within, the colored sunlight danced upon silk tapestries from the East with their scenes of exotic birds and veiled women. He welcomed me there with cool politeness and served me a fine claret as I warmed myself before his hearth.

"I come seeking your help," I said when we had exchanged pleasantries.

"It is time," he said, his black eyes glittering, "now that you have nearly cut your own throat. For once I find myself in agreement with my lord Arundel. You have been behaving like a spoiled child, and if you persist you shall be beyond any help I might tender."

"Do you refer to my refusal to meet York in the lists?"

"I refer to your flaunting of a Welsh peasant girl in the faces of the peers of England." He set down his cup with a clatter. "God's blood, Harry, what can you be thinking? You have never lacked for lovers. Why then must you create such scandal?"

"What do you suggest?"

"Get rid of her."

"No."

"Why not?"

"Because I love her."

"Love her? How can you love a lowborn wench?"

"How could my grandfather love your mother?"

His face darkened. "How dare you to compare the two! My mother was no lord's daughter, but neither was she a peasant bitch. Her father was a man of some means."

I ran my finger around the rim of my cup. "Good my uncle," I said, "I came seeking your help. I intend to rule England, rule her well, and I want you by my side. Nevertheless I shall rule without you, if need be. The choice is yours." I smiled at him. "I know that you deem yourself a keen judge of men. Well, you have known me since childhood, and you see me with a clarity these others lack. Do you then doubt what I say?"

He was silent for a very long time, and I was content to sip my wine and watch the logs crackling upon the hearth.

"What is it you want?" he asked at last.

"I seek the aid of the merchants of the realm, especially the Londoners. You can ease my way if you will."

He smiled. "My dear nephew, where are your vaunted scruples?"

"Who are the most powerful men in London?" I asked, ignoring his question. "Richard Whittington and John Hende?"

"Aye, that would be right."

They would do nicely. Dick Whittington in particular was beloved by the people, for he rose from humble beginnings to be a popular Lord Mayor of London. "You know them well, I believe?"

"Aye."

"I would meet with them and any others you deem valuable. Especially I am interested in those who sit in parliament and those whose dealings with the peers might put them in positions to be, shall we say, financially persuasive."

"And would you also know those who have their hands in the purse of the Archbishop of Canterbury?"

"I would be most interested. But is it possible to reach Arundel?"

"Perhaps. He has powerful friends of his own, you know. The victualers in particular support him."

"Aye. The most corrupt men in London, they are."

"Harry, you shall find no honest men in this venture of yours. Indeed, none would name you so when you are done with this. Nor shall it be simple. Arundel is an old hand at deceit. He shall not easily be run to ground. And should the King regain his health—"

"Yet in the end I have more to offer, do I not? I am the future."

"And in the future you must make good on what you offer."

"Still, I shall do nothing that is generally hurtful. I shall stop short of that. As for the deceit—well, it is in a good cause."

"Harry, Harry. I do tremble to see such an innocent cast in with the wolves. You are not ignorant of evil, but you seem to think that some are able to avoid it. No one can escape sin, nephew. Some sin more efficiently than others, that is all."

There was at once a mutual understanding between the London merchants and myself which my uncle fostered. To a man they shared my dislike of the peers with their pretensions and arrogance. Neither the nobility nor the King appreciated the problems of commerce, the importance of the continent, they claimed. They bemoaned the corruption of the Church and the high-handed rule of Arundel, with his threats to burn those who spoke for reform. Most of all they complained that my father's illness had set England to flounder like a rudderless ship. They left unspoken what I know they all felt—that the King's cheating of the grave was no good thing. Easy it was to reassure them, to muster their pledges of support. Easy it was to reassure myself. These were congenial men, men who understood my problems and frustration. I had feared their ambition, their greed, their disregard for the poor. Yet I was put at my ease by men like Dick Whittington, the wealthiest man in the kingdom, a bluff and hearty old merchant, a common man famous for the founding of many almshouses and hospitals. He put me in mind of my grandfather, and I was not unhappy to be his ally.

I pledged stability and personal favor in return for financial pressure upon Arundel and the peers. Nor would my father escape their attention, for Whittington and Hende had loaned many pounds to the Crown. They would pressure the King with kind entreaties only, I insisted. I dismissed the last of my misgivings by reminding myself that here was no blood spilt. The working out of details I left to my uncle Beaufort. We agreed it would be discreet if I retired from London for a time. Monmouth was out of the question, for I must needs be in constant contact with my uncle and the merchants. I therefore chose Berkhamsted, only a short ride from London, where Lancaster held a small castle little used by the court. There I removed in the springtime with Merryn and my household, and there I lived for many months.

It was no idle time at Berkhamsted. Messengers streamed back and forth to London keeping me ever informed of the doings at court. The merchants consulted me frequently, as did many humbler souls who had received no justice from the Crown. From afar I learned of my increased favor among the people. I labored ever harder, spending most of the day at my desk.

On sunny days I was wont to work in the garden amid the primroses and daisies, Merryn at my side studying her lessons or otherwise amusing herself. It was not so at first. Merryn had grown more subdued and moody away from her Welsh hills. Nor, given my preoccupations, could she command my full attention as she once had. For a time, a wall went up between us and we had little to say to one another. At last, we fought on a rainy day in May when I found her in the solar weeping and flinging her books about in anger.

"I know not why I stay here!" she cried when she saw me. "It is hateful. See how flat this English land is. It bores me, Harry. My lessons bore me. And you bore me as well. Never do I see you save when you come to our bed seeking solace from my body. I wish I were tending my sheep again upon the Honddu."

"Do you indeed? Then why do you not go? It has been unpleasant enough to have you around with your mopings."

"I mope because you pay me no attention."

"What then do you expect? It shall be worse when I am King. Will you badger me then?"

"I shall not be here then. I shall return to Wales. I know not why I have stayed so long."

Now I was frightened but would not have her know it. "So little does your promise mean to you," I said. "You pledged to stay with me, yet I'll warrant you never loved me. It is only that you had no place to go, knew not what to do, while I gave you food and shelter."

"How dare you say it?" she cried. "Do you name me a whore that I would fuck you for my keep? It is you who know nothing of love. You only cling to me because none else has loved you."

I could but blink at this last, and swallow a lump in my throat. "It is not true," I said feebly.

"Who has loved you? Who? Your father?"

"Jack," I said. "Joan. Joan—

My voice broke. She put her hand to her mouth then.

"Oh, Harry! Harry! I did not mean it. Why have I hurt you so, my poor Harry?"

She put her arms around my waist and laid her head upon my chest. My first impulse was to push her away, but I did not. I put one hand upon her head.

"Am I so difficult to love? Am I so cold, so distant?"

"No, Harry, no, no. Easy you are to love. I am at fault. I have been peevish of late. You must forgive me."

I did not believe her, but I pressed her no further.

"I do admit I have neglected you," I said. "I give you my word we shall be together more often. We can ride our horses as we did of old."

"And may I study with you as you work?"

"Aye."

Four days later I gave her a black spaniel, sent at my request from London. Rhodri we named him, after the legendary Welsh prince. Now did all seem with us as before, and we ever sought one another's company, even while working. Once while riding abroad we stumbled upon a secluded pond clotted with floating masses of water plantain. There we went once a week to bathe naked in the cool waters and then to make love upon the slippery grass beneath a spreading willow tree. I came to know her body as well as my own, every mole, every soft fold of skin, each tender place to kiss. Familiarity did not diminish my passion and I enjoyed our lovemaking as ever—the teasing, the intoxicating possession, and the wet exhaustion afterward. But I learned to treasure as well the holding of her only to know her closeness, to taste of her skin, to feel her breasts rise and fall against me and the tickle of the hair of her groin upon my thighs. With my fingers I would bless every part of her even as she slept, and often I would wake to the gentle caress of her hand against my manhood. Despite our hurts we grew still closer until it seemed as if we drew even a common breath, and if one heart should cease to beat the other would surely quit as well.

By harvest time of 1409 my efforts to influence the court and parliament had begun to bear fruit. My father had recovered remarkably from his illness of the previous year, yet even his renewed vigor did not stem the tide of power that now did flow toward Berkhamsted. Men sought me out from every corner of the kingdom for my favor with the merchants, even the fierce marcher lords swallowing their pride. I knew how well I had succeeded when I negotiated a loan for Lord Grey of Ruthin, he who had lost his fortune in a ransom paid to Owain Glyndwr.

In November, messengers rode north from the court. The King's health being much improved, he would undertake a royal progress to visit those parts of his realm that might benefit from his presence. It was his desire to stay for two days at Berkhamsted, there to be entertained by his beloved son Henry, Prince of Wales. I received these tidings with both triumph and misgiving. That my influence now reached even into the court I had no doubt, and this visit must be evidence of it. That Arundel knew what means I had employed I was equally certain. But I knew not what word he might have given my father. Nor could I be sure how the King would receive Merryn's presence.

It takes much effort and expense to entertain the court. Indeed, one reason for the journey was to relieve London for a time of the burden of providing for the King. At Berkhamsted there were victuals to procure, to provide the King with venison and trout and bread, and subtleties to be fashioned by a special cook dispatched from Westminster. The kitchen must be more fully staffed and the bedchambers prepared, the King's favorite wine set in, and floors swept clean of refuse and strewn with fresh rushes and mint. These tasks were overseen by the eminently competent Scrope, come from London at my bidding, with some awkward help from Merryn. This was no amicable partnership, for Scrope had not changed his opinion of our love. He dealt with Merryn as little as possible and then but coldly, so that she complained to me, "He likes me not. Sometimes when he glares at me I think he does hate me."

Once I reprimanded him, yet I could say but little, for never did he openly insult her and he managed my household ably. Stung by Scrope's aloofness and mindful of our humiliation at Ewyas Lacy, Merryn resolved to avoid my father at all cost. She would eat in the pantry and otherwise tarry in our bedchamber with Rhodri. I grieved that she must secrete herself, but I knew her to be right. Discretion would be the sanctuary of our love.

King and court arrived on the twentieth day of November, Father borne from his coach by four servants on a litter hung with cloth of gold. He was accompanied by my youngest brother, Humphrey, now a man of eighteen years. Of this brother it was said he possessed a sharp eye for women and a hot temper. Indolent he was named as well, and those who knew me not often compared the two of us. He was grown tall, surpassing my own height, but thin. His hair was curly as ever and his eyes brimmed with mischief. He called for wine as soon as he did enter the hall, and seldom was he without a cup in his hand.

We feasted royally that night, thanks to Scrope. Father lay next to me on his litter, propped up by pillows, for he had lost all strength in his legs. Despite this his appearance was better than in years, his face scabrous but not pustular and his eyes clear. He was duly impressed by the show of my hospitality and said so, to my surprise.

Next morning Humphrey and I sat with him before the hearth in the solar.

"I hear your name often these days, Harry my son."

"Indeed?"

"Everywhere in the city there is praise for you. At court you are spoken of even by those who once held you in little esteem. Everyone wishes to know, 'What does Prince Henry think of this or that?'" He raised a quizzical eyebrow. "Whence comes this newfound respect?"

"My lord father, I know not, save that I have tried to make amends with those I have previously offended."

Humphrey laughed. "Well spoken, brother. You have made your apologies so well that many gentlemen do say their prayers even as they count their treasure."

I shrugged and said nothing. Father rocked back and forth, a sardonic smile upon his face.

"For what purpose do you do this, Harry?" he asked.

"I merely follow the advice of your very wise chancellor, Archbishop Arundel, who chided me for my frivolity and bade me look to my future."

"Beaufort's hand is in this, I'll wager."

"You must ask him that."

"It is not the method an honorable knight would choose."

"My lord father, you know by now I am no respecter of chivalry. In this I have learned well from my father, who has shown himself capable of most unchivalrous deeds to gain and hold a crown."

He glared at me beneath hooded eyelids. I raised my eyebrows and smiled.

"You would not joust with York," he said.

"He would have slain me."

"At least you are plain about your cowardice. Now you find your defense in merchant's gold."

"And in my wits."

"Afore God, you do not lack those."

"It is pleased I am to at last have some compliment of you."

"Long have I despaired of you, Harry. You have brought shame to me and to Lancaster, and still you do. But in one thing have I been wrong. I had feared you would frivol away the royal legacy I have struggled to maintain for you. I would hazard now you will hold the crown. You shall not hold it honorably, but, by Our Lady, you shall hold it. Perhaps as I grow old and weak I learn to be satisfied with less."

"As do I."

"One thing more, and that is a warning." His voice now held a dangerous edge. "My lord Arundel is alarmed, for he sees you as a threat to me. I wonder myself. I say to you, Harry, save your newfound influence for such time as these bones of mine lie in the tomb. You may bully Lord Grey if you like, but do not interfere with me. Do you mark my words?" He pointed a bony finger. "I am yet King, and if you forget that, it shall go ill with you, son or no."

"Your grace, I have never imagined that my kinship to you afforded me any special claim to your affection."

He grunted and then said, "Dick Whittington does hound me to see you situated in the city. I have a house there, Coldharbour it is called, in Thames Street hard by the Ropery. It is a large house, a fine one, and near your new friends. Do you want it?"

"I am honored by your offer and I accept it."

"Then it is done."

"Actually it was not Whittington who moved Father to this generosity," Humphrey said. "It is the tavernkeepers and whores of London who speak for you, for they do miss your coin."

"You are tardy in your news of me, brother. I go no more to brothels."

"You are not serious about the Welsh bitch?"

"You shall not speak of her so. I shall not have it."

He flushed in his confusion. "She is but a—"

"Enough, Humphrey," Father said. He looked at me keenly. "Still you sleep with that one?"

"Aye."

"And no other?"

"No other."

"What!" cried Humphrey. "Does she chain you to your bed at night?"

"Enough!" Father said again. He turned back to me. "Where is she? I saw her not last night."

"We thought it best that she stay hidden away. We would not offend you as we did the House of York."

"I would see her."

"Why?"

"I would know what sort of woman could command such loyalty in you. I would judge for myself how it is a baseborn wench could lead you into such a scandal as you have raised."

"I would not subject her to your examination as though she were a meat pie on display at market."

"Fie! I mean her no harm. I am curious, that is all. I yet enjoy the sight of fair lasses, even though they are no longer enchanted with my own appearance."

Reluctantly I sent after her. The fear was plain upon her face when she entered the solar, and her eyes sought mine for reassurance. She curtsied awkwardly, for she had never learned such courtly graces, and stood before the litter with eyes downcast.

"Come closer, child." Father gestured impatiently. "I may look a monster but I am not, in truth. Sit here between us."

He motioned to the bench next to me. I took her hand as she sat down.

"My father the King," I said, "and my brother Humphrey. This is Merryn."

"You are Welsh," Father said.

"Aye."

"How is it that you understand what I say?"

"I have a tutor and I learn Latin and English."

"A tutor? For one of your station?"

"She has a fine quick mind," I said. "Why should she not learn to read?"

"Harry," Merryn whispered, "you should not speak so."

"Eh? What was that?" Father asked.

"P-Pardon," she stammered. "I did but chide Har—the Prince for his tone of voice, that he should speak so to his father."

His eyes narrowed. "Indeed?"

"I would not have you quarrel over me," she added.

He laughed. "We do not need you to quarrel. We are ever at each other like a pair of fighting cocks, are we not, Harry? Indeed, I would know of you how you command the love of this fellow, for I cannot do it."

"He has suffered much hurt from you," she said. "He thinks you love him not."

I shifted upon the bench. "That is enough, Merryn," I said.

"No, Harry, it is not," she answered more boldly still. "You do love your father, though you will not admit it. And now that I see him here as but a man, I think he must love you as well. It is that you are both stiff-necked."

The silence which followed this outburst was the most uncomfortable I had ever endured. When I could bear it no longer, I said, "My lord father, I beg that you allow Merryn to take her leave. This audience has no further purpose."

"I am not done with it." He laid his head back and closed his eyes. "What part did your kin take in Glyndwr's rebellion?"

"My father and brothers fought for Glyndwr, believing his cause to be just, and they died in his service."

"And you? Do you believe Glyndwr's cause to have been just?"

I held my breath.

"Aye," she said.

"Jesu," I whispered.

"Those sentiments are treasonous," said the King.

"If such be the case," I said, "then I too am a traitor, for I do judge Glyndwr's cause to have been just. He was wronged, and he sought redress for himself and his people." Merryn's slender hand gripped mine tightly. "You claimed you meant no harm in calling Merryn here. Why then do you charge us so?"

"I charge you with nothing. I merely mark your rashness."

He reached out suddenly and took Merryn's hand from my grasp.

"How came you by this ring?" he asked, and pointed to a gold band upon her middle finger.

"It is from Harry. It is a sign of our love."

"How many rings and baubles has he heaped upon you?"

"Only this."

"Only this? Do you mean he does not entice you with jewelry? You have struck a bad bargain."

"Merryn does not desire jewels of me," I said. "Such things matter not to her."

"Indeed?" His scabrous, twisted claws still held her. "And if Harry's hands were such as mine? Would you still be enamored of him?"

"I would love him still. He would yet be Harry beneath his disfigurement, just as you are yet yourself."

He dropped her hand and settled into his pillows. "You offer my son more than he deserves," he said in a tired voice.

"I freely acknowledge it, my lord father," I said. "And now if your curiosity has been satisfied—"

He waved his hand.

"Go on, then," I said to Merryn.

She curtsied again and ran from the solar.

"Is she with child?" Father asked.

"No, to our sorrow. Why do you ask?"

"I only wondered. I have no grandchildren. I would not shut her up all the day, Harry. Bid her know she is free to come and go as she pleases."

"I marvel at your kindness."

"Do not think I thereby approve of this affair. I do not. It is shameful. Still, I would not be cruel to her."

When the court had gone on its way to Stony Stratford, Merryn and I sat together in the garden.

"I liked him," she said. "I did pity him. He is so lonely and sad."

"He tried to affright you."

"Perhaps he did but test me. I wish you could be reconciled to him. He needs you."

I feared she would say he reminded her much of me, but she did not.

"You do not understand," was all I said in reply.

*   *   *

Father had spoken truly of Coldharbour, for it was a grand house. It perched upon the banks of the Thames, five floors in all and with its own dock. It had high oriel windows, and the chambers were spacious and light. A jewel of a walled garden with pear and apple trees and a maze brought delighted cries from Merryn, and we both marveled at a padded tub for bathing which would accommodate two people in comfort.

Soon after our arrival, I summoned Archbishop Arundel to Coldharbour. He came with great pomp, arrayed in a tall white mitre and a scarlet cope encrusted with jewels. With him he brought a troop of armed men bearing the insignia of Canterbury. They swaggered impatiently about the courtyard, for I would have but two of them inside.

"'Tis quite a display, my lord of Canterbury," I said. "I am impressed, as I am sure I am meant to be."

He bowed. "When summoned by his prince, a prelate should not hide his own dignity," he replied in his high, thin voice. I motioned for him to sit, but he demurred. "I prefer to stand."

"In faith," I said with a smile, "it would be most uncomfortable to sit upon so many jewels."

"Did you call me here for some serious purpose or for childish mockings?"

"My purpose is quite serious, I assure you. I merely observe that you have sought to overawe me with this display. As for myself, I am more commonly arrayed, as you can see."

I was dressed in a robe of plain green wool.

"You are clad as commonly as you are ever accompanied," he said. "As for intimidation, I need not resort to it. I know well the power of the Church, which is far greater than the power of any prince."

"Proudly spoken," I replied. "I call you in recognition of that power and to inform you that I have taken to heart your reproof of a year ago, when at my father's sickbed you did bid me to take heed of my peril. I have taken heed and I have been moved to action. Now I have a request of you."

"What may it be?"

"I would like you to resign the chancellorship."

He blanched but regained his composure at once. "You are mad."

"No, not mad."

"Do you expect that I shall simply do as you bid?"

"Your grace, there are a number of men in parliament who are not friends of the Church. They cry out for reform. I have it on good faith that when parliament next sits, a petition shall be presented which calls for a confiscation of the wealth of the Church. The Church is very wealthy, is it not?"

"Do you threaten me with this fantastic scheme?"

"It is no idle threat. I tell you, if you cross me in this, it shall happen. Many merchants there are who would love to plunder the coffers of the Church, and many men in parliament who owe me favors. They shall back this measure if I bid them to."

"The King would not stand for it."

"The King may have no choice."

"Do you threaten rebellion?"

"I do not tell you what I threaten. But if you are yet unconvinced of my strength, I know well a man who owns some part of those jewels you flaunt. Know you of whom I speak?"

He glared at me with impotent hatred.

"Come, Arundel," I said, "here is a splendid opportunity to act the part of a saint. Throw defiance in my face. Tell me you care not a fig for wealth, that faith alone guides your life. Go you to your prayers poorer but holier."

He stepped toward me menacingly, then seemed to shrink, to crumble before my eyes. Conscience smote me, leaving no room for the triumph I had thought to feel at this moment. I hesitated.

On with it, I urged. He does richly deserve this. I took a deep breath, unable to look at him.

"Your answer?" I said.

He turned and strode from the chamber. I sat down as a wave of nausea washed over me.

Three days after, Arundel resigned as chancellor of England.

The strain of my father's recent journeying had sent him once more to his bed. Besides his usual ailments it was said he had lost all feeling in his feet. Affairs of state were beyond his competence. Arundel, I was certain, would spew forth poisoned incriminations against me. At once, then, I sent another uncle of mine, Thomas Beaufort, to court to speak for the chancellorship. With him went Richard Whittington and John Hende. They reported to me that the King was much disturbed, yet weak and confused. He prated of "Harry's impudence" but they soothed him with praise of my willingness to bear responsibility during his illness, and this he seemed to accept. Thomas Beaufort came away with the chancellor's seal, and on the feast of the Epiphany my own Lord Scrope was appointed treasurer of the realm.

This Thomas Beaufort was younger brother to my uncle Henry Beaufort, Bishop of Winchester, who came to me much incensed upon learning he had been passed over for this high position.

"Afore God, Harry," he cried as he paced before my fire, "I brought you to this! Now you do push me aside. I should leave you for this insult."

"Where would you go?" I reminded him.

"To Tom."

"You would have to slay me, then."

"Do not tempt me."

Merryn, who sat sewing in the corner, looked up fearfully.

"Uncle, this was meant as no insult. You must hear me out."

"What is your defense, then?"

"My supporters are wearied with powerful clergymen, and they wanted none for chancellor. I must mollify the Lollards among them for that I do not support their petition."

"Perhaps you speak truly," he conceded after a moment.

"Never fear. You shall be no idler as we set about governing. I would have you address the Commons when they sit at the end of the month. And I will have you ever at my side to advise me."

More I did not tell him, of how I feared his ambition and his power. Thomas Beaufort had no experience, and I thought to find him pliable and deferential. He would not chafe to be my subordinate. But my good uncle the bishop—at times I judged him but Arundel in another guise. For my part, I longed to rule not by the means I had employed to gain this power but by love. I hungered to have my subjects vouchsafe me their affection because I did govern them well and justly. My uncle Beaufort would take no heed of this, and I would not have him chancellor until I might establish myself more firmly.

Jack Oldcastle came to parliament for the first time as Lord Cobham from Herefordshire and lodged with us at Coldharbour. Many of his friends, men with a keen interest in religious matters, would call upon us there, and we held forth on questions of theology long into the night. Many of their opinions I found congenial, for I was well aware of the decay into which the Church had fallen. Two rival popes there were, one in Rome and one in Avignon, each claiming to be the true successor of St. Peter, each as debauched and cruel as the other. Everywhere could be encountered corrupt clerks for whom chastity was unheard of, who lived lives of luxury at the expense of the poor, who neglected their flocks even to the failure to administer the sacraments. I did not need to be reminded of the machinations of Arundel or of the greed of the canons at Llanthony who had brought Merryn near to starvation. Still I could not bring myself to accept Lollardy. Its teaching concerning the Host, that it was not the Body of Christ but a mere inanimate object, less wonderful than even a living toad or snail, I could not abide. It seemed to me I must cling desperately to the mystery of Christ's presence and grace as to a raft in a wild sea, or what hope of salvation had I as I trod the path of kingship? I disputed with Jack's friends and honored them in their searchings, but throw my lot in with them I could not, much to their chagrin. Some were narrow and intolerant and would no more avail themselves of my company when they deemed me a lost cause. Others were less peevish, and I looked forward to their visits on the snowy winter's nights, for

they had some compassion for my yearnings. Merryn enjoyed them as well
and listened enraptured to our conversation, but never did she venture an
opinion.

Soon after the opening of parliament a man was arrested by Arundel,
tried by the Church, and found guilty of heresy. The unfortunate's name was
John Badby, and he had been among those who sought a place at my hearth.
An intense, wiry little fellow, I recalled, he had been angered by some of my
convictions and had not deigned to return after his second visit. He had not a
seat in the Commons himself, being a tailor of modest means, but had come
from the west, Evesham, I believe, in support of the reform measures being
aimed at the Church. Since his arrival he had noised his views about London
heedless of any peril and had been an easy mark for Arundel. I viewed these
proceedings with considerable uneasiness because of the man's presence at
Coldharbour. Sure I was that Arundel would have had him tortured. What
this might portend I knew not, but I resolved to continue as before until
such time as I had more cause for worry.

That time was soon in coming, for Badby was sentenced to be burned at
the stake. The next day a scarlet-liveried messenger with a summons from
the Archbishop of Canterbury arrived at my gate. I was "requested" to
represent the Crown at the heretic's execution. My failure to appear would
"cast grave aspersions upon the orthodoxy of the Prince of Wales, since the
condemned man was one of his companions."

I told Merryn nothing of this matter, but tossed and turned all the night
as I pondered what I must do. To go would seem to make me complicit in
Arundel's burnings; to stay away would be extremely dangerous. I must go, I
decided, distasteful though it be, else I would play into Arundel's hands. I
rose at dawn and made my way to the site of the burning at Smithfield.

Arundel was already there with a score of black-robed clerks. I did not
acknowledge him with any sign of respect, nor did I even dismount my horse
but sat at the edge of the crowd, my face a studied mask. Packed about me
was a throng of Londoners from all stations of life, many of whom I knew.
Some would be there in silent support of Badby, others for the spectacle of
seeing a living man consumed in flames. The cries of hawkers could be heard
here and there, preaching the virtues of hot trotters and apple cider.

Badby was bound securely to the stake and bales of straw and small logs
were piled about him as high as his thighs. His face was blue and swollen
from some beating, and he shuddered visibly in the winter air, for he wore
but a woolen robe.

"'E shall be warm enough by and by, Jack," a drunken voice called.

Arundel read aloud a statement attesting to the many heresies of John
Badby and declaring the findings of the ecclesiastical court which had judged
him deserving of death. He offered a prayer that, ere Badby's soul departed,
the flames might burn away all offending opinions and leave him purified

and ready to receive salvation. Then he read the order of execution signed
by the King, and a hooded executioner flourished a flaming brand and set it
to the straw in three different places while the clerks intoned the name of
Father, Son, and Holy Ghost.

My stomach churned as the flames leaped through the kindling.
Badby's eyes were closed, his lips moved silently. Wreaths of smoke masked
his face. When it reappeared he was gasping for breath as the air about him
became an inferno. His mouth twisted, opened; his head lolled back against
the wooden stake.

I found myself sliding from my horse, pushing frantically through the
crowd, grabbing the black-cowled executioner by the arms and shaking him.

"Quench the fire!" I cried.

Beneath the hood his eyes, like two live animals, rolled at me.

"Quench it, do you hear!" I screamed. "I am the Prince of Wales! I
command you!"

I thrust him from me so that he nearly fell, then I began to kick at the
blazing pile. I called for the armed men of my household who had accompanied me, and with their pikes they dragged away the burning debris and
beat at the flames. Badby sagged against his ropes as a trail of orange flame
wound its way up the skirt of his robe.

"Cut him loose and smother the flames," I ordered. "There is yet life in
him."

The crowd murmured in amazement and pushed to get a better view so
that the Archbishop's men must hold them back. A powerful hand grabbed
me roughly and yanked me around. Arundel's livid face was but inches from
mine.

"What do you think you are doing?"

"I am stopping this atrocity!"

"You cannot stop it! You have not the power."

I swallowed. "Has not the Prince—"

"The Prince has no say in this save to acknowledge it. The Church has
found him guilty and the King has signed his warrant. You cannot gainsay it
unless you wish to find yourself at the stake, and I swear before God and all
His angels, if you interfere with this I shall put you there."

I blinked back tears of rage. "And if he recant?"

"Then he is saved," Arundel said. "Yet he has ever refused before. And
I judge him in no condition to repent now."

Badby had been stretched upon the frozen ground. His robe was in
charred tatters from the waist down, exposing his badly burned legs to the
cold. I knelt beside him.

"John Badby," I said in his ear. "You do know me. It is Henry, the
Prince of Wales."

He moaned. His eyes were shut and his eyebrows had been singed away. There was about him the salty smell of a smokehouse.

"Badby," I begged, "you must recant. Do you understand me? If you but recant your earlier statements I may save you. Jesu, man, is it worth this? The sacraments shall keep their value whatever you say. Do not let Arundel have you. For God's sake, man, recant."

His cracked lips parted and I bent to catch his words.

"No," he croaked. "Get behind me, Satan."

I stood up and looked into the mocking face of Arundel. While I returned to my horse Badby was tied once more to the stake and the bales set afire. I sat with head bowed until the flames blazed above his head and then I rode back to Coldharbour, leaving the stunned and silent crowd in my wake.

"God save good Prince Harry," a woman called as I departed.

"Indeed," I muttered.

"In God's name, Harry, I would not have thought this of you," Jack raged.

"Jack, will you leave me be! Is it not enough that Arundel torments me?"

"Do not prate to me of Arundel! It is you I speak of, not Arundel. Do not hide your sin behind his. It is bad enough that you went to that place. Then must you tempt Badby as well into a recantation? You imperiled his very soul. Thank God he stood firm."

"I was but trying to save him. I tried to stop it, but I could not. Arundel did threaten me with the stake. What was I to do?"

"You could have gone to it. You are no better than Badby."

I threw up my hands. "You speak foolishness. I am no Lollard."

"Indeed, I know it now. I had hopes for you, Harry. You did seem to have some interest in our beliefs."

"So I do."

"Oh, aye, but in the end, when all is said and done, you are a prince, are you not? You believe in nothing save that which advances your cause. Oh, you speak incessantly of doing the right thing. You do weary me with it. But you mean not a word of it. There is a special place in Hell for such as you."

"No, Jack, it is not true!" Merryn sprang to my defense. "You are unfair and hurtful."

"Is this all our friendship means," I said, "that you would say such things to me?"

"Our friendship is forfeit."

"No, Jack," Merryn cried. "You must wait until your temper has cooled. It speaks for you now."

"You defend him, but will he defend us? Suppose Arundel catches me in his net? Will brave Harry Monmouth speak for me, or shall he protect himself?"

"Jack, you know—"

"Answer me this, Harry," he interrupted. "What if it were Merryn at the stake? Would you walk away from it?"

"You insult me. How can you suggest that I could ever let Merryn die unless I did die myself in the protecting of her? I would risk anything for her. In any case, she is in no danger."

"Indeed?" He raised his bushy eyebrows. "Tell him, Merryn."

"Jack," she said, "I know not if—"

"Tell him! It is deceit to keep it from him."

"Merryn, what does he mean?"

She came to me and placed her hands in mine. "I did not mean to deceive you but only to spare you worry, for you have much to trouble you already. I want to be no trouble, but only a solace. I think now I was wrong to keep this from you."

"Go on."

"I have been reading the scripture. Long ago, when I was first at Monmouth learning to read, and you were away in London, Jack left with me a gospel of St. Luke written in the Welsh tongue, and I did read it. Do you recall when we stood upon the Kymin and I assured you of God's love for you? I had read of it in the scripture. I still read the scripture, now in Wyclyf's English."

I dropped her hands and turned from her.

"Do you see?" Jack said. "Where is his love for you now?"

"Harry, you must try to understand. I am no Lollard, despite what Jack says. I do not agree with him on many points. But I cannot stop reading the scripture. I read the most marvelous things—of God's love, and how in turn we are to love our enemies—"

"You must stop," I said. "It is against the laws of the Church for anyone but a priest to read the scripture."

"I cannot stop," she said. "You are prince of England, but you are not prince over me and you may not order me to stop."

I sat and buried my face in my hands. "And what if Arundel learns of it? He has spies about. How better to harm me than to charge you with heresy? Jesu, I cannot bear to think on it."

"We must pray that it does not happen." She stroked my hair. "I pledge you this: I shall read my scripture only when I am alone, and I shall not publicly dispute these matters. I have been quiet until now and I shall remain so."

"Bah!" Jack cried. "And where is the integrity of your witness? More and more I care not who knows my beliefs, and shall tell them to Arundel himself if he asks."

"That is up to you," Merryn replied. "Yet I cannot say that God would wish us to bring hurt upon those we love if it is not needed. Nor need we seek martyrdom. If God wishes martyrdom for us, it shall come. For myself, I shall study God's word and I shall love my Harry. I am content with it, and I pray God is content as well."

"You speak as though Harry were worthy of your love. Know you what else he does? He connives with the most corrupt men in the kingdom to pursue power. He sells his very soul for power. And he uses his friends as well. You do not intend to back our petition to confiscate the wealth of the Church, do you, Harry?"

"No," I said wearily, naked of all defenses.

"I thought not. I was the greatest fool in Christendom to have trusted you."

"Jack, I gave my word to Arundel that I would oppose the petition if he would step down as chancellor. With him out of the way, some good may be done. Nothing so drastic as what you propose, but—"

"You play games with me."

"I cannot alienate all the Church. I shall need her help when I am King. The people shall need her help. I would cure her ills, but I fear your remedy is worse than the disease. I cannot agree with you upon the sacraments—"

I stopped, hard put to continue.

"What is the use?" I whispered. "You are set against me."

"I will stay not a night longer under your roof, and I part no friend of yours."

He stalked out, slamming the door behind him. I sat still.

"I am sorry," Merryn said. "Perhaps he shall be back. Your friendship goes back so far."

"No better friend did I have than Jack Oldcastle, and now he is gone. How long, I wonder, until you follow him?"

"You must not fear that."

"Why not? You see what I am, and you read your scriptures and learn of holy men and their deeds. How long shall it be before I disgust you?"

I left her then, and would not go to our bed that night but sat in the chapel until I fell asleep in my chair. She found me there as the dawn glowed pink upon the glazed windows, and she woke me and pillowed my head upon her breast.

"I did try to save him," I mumbled.

"I know it. I love you for trying."

I did not tell her how I had passed the night, how I had watched the dancing shadows while the candle I had with me yet burned. When its flame was spent there was but a shaft of moonlight from the window. The altar was all dark save for the glint of the gold crucifix. It was the temple of God, and there was no comfort there.

10

For two years I was the uncrowned King of England. Father's malady had affected his limbs so that he could move them but little. He suffered in mind as well, for his headaches continued and he was often disoriented. Even Arundel gave up on him and retired to Lambeth to sulk. I set out unencumbered to keep the promises I had made to my supporters, and Scrope and I spent many a long hour at the tedious task of putting in order the finances of the realm. Most of all, though, I was fascinated by statecraft and I turned my attention to France.

A woeful time it was indeed for that fair land. Her king, Charles the Sixth of Valois, was a madman. During our King Richard's reign, insanity had overtaken him as he rode out with his troops to face a rebellious nobleman. Never a strong man, Charles had traveled many hours beneath a white hot sun amid the flashes and glints of his company's armor. The sound of a sword clattering upon a shield, so I have heard, unleashed a bevy of demons upon his enfeebled brain and, thinking himself under attack, he threw himself in murderous rage upon his own attendants, so that they did wrestle him raving to the ground. It was said he slew several of them ere they did subdue him, and blood was spilled which has not ceased to flow in unfortunate France.

A king may be mad, or a babe, or an invalid as was my father, yet someone must rule. In France there were many hunters who wished to slay the deer. The King's uncle John, called the Fearless, Duke of Burgundy, was one such, a powerful and ruthless lord. Another was Louis, Duke of Orléans, the King's younger brother. Burgundy and Orléans hated each other. Louis was even more vile than his uncle. He oppressed the poor of France in countless ways, even to abducting their daughters to use for his pleasure and then turning them out to their fathers the next day. When his star rose the people groaned, for he taxed them unmercifully to support lavish entertainments where, it was whispered, women danced naked for his enjoyment. Such debauchery has been all too common a badge of the nobility of France.

There was rejoicing, both singing and dancing, in the streets of Paris when Orléans was murdered there in 1407 by the retainers of the Duke of Burgundy. Sadly, this deed brought no end to the dispute, for Orléans had a son, Charles, the very man who had wed my childhood love, the delicate Isabel. Charles was no better than his father. I heard this with sorrow for the sake of that fair lass I have named, who was fated to die soon after in the bearing of Orléans' child.

Charles of Orléans gathered to his side his royal uncles of Berry, Bourbon, and Brittany to oppose the ambitious Burgundy. Then did the warring begin in earnest, and the weeping of widows and orphans carried even across the Channel to England. Of all wars, none is more cruel than civil war. As with all wars of chivalry, this one was fought with reckless abandon. The savage armies ranged widely across the land, cutting down any wretch who ventured into their path and devouring the provender of the land. Little enough damage did these brave knights to one another.

I pondered the plight of France with disgust and could not help but hark back to my earlier musings. Suppose one man, one strong man, were king of all? Suppose that man ruled justly, so that none of the peoples under him need complain of ill treatment? Would this not be a blessing to Christendom and the best hope of peace? I thought on it carefully, and when both French parties sought aid from England, I was ready to act.

The Armagnacs, as the followers of Orléans were then called, I sent bootless away. With the Burgundians I treated, and I resolved after much inward debate to send an army to their aid. I attached the condition that no English soldier would ride on the pillaging chevachees and that Englishmen would be employed soon in a fixed battle for some purpose or else sent home. These instructions I charged to my captains, one of whom was Jack Oldcastle.

Jack's anger had kept him from me for a year. Then one day I found him waiting at my hearth, a welcome sight indeed. We embraced awkwardly.

"I came to beg your forgiveness," he said. "It has taken me these twelve months to swallow my pride. I played the hypocrite, for while I badgered you about your courage I had not found enough myself to declare my faith to the world, and still have not. I asked more of you, who are no Lollard, than I did of myself. I hurt you, and I am sorry. I yet would name myself your friend."

"Friend indeed you are," I said, "and ne'er had any man a truer one."

Merryn came from wandering about the markets of Billingsgate to find us laughing before the fire. Yet was there a constraint between us which I feared would never be gone, as each of us wondered what new testings of our love we would be led to. We did not speak of such things, and Jack went as my servant to France, a surety that the campaign would be conducted as I wished.

Many were not happy with my choice of allies. Charles of Orléans and his uncles were deemed the very exemplars of chivalry, and most of England's peers were in sympathy with the Armagnac cause. Tom came to me to voice their opposition.

"The French court is the jewel of Christendom," he argued. "All look to Berry, to Bourbon, as patterns of gentilesse. Burgundy, on the other hand, is a renegade, though royal blood does flow in his veins. Look at his cowardly murder of Louis of Orléans, his own nephew. He dared not meet that chevalier in the lists as would a true knight. Instead he employed the most common sort of men to stab Orléans while he rode in a dark Paris street. Why support such a craven?"

"Why? Because he shall win."

"Harry, how can you say it? The flower of chivalry fights for Orléans. Burgundy relies upon a mercenary rabble."

"And that is precisely why he shall win. The French peers are more foolish than the English, if that is possible."

He threw up his hands. "How may I convince one so pigheaded?" he moaned.

"You cannot. You must be patient with me, that is all. I am not happy to aid Burgundy, mind you. He is, as you say, a foul murderer."

"Your dealings with him force you to wallow in the muck."

"You speak as though Orléans were pure. He is not, brother. No, the alternative to Burgundy is to do nothing. I have considered that. But inaction will not help the French people who suffer through these knightly games. So, I hold my nose and seek to force an end upon these warriors. And perhaps I may do so at some terms favorable to England. I'll not fight just any war, Tom. There must be accomplishment in it."

"And I may not change your mind?"

"No."

"Father will be most displeased. He was incensed over the murder of Orléans four years ago. I say it plainly, you dishonor him by pursuing policies he would abhor."

"I must do what I must do. Nor shall Father's lack of judgment deter me."

"What shall you do if his condition improves? It has happened before."

"I shall take that as it comes."

Of all my critics, the most difficult to answer was Merryn.

"You have sent Englishmen to fight in France?"

"Aye."

"Oh, Harry, that means you have sent poor men to their deaths."

I shuddered, for we were walking at dusk in the garden at Coldharbour and the wind from the Thames was chill.

"None went to France under duress," I countered. "All freely chose to go."

"Still, it was you who sent them."

"What if I did? I had good reasons of which you know nothing. There is civil war in France, and someone must end it."

"Is there not a better way? Can you truly end war with more war?"

"What would you have me do? Hold their hands and beg them to drop their weapons like good children?"

"There is no need to mock me. I do not say it would be easy, or even that you would succeed. But God would be pleased if you did try."

"Would He? You are sometimes too glib with your advice. Why does the Church speak no word of condemnation for what I do?"

"Well you know the corruption of the Church. As for the scriptures, therein Our Lord does say, 'Blessed are the peacemakers.'"

"Yet Our Lord was no earthly king," I said. "Perhaps He cares not for kings and princes but abandons us to the Devil while He concerns Himself with the saints."

She parted from me to stand in a shadowed corner of the garden. I left her alone for a time but finally stood behind her and set my hands upon her shoulders. She did not respond.

"I would not quarrel with you, Merryn. I am peevish, I do admit it. And so have you been of late. You do not laugh often these days."

"I am weary of London," she said. "As summer comes upon us I long for Wales, I long for the mountains. I dream of tending my sheep again. It has been long, Harry, so long. Two years have I been from Wales, and I am sick for it."

"Well," I said, trying to hide my hurt, "you may return if you wish. Joan would be glad for your company, I am certain."

"Would you not come? Then I would not go! Harry, my love, I would have you out of this place as well. I like not what it does to you. You grow so cynical and calculating."

"My days are full now," I protested. "The realm—"

"—is ably served by the chancellor and Scrope. It is not so far to

Monmouth. You could do much business there and return quickly if need be. But three months, Harry, 'tis all I ask. To wander the green hills for but three months. With you. It shall be as before."

I took her in my arms and kissed her hard upon the mouth.

"More there is," she whispered as she clung to me. "All these years I have lain with you, yet I bear you no child. I want to so badly, and I pray and pray, yet I do not conceive. Perhaps I am too far from home. Harry, would you not like a son, with hair of brown and wide eyes like your own, and his father's dimple upon his chin?"

"I should like a daughter who was a twin of her mother."

"Then take me back to Monmouth and love me there. Then it will happen, I know it will. There is magic at Monmouth."

"I knew not this had troubled you so. Perhaps it is all for the best. My own mother was worn out with bearing six babes in six years, and so I lost her. I would not have it so with you."

"Yet to bear you no children! It grieves me to think of it. I want a child to live after us, a sign of our love, no matter what happens to us. Your child."

"Hush, then. I cannot long gainsay you. We shall summer at Monmouth if you wish it so."

We sat upon the brow of the Kymin beside the fairy castle and surveyed the emerald-green valley.

"Do you know what I should like to do?" Merryn asked dreamily.

"Herd sheep all the summer."

She poked me in the belly. "You may laugh, but it would pleasure me. Still, what I had in mind is even more wonderful. Is it not true that Arthur's sorcerer, Merlyn, sleeps deep in a cave awaiting Arthur's return, when he shall rouse himself and work his spells once more?"

"So it is said."

"And does this enchanted cave not lie here in Gwent?"

"So the old people say. Do not tell me you would seek this cave?"

"I would!"

"Shall we seek throughout all Gwent?"

"If we must. We shall find it. I know it in my bones. And when we do, we shall return to it upon our last day in Monmouth, and there we shall make love. Merlyn's magic shall give us a babe."

For many weeks we rode up and down Monnow and Wye, and even into the Forest of Dean, and we found several caves, but none was enchanted.

"Has all magic fled from the land?" Merryn lamented as we sat upon the bank of the glittering Wye casting for fish.

"All magic fled and dragons slain, and the fairies are in hiding, Joan says."

"I'll not believe it. Something there is which blinds us to it, that is all."

In July, messengers came spurring their horses from London. I read their dispatches in the solar and then sought Merryn in the garden, where I found her romping with Rhodri. She froze when she saw my face.

"You have bad tidings?"

"Not so bad. There has been a battle in France. At a place called St. Cloud it was, near Paris. The English and the Burgundians did carry the day."

I knelt to stroke the spaniel's silken ears.

"Jack?"

"He is well. The dispatches say he fought bravely."

"Jesu be praised for his safety. And how many slain?"

"Forty-one Englishmen. Two hundred of Burgundy's men. Some four hundred of the Armagnacs."

"Oh, Harry," she whispered, "so many. So many men, and their poor wives weeping for them. I cannot name such loss as victory."

"Do not think I rejoice in it. But what could I do? The French would have fought among themselves anyway, would they not? Now at least Burgundy controls much of northern France. Soon he shall be in Paris itself, and the strife ended."

"No, it shall not end, for children who have lost fathers at St. Cloud shall grow up with their mothers' bitterness for food, and they shall learn to hate this side or that and plot vengeance, and they shall slay the father of some other child and make more orphans still. Where shall it end? It shall not, I fear, until there are none left to slay."

A sharp pain tore through my belly so that I wanted to cry out, but I only flinched. Slowly I sat down.

"I can defend myself against all save you," I managed to say.

A fortnight later we found another cave, this one near to Symond's Yat, but there was no magic in it and we did not make love. Nor was Merryn with child when we returned to London.

Soon after we settled into Coldharbour came the controversy that would lead to my downfall. Arundel had carried his heresy hunts even into the universities, and soon all Oxford was in turmoil. There John Wyclyf had been venerated as a saintly man and his teachings were studied by many clerks, even those who were not Lollards. Arundel resolved to root out this treacherous influence and called for a burning of each parchment which bore Wyclyf's work, as well as an examination of every master and student in the university. To my good friend Courtenay, who was yet chancellor at Oxford, few things were more repugnant than the burning of books and the subsequent degradation of ideas. When Arundel went to the university church of St. Mary's to read his edict and carry out his threats, he found the doors locked against him. Then was he furious, for he knew Courtenay to be my confidant, and called upon him to relinquish his post or face excommunication. Brave Courtenay in his turn reminded the Archbishop that Arundel was himself a former student of Oxford and had therefore sworn a sacred oath to uphold her ancient privileges against all meddling. If the good Archbishop pressed his demands, Courtenay proclaimed, he would himself be excommunicate for perjury of his oath. As for the young clerks of the university, many had armed themselves to resist by force, if necessary, Arundel's threat of inquisition. Here matters stood until I intervened.

My lord of Canterbury was not pleased with the terms I negotiated. Oxford would recognize his jurisdiction, but only if he agreed not to exercise it. Courtenay would step down as chancellor, but the university proctors were free to re-elect him, which they did soon after. Shaken and humiliated, Arundel returned to London to lick his wounds and plot my removal once and for all. I thought myself reasonably safe, for Father was yet quite ill. In this I underestimated the lengths to which Arundel would go.

Early in Advent I sat at Westminster with the King's council, reviewing the revenues of the wool staple. Into our presence burst four men wearing the royal livery and armed with swords. Arundel followed them into the room.

"A proclamation from his royal grace, King Henry," one man cried.

Arundel smiled broadly and unrolled a parchment. "My lords, and your most royal highness." He bowed low before me. "His grace bids me preface this order with a reading from that renowned father of the Church, John of Salisbury: 'Any authority which a prince has received is from the Church.'" Here he looked pointedly at me. "'Therefore is the prince servant to the priest.'"

I looked at Scrope, who rolled his eyes skyward.

"My lords," Arundel continued, "I now read to you the words of the King. 'The Prince of Wales, our son, has shown himself irresponsible and requires chastisement. He has grossly interfered with Holy Church in her efforts to maintain the teaching of true doctrine, as the Archbishop of Canterbury has complained to us. Likewise has he offended his sovereign by the adhering to foreign policies which are repugnant to us. Here we refer to the spilling of English blood in the service of the renegade Duke of Burgundy. Therefore we declare the Prince of Wales removed from our council, never to sit upon it again in our reign. Nor shall he again enjoy our confidence. His brother Thomas we create Duke of Clarence and set to represent us on the council. Likewise are Thomas Beaufort, chancellor of the realm, and Henry Scrope, Lord Masham, treasurer of the realm, removed from their positions of trust.'"

Arundel waved the parchment. "'Tis signed by the King, my lords," he said, "and so I bid you good day."

"Signed by the King!" I exclaimed and strode to him, snatching the parchment from his hand. There was a signature upon it, so shaky as to be indecipherable save for a large jagged H.

"If my father indeed signed this he was exceedingly weak," I said. "What did you, my lord? Did you hold the quill to his hand yourself and force him into these strokes?"

"This signature is the King's, freely rendered, and these sentiments as well. He is not too weak to be appalled by your behavior. And he is yet King of England."

"I demand to see him, to hear this from his own mouth."

"It is impossible."

"Do you tell me I cannot go to my own father?"

"Your highness, you are estranged from him. He will not see you."

None of the men on the council would meet my eyes. Arundel's escort had placed their mailed hands ominously upon their sword hilts. A sudden fear presented itself, that if I said one word more in protest I would be cut down where I stood and then declared a rebel against the King. I turned and left the hall, Thomas Beaufort and Henry Scrope scurrying behind me.

No one spoke until we had called for a barge and had put safely out on the murky Thames toward Coldharbour.

"Jesu, Harry," said Scrope, "if such is his mood, lucky you are he did not disinherit you."

"He knows I would not have stood for it," I replied grimly.

"Have a care, nephew," said Thomas Beaufort. "Your words are close to treason. As Arundel said, he is yet the King. It would go ill for you if others heard you."

"Master Barnes," I called to the bargemaster, "I have changed my mind. I would put across the river to Kennington."

"Why?" Scrope said.

"Tom lodges there, and I would speak of this with him."

"Is it wise?" Scrope asked. "He has much to gain."

I leaned back and regarded the gray wisps of cloud scudding dizzily overhead. "Tom has ever been straight with me."

So he was once more. "Father is yet ill, but his senses are more and more about him. And he did sign your dismissal, for I was present when he did."

"And the wording?"

"Arundel's, of course. But he speaks truly, brother. Father is most wroth with you, and he will not see you. I did warn you. He thinks you seek to set him aside, and Arundel encourages him to believe it despite my reassurances. Harry, heed my advice. Leave London at once. Get you as far away as you may and do nothing until your time comes."

"No. I shall not leave. I shall not give Arundel the satisfaction."

"Listen to me, you dolt. Arundel is after you. He did suggest that you be stripped of your inheritance and imprisoned in the Tower, and that I be created Prince of Wales."

"What?"

"I thought as much," Scrope muttered.

"Harry, I am loath to wound you by the telling of it, but Father did hearken to the idea. Only when I said I would have none of it did he let it go. I swear to you, and you must believe me, I did vehemently refuse such a plan. I am loyal to you, brother."

His brown eyes were pleading and he gripped my arm.

"I dispute much of your policy," he said, "and I have my own ambitions, but before God, and His Son, and the Holy Mary, never could I seek to supplant you. No true knight would, nor true brother."

"In faith," I said, "I do believe you."

He sighed. "That is good. Now flee, as I bid you."

"No. I shall not quit London."

Nor did I, but returned to Coldharbour and threw myself into the Yuletide preparations of the household. My uncle Beaufort urged me to pressure Arundel through the merchants, but I deemed it imprudent, given my father's temper. A fortnight later I was summoned to court to accept command of an English force to be sent to France to aid the Armagnacs. I would not go near the palace but sent a curt note of refusal. Tom was then given the post, and Jack and his men were called home. With fresh troops and coin, Orléans and his uncles terrorized the countryside with slashing raids, as if the peasantry and not Burgundy were their enemy. Tom wrote to me that every man in his company had made his fortune from his plunderings. Burgundy retreated without gaining Paris, and all the deaths which had caused me such agony were indeed for naught.

Merryn took calmly the news of my disgrace. "Now I shall have you about more," was all that she would say.

I grumbled at her, but her happiness was infectious and soon I joined in it. My days were more idle than they had been in years so we were often together, and the strain of the year past vanished. Together we explored London town. The people did love to behold their prince wandering about in a plain black cloak, hand in hand with his lady, sampling the wares of the hawkers and lifting a glass in the alehouses. Now more than ever I knew their hearts belonged to me, and this I deemed more valuable than gold.

Nor could my predicament taint the joy of that Yuletide. Jack had returned from France and was met at Coldharbour by his wife, Joan. Courtenay came to apologize for the trouble he feared he had caused me, and he too stayed to celebrate with us the twelve days of Christmas.

On Christmas Day we feasted upon boar's head and roast swan and a

steaming mound of plum pudding. Merryn it was who found the shiny silver
coin hidden within her portion, and the company toasted her with wassail.

"'Tis our Welsh lass who shall enjoy good luck this year," said Jack,
"and none does deserve it more, I say."

"And what shall your luck bring you?" Courtenay asked.

"You know it is bad luck to tell," she replied with a blush, "yet I'll wager
Harry can guess it."

I knew that she hoped for the babe, and I squeezed her hand beneath
the table.

When we had supped near to bursting, Merryn and I entertained the
company with song. She had learned the recorder and I played upon my
harp and sang "Lullay, Lullow" and a lilting Nowell. We performed as well a
carol of my own composition, an Ave Maria penned out of love for the
Virgin, but when I sang that Lady's praises it was Merryn who was ever
before my eyes.

Spring was late in coming that year, and April brought snows as heavy as any
in January. Merryn and I wandered the riverbank as though in a dream
while great ragged flakes like lacy handkerchiefs wafted down. All London
was bewitched, the usual raucous din engulfed in white silence. The tattered
inhabitants ambled with awkward grace through the drifts, snowy mantles
draping their shoulders as delicately as any noble lady's cape.

We came home that evening apple-cheeked from a romp in the snow
with Rhodri and supped well on a savory mutton stew. With winks and
smiles we made promises of the pleasures of the night to come, and we
retired early, bearing our candles before us. I had just set my taper upon a
table beside our bed when I heard the low rattle of Rhodri's growl. My
downturned gaze fell upon the brown tips of a man's boots just protruding
from beneath a hanging tapestry.

He burst from behind the arras ere I could think, his long slender knife
flashing in the candlelight. Merryn screamed. I had just time to throw up my
arm. His hurried thrust at my throat was wide of the mark, and then he fell
against me and we both crashed to the floor. I landed upon my back and
struck my head hard upon the stone but did not lose my senses. The man
thrust again with his knife. I grasped his wrist and with all my strength held
him back. The point of the knife quivered but an inch from my eye. His
breath fell foul and hot upon my face. The vein in my temple throbbed, and
his face burned red before me.

Then the weight was torn from me, the man pulled away by my attendants and pummeled into submission. Rhodri was yapping wildly. Merryn
leaned weeping over me.

"Oh, Harry, my Harry! Are you hurt? I feared he would slay you before
my very eyes."

For some reason, her clinging irritated me. "Leave me be!" I said.

I knew this rough answer must hurt her, but I cared not. I lay quiet as I gathered my strength and sought to still the trembling of my limbs. At last I sat up and looked to where my would-be assassin lay trussed like a pig at market. He was a rude, dull-looking sort, and I knew at once he could not have acted of his own. Wine was given me, and I drank and stood up shakily.

"How did he get in?" I asked the frightened attendants. They dropped their eyes in confusion and said nothing. A fury gripped me such as I had never known in my life. I flung my cup clattering into the hearth.

"In God's name, answer me! How did he get in?"

They fell back before me.

"I-i-in truth," one stammered, "we know not, your highness."

Scrope had entered the chamber, and it was he who said, "There were some workmen about today. Perchance he slipped in with them."

"And whence came the workmen?"

"From Westminster. I engaged the royal masons to repair a privy upstairs."

"From Westminster."

I knelt before my assailant, grasped him by the shirt, and raised his head. His eyes lolled white.

"Who paid you?" I demanded.

His mouth opened to reveal a row of blackened stumps of teeth.

"Who paid you?" I shook him.

"I'm to say naught," he moaned.

"Afore God, you shall talk ere we are through with you. Scrope, take him at once to the Tower. I would know whose agent he is."

Scrope nodded, and with the attendants he hauled the man away like a sack of oats.

"Harry," Merryn entreated tearfully, "you are overwrought."

"Leave me be!" I shouted.

She shrank back. "You shall not have him tortured?"

"If I must. Yet I think it shall not be necessary. He is already frightened out of what wits he had."

"If he was paid to do this, he must have been desperate. Perhaps he needed food for his children. Promise me you shall be merciful with him."

"Merryn, you seem not to understand. Were it not for the dog, I would have died this night."

"I have never seen you so harsh as you are now."

"Do you listen to me? I might have died! Do you not care about that?"

"I, too, came after you once with a knife."

"So you did." I paced back and forth.

"Well?"

My anger could no longer be reined. I gripped her shoulders roughly.

"I am weary of your childish questions," I said. "I am weary of your judgments of me."

"Harry, you are hurting me."

"You wonder that I am harsh. That man was sent to slay me, and do you know by whom? By my beloved father! Would it not harden a saint? At last he has had enough of me, and so he does what King Richard and Harry Percy would not do for him. He will have me killed."

"You are not yourself. It is your fear that speaks for you. He would not do such a thing."

"Why not? He bears me no love."

"He does love you."

"He hates me! Twice he abandoned me to his enemies. Do not preach to me. You know nothing of what it has been like."

"It must have been Arundel. It could not have been your father. As for your estrangement, you are not yourself blameless—"

I could bear no more reproach. I struck her a blow across her face, so that she staggered. Bright red blood trickled from the corner of her mouth where the tender lip had been split.

We stared at each other in horror.

"Jesu! What have I done? Merryn, never had I thought to strike you."

I took a step toward her. She stiffened.

"Do not touch me. Never touch me again."

She fled from the chamber.

I looked at the hand that had dealt her the blow. I longed to cut it off, to fling it from me. I was overcome with self-loathing. No wonder my father had sought to slay me. I did not deserve to live.

My despair drove me out of Coldharbour and into the black London night. Two of my retainers sought to stop me but I ordered them away and they withdrew, still calling to me of the perils which lurk in the dark. I pushed my way through the snow to Botolph's Wharf, where sailors gather who would not know me. It was a mean area of twisting alleys, its buildings little more than wattle huts. I found a dingy hole of a tavern packed with rough fellows from many lands seeking shelter from the cold. I pushed my way into a corner, called for a quantity of cheap wine, and drank myself into a stupor.

The din of voices became a soothing murmur. My memory blurred and I began to nod. Once in a while an impassioned outburst of Portuguese or some such tongue would rouse me. Merryn would cry at me again, and I would drink some more.

A hand grasped my shoulder and shook me. "'Ere you! I'm closing. Pay up and get out."

He was a wavering specter to me. I groped for my purse but could not open it.

'Ere," he said again, and opened it himself.

"Gold pieces," someone said from a distance.

"Not here. Outside."

"What?" I muttered. "What is the trouble? Is my coin not good?"

They hoisted me up.

The cold air cleared my head a bit. Three men carried me roughly along. We came to a small snowy enclosure, an alley, perhaps.

"Where are we?" I moaned.

"Let us 'ave the purse then," one man said.

The purse was ripped from my belt.

"There be a fine ring upon 'is finger. Take it before we dump 'im."

"Fine indeed. Who d'you think 'e be to show 'ere alone with gold?"

It came to my muddled brain that they might mean to slay me, and I struggled awkwardly to free myself. Something hard struck me in the belly, so that I bent double in pain and gasped for breath. A blow to the face dropped me to my knees. Arms went around my neck and lifted me so that I choked. As I struggled, fingers raked at my eyes, my mouth. I found one finger with my teeth and blood spurted hot in my mouth. The wounded man screamed and flung me against a wall. Another boot in the ribs, and I blessedly lost my senses.

I woke deep in a snowdrift. My cloak was gone, and I shivered uncontrollably. I tried to rise. I retched and puked the sour wine. Each heave sent pure fire coursing along my battered chest. At last I managed to pull myself up, to stagger and fall and finally crawl through the snow to the alley's entrance. Here my strength deserted me. I sank into a drift and thought that the snow might warm me if I could but pile enough of it over me.

A shaft of light fell across the snow. A door had opened near me and several laughing men emerged.

"Help me," I cried as loudly as I might. "Help, in Jesu's name."

I do not believe they heard me, but one saw me then.

"Here, Bet!" he called out. "Here is a lusty fellow to take into your bed."

The others laughed again.

"Is 'e drunk, then?" a woman's voice said.

"So it seems."

"'E shall freeze to death where 'e is. Bring 'im inside."

"No, leave him be," one man protested. "I am too tired to lift such a weight."

"Bring 'im in at once, Will," the woman said. "I'll 'ave no frozen corpse without my house to give it a bad name. Someone may think I did 'im in."

I cried out when they lifted me and nearly fainted when they dumped me before the hearth.

"We're off, then. Enjoy your new friend."

The fire crackled near my face but I could feel no warmth, nor could I move.

"'Ere, then," the woman said, quite close. "You've been beaten on. No cloak either, and wet with snow."

Her arm went around my neck, lifted my head.

"Drink this," she commanded.

It was a strong potion which splashed my insides with reviving fire. She undressed me, covered me with a heavy blanket, and pillowed my head.

"Thank you," I whispered through battered lips.

She sat beside me. "Wot's your name?" she asked.

"Harry." I shivered.

"Are you yet cold?"

"Aye."

She slipped beneath the blanket and lay beside me so that the warmth of her body comforted my naked skin.

"Who did this to you?"

"I knew them not. They robbed me. I had been drinking."

"Those boots I pulled from your feet, they were fine boots. You are a gentleman, are you not?"

"No. I am in service in a rich household, that is all."

"Where?"

"At Coldharbour, with the Prince of Wales."

"The Prince! There is a lad! Once I saw 'im, in Candlewick, it was, on 'is way to someplace important, I suppose. 'Tis 'andsome 'e is, as a prince should be. 'E—"

She lifted her head and studied my face in the firelight.

"'E's 'arry as well, is 'e not? The Prince?"

"Aye, we have the same name."

She lay still, and I fell asleep.

When I woke I was in her bed, and it was day. She sat near the fire.

"Hello," I said and smiled.

"'Ello."

"How did I get in bed?"

"When you was warmed up, I walked you to my bed. I do think you was walking in your sleep."

"How long have I slept?"

"All the day. But an hour more and night will fall."

Merryn shall be frantic, I thought. Then I recalled our parting and my shame returned. I shut my eyes against the memory.

"I shall wait until dark," I said, "and then I shall leave. That is, if I am no burden to you?"

"It matters not to me. Are you well enough to move about?"

"I think I am." I sat up slowly, painfully.

"Your clothes are 'ere. I dried them by the fire."

"You are most kind."

"And I 'ave been out and bought you a pork pie. I pray that shall satisfy you."

"I promise you I shall repay you when I am able."

"Never mind. Shall I wash your face? It is all bloodied."

"No, it shall be tended soon enough."

She helped me to dress, clucking over the knot on my chest.

"I fear I have cracked a rib or two," I said.

"Aye, and your face be black and blue. But it shall 'eal and you shall be 'andsome as you were the day I saw you."

"What?"

"I told you I saw you once in Candlewick, and 'andsome you were." She smiled archly. "Many men I see, but I forget none of them."

"So I have not fooled you."

I sat gingerly at her table and helped myself to a slab of pie. She sat across from me, her chin in her hand. Young, she was, and drab, her stringy hair a lifeless brown, her face long and freckled.

"Your name is Bet?"

She nodded.

"How long have you taken on men?"

"'Bout a year."

"Why are you not in a house with other women?"

"I was, up in Love Lane, but I 'ated it there. Noisy it was all the time, and they was mean to me."

"Is it not dangerous by yourself?"

"I don't know. Nothing's 'appened yet. I got a man to look in on me from time to time. 'E brings me business, too."

"Do you like this life?"

"'Course." She tossed her head. "Why'd I do it if I didn't?"

"You do not fool me any more than I fooled you."

"Will you preach at me then? I 'ear you've spent some time with 'ores yourself."

I smiled, and she was suddenly abashed at her boldness.

"It is wot I 'eard," she murmured.

"You heard right. Yet it has been a few years since I visited a whore. Tell me, why do you do it?"

She stared at her hands. "'Cause I got a mother in the Stews with ten brothers and sisters, and me the oldest, is why. 'Cause they got to eat, is why."

"This pie would feed the lot of them, would it not?"

"Well, I feared you would take sick. And I thought you should 'ave something grand. I got nothing else is grand, so I bought the pie. Never mind. I 'ad a good night last night."

We talked on until sunset of her family, of men and women, of love.

"'Ave you a woman?" she asked shyly.

"Aye."

"I thought so. She is lucky, that one."

"No, not so lucky. 'Tis a hard life I have given her. I have treated her roughly of late. I hit her."

"Wot, 'it 'er? Why, 'tis nothing. My man does take after me regular."

At sunset I stood shakily to go, hopeful that then I would not be recognized on the streets. Bet followed me to the door, and I bent and kissed her freckled forehead.

"Will you not stay the night?" she asked. "I care not that you have lost your coin."

I hesitated. She would indeed ask nothing of me, not coin, not forgiveness.

"No, I must go home. But I am honored by your offer."

"You're back to your woman, then?"

"Aye, back to my woman. Have you men coming this night?"

"Aye."

"How much shall you take in?"

"Four shillings, five if I please them specially."

"Come to Coldharbour on the morrow. There shall be a position there for you at twice that."

Her amber eyes filled with tears. "I want no alms," she said.

"No alms. There is plenty of work to be done. Say you shall come."

"I shall come," she said.

But I knew she would not come, and indeed she never did.

Merryn sat upon a bench, alone in the hall, and stared into the fire. She did not look at me as I hobbled across the tiled floor and sat next to her. I despaired at her coldness. A dark bruise smudged her cheek, and there was a blood-red cut at the corner of her mouth. I gathered my courage and spoke her name. She did not answer, but her compressed lips quivered as she fought back either tears or anger.

"A long time ago," I plunged on, "you spoke fearfully of our love. You said that perhaps we should not be lovers, for we would wound one another so much. I see now that you were right, for never had I thought to hurt anyone so much as I have hurt you. I told you once that I needed you and I sought your pledge that you would never leave me. I need you yet, but I would hurt you no more."

My speech was slurred for my lips were yet thick and tender. Awkwardly I sought the words while scalding tears slipped unbidden down my cheeks.

"I love you too much to hurt you any more." A sob caught in my throat, and I covered my face with my hands that she might not see me weep.

"I was only angry for a while," she said. "And I shall never leave. Never, ever. You cannot order me from your side, for I shall not go."

"You are a fool," I said through my tears. "This shall only get worse. What shall you do when I marry and get a son by my queen? What shall you do if I go off to fight? What shall you do with my rages? I cannot be as good as you wish me to be."

She rested her head upon my shoulder.

"I should push you away. I should force you away for your own good."

"You cannot," she replied. "I have bewitched you, Harry Monmouth, and so you shall never be rid of me."

I buried my hands in the mane of hair that tumbled down her neck and pulled back her head that I might seek her lips. For the first time she saw my face and gasped.

"Harry, what happened to you?"

"I got drunk down by Botolph's Wharf and was robbed and beaten and left for dead in the snow and rescued by a whore named Bet. I offered her a position in our household, but I doubt she shall take it up."

She burst into laughter.

"What is so funny?" I demanded. "I thought you would be frantic with worry."

"Did you so? I did worry a bit, but I thought you had gone to stay at the house of your uncle Beaufort." She giggled. "In truth, I should know by now that you will act like no prince. That is one reason I love you. But what would my lord Arundel say?"

I swatted her rear. "Fie on you!" I laughed and then winced at the pain in my ribs.

"Oh, but you are hurt, poor dear, and I should not laugh at that. It is a wonder you did not die."

"My life is charmed these days. And it is not serious. A few ribs to mend."

"You should see your face. It is a lovely shade of black and blue. And your mouth is worse than mine."

"No, not worse, for it was I who wounded you." I touched her lip with the tip of my finger. "Never on this earth shall it happen again."

"Kiss me," she said.

I did so, gladly.

"Now it is healed," she said, "and so we must see to you. You shall have a hot bath, and then I shall wash the blood from your face and bind your chest."

When we were in bed I ran one hand down the curve of her body.

"I am passing sore," I said, "but I would try to love you."

"Aye. It is meet that we love this night."

11

The day following my return home brought my uncle Beaufort pounding upon Coldharbour gate, Scrope in his company. They burst in upon Merryn and me as we broke our fast in the library.

"What happened to your face?" Scrope said breathlessly.

I laughed. "I was robbed by some fellows who made a far better job of assaulting me than yon unfortunate assassin."

"You are in a lighter mood than when I last saw you," he said.

"You would do better to be sober," my uncle broke in.

"What tidings bring you?"

"It is the assassin," Scrope said. "He is dead."

"Dead?" I sat back from the table. "I gave no order for his death."

"No, it was Arundel who so ordered."

"Arundel? How did he get custody of the fellow?"

"He was at the Tower when I arrived there with the prisoner, and he took the man from me. I asked for his authority, and he replied that the King would wish the man to be properly interrogated. I knew not what to do, for he had the royal seal with him and a large guard. He spirited the man away at once, and I could not think how to get him back. I returned here and this woman of yours said you had left and she thought you at your uncle's house. When I found you not there, Beaufort and I went next day to the Tower,

239

where we waited until last night for word of the interrogation. Then a man of
Arundel's came to us and said the assassin had been executed. He said the
man would only say under torture that he was in no one's pay, that he acted
upon his own. Arundel had him sewn into a large sack and thrown into the
Thames."

My uncle had been pacing the floor. "Do you not see, Harry?" he cried.
"Arundel silences him ere we can learn who employed him. And even now
vicious rumors are put out at court that it was I who paid the man. I! It is
absurd, of course. This poison spreads quickly, but you must not heed it."

"Quiet!" I said. "I must think."

Outside the solitary cry of a boatman echoed upon the river. Somewhere beneath the cold waters must float the body of the wretch who had
wielded the knife.

"That Arundel is behind this plot I have no doubt," I said. "But the
King, the King— What think you, Uncle?"

He looked shamefaced. "Perhaps," he muttered. "Perhaps he had reason."

"What mean you?"

"I went to him a week ago—without your permission, I know—to speak
on your behalf. I told him of the arrogance of Arundel and how the people
detest him. I recalled for him his own declining health. And then I urged
him to abdicate in your favor."

"You *what?*" I was in shock. "You asked him to give me the crown? This
is beyond belief! Is this my uncle of the cool political judgment? Or is it my
uncle of the overriding ambition? God's blood, you have put me in peril.
Small wonder this attempt was made upon me."

"I did but what I thought would help you. He is my brother. I thought I
might reason with him. I had no idea he would act this rashly."

"Did you not know that Father wished to set Tom in my place? He does
not want me as Prince of Wales, much less as King. I find it difficult to
believe you thought he would heed you. You are not so stupid."

"Of what do you accuse me?"

"I accuse you of impatience and ambition. I accuse you of seeking a final
breach between my father and me which you hoped would lead me to
overthrow him—at your urging, of course."

"What would I gain by that? He has not long to live."

"So we thought five years ago, but he holds on, does he not? He may
suffer on for another five years, for all we know. And then there is Arundel.
If I succeed peacefully to the throne, he would yet be Archbishop of Canterbury. And well I know who covets that position of power."

We faced each other like fighting cocks.

"It is well you trust me so," he said.

"Do not speak to me of trust, Uncle. I have looked to you for much, but never with trust. You would turn to another in an instant if you lost your advantage with me. You it was who taught me the ways of power, and never did you speak to me of trust."

Scrope stepped between us. "You waste time with your wrangling. The question is, what is to be done? Whatever it is, it must be done quickly."

"Indeed," I replied. "It is a surprise to me that I am not already locked in the Tower for plotting treason. I see now my brother's advice was sound. I must quit London at once."

"Where shall you go?" Beaufort asked.

"I shall tell no one save Scrope until I am safely there. Scrope, I would have you remain to keep me informed of the temper of the court. As for you, Uncle, you shall seek another audience with the King. You shall assure him that your suggestion was your own, that I disavow it. Do this and you return to my good graces. Otherwise I want nothing more to do with you."

He bowed stiffly, his face a mask. "As you wish."

"Scrope, set my servants to packing. I would depart as soon as the sun sets."

When they had gone I sat upon the bench where Merryn yet cowered.

"Are you frightened?" I asked.

"Aye."

I kissed her forehead. "I do pray this shall yet be set right."

"Where shall we go?"

"I shall make for Coventry. I have a manor there. It is near to Wales if I must flee, but yet not so far from London. And it is hard by Kenilworth, a strong fortress if I have need of it. But I wonder if you should come."

"Why not? I want to be with you."

"Merryn, I know not how far this has progressed in my father's mind. He is ill, and Arundel feeds him daily with lies about me. It may be that I shall be set upon and arrested, or that another assassin is hired. I would not have you in harm's way if that happened."

"There is danger wherever I be. If you are taken, I would be at your side to offer what love that I can. I could not bear to think I had deserted you."

She went, of course, though the journey was unpleasant enough for her. She took ill early on and abandoned Fille's broad back to ride in a drafty, swaying coach. When this became mired in the mud I took her up before me and kept her warm as best I could. Anxiously I felt her forehead, but there was no sign of fever.

"You should not have come," I said. "This is a strange illness, and I would have you cared for in bed."

"Hush," she replied. "It is not serious. It is but my woman's time."

Her woman's time had never gone so hard with her before, but I knew I would not overcome her stubbornness by pressing her, so I fell silent.

We came without further incident to Coventry, and I sent Merryn at once to bed. I would have slept myself but for a messenger who arrived hard on our heels. He came from Coldharbour and his news was ill. Hardly had we quit London when the King's men arrived. Upon finding no one at Coldharbour save Scrope, they arrested him and even now he was lodged in the Tower, having only enough time to whisper my whereabouts to a trusted retainer. His crime was said to be in assisting me in the misappropriation of the royal finances, an absurd charge. I would have been arrested as well, it was rumored, but my flight had put my enemies in a temporary state of confusion.

All thought of sleep left me, and well into the night I paced the floor. Before sunrise Merryn came to me.

"I woke and you were not beside me," she said. "What has happened?"

I told her of Scrope's tidings.

"What shall you do?"

"Wait. My uncle yet seeks an audience with Father. Perhaps he may set things right."

She sat next to the fire. "Come," she said, "lay your head in my lap."

I obeyed her, and she ran her supple fingers through my hair and across my temples.

"You should be in bed," I said, "but in truth I cannot send you there."

"Sorry I am that you have worried about me. That is one burden I can take from you now. My illness, it is no illness at all. It is a babe, Harry. I carry within my womb your babe."

I sat up straight. "A babe?" I whispered. "Can it be true?"

"It is true. It is what I have prayed for." The joy was warm upon her face.

"But—but why did you not tell me? Now I have let you make this arduous journey—"

"That is why I did not tell you. I feared you would leave me behind. There is no need to worry. I have this sickness in my stomach, that is all. It shall pass soon, I am told."

"All the jostling—"

"Fie! My own mother worked as hard as ever up until the days of her lying in. Oh, Harry, I would have told you sooner, but it was only of late I was sure myself. So often have I hoped, only to be disappointed."

I set my hand to her belly. "You do not yet show."

"No, but soon, soon the world shall know that I carry Harry, Monmouth's child. Are you not happy?"

"Aye, happy indeed." I rested my head upon her belly and felt the rise and fall of it as she breathed. Happy, I thought, and frightened, but that I did not tell her.

Several weeks passed. Once more word came from London, and it could not have been worse. My uncle had been refused audience with the King and threatened with arrest for his associations with me. Moreover, it was known at court that I lodged at Coventry, and Arundel had announced that I gathered an army there for the purpose of seizing the throne. There was yet no formal charge of treason, but that was sure to follow.

Whatever you do, my uncle's letter ended, *in God's name, do it at once*.

"Is there none you can turn to for help?" Merryn cried. "What of Tom? He said he would not let them set you aside."

"He can do nothing from France. It is why Arundel acts now."

"And the merchants? Whittington?"

"They can do nothing against the King. He suffered them to help me for a while. But Arundel has his mind now, like the very Devil himself clinging to a lost soul. No, only the King can save me, and if he wants me dead I am lost."

"You speak as though my babe may have no father. Do you give up, then?"

"No, I do not give up. You must be prepared for the worst, though. Soon I must leave. When I am gone, you must take yourself to Joan Waryn at once, do you hear? I shall arrange an escort for you. If the babe is a boy he may be in danger. You must conceal this pregnancy as long as you can until the outcome of this affair is clear. And if anything happens to me and we have a son, you must hide him in the Welsh hills. Promise me you shall do it."

"I promise."

"I know your mettle. I would trust no one with this more that you. Now heed me well. I must leave this very night, and you upon the morrow."

"So soon! What are you going to do?"

When I told her what was in my mind her eyes widened in fear.

"Oh, Harry, it shall be perilous!"

"Aye, but less so than doing nothing."

It was a hard parting. We clung together in the torchlight of the manor hall.

"If all goes well, you shall be in London well before the babe's birth," I said with more cheer than I felt.

"Aye, so I shall." She studied my face as though she sought to memorize every line of it. "It is proud I am that you choose this way."

"I love you," I said. "You have been the joy of my life. I would not part without saying that to you, and you must tell the babe if I cannot."

She touched the cleft of my chin. "*Rwy'n dy garu di,*" she said in Welsh. "I love you. I would be with you when—"

Her voice broke, and she hid her face in my cloak.

"My lovely, lovely Merryn," I murmured. "Kiss me once more, and I must go."

Her lips were moist and sweet, and never did I anything harder than to leave them. Somehow I forced myself from her embrace and rode away into the forbidding night, uttering a prayer for her safety as I went.

I had spent my time at Coventry laying my plans, calling to me men who had served me loyally in the past. They came from Monmouth, from Hereford, and from my London household. I knew them all. Most had been with me in Wales and at bloody Shrewsbury. To these men, some three hundred in all, I entrusted my life.

It would not go unnoticed by royal spies, this gathering of troops, and would only fuel the rumors that I had revolted against the King. I tried to allay suspicions in a letter dispatched to my father. I denied any intent of usurping the throne and claimed that I gathered soldiers to offer for service in France. It was a lie, of course, and I hoped only that it would reach my father and cause hesitation on his part, that I might have more time to act.

Scouts brought word of a royal troop south of Berkhamsted. We avoided them by sheltering in a thick wood until they had passed. It appeared that they rode toward Coventry, and I prayed that Merryn would be away ere they arrived. None others did we encounter on our journey and so came to London town, with God's help. I began to believe that this desperate ploy might work. By his charges of usurpation, Arundel had thought to force me to call men for my defense, perhaps at Kenilworth, thus giving the King cause to come against me. Never would he dream that I might do anything so rash as appear on his doorstep. I would have given a sackful of crowns to see his face when he learned of my arrival.

We entered London after dark, the gates opened for us as arranged and then shut fast behind us. Armed prentices stood watch all the night. Word would travel like lightning to Lambeth, and Arundel would rush to Westminster, if he were not already at my father's side, and whisper in the King's ear that the Prince had occupied the city with an army. How much more evidence of treason could be needed?

Inside the city walls, all was in turmoil. The Londoners knew of my plight and had taken to the streets to bellow their support. I passed through their midst by torchlight, astride a black charger, and waved as they called my name. Another day, perhaps, this show of strength would buy me ere Arundel would decide how to move against me without himself falling prey to the people.

I lodged with my men at my uncle Beaufort's house, which he had prudently abandoned for the more peaceful atmosphere of his bishop's see at Winchester. I slept fitfully for a few hours and then rose well before cock crow. Carefully I made my toilet and dressed myself in a robe of lush green velvet. About my shoulders I wore a gold collar of linked S's, which is the insignia of our house of Lancaster. I slipped the embossed garter of the Prince of Wales upon my arm. All this finery I concealed beneath the gown of an Oxford scholar and covered my head with the hood. Then I passed through Ludgate and quit London with ten brave men in my company.

We came to Westminster Palace in the gray light of early morning. I ordered my men to wait hard by the abbey with the horses and strode on alone. The bulk of a guard loomed in the swirling fog next to the gate.

"I come from the city with news for the Archbishop," I said.

"Does he expect you?" the man asked.

"He does not. I come straightway with the urgent news of the Prince's treasonous plans, which I overheard from a drunken servant of his. I have risked my life to leave London. Now I beg you, let me pass."

"Very well, then. He lodges hard by the Painted Chamber. Present yourself to his guard there."

He stepped aside, and I passed through the gate to the entrance of the great hall. Here was yet another guard. I repeated my story and was allowed to enter.

The vast hall was empty, and my footsteps echoed eerily from its roof of hammered wood. Here had King Richard been formally deposed; I wondered if his shade might linger watchful in the shadows. With heart pounding I walked to the hearth in the middle of the hall and removed my dingy scholar's gown. The band of gold upon my arm glowed in the soft light. At the far end of the hall whence I had come there were footfalls. I turned to see the guard staring at me.

"What means this?" he cried in alarm.

I unstrapped the sword from about my waist and held it above my head.

"You see I am unarmed," I called back.

I set the sword before the fire and entered the palace proper. Behind me a hue and cry was raised, and I knew my time to be short. I prayed that my father would be in his bed at this early hour and made my way toward his private quarters. The palace had just begun to stir. Here and there I met a servant who would shrink from me in disbelief, but none dared to stop me. Scarcely able to breathe, I burst into my father's apartments only to find them empty save for a woman tossing the featherbed. I nearly wept in my desperation, sure I would be taken now and with no chance to defend myself before the King. A man entered the room. It was my brother John.

"John!" I cried. "Where is Father? Tell me at once!"

"Harry! What in God's name? Do you not know your peril?"

"I know it well, and that is why I must find Father. I must plead my case. If you love me, brother, help me."

Good, stolid John. As a child he had stuck to me like a shadow and had sometimes lied about my doings to spare me Father's wrath.

"He is in the library. He likes to lie before the hearth there. Harry, what will you do?"

There was a commotion outside. I ran from the apartment just as a dozen guards spilled into the head of the passageway, their swords drawn. Even in my long robe I was swifter of foot than they, and I bolted down the corridor and into the library. Father lay in a litter before the fire. His attendants leaped up in alarm at the sight of me and brandished their swords. The guardsmen poured into the chamber and I stiffened in expectation of a sword thrust between the shoulders. They stood in a ring about me with the points of their weapons poised an inch from my throat and chest.

"Father," I said, "I do not come against you."

I halted, for my well-rehearsed speech had fled me. The room was filled with the stink of rotting flesh, my father's flesh. His hands which lay unmoving upon the coverlet were a bloated green, as though he were already a corpse in the grave. Only his eyes seemed alive, and they were white with fear.

Arundel burst in then, with John close on his heels.

"Your grace," the Archbishop said, bowing low, "your rebel son is taken ere he could carry out his treacheries."

"No, Father," John said. "Harry has come of his own free will to plead his case."

The eyes flitted back and forth from one face to another. I shifted my weight, and the sword tips raised threateningly.

"My lord father," I said, "Arundel lies. Never have I sought your throne. I would have denied these foul charges before now if only I had been allowed to see you. I am loyal. May I yet approach and plead my case?"

"Arrest him," said Arundel.

Strong hands pinned my arms to my side.

"No!" I cried. "What have I done? I am unarmed!"

"Wait. Wait." Father's voice was but a low croak. "What would Tom say to this?"

John stepped forward. "My lord father, Tom has ever named Harry a loyal and true son to you. He would have you hear Harry."

"Your grace," Arundel said, "the Duke of Clarence knows nothing of this treason, as he serves you loyally in faraway France. Were he here, he would renounce his traitor brother."

"Yet this is my son, however prodigal. Should I not hear him, at least, ere he is sent to his death?"

"Father, may I come to you?"

"You may."

The guards loosed their hold on me and I knelt by his side.

"Your grace," I said, "when my uncle Beaufort suggested that you abdicate in my favor, he did so without my knowledge, without my permission. He is penitent. Had you seen him, he would have craved your pardon and told you this himself. As for me, I have been denied audience with you since I was dismissed from the council. During my absence you have been told lies about my actions. I have been accused of misusing the finances of the realm for my personal gain. I have never been a lover of money, and well you know it. I have with me records that prove the falseness of these charges."

I pulled the parchments from inside my robe and gave them to John.

"I have been accused of plotting your overthrow. It is a fantastic charge. I gathered troops to me only for protection, for I feared I might be slain ere I could speak these words to you.

"Never have you loved me, and you have long mourned that Tom is not your heir. This I know well enough. Yet, Our Lady as my witness, I have tried to earn your love."

The hurt welled up in me and my throat tightened.

"Never have I known how to be what you wished me to be. There was a time, when I was a boy, when I dreamed of saving your life. In my mind, I would take some blow for you and die in your arms. Then, I thought, you would love me. But ever it has seemed to me that in truth you would rejoice at my death. Not long ago, an attempt was made upon my life. I wonder, did you know of it? Did you?"

He would not meet my eyes.

"John," I said, "come here."

John knelt beside us.

"Place your dagger in Father's hand."

He looked at me in surprise.

"Do as I say," I urged him.

"It is a trick," Arundel said. "He shall slay the King."

But none moved, as though they were bewitched by the slender silver dagger John removed from his belt. He set the jeweled handle in Father's hand.

"What is this, Harry?" Father said. "What is this?"

"I know you cannot hold it alone," I said, "so I shall help you."

Gently I placed my hand upon his so that his swollen fingers grasped the handle more firmly. Then I slowly raised the weapon so that the point rested firmly against the vein which throbbed in my throat.

"You have strength enough to thrust, do you not? Then slay me if you hate me so. Slay me if you think me a traitor. Go on. Tom shall be king."

His hand trembled, and the point bit into my skin.

"My son," he implored me.

"I do not ask for your love now," I said. "I wish only to know that you did not hire the assassin."

He began to weep. "I knew nothing of it. I did not know you were attacked. You should not accuse me of it."

His fingers went limp, and the dagger clattered to the floor. I sank forward against the litter and buried my face in my arms.

"Leave us," he said. "Leave me with my son."

"Your grace, is it safe?" Arundel protested, defeat in his voice.

"Leave us, my lord of Canterbury," Father replied.

We were silent for many minutes after they had gone.

"You sent troops to Burgundy," Father said at last. "You overstepped yourself. I did warn you at Berkhamsted that I am yet King."

I leaned back wearily. "I did what I thought best for England and for France. I could not stomach Orléans. Had I the decision to make again I would do the same."

"It is a stubborn, impudent young pup you are, Harry. As ever."

"Aye. Nothing changes."

"How is the lass?"

"Merryn?"

"Is there another?"

I blushed. "There is not. She is with child."

"Indeed? Then shall I have a grandchild at last. Oh, I am sure the others have bastards scattered around, but they do not know of it for they can never abide the woman long enough to find out. How far along is she?"

"Only a few months."

"I am dying, Harry. I know it now. Yet perhaps I may draw breath long enough to see the babe."

"I pray you shall."

"And I pray if it is a boy he is not like his father. Ah, but at least you do not feed me this prattle about having many more years left to reign. Perhaps if you did not know me to be dying you would have indeed come against me?"

"No, I would not."

More silence, and then he said, "The lass. When I was at Berkhamsted, she rubbed my head in a most soothing way. It did ease these headaches. Do you think she might come to me here and do the same? The pain torments me."

Beneath the thin red hair his scalp was foul with sores.

"I am sure she will come," I replied. "Yet there will be a condition."

"And what might that be?" he asked warily.

"I must be allowed to come with her."

I went to Monmouth to fetch Merryn. Word of my approach had preceded me to the castle, and scarcely could I alight from my horse ere Merryn had flung herself upon me and smothered me with her kisses.

"Soft!" I exclaimed. "You shall crush the babe. Already I can feel the bulge of your belly. This little one has prospered in my absence."

She laughed gaily. "Every day I have patted my belly and said, 'Patience, child, your father shall come for you soon.' Then I would pray that it really be true. And here you are in my arms at last. Was there danger, my Harry?"

"There was."

Nothing would do but that I sit down and tell the whole story to Merryn and Joan. They beamed with pride when I told them of my reception in London, and cried out at the image of my fleeing the palace guard with their drawn swords. Finally they wept when they learned of my father's condition, and how he had dropped the knife and named me his son.

"Glad I am that you are reconciled," Merryn said. "He does suffer so."

"And what of that serpent Arundel?" Joan demanded. "It was he who caused this trouble."

"Joan, ne'er have you met the man," I said with a grin. "How do you then judge him so harshly?"

"Good for him we have ne'er met. I would box his ears harder than ever I did yours."

"He still has Father's favor, yet he has been set in his place," I said. "Defeat was in his face. He knows that I shall now be king, and he lives in dread of that day. Still, I shall not take him lightly. The wild boar is most dangerous when cornered."

Merryn and I lingered in Monmouth for several weeks and then set out for London. Our pace was leisurely, for I would not have Merryn jostled or fatigued. We were blessed by pleasant weather, warmed by the sun of early summer and refreshed with balmy winds. Thrushes serenaded us from spreading oaks, and fields of clover and young corn delighted our eyes. My heart filled with the beauty of the land, green England. Soon God would entrust her to my care. On a summer's day the prospect was not frightening, but a sacred trust that inspired visions of selfless service.

Twice a week, upon our return to Coldharbour, Merryn and I would take a barge up Thames to Westminster. There we would pass the day, Merryn tending to my father while I saw to some task or other of government. Father refused to restore me to the council, complaining that I had betrayed his trust. A chastened Arundel he retained as chancellor. Yet he seemed glad enough for what help I might give with the finances, or in the granting of charters or the judging of petitions which he had not the strength or will to consider. He would moan to Merryn of me, how I had never heeded his advice, and he would list the ways I had brought shame to him. In the next breath he would say, "Harry, my son, I am beleaguered by these quarrelsome fellows in Derby who dispute eternally over some boundary line or other. They claim my officers have not satisfied them. Will you not see to it?"

Merryn would smile at me and I would answer, "Aye, my father."

I learned much of patience in those months.

Never at any time in my life was I more in my father's company. Never did we truly quarrel. Much was due to Merryn, who made plain her love for us both. Little enough could she do for my father's pain. She dared not touch his sores, and so she would rub the few unblemished patches of skin at his temples and at the back of his neck, ignoring the stink of his flesh. He was grateful for even this pitiful bit of comfort.

One day we sat in the library before the fire, Merryn massaging the King's neck and I plucking at my harp, which I was wont to do to break the tedium of my work.

Merryn sat suddenly straight and cried, "Oh!" Her gray eyes widened. "The babe! I felt the babe. It moved."

I was beside her in an instant and set my hand to her belly. I felt a small, sharp movement.

"Feel, your grace, feel!" she cried and placed one of my father's bloated hands upon her belly. His eyes glowed and he nodded.

"A frisky bastard," he said. "This one shall keep you awake at night."

In truth we both lay awake that night, too excited for sleep. I cradled Merryn's head upon my shoulder and we spun our dreams.

"My mother was Ceinwen," she said. "That name I should like well, if this be a girl."

"Aye, and if a boy, then Owain, after Glyndwr. 'Tis the proudest name in Wales."

"Shall he speak Welsh, then?"

"Of course. He shall be a true son of Wales."

"Shall he be scorned, do you think, that his mother is a shepherdess?"

"Not while I draw breath shall he be scorned!"

She giggled. "Owain of London. 'Tis a singular name."

"'Twill be a singular babe."

I longed to make love to her, but it is perilous to do so after quickening. I contented myself with rubbing against her. When she saw how it was with me, she generously caressed me until I gave up my seed to her gentle ministrations. Such a woman she was, the joy of my life.

The months fled by, the leaves assumed their bright autumn hues and then fell in crackly brown mantles upon the London streets, and the wind blew chill. As the time of Merryn's confinement drew nigh, the journeys to Westminster came to an end. Midwives were secured, the finest in London, who had delivered many noble ladies of their babes. Merryn was busied with the fashioning of tiny gowns of wool such as would warm a little one against the wintry drafts.

When she was big with child and soon to be delivered, she came to where I worked and sat silent with face drawn.

"Is something wrong?" I asked.

"It is the babe."

"Is your time come? I had thought a fortnight more, perhaps. Shall I call for the midwives?"

"No," she answered, her voice so low I could scarcely hear. "The midwives have been here this morning. It is the babe. The babe does not move. They fear it is dead. The signs are not good, they say."

My blood froze within me. "Nonsense. They are mistaken. The babe cannot be dead. It rests, that is all. It tires as we do."

"Harry, it has not moved these two days. I feared to tell you. I waited and prayed, and hoped it would move again. But it has not. I tried to be cheerful for your sake, but I could bear it no longer. I called the midwives to me."

She gripped my hands and her fingernails bit into my flesh. "It does not move!" she cried. "It cannot be dead, my little one! What shall I do?"

I tried to calm myself. "We do not know for certain how it is with the babe. We do not know. We must be patient and faithful. We must trust to God."

She spoke of her fears no more, but the days passed and the babe was yet still. Death chiseled its lines in Merryn's face, and she moved as though a heavy weight dragged at her every step. I wrote urgently to Courtenay at Oxford and begged him to come to us. We settled in to wait.

Courtenay arrived upon a rainy day late in November, and we took some cheer at his presence. A week later, in the middle of the night, Merryn's time came. Wordlessly she dressed herself in a shift and lay in our featherbed, giving herself up to the ministrations of the midwives. I sat on the edge of the bed and held her hand, squeezing it reassuringly when the pain was upon her. Then I was shooed from the chamber by the chief of the midwives, a heavy woman with a crisp white kerchief, for there must be no man present during the birthing. I left them to their birthing stools and boiling water and joined Courtenay before the hearth.

The bedchamber was at the top of a short stone stairway at the near end of the hall. Merryn's muffled cries carried at intervals through the heavy oaken door. I looked at Courtenay.

"It is ever the way of it," he said. "Thus did you and I come into the world. God shall not give her more pain than she can bear."

It was small comfort to me. I poured a cup of wine and drank it moodily.

The door opened and Merryn's cries filled the hall. The chief midwife lumbered down the stair and came toward us.

"Why do you leave her?" I asked. "She yet cries out."

"I have come to fetch this priest," she said, "and to bring you bad tidings."

"What tidings?" I whispered.

"Her waters have broken and they were poisoned."

"Poisoned?"

"Aye. Foul and black. When the waters are poisoned, never is the babe born alive. This good clerk must baptize it ere it emerges, that there be some hope for its soul."

Courtenay gripped my arm. "Indeed I am sorry, Harry. I shall come back to you as soon as I may."

I sat down. The door closed once again and Merryn screamed. It was a shriek of naked torment, and I buried my face in my hands.

"Must she suffer so for a dead babe?" I muttered. Her cries were constant now, never-ending, piercing my brain, my belly, curdling the very marrow of my bones. I blinked back tears of anger.

Then all was silent. I strained to listen. Now should the air have been rent by the thin squall of an infant. Nothing there was but the popping of the fire.

The door creaked open. Courtenay emerged with a tiny white bundle in his arms and descended the stair, his finely chiseled features strained with grief.

"It is a girl," he said. "She is dead."

I bowed my head in sorrow and crossed myself as the tears slipped down my cheeks.

"Ceinwen?" I asked.

"Ceinwen. So I named her before God."

He raised the edge of the coverlet. The tiny face was very white, its eyes and mouth nearly invisible, so tightly were they squeezed shut. A wisp of brown hair lay flat upon the top of the round little head.

"I cannot tell what color her eyes are," I said. "I wonder if they are gray."

"The servants shall lay out the body," he said.

"Aye. Does Merryn know?"

"She does. She weeps even now for her babe."

"Then I must go to her. I must comfort her."

I started past him but he stepped in front of me.

"Harry," he said, "there is more you must know."

I had not the courage to ask what it was.

"The midwives say—the midwives say that when the waters are poisoned, the woman usually dies as well."

"No." I shook my head. "No. It is not so."

"They say you may send for a physician, but it shall do no good. Merryn will take a fever and die within a few days."

"No! Do not tell me this! Jesu in heaven, it cannot be!"

I sank onto a bench and wept like a child. Courtenay's arm went around my shoulders.

"Why? Why would God take my Merryn from me? Have I sinned so gravely that He must have her?"

"It is the lot of women. They bring forth children in pain, and often they die. It is Eve's sin, not yours."

"Call for Scrope. He must ride for Westminster and fetch my father's finest physician. Have him call for prayer at the abbey and St. Paul's as well. I swear she shall not die. She shall not!"

"As you wish."

"I must go to her," I said through my tears.

"First you must compose yourself."

"Very well. See to the babe. I shall curb my weeping. I would not affright her."

Carefully I washed my face in a basin of cold water and went to her. I ignored the midwives, who had finished their cleanings and had prepared to depart. The chamber smelled of warm blood and something else, something nameless which hovered in the air.

I approached the bedside.

"Merryn?" I whispered. She was very small in the bed, and her hair spread like a dark fan across the pillow. Her eyes were red and moist from weeping.

"Harry?" she said weakly. "Oh, my love, I am sorry. Our Ceinwen is dead."

I kissed her forehead. It was cold and clammy, and wisps of hair stuck to it.

"You must not fret," I said. "You must husband your strength."

"Your eyes are swollen. Did you weep for her?"

"Aye. I wept for her."

"Courtenay was very kind to me."

"And to me as well."

She shivered. "I am cold."

She was well covered, but I ordered the fire to be banked high with logs and tucked another blanket about her.

"I am very sleepy," she mumbled.

"Then you must sleep. I shall sit here with you. And when you wake there shall be hot broth for you."

"You are so good to me."

I paced the floor until midday, when the royal physician arrived from Westminster. He was a thin, swarthy man, a Lombard, and well spoken of at court. Once more I waited with Courtenay in the hall, lightheaded from anxiety and lack of sleep. The physician was not long in his examination.

"I am sorry, your highness," he said, "but I must be plain. She is dying. Already the fever has set in and there is corruption in her female parts. I have bled her but more I cannot do. It was a hard birth and she seems much weakened by it. I do not believe she has long. She should be shriven as soon as possible."

"I shall see to it," I heard Courtenay say.

The world had become a blur. I groped for the wall and leaned against it.

"She must be told," Courtenay said. "Shall I do it?"

"No," I said. "I shall tell her. Leave me alone with her."

I tried to still the trembling of my limbs and climbed the stair.

"Harry," she said when she saw me, "I am so glad it is you. Will you sit with me now the physician is gone?"

I forced a smile. "Indeed I shall. As long as you like."

I perched on the edge of the bed and felt her forehead. It was so hot that my fingers did tingle.

"Hold my hand," she pleaded. "I have not the strength to take yours."

I studied her slender fingers. "I must tell you something," I said. "We have faced trouble together before, you and I, ever together. Now there is one thing more."

Her eyes were calm. "I think I may guess what it is," she said.

I looked away and my tears returned. "I promised Courtenay I would be brave for your sake," I said.

"Oh, my Harry."

I stretched out next to her and held her, and we wept in one another's arms.

"Always I said I would never leave you," she said at last, "and yet now I must. My poor Harry."

Then, "You will lay me at Monmouth, and Ceinwen with me?"

"Aye, whatever you wish."

"At the foot of the Kymin?"

"Aye."

Her lips moved against my cheek. "I do not want to die. My life has been passing short. So it ever seems to the dying, I suppose. Yet I cannot complain too much to God. Few people have known such love as you have given me, and I am grateful for that. Oh, but I do hate to leave."

"Would that I might die as well."

"Oh, no, Harry. You must live for England. You must love her as ardently and truly as you have loved me. And now you should summon Courtenay, for I would be shriven."

I knelt beside the bed while Courtenay prayed, the familiar words of the Confiteor tolling like bells in the quiet chamber.

"*Kyrie eleison,*" he intoned, and Merryn faintly mouthed the words after him.

"*Christe eleison.*"

Without the door, many of the household had gathered to tell their beads and to pray, for they loved her well. Then everyone withdrew, and once more we were alone.

We were quiet for a time, and then she slept. I had vowed to keep awake, but seeing how easily she breathed, I nodded off upon my chair. When I started awake, night had fallen once more. Merryn lay staring at me in the candlelight, an expression of utter peace upon her face.

"You look so like a child when you sleep," she said. "I have been watching you, and praying all the time."

Gently I ran my fingers through her hair.

"*Ma plus belle fleur,*" I said.

She smiled. "I have been thinking that I shall keep my promise to you after all," she said. "I shall never leave you. I have been remembering how it was but a few months ago, when you rode away from me at Coventry and I feared I would not see you alive again. As each day passed I wept and imagined the worst. But when I closed my eyes, there you were with me again. And then I thought, Even if he be slain, he shall not die, because I love him. As long as I love him, he will live. And I shall love him forever, even beyond this life we know. It shall be no different now, Harry. It is our love that tells us we shall live forever. Do you not see how it is?"

"I am trying to see."

She was exhausted by this effort and shut her eyes. "Would you hold me in your arms? I would have them be the last of this world I know."

I slipped beneath the covers and nestled her against my chest.

For a time I thought she slept, but then she said, "Sing to me, Harry. Your voice is so lovely."

"What would you have me sing?"

"The Salve Regina. The one you composed at Monmouth last year."

Softly I sang, "*Salve regina, mater misericordie . . .*"

Thrice I sang it through, until she had fallen into a slumber from which I knew she would not rouse. Far off, the great bells of St. Paul's tolled. Her breathing was more labored now. I kissed her hair, touched her face, listened, wept. Not until the shadows of dawn had passed over her face in benediction did she catch her breath and sigh. Then she was still.

I held her until the warmth had left her, rocking back and forth in a trance. Then I stretched her upon the bed, closed her slightly parted lips, folded her arms across her breast, smoothed her hair. I sat in a daze, for how long I do not know. When I was so weak from fatigue and lack of food that I could scarcely sit, I left the chamber and made my way to the hall.

From close by I heard Courtenay ask, "Is it over then?"

"I do not know," I mumbled. "She said it is not."

The floor raised up and someone caught me.

"Take him to bed," a voice said. "To bed."

She was sewn into a white shroud, the babe in her arms, and lowered into a narrow grave at the foot of the Kymin. Joan Waryn was there, and Jack from Hereford, and Courtenay. It was a fiercely cold day, but I would not leave her side until the last clod of dirt had been shoveled on and stones piled high to keep away the wolves. Jack kept watch with me.

"Come back to the castle, Harry. It is done."

"It is so cold to leave them here. The earth is so hard."

"Come, Harry."

The fairy castle on the brow of the hill was barely visible beneath a thin powder of snow. Beside it a yew tree thrust its claws skyward.

"Never shall I return to Monmouth," I said. "Never."

I turned and walked away, and ever after I kept my word, despite Joan's entreaties. Never did I return save in my dreams, and in time not even then.

IV

1413-1415

We few, we happy few, we band of brothers.

—Henry V, act IV, scene iii

12

I passed the Yuletide in seclusion at my manor of Kennington. The King sent for me to attend the festivities with the court at Westminster, but I declined. John and Humphrey came once to me, and from them I learned of Father that he was "sorry indeed to hear of the lass and the babe."

My brothers urged me to go to him, and at last I did. We sat in silence, each contemplating his own misery, and when I left he had fallen asleep.

Soon after, Father's attendants bore him through the wintry lanes of Westminster to the abbey church, where he prayed before the jeweled shrine of St. Edward Confessor. There he swooned and was taken to the Jerusalem Chamber of the abbey, so called for its paintings of the Holy City, to recover so that he might be returned to the palace. But he did not recover, and late that night messengers were pounding upon Kennington gate, summoning me to yet another death watch.

He was barely conscious when I arrived. The chamber was filled with spectators, just as when he had earlier lain close to death. Many lords and knights there were, but only John and Humphrey did I seek out.

"It is truly the end this time," said John. "Tom shall be distraught that he was not returned from France in time."

Arundel approached, his face a mask.

"The King asks for you, your highness."

"Is he shriven?"

"He is."

I knelt by the bedside.

"It is I, my lord father, Harry."

"Harry?" he rasped. "Harry? Where is Tom? Has Tom yet returned?"

"No, your grace, he is yet in France, unless he has taken ship by now."

"I would speak with him. I would speak with you both. The pair of you are stiff-necked. There are those who would set you at each other's throats, those who love not Lancaster."

"No, your grace, it shall not be. We love one another too well."

"I fear for you, Harry. What shall become of you? Ah, I would die easier if Tom were the eldest. My enemies say I do not hold the crown by right. Barely have I maintained myself against them. How shall you rule then?"

My cheeks burned with mortification. I knew every ear in the chamber had caught these words with great interest.

"My lord father," I said clearly, "I shall guard the crown with my strong right arm, even as you have."

His mind wandered.

"Richard," he said. "I recall Richard—"

The ghost of the murdered king hovered over his bed.

"It is done," I said, "and you are shriven."

"Shriven, aye, but I had thought to make expiation. It was once prophesied to me that I would die in Jerusalem. I took it to mean I should one day lead a crusade for contrition's sake against the infidel. It shall not be. This chamber be a smaller Jerusalem than I had foreseen."

He clapped his dry gums together and tried to swallow.

"Water," he whispered.

He was given to drink, and the water ran in rivulets from the corners of his mouth down his scraggly red beard.

"I have spoken to Arundel of you," he said. "He pledges he shall serve you faithfully. Likewise have I sent to my staunchest supporters among the great men of England. They, too, shall be pledged to you. More I cannot do for you, Harry."

These were the last words he spoke. When he had lapsed into unconsciousness I yet stood beside him and prayed. His uneven breathing brought visions of a dying Merryn to me all unbidden. I fought back the tide of hurt that welled within me and concentrated on the sounds in the room. There was much uneasy coughing and shuffling of feet, and a steady murmur of voices which I have ever thought unseemly in a deathroom.

". . . England a laughingstock," I heard whispered in a far corner. I clenched my fists. The smell of tightly packed bodies overcame even the stench of my father's rotting flesh. I longed to escape, to make my solitary

way along the black ribbon of Thames. Yet there would be no escape this
night, I knew, nor none thereafter.

Within the running of an hourglass the death rattle escaped his throat.

Arundel bent over him, closed his eyes, and said, "My lords, King
Henry is dead. May God rest his soul."

I pursed my lips and stared at my feet as I crossed myself. How then
should I mourn? The tall, golden-haired chevalier I had both worshiped and
feared had died long before this night. As for the twisted, tormented king,
he was freed at last of his burden.

A hush had fallen over the assembly as though all held their breath in
unison. Then a peer in the front rank, the Earl of Salisbury, said, "Long live
the King! Long live King Henry the Fifth, and may God save his grace."

"God save the King," the others echoed. There was a rustling of many
gowns as they knelt together and left me to stand alone. I stared at them,
earls, knights, bishops, all with bowed heads. King, they had named me.
Henry the Fifth, King of England. I realized that I must address them.

"My lords, you may rise."

Uncertainty I read in many of their candlelit faces, contempt in others.

"I thank you right well for your homage," I said, "and for your past
service in my father's behalf. I know that you love England as I do, and that
you will strive with me to preserve her in good fortune."

How to dismiss them?

"And now, gentle lords, I would pray alone by my father's body. I
beseech your understanding."

They hesitated and then shuffled out one by one, until none remained
save my brothers and Arundel.

"Har—your grace," said John, "may we keep vigil with you?"

I nodded. "For a time. They must prepare the body soon, I suppose."

"Will you take your rest at Westminster, your grace?" Arundel it was
who spoke. His face was collapsed in wrinkles of grief, and I realized with a
start that whatever else he had done, he had indeed loved my father.

"I cannot yet rest," I replied, "until I have faced this thing which has
come upon me. I would find a quiet place here in the abbey that I might
pray."

"I shall speak with the abbot," he said.

"I thank you, my lord of Canterbury," I said. He bowed and took his
leave.

"He has aged this night," John observed.

"Indeed," said Humphrey. "He does fear that Harry shall call for his
head upon a platter."

"Enough!" I said. "It is no time for foolery."

The monks of Westminster, a chanting double line of cowled figures, escorted me to St. Benet's chapel, where I knelt in prayer until just before the dawning. The familiar odor of incense and damp stone walls gave me some solace. Faintly I could hear the criers without the abbey.

"The King is dead," they shouted. "Long live the King."

Again I was named king. This title did chafe me as roughly as a stiff new boot. I had no strength to face it, heartsick and lonely as I was. Why had God taken Merryn from me now, when more than ever I needed her? Why had He left me alone with the crown? Yet even as I wondered, I put these doubts from me. One did not question God, Who ever acted for the good. Especially must the King not question, whose soul already hung so precariously over the yawning pit of Hell. Safer it was to trust.

"Jesus Christus, I am your liege man," I said. "I seek to do your will, only you must show me what it might be."

There was no answer save for the muted echo of a chanting monk somewhere in the abbey.

"A sign, my Lord, give to me a sign," I pleaded. I listened to the thumping of my heart. It shall come, I promised myself. A sign shall come. Only be alert for it. I lit two candles and set them before the altar, one for my father, one for Merryn.

The abbot of Westminster came to me after Matins.

"Your grace," he said, "there is a holy man within our precincts, a hermit. Not once in a score of years has he left his cell but devotes himself ever to prayer while our lay brothers tend to his meager bodily needs. A fortnight ago, he forecast that the King was soon to die and asked that, when that happened, you might be brought to him. I know not how you are disposed in your time of grief."

"I will go to him," I said at once. "I will go to him now, if that may be."

He was a twisted old man clad in a habit that could not have left his body since he entered his hermitage. His hair and beard were stained and matted, his fingernails black. A holy light did burn in his eyes.

"Kneel with me, my son, and pray," he said, without paying me homage.

I sank down next to him and waited for him to speak, but his prayer was silent. The air in the cell was close, fetid, and the hard stone of the floor bit into my knees so that I wriggled in discomfort. Still he prayed. At last I could bear the pain no longer and struggled to my feet. The hermit stirred at this disturbance.

"Forgive me," I said. "I could kneel no longer."

"You are not so accustomed to prayer as you should be."

"Indeed I pray often, but never in such a position for so long a time."

"It schools the flesh," he said, "and so is good for the soul. But you may sit if you like."

He motioned to a rude straw pallet in one corner. I sank down onto it and buried my face in my folded arms.

I knew not how long we prayed thus in silence but it must have been hours. When at last he spoke, the shock of his voice made my flesh to crawl.

"You are the man," he said. "Long have I waited to give you this word. You are the fourth king in my lifetime, and the most favored, but you are the most burdened as well. You must purify the Holy Church and restore Christendom. That is the charge given you by God."

"How do you know this?"

"Have I not prayed for it these many years? Think you that God would hear my supplications for so long and not answer them? You are the man. I see it in your face and I hear God say it in my heart."

"Was it for this that my father usurped the throne?"

"God has worked through your father's treachery, aye."

"I have wondered. I have sometimes thought . . . how must I do it? Restore Christendom, I mean?"

"However you may. You are God's instrument, to forge His will. Yet heed this, young sovereign. Our Lord said, 'Everyone to whom much is given, of him much will be required.' You must bend your life to God's purposes, shutting out all else. If you do not, God shall break you as He did King Saul. Pick up the sword therefore and smite the enemies of God."

There were many stirrings of discontent abroad in the land in those days. It was said by some that good King Richard was yet alive in Scotland. Now that Bolingbroke's weakling son sat upon the throne, Richard would sweep down from the north to reclaim what was rightfully his. This was nonsense, of course, and only the ignorant believed it. But there was another threat I could not ignore so easily.

Richard, being childless, had named as his heir his young cousin Edmund Mortimer, brother to Lady Anne. It had been easy enough for my father to sweep aside Mortimer's claim. Edmund had been but a child, younger even than I, and he could not resist so willful a knight as my father. The peers knew that my father fought for their privileges against Richard's capriciousness, and so Edmund Mortimer had been placed under guard at Windsor, where he yet remained. Now, though, was mighty Bolingbroke fallen and Mortimer grown to manhood. Who should claim the allegiance of the great lords? There was little enough love for me among those gentlemen. Nor was Mortimer the only challenger. Some of the younger peers laughed behind their hands and said that the brave Duke Thomas would return soon from France with his army and sweep his brother into the Tower.

The Turkish sultans have a solution to such a problem. They round up all competitors—brothers, cousins, pretenders—and lop off their heads.

This I would not do even though my own head roll for it. I must be a Christian king or no king at all. After much thought I did what was least expected, but which seemed to me both right and prudent. I released Edmund Mortimer from custody, restored his goods and lands, and created him Earl of March. I thought of Merryn even as I did this, for it seemed to me she would have approved. And as I lay lonely in my bed that night I tried to conjure her, to feel her close to me as she said she would be.

"If you are watching," I said, "see what I have done, how I have bestowed favor upon one whom some would make my enemy."

For one fleeting moment her face was clear before me, and she smiled approvingly. Then she was gone, and I left to warm myself in my bed by scrunching up into a ball with the bedclothes wrapped tightly about me.

The night before my coronation snow fell, so that by morning the drifts lay high as a man's knee. Nor did the snowfall cease throughout the day. Many sought to know what this might portend. Some said the snow was the King's pure justice dealt to all equally, regardless of station. So spoke the common folk of England. My enemies did name it a sign that England now faced winter, a season of decline when shame would blanket the land as thoroughly as did this blizzard. For myself, I tried to ignore all talk of omens, but fasted for two days before my hallowing and sought the word of God. My uncle and brothers urged me to eat, for they knew the ordeal that I faced.

"What joy it shall give the purveyors of portents if you swoon at your coronation," Beaufort said.

"If God means for me to rule," I replied, "He shall sustain me."

It is a tradition that the King of England should go to his hallowing unshod. I trudged barefoot through the snow from the Tower to my horse and rode in that manner with my escort through London to Westminster. My feet stung at first, then were numbed by the icy stirrups. I longed to wrap my legs tightly about my mare and warm my feet against her flanks but I dared not, for the way was lined with cheering Londoners and I must be dignified before them. Happy were those kings crowned in the summer.

I could scarce walk when we reached Westminster and stood in agony upon the stone floor of the porch while the procession formed. There Richard Courtenay came to me, stood close by so that the hem of his gown trailed over my feet, and rubbed his boot back and forth over them so that some painful feeling was restored.

"This I shall not forget, my friend," I whispered.

I entered the abbey with an awning of silk borne over my head, amid the bishops and great men of the realm, all arrayed in a splendor of scarlet and gold. Crosses they bore, and scepters and swords, and they walked with measured step and stately mien toward the high altar while choirs of boys sang with cold purity. There was a sound as of a rush of wind, for all those assembled strained forward in unison as I passed into view. They must see me, judge me, trap me living within their ken, and hedge me about with their myriad expectations.

The procession halted upon a platform above the high altar. I stood in full view of the multitude and swore upon the Host that I would defend the Church and rule according to her teachings of goodness and justice. Then was I stripped of all clothing save for my hose, as is the custom. The draft in the cavernous abbey church raised chillblains upon my bare arms, and I shivered. The gathered people were a faceless mass, but I could feel their eyes upon me, alive, piercing. They bore through to my very marrow, dispassionately dissecting the poor, naked man who stood so miserably before them. So it seemed then. Later I was told what a fine figure I had cut, with my head held proudly and my face "that of an angel." Those women present were quick to praise my lithe body. This last I heard from Humphrey, who claimed that every lady in the abbey had fallen in love with me that day. It mattered not a fig to me.

After my anointing with the sacred oil, the royal robes were draped about me. These were so weighty that the wearing of them made breathing difficult. So heavy did they bear down that my shoulder blades did bend in upon one another until I tightened my muscles and set myself to carry their burden. Arundel, who stood in his place as Archbishop, handed me the great Sword of State and charged me solemnly to wield it to crush the enemies of the Church. His eyes gleamed as he spoke, and I knew he thought of Jack.

At last came the crown. Never was anything so hateful to Arundel than to set it upon my head, I am sure. Yet if he had but known the pain it brought me, no doubt he would have reveled in it. So heavy it was that I feared my neck might snap from the strain. At my father's coronation he had set his hand to the crown, and gossip had spread that Richard's birthright sat uneasily upon Lancaster's head. I would have no such thing spoken of me. The pressure upon my brow was sheer torment, and I longed to cast the bejeweled weight upon the ground. All through the mass which followed I must bear it, the blood pounding in my head, and more than once I feared I might swoon. The air had grown stale, and Arundel wafted the hot incense in great clouds about my head. Somehow, with God's aid, I persevered, and stumbled into a wardrobe where the crown and robes were removed and lighter ones substituted. That these latter are not used from the beginning I can only attribute to a desire for the suffering of God's anointed. A dark red band was cut across my forehead where the crown had rested, and it did not disappear until the next day.

I did not break my fast at the banquet but sat solemnly through the feasting. Scarlet-clad retainers on horseback rode through Westminster hall among the long trestles bearing steaming platters of roasts and glittering subtleties. Haunches of venison, stews, and flampets passed before me, but I would not touch them despite my growing weakness, nor drink of any wine. Custom decreed that I sit apart from my subjects, and so I watched, lonely and desolate, while the gentlemen and their ladies made merry. Without the hall, the conduit flowed red with Gascon wine and the common folk roistered despite the snow. I heard them long into the night as I lay abed at Westminster, heard them glorying in the moment's respite from the harshness of their lives, and I lifted their well-being to God.

From the beginning I sought to do what was right and to make restitution for the wrongdoing of Lancaster. Throughout the kingdom I established alms-houses for the poor, and I restored the monasteries plundered by the fighting in Wales. Owain Glyndwr I pardoned, though he never acknowledged it and it was rumored that he had died. My old enemy, Richard of York, I created Earl of Cambridge. Most precious of all to me was the reburial of the body of King Richard. My father had consigned Richard's bones to an igno-minious grave at Langley, while Richard had ever meant to lie in effigy at Westminster Abbey near the Confessor's shrine. There I had him laid with great pomp and many masses in the same tomb as his beloved first wife, Anne of Bohemia.

Arundel I removed as chancellor and in his place set my uncle of Beaufort, but I did not punish the Archbishop for his plottings. Punishment enough to see me king, I decided. Like my uncle, at last rewarded with high office, Richard Courtenay profited from my accession, for him I named Bishop of Norwich. I relied upon Courtenay for much advice, but more than coun-selor he was boon companion. He accompanied me in June to the palace of Eltham, where I went to escape the heat and the memories of London.

It was at Eltham that Jack Oldcastle came to us from his castle of Cooling in nearby Kent. He brought with him a troupe of wrestlers, strap-ping brown-skinned Kentish men who threw one another as we wagered. Most of the coin I took, for I was a skilled wrestler myself and a keen judge of what is in a man.

"What need have you for such fortune?" Jack said as I counted my winnings. "You are King. The treasury of England is yours."

"He has great need of it," Courtenay said. "He must cover his losses at tables."

"It is true," I admitted. "Scrope and Courtenay do take my measure there. And the treasury of England has weightier claims upon it than my gaming losses."

"I am glad to hear there is some pleasure in your life," Jack said. "The kingship seems to go hard with you, Harry, for you look weary."

I shrugged. "I keep long hours."

"He must have a hand in everything," Courtenay said. "He should leave more to his ministers."

"I shall, I shall. But my father's illness left the realm in chaos. I would have my subjects know from the beginning that a firm hand governs them."

"You cannot long bear such a burden," Courtenay said.

"Well," said Jack, "if it is burdens you bear, I fear I must add to them. I have not come to you for pleasure only. I crave an audience with you, Harry. Alone, if Courtenay will forgive me."

All jollity was gone, and his face was hard.

"Very well. The park is cool and refreshing this time of day. Shall we walk there?"

We took our leave of Courtenay and made our way beneath the spreading oaks, hands clasped behind our backs.

"I have a summons from Arundel," Jack said. "He has seized books I ordered from a limner in Paternoster Row. I am to answer charges of heresy."

I stopped, horrified. "Is this how he deals with me? Will he strike at me through you?"

"So it seems."

"What books, Jack? Are they indeed heretical?"

"I suppose Arundel would deem them so."

"And what do they contain?"

"I am not certain. They are translations from the continent. I was to pick them up in a few days and then I would have read them."

"Then you do not know their contents. You must say so when questioned. You must play the innocent, do you hear?"

"You do know of my views. Would it not be deceptive?"

"Deceptive? To claim no knowledge of books you have never read? Jack, you must do as I say. I am trying to save you, but you must help me."

"There is another way," he said.

"What way?"

"Come over to our side, Harry. You are the King. You can do as you will. If you stand with us, we can purge the Church of all evildoers, and turn her into the path of true doctrine."

"And what must I do?"

"Repudiate the two false popes and, indeed, all popes. Close the monasteries, confiscate their wealth, and give it to those with true faith. Stop the false teachings about the Host."

"What of those who resist these changes?"

"If they resist they must die as corrupters of the faith who would bear poor men into Hell with them."

I shook my head. "You sound too much like Arundel for my ears."

"Do not reject me so quickly. Think upon it, Harry! I know there is much you would do for England. Every friar's head that rolls will mean a gold noble for your treasury. Think on it."

"With all my heart I seek the reform of the Church," I said. "Now that I am King I may be able to halt this farce of two competing popes. I may help the monasteries to recover their simplicity. But I can never do what you ask. I have sworn upon the Host to defend the Church. Nor can I accept your doctrines of the sacrament. Never."

"You are rejecting Merryn, who believed as I do."

"Jack, in Jesu's name it is not true, and never say that to me again."

"Then there is nothing more to be said."

"Nothing save that my offer of help still stands. I will defend you before Arundel. Your own actions are upon your head." I regarded him with sorrow. "You speak of slaying friars as though of wringing the necks of geese. Could you come to speak so easily of slaying kings for your faith?"

"Do not suggest such a thing," he said uneasily. "Afore God, I mean you no harm."

We returned to the palace in silence, and Jack took horse for Cooling within the hour. Afterward Courtenay found me wandering in the garden.

"Jack is in trouble?"

"Aye. Arundel charges him with heresy."

"Jesu! What shall you do?"

"I shall do whatever I can to help him. I would be no true friend if I abandoned him now. Yet am I also King, with the welfare of England to consider. I know not if Jack understands it."

Jack appeared before a convocation of clergy at my own manor of Kennington. This was at my insistence, that I might be easily in attendance and that Arundel might find himself in unfriendly surroundings. Indeed the row of black-robed clergy did seem intimidated, and throughout the hearing I caught them stealing furtive glances at me as though to judge my thoughts. As for Jack, he was subdued and I thought it boded well that he was in such a state of mind. He cast his eyes down as passages were read from the offending books. The sentiments contained therein were those I had heard before from Jack and his friends—that the Host was no true Body of Christ, that the pope was Antichrist, that the Church had no business to interpret the holy scriptures for a man. When the reading was done, Arundel cast a malevolent eye upon me.

"Are you not shocked, your grace, at such sentiments?"

"I am indeed."

"And you, Lord Cobham?" He addressed Jack. "How do you respond to what was just read?"

I held my breath.

"I share the sentiments of the King," Jack said. "Such a book is worthy to be condemned."

Good, I thought. Good.

"Then how came such books into your possession?" asked Arundel.

"I only just ordered these books. I had but glanced at them and knew not the substance of their content."

Arundel sat back in his chair. I took advantage of his confusion to stand and address the convocation.

"Good fathers," I said, "I have known Lord Cobham for many years. He has been true knight and true friend. I find myself this day satisfied with his answers, and I urge you to drop these charges."

They stared at me in stony silence. Then Arundel gathered his wits and said, "There is other evidence, your grace. We have the testimony of recanted Lollards that they have heard Lord Cobham utter with his own mouth such heresy as is found within these volumes. Not only is he named a Lollard, but the chief of these madmen in all the kingdom. The others look to him, it is said."

My heart sank then, but I was not finished. "If you are so sure in your knowledge of Lord Cobham's beliefs, why bother to call us here? In any case I beg a suspension of these hearings, out of the love I bear for Lord Cobham. I would give him time to be prepared once and for all to reject any heretical ideas you might impute to him."

They were not happy, of course, but they could not deny such a request from their King. When they had made their sullen way back to Lambeth, Jack sank wearily into a chair.

"How much must I say?" he moaned. "How much can I say?"

"I fear you must recant every Lollard belief you hold, or it may do no good. Arundel is determined in this, the whoreson bastard."

"I know not if I can."

"It is the only way I can keep you from the stake. I saw that in their faces. They will not relent."

"And would you have me sell my very soul to keep me from the stake?" he cried. "It was wrong, what I did today. I lied! Others have been faithful and gone to their martyrs' deaths, but I lied! At your behest, Harry, I lied!"

"I have done this out of love for you. I do not ask you to forgo your conscience. I beg you to change your mind. Recant, Jack! For Jesu's sake, and your own, recant!"

"No! It is you who should recant. It is you who are wrong, and you drag the souls of poor Englishmen into Hell with you."

"My friend, my friend. How we do hurt one another. We cannot both be right. But perhaps I was wrong to ask you to hide your convictions, though I did it from love. Perhaps, if God be merciful, we are judged according to how we defend our consciences, and not by whether we be right or wrong."

"No." He shook his head stubbornly. "There can be no salvation from false doctrine. It is that you are King, there is the rub. You seek self-preservation over the right. It would endanger your precious crown to embrace Lollardy, and so you will not consider it. Well, I have had enough of self-seeking. I shall play your games no longer."

Jack went to his castle of Cooling, and I to Windsor. I could not bring myself to believe the years of friendship had been for naught, and sent for him. To my joy he came at Lammas, once more bearing with him his troupe of wrestlers. Yet we saw at once how it was, and he did not stay long. We parted at the castle gate.

"Forgive me, Harry," he said. "If ever we meet again, it must be as enemies."

"I would not put it so plainly," I protested. "I am not done with you yet."

"Why would you wish to do more? For I swear to you, from this day forward I shall fight for my faith, even if it means setting you from your throne. There, I have spoken treason. Now shall you have me arrested?"

"Of course not."

"You were ever a fool, as I have said to you before. Your scruples show most clumsily."

"'Twas not so long ago you accused me of sacrificing my principles for self-preservation. It cannot be both ways, Jack."

"But it is, Harry. With you, it is both ways. And some day, when one part of you has defeated the other, you shall die. As I soon shall."

In August I wrote to Archbishop Arundel, telling him I had failed in my efforts with Lord Cobham, who was now loudly proclaiming his convictions. Thereafter Jack was arrested, imprisoned in the Tower, and brought to trial at St. Paul's. This time I was not present, but I heard how Jack spoke plainly and named both king and clergy instruments of Satan who endangered the souls of poor men. He stood condemned and was sentenced to be burned, and was sent back to the Tower to await execution.

Now I played my last and most desperate card. It was not unheard of to grant heretics a stay of execution that they might have one more chance to recant. This I requested for Jack, and again none would gainsay the King. In the month that followed, I sent priestly visitors daily to seek a recantation from the prisoner. In the meantime I was at work through my spies. Lollards I sought out in London, men like the limner William Parcheminer, fanatical followers of Oldcastle who would risk their lives for him. My search was anonymous, that suspicions might not be raised at the King's involvement. Likewise, many guards at the Tower came secretly into possession of gold nobles. The keeper of the Tower was relieved of his duties for a few days. Finally, a note was placed in Jack's hands from Parcheminer, telling him that he would find the door of his cell open at midnight of October nineteenth, and the guards looking the other way. He was to make his way to the limner's, where gold coin awaited him, and thence to the west, where he must hide himself in the mountains of the march, never to be seen again in England.

I myself was at the priory of Merton on the night of his escape. I lay awake at the tolling of the midnight bell and imagined his dark, fleeting form slipping into the crooked lanes of London, and thence away.

"Farewell, Jack," I whispered to my pillow.

Arundel was furious, and even more so that I delayed eight days sending notice of the escape. That he suspected my complicity I was sure, but equally certain that he could do nothing. One person only I told the truth and that was Richard Courtenay, who swore to bear my secret to the grave. For a time rumors were abroad that the King had set Oldcastle free, but these died with time and the people set their minds upon the harvest.

Yuletide approached once more, the second since Merryn's death, and I vowed I would not be so lonely as in the year past. I went to the palace of Eltham, set like a jewel in its great park beneath dark green fir trees, and called to me my three brothers. Tom was now home from France, having rushed to pledge his support of me, to the disappointment of the young peers. Likewise I had with me my uncle Beaufort, Courtenay, and Scrope. I recalled the festivities of my youth at Monmouth, when mummers had set my brothers and me shrieking with excitement at their sword dancing, and so made arrangements in the city for a large troupe to entertain us upon Twelfth Night. The ever-efficient Scrope saw to the details of the festivities, even to setting in casks of fine Burgundy at my request.

"Burgundy is Tom's favorite, and indeed I prefer it myself," I said to him cheerily.

"It is a fine, rich, wine," he acknowledged, "fit for royal merrymaking. And there is one thing more I would add to the festivities."

"What can there be that is not already done? You have seen to everything from the minstrels to the pudding."

"I have not yet seen to the women."

"Women?"

"Your brothers would enjoy a woman in their beds during their stay. I know, for Humphrey has already asked. And it would do you good as well. It has been a long time—"

"No! I will not hear of it. Humphrey may take his whoring elsewhere."

"What, Harry, will you become a monk over this peasant girl?"

"Aye, a monk! And if ever you mention her again in such a tone of voice, or suggest such a thing as this, afore God I shall set you out of my household."

I knew his anger must match my own, but he ever hid his choler, Scrope, and so he only bowed, regarded me a moment with his eyes half shut, and took his leave.

Christmas passed pleasantly enough, and the New Year. I was much with Tom and we had great delight in one another's company, for we had both been apprehensive at the rumors of our estrangement. Day after day we rode together to the hunt and spent our evenings before the blazing Yule log in Eltham hall, sipping our burgundy and reminiscing. Tom spoke with sorrow of our father, that he had been absent at his death.

"He was so frightened to die," Tom said. "Once he confided that his illness had been sent as a punishment for the deaths of Richard and Archbishop Scrope. He told me how the sores of his body would burn, and how he feared they were a foretaste of that fire that awaited him in the next world."

I shuddered and crossed myself. "God forbid it. Daily I have masses said for his soul. I pray that is enough."

On one of our hunting forays we ran a huge boar to bay. It was a young one and slew two of our baying alaunts with its slashing feints ere Tom stood his ground and ran his pike through the quivering body.

"This fellow shall be the finest trophy upon the table tonight," John said.

My mouth watered at the thought of the tender meat and the crispy skin crackling between my teeth. We drank wine from flasks and watched as the servants dressed the meat, the steam rising from the still warm flesh. The task had not been completed when one of my retainers came galloping from the palace, waving his arms in agitation.

"You must go to the palace at once, my lords," he cried. "The King is in danger. You are all plotted against."

Not again, I thought as we rode hard for Eltham. Who might it be? Richard of York? Edmund Mortimer? Perhaps Arundel. I shall throttle the old man myself if he be guilty this time, I promised myself.

We were met in Eltham hall by one Thomas Burton, a man in my employ with connections among London's Lollards who had helped to arrange Jack's escape.

"Health to your grace and safety in this time of peril," he said as he knelt.

"What are your tidings?"

"You must not hold your mumming this night," he replied, "for Lollards shall be the mummers. They mean to seize your grace and your brothers, and to set Sir John Oldcastle to govern England."

All those assembled gasped in horror. I would not believe it.

"How do I know you speak truly?"

"Your grace, you need but send to a certain carpenter's shop without Bishopsgate this very moment and there you shall find false mummers and their costumes. They will tell you all you need to know, I'll wager. And there is more to this plot. Even now, they have bragged to me, Oldcastle rides for London with armed men at his side. Likewise Lollards with swords and other weapons are at this moment marching for London from all parts of your kingdom. They shall meet in St. Giles' field and enter London through the connivance of their friends within the city. By that time your grace should have been taken and clapped into the Tower, and all clergy shall be driven from the realm and Oldcastle shall rule."

"What monster is this?" John cried.

"Monster, indeed," said Burton, "and his followers with him. They boasted to me this day of how many heads they would lop off, and how they would divide the spoils of the monasteries among themselves."

"In Christ's name, Harry, what shall you do?" my uncle Beaufort asked.

"Patience with me, Uncle, for I am much shaken. I would have these mummers taken and hear this story confirmed."

"Jesu, Harry, there is no time!" cried Humphrey.

"There is time," I answered. "My lord Scrope, see to the arrests."

"It may be that Arundel is in danger," Tom said. "You should send to him at once."

The idea of it filled me with revulsion, but I knew he was right. "Go to him at Lambeth, Tom. He does trust you. Ride straight with him to Westminster. If all is as Burton says, we shall join you there shortly."

I sent them all from me save Courtenay.

"Is this how he repays me?" I said.

"Likely he does not know it was you who set him free from the Tower."

"Yet to come against me—the fool! Does he not know I have spies about? How could he imagine that the powerful men of England would accept him as their ruler? God's blood, they can barely stomach me! I would weep for this folly, but I cannot. I have had no tears since Merryn died."

"I am sorry, Harry, truly sorry."

"I know you are. You are true friend, Courtenay, and you are all that I have."

"It is not so. Your brothers do love you well and are faithful. There is your uncle of Beaufort. And what more trusted minister than Scrope?"

I took no comfort from his words but sought what solace I could in prayer. I was yet upon my knees before an image of Our Lady when my uncle brought word that the conspirators had been taken and Burton's report confirmed. One of the would-be mummers was Jack's own squire.

"Well, Harry," Beaufort said. "Will you be king or no?"

The carved madonna smiled down at me.

"I shall be king," I said.

We rode straight for London, where I ordered the gates of the city shut and guards set at every entrance. Thence we made for Westminster. Tom had already arrived with Arundel, but I refused the Archbishop an audience for I could not bear to set eyes upon him. That night, scouts brought word that the first contingent of rebels was approaching the city. I stationed myself with a large troop at St. Giles' field to await them. There was no moon, but once the sky was lit by the trail of a fiery comet which roused fear and wonder in us all. It seemed an ill omen for someone, but we knew not for whom.

The first of the Lollards loomed suddenly, ghostlike, out of the night. Even as we saw them, they likewise spied us. Chaos followed as they turned to flee, tripping one another in their haste. The darkness rang with muted cries of animal fear. Only a few hotheads were slain, for I had given strict orders to seek the rebels' surrender. They milled about in confusion, encircled by my soldiers, who drove them tighter and tighter together until they could not move. I sat motionless upon my horse as they were disarmed and marched off to gaol. All through the night they continued to arrive, thousands of them, only to be caught in the same way or to flee under cover of darkness.

Not until dawn tinged the sky above London town did I return to Westminster. I was met at the gate by Arundel, resplendent in cope and mitre, his arms upraised in triumph.

"Thus perish the enemies of the Church!" His eyes glittered, and the vein in his neck throbbed. "Will you not come to the abbey to offer thanksgiving, your grace?"

Only forty Lollards did I have executed for treason. The rest I sent home pardoned. Somehow Jack had slipped away under cover of the night and remained at large. After much agony, I offered him a pardon as well, his life and my pledge that I would not search for him if he ceased to seek my overthrow. I heard nothing for months, but one day I was delivered in secret with a worn parchment bearing his familiar scrawl.

We are too far gone for trust, Harry, he wrote. *After all, you are a king.*

As for Arundel, in February he was seized of a strange malady of the throat. For two days he could not speak, and he died at last of suffocation, his windpipe constricting and his eyes bulging from his head. The people whispered that it was the hand of God that strangled him, and I will not dispute it.

13

It was the sack of Soissons that made up my mind to go to France.

Armagnac and Burgundian continued to fight their civil war, and throughout Christendom there were turmoils and bickerings among the petty duchies and principalities ruled by ineffectual and debauched puppets. Bands of armed mercenaries roamed freely from the Danube to Portugal, and when they could not hire themselves out to some lord they fell upon the poor folk of the countryside. Nowhere was there peace. It did seem to me that the people called out piteously for a deliverer, and I knelt daily to ask God, "Am I the one?" I came to long with all my heart that it be so, for I craved the love of the people, that I might live for it.

I searched for signs of what I should do. My deliverance from Jack's plotting seemed to augur favorably, though I grieved over the loss of his friendship. The clergy now hailed me as a hero for that the Lollards had been chastised. Often they spoke to me of uniting Christendom in a great crusade against the Turks, who held the Balkans, threatened Constantinople, and ranged as far as the Danube. Soon the way to all Christendom would be open, and our unhappy divisions would render us helpless before them. Even the Church remained rent asunder by its two corrupt and rival popes. Would God endure this long ere He raised up a champion?

I was troubled by the foul way in which Lancaster had seized the crown of England. Was not Edmund Mortimer true king? Yet he was but Earl of March, and God had seen fit to raise Harry Monmouth to the throne, who had never thought to sit upon it. The longer I studied, the more I began to perceive the hand of God at work. That I had not died of my infant illnesses, that I had been preserved through numerous plottings and protected at Shrewsbury field, seemed to me providential.

I pored over the histories of wars and diplomacies and studied the maps of Christendom. Wales I had taken in four years, and that when little more than a boy. Now I was a man of twenty-six. Could I not take Normandy in four or five years, and all France in eight or nine? Burgundy, Flanders, and the Rhineland in another five? Of course, I might gain much with diplomacy as well. Lombardy, Tuscany, Bavaria. With the might of England and France and the will of God to support me, how would any withstand me? I thought I could accomplish it ere I saw my fiftieth year, if God in His grace would preserve me so long. And if I begat a capable heir to succeed me . . .

I had other, less exalted motives, I must now admit. The peers yet grumbled against me, and the Lollards' uprising had disquieted them further. There were vague rumors of plottings, of growing support for Edmund Mortimer. The fate of King Richard haunted me, and I knew not how much longer I might rule unless I acted boldly. Still I was reluctant to save myself at the expense of those who would perish by my warring. There would be no help for my soul if men lost their lives only to keep me upon my throne. Then came Soissons, and I put aside my doubts.

She was the Duke of Burgundy's city, Soissons, and the King of France came against her with a great army. King Charles had for the moment regained his sanity and thrown in his lot with the Armagnacs out of distaste for the poor people of Paris, who supported Burgundy. So Charles besieged Soissons and after gaining entry turned his soldiery loose upon the town. Such brutality as happened there made even the excesses of Attila seem gentleness. Men were pulled from their homes and savagely murdered in the streets. Women, girls, even nuns were ravished, and babes ripped from their mothers' wombs by the swords of the attackers. Drunk with the smell of blood, the soldiers would dip their hands into the gory wounds of the men they had slain and smear them over the bodies of the wives and daughters as they defiled them. Children were thrust through with daggers and impaled upon the timbers of their houses. Some five thousand people perished in Soissons.

"Jesu, Harry," said Courtenay when he heard of the massacre, "I cannot imagine you so using a town of your own realm."

"Nor any town," I said. "By Our Lady, I would go to Paris this very day if I could and cast down those who have done this thing."

"I have been watching you closely these days, and I think you are serious. Have a care. It is a perilous thing to unleash the hounds of war."

"Already they are unleashed. Nor did I do the loosing."

"Yet you may only make the situation worse. And if you lose . . ."

"I should not lose. And I would bring stability where there is chaos. I would go to France not as conqueror but as governor."

"You are farther along in these plans than I had thought. Have you confided in anyone?"

"Beaufort. Tom. They urge me to it."

"And why have you not told me?"

I hesitated. "I knew not if you would approve."

"Nor am I sure that I do. Harry, you must know that more Merryns shall be orphaned."

I brought my fist crashing to the table where we sat. "In God's name, do not bring her up to me! I see her now in every maid who was violated and slain at Soissons. Somehow it must stop."

He chewed his lip. "A certain amount of force is justified in defense of the weak," he said.

"Of course," I said. "Of course." I stood up and paced restlessly. "I shall need your help. I want an ambassador to treat with the Armagnacs, and I would have you."

"Why me? I have no experience."

"Because I trust you with my life."

He sighed. "At least you seek peace ere you would go to war. Perhaps we may settle this without bloodshed."

"Aye. Perhaps they shall listen."

I did not tell him that I had already made up my mind to the invasion. I had judged of the Armagnacs that bargaining would do no good, for they had even broken their promises to my father, their ally. Still, chivalry demanded that I treat with them. I would play their diplomatic games, but only that I might gain some advantage from them. Even as Courtenay was on his way to Paris, I was in touch with the Duke of Burgundy.

I had qualms about deceiving Courtenay, but who better to carry out this mission than my innocent and earnest friend? He went to Paris and spoke with sincerity to the court of the English desire for peace, even as he presented my demands—the crown of France and the hand of the King's daughter Katherine in marriage.

"Is it not exorbitant to demand the crown of France?" Courtenay wondered. "They would never accept it."

"Always it is good diplomacy to ask for more than you expect to receive," I assured him, "for when you compromise you shall then have what you want."

The Armagnacs laughed at my demands, and I ordered Courtenay to refuse their paltry counter offer. Courtenay returned home, and in the meantime my alliance with Burgundy was solidified and my preparations for the invasion nearly done. Some of the more astute leaders among the Armagnacs became alarmed and sought a hasty peace with Burgundy. Now they thought themselves safe, for they had heard from their English counterparts that I was not capable of doing them any damage. A year or two, and the usurper Harry Monmouth would be driven from the throne of England. Burgundy cheerfully pledged them aid, even as I had his secret assurance that he would sit idly by while I entered France. I had no illusions about Burgundy. He saw me as a useful diversion to occupy Orléans while he sought the throne for himself. There would be time later to manage him.

Upon the eve of Courtenay's arrival from Paris, I was assailed by doubt. I had misled my friend and I had plunged into a web of deceit and intrigue for the purpose of making war. What of the boy who long ago had blanched at the bloodshed in Wales? And what would Merryn say to all this? Never mind, I told myself. The boy is dead. Merryn is dead. For two years she has been dead. I tried to conjure her but her face was a blur. I could not recall how her voice had sounded or what her smell was like.

"I love you still," I whispered upon my bed, "but you are not here as you said you would be. Is it because of what I do?"

I shut my eyes and saw nothing but darkness. . . .

I received Courtenay at my castle of Kenilworth.

"Faith, they are an unsavory lot, the Armagnacs," he said. "They speak of their people as of dogs. And the debauchery! All the talk is of who is in whose bed. The men are adorned like peacocks and wear pointed shoes with toes curved in such great arches that they must be tied at the knees. They are filled with idle chatter. I must say, you have given them some amusement. There is a joke current at the court which they made certain to repeat to me. It seems they threaten to send you a ton of tennis balls with which to occupy yourself, since you are such a foolish little boy."

"Indeed? And how far is this story spread abroad?"

"All the French court did laugh at it behind their hands, and those who waited upon me have brought it back to England. I fear they base their notions of you on reports from our own peers."

"Well do I know it. Yet do not let it trouble you. You have served me well."

"Have I? You would be better served, perhaps, if I spoke plainly of my fears for you and refused to help you along this road you travel. But I would not abandon you. That is what I fear for you. You keep no company save the cursed crown."

I sat brooding for many moments. "I have run from the crown since I was twelve," I said at last. "I am weary of running. I would take it up, Courtenay. God has thrust it upon me, and if it be my damnation, then so be it. But I would be king."

"And your ideals?"

"I have not lost them. I shall rule justly and strive for the good. That I will not compromise. But mark this, Courtenay, I will not trouble with honor when it does defeat good purpose. If I must commit small wrongs to accomplish greater good, I shall do it."

"It is a seductive way you choose. Easy it would be to lose yourself."

Soon after our conversation I fell ill and was abed for a fortnight. A fever it was, and some malady of the belly. Memories of my sickly childhood affrighted me, but I fought back and was well enough by the time I must tell the English people of my plans.

My uncle Beaufort presented to parliament my intention to invade France and recounted the history of English slights at the hand of the French. William the Conqueror, he explained, had brought to England with him the title to the Duchy of Normandy. Henry the Second of England was also a Frenchman and had held Anjou, Touraine, and Maine. Through marriage he gained Aquitaine and Poitou for the English crown. All these lands had been illegally confiscated by the French king Philip Augustus, so that only the city of Calais remained to the English king, and a small patch of Aquitaine surrounding Bordeaux. Not content with thus impoverishing England, even now the Armagnacs attacked Aquitaine, to the detriment of peace in that sun-kissed land.

"Our great King Edward the Third won back much English land," Beaufort intoned, "but once more was it falsely taken during the reign of the late King Richard the Second. Since then the French king has given aid and comfort to the rebels in Wales and has constantly harassed our shipping in the Channel. This sad state of affairs may only be righted if our King does claim his own."

He then went on to set forth my claim to the throne of France. He showed how King Edward the Third had been rightful King of France, as eldest grandson of the French king, but that his claim had been set aside by the French on the pretext that he would have inherited through his mother. They would have no foreign king, they said, and so set a Valois upon the throne, an ancestor of the present mad Charles.

"Thus is France buffeted by an insane king and cruel civil war, while her true sovereign, who would bring her justice and good government, is scorned and mocked by the haughty Duke of Orléans and his followers. But, lords, with the help of God, these wrongs shall be redressed."

Next spoke my new Archbishop of Canterbury, Henry Chichele. Chichele was reputed a wise and holy man, but he was of common parentage and my choice of him had brought much grumbling from the peers. I had ignored their complaints, for only Courtenay would I have had before this man, and he had refused my offer.

"You must recall Thomas Becket and Henry the Second," he had warned, "how they were boon companions till that Henry gave Becket the see of Canterbury. Do not so test our friendship. Leave me be, I pray you."

His reticence had been in marked contrast to my uncle Beaufort's fury at being overlooked, for he had coveted the see of Canterbury above all other positions.

"It would be a disaster, Uncle, and well you know it," I had said to him.

Still he raged at my ingratitude, but having no recourse he settled down soon enough and made me a hard-working and faithful chancellor. He watched now impassively as Chichele swept by him clad in the billowing robes of Canterbury to face the assembled Commons.

He was not an orator, Chichele, and he spoke but briefly. The King's quarrel was a just one, he explained, according to the teachings of Holy Church.

"The Church may bless these military enterprises which are undertaken to accomplish a greater good," he said.

He read from a parchment prepared by his clerks, squinting and holding it close to his nose, for he was shortsighted.

"France is ill ruled and her people oppressed," he continued. "Our King would restore to her peace and good government, and to England would he bring honor and achievement. It is a most worthy cause to which the Church may add her blessing and prayer."

The bored Commons shifted their weight upon the hard benches and stared straight ahead. They had known all they wanted to of this venture when they tallied their likely profit from provisioning the army. I wanted to stand and shout, Listen to him, fools! It is the fate of my soul he speaks of, and your own as well.

The financial support of the Commons being assured, preparations for war went forward. Great magnates, lords, and knights all rushed in to pledge their eager support and muster their men-at-arms. A fight at last! they cried and slapped one another upon the back. It was as if all England sighed with relief. After the years of Richard's well-intentioned bumblings, after the internal dissension which tore at England's gut under Bolingbroke, at last to have someone to fight! I watched overawed as the mood of my England rose and festered like a sore which threatens to break and spread its poison. How did one stem such a tide, once released? To even try now, I realized, would be suicidal. I had set my feet upon this path, and there seemed little hope

now to leave it. Yet even so I hesitated. My dreams were more and more
foul, haunted by scenes from Wales and Shrewsbury—the burning huts, the
gory bodies of the fallen. Merryn came to me in my sleep, laughing and vital,
only to shrivel and rot before my very eyes. I sat up in bed with a scream that
awakened Scrope, who was sharing my chamber.

"I cannot do it," I said to him.

He stared at me as though all sense had left me. I lay back down to a
sleepless night.

When ambassadors arrived in June from the French court, I was ready
to treat with them. I received them at Winchester in the company of my
brothers and advisers. We made an impressive sight, we four princes of
Lancaster. Straight and slim we were, and young, brown-haired and fair of
face. I stood in the center arrayed in a robe of glittering cloth-of-gold and
shared with the Frenchmen a chalice of wine and spice, as is the custom
when offering hospitality. Upon their lips were the usual formal greetings,
but in their eyes I beheld only judgment and contempt. I spoke of this to
Courtenay when they had retired.

"I fear to tell you this," he said. "They were impressed today, but not
with you. 'Twas Tom they most readily admired. It is a false judgment to my
mind, but he is taller than you, Harry, more sturdily built and fiercer of
mien. The Count of Vendôme told me Tom seemed to him a chevalier
reminiscent of the Black Prince. You, he said, he would have taken for a
churchman had you not worn the cloth-of-gold."

I sighed in exasperation. "I fear I have overstepped myself and would
settle with them. But I must receive something in return or my situation in
England shall be precarious indeed. Will they take me seriously, do you
think?"

"I shall continue to encourage them to do so."

The head of the French embassy was the Archbishop of Bourges, a
portly and worldly prelate of the type well known to me in Arundel. I stood
with him before the entire company and made my final offer: the hand of
Katherine, the French princess, in marriage, along with a suitable dowry.

"As well," I added, "I would ask a cessation of the assaults upon Bordeaux."

He nodded. "We are authorized to honor such a request."

There was a murmur of disappointment from the English lords in the
hall.

"They have spent much coin already to arm themselves," Tom had
warned when I told him of my misgivings. "They will take it hard if you back
out of this expedition."

I studied Bourges intently. If I was to emerge with my prestige intact, I must not appear weak before him. Unfortunately he seemed to me a proud man, and not easily intimidated.

"English kings have heard many fair promises from France," I said, "yet few are kept. If this marriage is to be, it must be done quickly ere you have time to change your minds. The wedding must take place in three months. If you agree, I shall send my ambassadors to Paris with you to make the arrangements."

He smiled and lifted his hands. "Your grace, it is too soon. We must have time."

I read the deceit in his eyes. Time, aye. Time enough for my disgruntled nobles to part me from my head.

"My lord Archbishop, you seek to play me false," I said in a loud voice. "If we are to come to terms it must be done quickly. I would remind you I have sacrificed much of what is rightly mine to make you this offer and preserve the peace. True King of France I am, yet I choose not to reproach yon Charles for that he does wear my crown."

Bourges's eyes glittered with contempt. "How do you make such a claim," he said, "when it is the heir of Richard with whom we should now treat? King of France?" He turned to my shocked nobles. "This fellow cannot even rightfully claim the throne of England! We might as well treat with a butcher's son."

His words rang their challenge throughout the hall, and I knew not who might take it up in the secrecy of his heart. My face flushed hot.

"Judge as you will my claim to the throne of England," I cried, "yet I do sit upon it! And God as my help I shall wear the crown of France as well. Get you gone, my lords. We shall meet again in Paris."

I swept from the hall ere he could reply, my entourage at my heels.

"The fool!" I said when we were alone. "The fool, to say such a thing! He left me no place to retreat."

"Nor did he mean to," said Beaufort. "They think they can beat you."

Humphrey was livid with anger. "It is unpardonable, what he has done. He has called your lords to treason, Harry, before your very face. You should have his head."

"No, brother." I waved him away. "Do we not have enough cause for quarrel?"

"You must go after them now," Tom said eagerly.

"Aye."

"You'll not live a month if you do not," said John.

"I will go."

"Never fear," said Tom. "They may think to defeat you, but they do not reckon with the honor of Lancaster. Did not Father boldly uphold the name

of our house in his many battles, and shall we not do likewise? We shall beat
them, I swear it."

Poor Tom. Poor, yet fortunate, Tom.

"Of course we shall beat them," I answered. "Never have I doubted
that."

From Winchester I journeyed to Southampton, upon the Channel, to see to
the organizing of the invasion force. We would cross the water to Harfleur,
the finest port in Normandy. Our destination was kept secret from all save
my brothers and Beaufort.

"Harfleur is deemed by the French to be impregnable," Tom complained. "Why Harfleur?"

"That is exactly what the Armagnacs shall say when we land there safe
and all unexpected. 'Why Harfleur?' they shall moan."

We lodged hard by Southampton in the stronghold of Portchester.
Many lords had joined us there with their companies of men-at-arms. Most
vital to me were the archers, the long-bowmen. I had studied the English
victories at Crécy and Poitiers under Edward the Third. While chivalry was
given all the credit, it seemed to me that it was the lowly archers, yeomen
all, who in fact carried the day for England. I called to me the best archers in
the land, from Cheshire and Hereford. Most heartening of all was the report
that a contingent of Welshmen was on its way to serve me. Men of Gwent
were said to be among them, men who had fought for Glyndwr but thought
highly still of Harry Monmouth. I had reason to rejoice in their presence
with me, for talk was rife of growing discontent among the peers. In vain I
set my spies to seek out any plots. Nothing came to my ears save vague
rumoring.

Late one night I sat talking with Beaufort, Courtenay, and my brothers
when Edmund Mortimer sought urgent audience with me. We puzzled over
what he might want at such an hour, and Beaufort counseled caution.

"Fie, Uncle," Humphrey said. "You see a plot behind every stone."

"I like it not," Beaufort replied. "The Frenchman's insult left a bad taste
in my mouth."

"Your point is well taken," I said, "yet surely we need not fear a lone
man. I will see him."

Edmund Mortimer was flaxen-haired and blue-eyed, as had been my
father, and Richard, and every King of England save Harry Monmouth. He
was plainly ill at ease, as well he might have been in the presence of the
family which had denied him the throne. He dropped to one knee and
bowed his head.

"Forgive me, your grace," he said. "I come to you to pledge my loyalty, to place my life in your hands, and to disclose to you a plan for most foul treason to which I have been a party until this very moment."

"You see!" cried Beaufort.

"Jesu," Tom swore, "what a time for it."

"What treason?" I asked.

"At your supper tomorrow you are to be stabbed to death, and your brothers and uncle as well. I was then to be set upon the throne."

I looked at Courtenay. "I should be used to it by now," I said, "yet I am not."

"Who seeks our lives?" Humphrey asked.

Mortimer hesitated.

"Go on," I said, "but know that likely you condemn men to death with your words."

"Richard of York," he said, "the Earl of Cambridge."

"It surprises me little," I said.

"Sir Thomas Grey, York's knight," he said.

He who had insulted me at Ewyas Lacy.

"I dread to say the next name," Mortimer said.

"Speak on."

"Your treasurer, Lord Scrope."

"Scrope!" the others cried together.

"Oldcastle as well"—Mortimer rushed on—"though he is not here. His Lollards were to rise in my behalf on news of your death. My lord of Scrope was to strike the blow, because it would be easy for him to get close to you."

The companions of my youth. Jack hidden in the hills of the march, awaiting word that I had been killed. Scrope, who had helped lead me to Alison's bed when I was but fourteen, wielding the knife.

"Where is Scrope?" Tom demanded.

"He is in Southampton, seeing to the victualing of the King's ship," said Beaufort.

"Answer me this, Mortimer," Humphrey said. "Why came you here tonight?"

"I have sworn an oath of loyalty to the King."

"Yet you said you knew of the plot previously to this night," John said. "Why did you not come earlier?"

"I—I do not know. I was afraid. I knew not what to do."

"Doubtless you realize now that you are no more safe than the King," said Beaufort. "A man of York's ambition would not let one such as you rest upon the throne. With the King dead, he would slay you as well and seize the crown for himself."

"I know nothing of that," he protested.

"You should arrest this man, Harry," said Humphrey. "He is as guilty as the others. He has plotted treason these many weeks."

"Your grace!" Mortimer cried. "I throw myself upon your mercy."

I came from where I stood alone by the fire. "Once more I would have the question put," I said. "Why came you here?"

"Your grace, I shall be plain. I have thought on it well. I would not be king, not for anything in this world. I do pity you, that you must wear the crown. It is a burden I do not want."

"A wise man," I said softly. "England has need of wise men. Go from me now, and have no fear. I accept your pledge of loyalty."

He trembled as he rose and took his leave.

"You are too lenient," said Beaufort.

"What shall you do?" Tom asked.

"I shall summon a council."

I called them all together, the lords of the realm, as though to discuss some matter pertaining to the expedition. They were much engaged with chatting and laughing when I entered the hall, and the traitors were blithe and jolly as any. I was careful to look at none of them save Scrope, whose face I searched for some sign of remorse. I found none, and turned coldly to my task.

"My lords," I announced when they had settled upon their benches, "a most disturbing report has reached my ear. It seems that treason is abroad in the land—indeed, in this very hall."

An uneasy hush settled over the assembly.

"I am told some of you seek my life, and the lives of my brothers and uncle as well. I can hardly believe it."

I looked straight at Richard of York.

"Know you anything of this matter, cousin?" I asked.

He had turned pale as any shade.

"Sir Thomas?"

Grey stood as though to protest, but said nothing.

"My lord Scrope?"

Never have I seen such terror upon a man's face.

"No! It is a lie!" he cried. "I was with them only that I might learn of their plans and warn you."

"The time draws nigh for the execution of this treason," I said, "yet my only warning has come from the Earl of March. Even my spies were able to learn nothing. It is not surprising, since you knew of their movements beforehand."

"No! Your grace—Harry—"

"Do not grovel, Scrope," York said. "We are betrayed. Play the man."

"Why came you against the king?" I said to York.

"You are not my king."

"You swore allegiance to me."

"As did Bolingbroke to Richard. My conscience would not let me stand idly by while you humiliate England. God's blood, I crave a fight with the French as well as the next man, but I would win that fight. Look at him, my lords! Is this the man to defeat the most chivalrous knights in Christendom? He is a tavern crawler, a libertine, and a coward. He knows not the meaning of honor. He shall bring shame upon you all if you do not turn against him now. Rise up, lords!"

The men of my household set their hands upon their sword hilts, as did my brothers. The lords squirmed on their seats, but none rose.

"Your challenge is not taken up, my lord of York," I said. "As for your slanders of my person, I shall answer them with my deeds."

I turned once more to Scrope. So pained was I at his betrayal that I must say more to him.

"My lord of Scrope, I confess to you that I am deeply wounded to find you here before me. You have served me well these ten years or more, with no sign of discontent. I named you my friend, and you have been privy to my deepest feelings. Why then would you plunge a dagger into me?"

"Tell him, Scrope," York taunted.

"You have had your say," I said.

"I will not answer," Scrope said.

"Come, Lord Scrope," said York, "what of your uncle, the Archbishop, foully murdered by Bolingbroke? And is it not truly that intimate knowledge you have gained in Monmouth's service which brought you to this? Tell the peers what you have told me."

Out of the corner of my eye I saw Beaufort motioning that I should silence him.

"Tell them," York hurried on, "how Monmouth sullied his honor by refusing to meet me in the lists. Tell how he skulked like a highwayman in the dark and robbed his own father's retainers, stole the coin of the realm. For such we hang men, my lords! Tell the peers how time after time this bastard King has shared with you his contempt for the nobility of England."

"Enough!" cried Beaufort.

"Tell them how he sniffed after a Welsh peasant slut like a mongrel after a bitch in heat."

I stood with clenched fists and motioned for the guards to take them away.

They were tried by their peers within five days, as is the custom, and beheaded. Two days after, despite warnings that it would now be unwise to leave England, I set sail with my army for Harfleur, leaving Beaufort and John to rule in my absence.

From the rolling sea, she appeared as a great crown, Harfleur, set upon a wooded headland where the Seine enters the Channel. We had crossed in two placid days. It had been quite a sight, the thousand small ships bobbing upon the glassy water, each proudly flying the banner of St. George. When we caught sight of the French coastline, a thin cheer took wing from the vessels scattered across the expanse of sea. This noise quieted soon enough when Harfleur came into view. Impregnable she looked, as the French had named her, and the men grew sober at the thought of taking her. I was more concerned that the French might have learned our destination and put men in the field against us, but we landed safely and unopposed. I sent at once to the town to seek their surrender, but my offer of fair treatment was refused. We settled in to the siege.

Scarcely had we landed ere tales of looting and pillaging came to my ears. This I would not countenance, for I had resolved to rule the French people rather than to terrorize them. I issued orders that robbery, rape, and murder would be punished by hanging. I paid a personal visit to one group of peasants abducted by my soldiers, to beg pardon for their frightening experience. Humbly I explained I had come to set them free from their oppressors. They stared, uncomprehending, at me but were glad enough when I paid them for their trouble and set them free.

My captains complained at once to me.

"An army checked from looting shall be a discontented army," said Sir Gilbert Umfraville.

Umfraville was a short, thick-necked man, given to wearing his sword at all times and swinging it to and fro in its scabbard as he spoke.

"We shall see, my lord," I said. "Yet chivalry forbids the harming of the innocent, does it not? My orders stand. See that your men follow them."

They had no reply, Umfraville and the Earls of Oxford and Suffolk. The beheadings at Southampton were fresh in their minds, and even as I was uncertain of their support, so they were wary of me. They kept apart from me, ever respectful, and yet I knew they must whisper of me over their cups at night and shake their heads. I could not bring myself to join them, to see the raised eyebrows and feel the questions hanging silent in the air. I left Tom and Humphrey to entertain them, and Courtenay alone I took into my confidence.

It was swampy, festering land which bordered Harfleur. The water was salty and foul, and the August sun bore down unmercifully upon armor and leather jerkins. Yet the men set to work with a right good will, placing the heavy guns and siege engines to assault gates and walls and digging their

mines to weaken the fortifications. Tom I sent with a goodly force to the far
side of the city, that she might be encircled. It was a far-flung operation, for
Harfleur was one of the largest towns in the north of France. I saw to every
detail of the operation myself. Even at night I walked abroad, supervising
the mines and challenging the sentries. Seldom did I sleep, three hours
here, one there, snatched at odd times. Courtenay often urged me to rest,
but I would not heed him. Nothing must go wrong because of my negligence, else it might prove the truth of York's charges against me.

'Twas upon my rounds one evening that I found the Welsh archers. I
was explaining to Humphrey the fine points of a siege engine when we
walked past them, a knot of ten or so roughly clad men eating their supper.
They talked incessantly, their crisp Celtic speech cutting through the heavy
vapors of the swamp.

"Leave me, brother," I said. "I would pass some time with these fellows."

"As you will. They are but archers."

So intent were they upon their argument over whether the women of
Gwent made better lovers than those of Powys that they did not note my
approach.

"A Powys woman has staying power," one man exclaimed, waving his
greasy fingers in the air. "She will grip you all through the night. A tanner's
daughter in Brecon I bedded for three days straight, mind you, and me
scarcely out of her."

"She must have been stone dead to have stood it," his fellow said, and
the whole lot roared with laughter.

"Dead or alive, she was a good lay," the first returned.

They groaned in appreciation.

The Powys man took note of me then. I was dressed plainly, as is my
wont, and he knew not who I was or that I had the Welsh tongue.

"Here's a slim English boy would be swallowed up by a Celtic woman,"
he said and winked at his comrades.

"Indeed it is not so," I replied in Welsh, "and I should have your balls
for saying it."

His face fell in astonishment.

"Where be you from?" another demanded.

"From Gwent," I said.

A cheer went up from several of the men.

"'Tis a man of Gwent you insult, Dafydd," one cried. "If he does not
have your balls for it, I shall." He took a long knife from his belt and tossed it
to me. "That should make good carving," he said. Then he stopped short, his
eyes wide. He was a tall and wiry man with a wild bush of red hair, and I
knew him then.

"Rhys?" I whispered. "Rhys ap Llewellyn?"

"Harry?"

"Well?" cried Dafydd. "Who is it I am to fight?" He swaggered up to me and thrust out his chest.

"It is the King," said Rhys.

It would be worth a sack of gold crowns to see their faces again. Not a jaw there that was not slack.

"Jesu, I am a dead man," Dafydd moaned.

I handed the knife to Rhys.

"I think that Dafydd will crave pardon without that," I said.

"Afore God, I did not know it was your grace," said Dafydd.

"That is not the same as an apology," I said, amused.

"I crave your pardon. I misspoke myself. You are obviously a most able man, a man among men. I am bad-tempered, you see; I say things but do not mean them." He laughed uncomfortably and wrung his hands. "I am your liege man. I took the oath at Southampton, I did."

"As did we all," Rhys added.

"How came you to it? You were all Glyndwr's men, were you not?"

They glanced furtively from one to the other.

"We were," Rhys answered, "but that is past. Not a man here who did not respect you, enemy though you were. For the other Englishmen we had only contempt."

"The respect was mutual," I said. I pointed then to the pot bubbling over the fire. "What have you there?"

"Hares we have snared by the river," Rhys said.

"Many a time as boys did we roast a hare together, Rhys."

"Well I remember, your grace."

"Harry," I said.

"Harry. I remember."

I smiled. "May I join you then?"

They shifted to make room for me in their circle and then sat timid and staring at their belts. I longed for them to be companionable with me but told myself it would take time. We ate in silence, and at last I looked at them regretfully.

"I fear I have spoiled your bantering," I said, "for you sit too much in awe of me. I shall take my leave, for I would have you jibe and laugh as before."

I stood to go.

"Wait!" Rhys said. "Would you not hear of Joan Waryn and Monmouth?"

Slowly I sat back down. "Tell me of them. When last were you there?"

"But a few months ago. I did not come down from the mountains until I heard you were King, for fear of your father's officers. I came home to find my mother carried away by a fever. My father had long been dead in Owain's service. Only my sisters were left, yet Joan had provided for them, and I took myself to the castle to thank her. Doleful she is. She pines for a sight of you."

"I have offered to bring her to London, but she will not come. She says she fears to leave the Welsh hills. England is unhealthful, she has heard."

"She told me of the lass."

"What lass?" asked Dafydd, keen to hear of a woman.

"A Welsh lass," Rhys replied, "and the King's own true love."

I studied my fingers, aware that all eyes were upon me. "A shepherdess from the Honddu," I said. "I loved her dearly. She died bearing my child soon before I was crowned."

Nearly three years ago. My lovely Merryn.

"Joan tends her grave," Rhys said. "She has planted roses all about it, red ones for Lancaster. Do you not wish to see it?"

I shook my head. "I could not bear it."

The men murmured all together in sympathy. Pride there was too in their faces, that the King should have so loved one of their own. A flask of sour wine was passed to me.

"Their lives be passing short, women," Dafydd said plaintively. "No sooner get attached to one than she be gone."

"What of your Brecon woman?" I tried to sound lighthearted. "Does she yet live?"

"No," said a thin, long-nosed lad they named Lloyd. "She died of Dafydd, do you not recall?"

We laughed in earnest then while Dafydd feigned chagrin. He was a short fellow, round of belly, black of hair and beard, with thick red lips and sleepy eyes.

"'Twas the pleasure killed her," he avowed.

The flask of wine went once more around the circle.

When they had quieted, I asked, "Why did you leave your Welsh women to toil here in this swamp?"

"Why not?" Rhys said. "Rebels and outlaws we have been these ten years. When I came again to Monmouth I found I had no taste for it. Tend swine for the rest of my life? Indeed, no. I would die of it."

"I came to serve Harry Monmouth," Dafydd declared. "The best prince in Christendom, so he is deemed in Wales, and I would bend my bow for him."

"You came for the wages," scoffed Lloyd.

"Aye, that too," said Dafydd. "And we shall earn our wages, shall we not, your grace? Yon city shall not fall so easily, it seems to me."

"No, not easily," I replied. "But she shall fall."

"Must we scale her walls?" Lloyd asked. "Many poor fellows shall be slain if it be so."

"I doubt it shall come to that," I said. "I took many of your Welsh strongholds, and with little loss of life. Mark you well, all of you. I pledge to serve you, even as you serve me. I have not brought you to France only to fling away your lives in reckless attempts to enhance my honor. There are those of my rank who do not value your lives at tuppence, and well you know it. It is not so with me. May God draw the very life from me if I do not strive with all my might to bring you safe out of France."

"It is all we can ask," said Rhys.

Dafydd was right, for Harfleur did not easily fall. Four weeks the siege dragged on with no sign of the town's surrender. Doubts assailed me, for many of my men sickened with the bloody flux. Harfleur, as I have said, was a swamp. Reeds grew in pools of black water, and the air was filled with noxious vapors. In such places foul miasmas hover to weaken the bodies of poor men. Disease spared neither highborn nor lowborn, and even sturdy Tom was felled by it. As soon as the tide was right, I had ships filled with the sick and sent back to England. Tom, I resolved, would be among them. He wept in frustration to hear he must leave.

"Now there shall be no glory for me. I would sooner die here than be sent away in my bed."

"Peace, brother. There shall be much to occupy you later, and I have need of you alive."

"If you fight them and I miss it, I shall never be content."

His servants bore him fretting in his litter to the waiting ship, and so to England.

Still more men were stricken, and several hundred died. I began to fear that the hand of God was against me after all. I had expected a lengthy siege, but the wholesale deaths of my men I had not bargained for. The old Earl of Suffolk breathed his last, and his son, also with us at Harfleur, assumed his father's title and command. This young Suffolk, along with Umfraville and Oxford, grumbled against me, calling for an assault that we might end the affair quickly. Day after day my guns and engines had battered the city. Many buildings were demolished, the barbicans protecting the gates were brought down, and the ramparts were destroyed so that the walls could not be defended. At night the French made their repairs with logs, stones, and all manner of rubble. I shuddered to think of the loss of life, both English and French, if I sent my men over the makeshift barricades. Once mounted, even a successful attack would be difficult to halt, and there would be a slaughter of innocents within the town.

"Harfleur shall not be Soissons," I said to my impatient captains. "I shall wait."

Then struck the cruelest blow of all. Richard Courtenay swooned before my very eyes, as we prepared one morning to break our fast, and was carried straightway to his tent, burning with fever.

I had not wanted him at Harfleur. "There is much to be done in England," I pleaded, "and I shall have no use of you in France. What, would you take up the sword?"

"Indeed not," he had replied. "I have grave misgivings of this venture, Harry. Yet do not claim you have no need of me. Who does not stand in need of a true friend? None in the realm loves you better than I do, and none may so prick your conscience either."

I could not gainsay him, for the pain of Scrope's treachery was fresh with me and I longed for companionship. Yet prick my conscience he did not. In the face of the deaths of my soldiers he did not urge me to quit the siege, even as he had protested but little as I planned my invasion. As the sweltering days dragged on he had fallen silent and taken more and more to his tent to pray. I saw him little, so engaged was I in the direction of the army. When at last the fever overtook him it seemed that he had waited for it, embraced it with open arms. Four days only he lingered.

"I die faithful, Harry. I did not betray you."

Those were his last words to me. When the breath had left him, I closed his eyes myself.

"Aye, gentle Courtenay," I whispered. "I am the traitor."

The ship sailed that very day which would have carried him to England. Instead it bore his body, to be laid in a place of honor in the abbey church of Westminster. I watched all empty as the white sails sank beneath the horizon.

"You should take your rest," Humphrey said. "You look like death itself. I fear you shall be the next to sicken."

"May it be so," I said. "May God take me and be done with it."

I turned from the shore and trudged back to my tent.

"Would that I might be drunk this night," I muttered. "Yet there is too much to be done."

A fortnight after Courtenay's death, Harfleur came to terms. Her supply of food had not run out but her people were said to be afflicted with the bloody flux as we were, and their patience was all worn down by the constant bombardment from my guns. In vain the garrison had waited for relief from King Charles and the Dauphin, his son, and held out from fear that I would use them harshly because of their fierce resistance. When at last the leading men of the town came before me in submission, it was with fear and trembling, for they expected to be executed and their goods confiscated. They left amazed that I gave them all their lives and further pledged that no man who swore loyalty to me would have his goods stolen.

"My lords," I said to them, "Harfleur is my town. I would not ill use any such place which is given into my care."

My captains again disputed with me when we met in the abbey of Graville.

"If you do not set your soldiers free to plunder, you shall lose their hearts," said the Earl of Oxford.

"No," I replied, "it was not so in Wales. If they were not paid their wages or if they had thought I used their lives carelessly, then would they have turned against me."

Only old Sir Thomas Erpyngham agreed. He had grown gray in the service of Lancaster and had been with my grandfather even in the days of Edward the Third.

"The King has been with the men day and night, walking among them and speaking to them," he said. "Never have I seen such high spirits in an army, nor more willingness to serve. Never fear, my lords. The King has their hearts."

"What of the French?" asked Humphrey. "Will they cease to fear you, Harry, if you do not appear strong?"

"It is one thing for them to respect me. It is quite another to fear and loathe me for my cruelty. Their respect shall spring naturally from my success, not from the killing of innocent people. This matter is closed, my lords. There shall be no sack of Harfleur."

We turned to plot our next move. This was a thorny problem which had caused me much concern. That we could not remain among the miasmas of the coastal marshes I was certain. But where were we to go?

"Back to England," said my captains.

"Why?" I asked.

"We have lost many men to disease," said the young Earl of Suffolk, clad all in black to mourn his father. "Of the others, half have been invalided back to England. You cannot have more than six thousand healthy troops."

"And only one thousand of them knights," Humphrey added.

"It is enough," I said, "to march into France."

"What?" Oxford exploded. "One thousand lances enough to face the chivalry of France?"

"No," I said with a smile, "it was the five thousand archers I thought upon."

"Your grace." Oxford spoke as though he addressed a small child. "Your scouts report twenty thousand of the cream of French knighthood are gathered even now at Rouen, with thirty thousand more lances of lesser degree.

You cannot seriously think to face such a host with five thousand country louts."

I raised my eyebrows. "Cousin of Oxford, if God willed it, I could beat the French with but five hundred of these 'louts,' as you name them. Yet I thank Him for the five thousand. They shall serve."

"It would take but one company of knights, mounted and armored, to ride down your archers," said Gilbert Umfraville.

"Not if my men have some protection," I said.

"What protection?" asked Suffolk. "Would you have us sully our honor by skulking behind trees? We would face them in the open as true knights, would we not?"

Here was a proud young man and smitten by chivalry. A young Bolingbroke, he seemed to me, with his thick mane of red-gold hair and his proud bearing.

"Indeed, my lord Suffolk, we shall face them in the open," I answered.

"I know you well, brother," said Humphrey. "Your mind is made up."

"It is," I said. "Do not think I act rashly, my lords. I have studied this matter since before I came to France. The disease we have suffered has altered my plans, I must admit. I had thought to take Rouen, perhaps even drive toward Paris on this expedition. We no longer have the staying power for that. Still, we need not go bootless back to England. We may strike them a blow from which they shall never recover. I would see something of these lands I claim for my own. I hear they are fair. I would know it for myself. I hear that the French lords have mistreated their subjects and squandered the land's plenty. I would know that as well, and show my new subjects that I mean to rule them justly. I shall march then from Harfleur to our city of Calais. We shall travel light, my lords. Eight days' food shall we carry. It is less than one hundred forty miles to Calais, and I would not be encumbered with supplies."

The skepticism was plain upon their faces.

"And suppose the French army bar our way?" said Oxford. "I know not yet why you are so sure you can beat them."

"It is because I know how they shall fight. I know how they think."

I dismissed them, and they filed dejectedly from the chamber, leaving Humphrey behind.

"I know well why you shall not return to England, brother," he said.

"Do you?"

"You fear you cannot hold the throne if you have but one city to show for this venture."

"Let us just say that the mistrust which ever has plagued me would not be quieted."

"Yet suppose the French do not come against you? If I were the French,

I should let you pass on to Calais and then out of the realm, unmolested but with nothing to show for your pains."

"I would do the same. But they will fight. After all, they have their honor to defend."

We marched from Harfleur on the sixth day of October, in the year of Our Lord 1415. It was later than I would have liked, but I must play games to humor my captains. I must, they said, challenge the King of France to single combat, that the issue between us might be settled in the most knightly fashion. I protested this as a meaningless gesture which would waste valuable time, but Suffolk and the others were adamant. It was a formality only, but a convention nonetheless. I gave in, for I knew that I had already sorely tried their patience. My heralds were dispatched to Rouen. It gave me much amusement to picture it—Harry, the inexperienced jouster, ranged against mad Charles, a drooling old man upon his charger. In the end this scenario proved too ludicrous even for the knightly Suffolk, and at his suggestion my challenge was sent not to the King but to the Dauphin. There was, of course, no joust, the Dauphin being a fat and indolent youth even less inclined than I to break a lance.

Upon leaving, I chose some two hundred archers to serve me as a personal escort. Rhys, Dafydd, and Lloyd I picked with a score of their Welsh fellows, as well as Englishmen from the marches. There was much swaggering and boasting before their comrades who had not been so honored, until I must threaten to send them from me again if they did not quiet themselves. Still, I was pleased to see such value set on serving me.

Upon the eve of our departure, I strolled with Erpyngham through the streets of Harfleur, to make certain that the men prepared themselves properly for the journey. Everywhere we saw the red cross of St. George, for I had ordered each man to wear one on his tunic that he might be readily identified as an Englishman. Then I could account more easily for the actions of my soldiers.

"An audience with your grace! An audience!"

The voice carried even above the din of the street. A burly fellow with greasy brown hair left the barrels he had been loading onto a cart and fell at my feet.

"Is this a matter of some importance?" I asked.

"Of utmost importance. Your grace 'as picked 'is own troop of archers and left me out of it, who would serve better than any man alive."

"Indeed? Stand up then and let me look at you."

Something familiar there was about the gravelly voice and pockmarked face, but I could not place him.

"What are you called?" I asked.

"John Wotten, an' it please your grace."

"And why should you serve me so well, John Wotten?"

He flashed a toothy grin. "Do ye not recall, your grace? Ye saved my wages once, at Worcester it was. An 'ard night's work ye put in for 'un. I would return the favor."

I knew him then, the guard at Worcester who had witnessed my brief stint as a highwayman. I threw back my head and laughed.

"Would you indeed? Under whom do you serve?"

"Sir Thomas 'ere be my liege."

"Well, Erpyngham, do you give him to me?"

The old man smiled. "If he be doughty as he claims, I ought not part easily with him. Yet for love of my king, I shall."

"You are mine then, Wotten. My men are lodged in the Hotel de Ville. Get you there at once."

"Aye, your grace, and most gladly."

He tugged his forelock and hopped away through the throng, his bundle of goods clutched to his chest.

"He is worth three earls to me," I said. "But never tell Suffolk I said it."

"Age should give me the freedom to chastise you, king though you be. Yet you put me too much in mind of your grandfather to do it."

I clapped him upon the shoulder. "No finer compliment could you pay me."

We set out for Calais as blithe as any hunting party. For a time I rode upon my gray courser and chatted with Humphrey and Suffolk, but they bored me with their talk of the comparative merits of the Black Prince and Bertrand du Guesclin. It was not long ere I dismounted and sought the company of the archers. They were in fine fettle, intoxicated by the morning air and the adventure upon which we embarked.

"'Tis a fine land, this," Dafydd said expansively. "'Twill be a pleasure to win it for your grace. And fine fellows these for companionship."

Before us, the thin line of the vanguard was a bright necklace draped across the tawny shoulders of the hills. Nothing ill could possibly touch us. Did we not laugh easily and often? Did the air not burn in our quick lungs? No enemy would dare to crush such vitality.

My spirit was chastened, though, as we saw more the countryside. The desolation was worse even than what I had seen in Wales. Hollow-eyed peasants stood as scarecrows in their fields and watched our passing. They did not run to gather their livestock in to safety, for these had long ago been stolen by Armagnac or Burgundian war parties. What need to fear the English? Only the women fled from us, guarding that treasure which, to their sorrow, may never be hidden from violation. They need not have feared us, for I swear before almighty God and His Holy Mother that none of my men harmed a woman on our march, out of fear of my punishment. This has often been marked upon, even by the French. The poor women of Fécamp were not so fortunate in their treatment at the hands of their own soldiers. In that town, knights sent by King Charles to oppose me lodged in the abbey Church and abused the women who had come to pray there. This we learned from several prisoners we took as we skirted past the town. These brave soldiers of Fécamp sallied out to oppose us as we marched past but were shortly driven by our archers' shafts back into the town, to the lamentation, no doubt, of the inhabitants.

I could have taken Fécamp, had I wished, but I did not linger there. Reports came to me that the great French army had departed Rouen and so would be marching somewhere to the east of us. Before us lay the vast river Somme with her marshy banks, and this obstacle I would pass ere we were brought to battle. We would move faster than the French for we were fewer and less encumbered by supplies and accouterments of chivalry than they would be. Still, I would not tarry, as it was said the Somme could be crossed in only a few places or not at all. The largest ford was at Blanche-Taque, near the river's mouth, and this we approached on the fourth day from Harfleur.

We were six miles from the ford when Gilbert Umfraville came spurring back from the van.

"The march must be halted!" he cried. "We are foiled!"

The bantering men around me fell silent.

"What mean you, Gilbert?"

"We have taken a prisoner, a Gascon. He claims the French hold the ford against us. They have driven stakes into it and now await us with an army of some six thousand lances."

"Are they on this side of the Somme?"

"No, the far side."

So they did not mean to fight us yet.

"Bring the prisoner to me, and call my captains to parley."

The Gascon swore by his story. He was a true subject of the English king, he said, on his way to trade in Calais. Barely had he escaped the clutches of the French himself.

"There are many, thousands." He waved his arms. "All on horseback they are. The Marshal Boucicaut leads them, so I have heard."

"He is a knight of renown," said Oxford.

"You come with so few," the Gascon said. "They will eat you alive, the French. Thousands there are."

"Enough!" I snapped. I looked around the circle of my advisers. "I sent word to the Earl of Warwick at Calais. He was to hold the ford."

"Then he has failed, has he not?" Umfraville said.

I read the reproach in all their eyes. So too have you failed, they said.

"Well, my lords," said Suffolk, "I hope you have enough money for your ransoms."

"Suffolk," I said, "if you speak so again, I shall turn you over to the French myself."

The youth flushed red and sputtered. "Your grace, I only say what—"

"There will be no ransoms. Is it clear? We live or we die but we do not ransom ourselves."

"Why, brother?" Humphrey asked. "It is not dishonorable."

"Look at these poor fellows we have brought with us," I answered. "They have no money for ransom, these archers of mine. Nor shall we buy our way safely home at their expense, my lords."

"Your spirit is admirable, your grace," said Erpyngham. "But the main body of the French must be approaching at our rear. If we are in a trap—"

"We are in no trap yet," I said. "But if ever we are, we shall fight our way out of it. And my lords, I would have you spend more of your time thinking on how to break free of traps than in counting up your ransom money."

We had not long to wait until our scouts confirmed the Gascon's story. The passage of the Somme was denied us.

"Shall we return to Harfleur?" asked Humphrey. "We have just enough food for it. If we move quickly, we may arrive safely ere the French catch us."

"No," I said. "I do not go backward. We shall seek a passage farther up the river."

"They shall shadow us on the far bank," said Oxford. "They shall block every passage."

"I have studied the map," I replied. "There is a sharp bend in the river. They must follow the outside of the loop, while we will cut across the neck. We can gain a day on them."

"I too have seen the map," said Erpyngham. "It will take several days of hard marching to reach that loop. Our food shall be gone by then."

"We shall deal with that when the time comes."

"They are on horseback," said Oxford.

"They shall not outdistance us," I said. "They shall want to keep an eye on us."

I needed no one's skepticism to tell me of our peril. I should not have gambled on Warwick's holding the ford, should not have insisted upon so few rations. I had been overly proud, overly certain of my own shrewdness. God would not bear with such arrogance long; He would seek out some other instrument to unite Christendom. I prayed that in turning from me, He would not desert my archers as well.

They muttered and looked about them warily, my men, when we

turned aside from the road to follow the river. I had not yet told them I expected to fight, and all their hope had rested in marching unopposed to Calais. Rumor blazed through their ranks that the French army waited even now at the head of the river to devour us when we arrived at last, weary and starving. The gentlemen would be ransomed and the archers slain, and that would be that. This tale I had from Rhys as we made ready our camp in a lush water meadow.

"What say you to it?" I asked him.

"I say the man I fought against in Wales was no fool. I say the boy I grew up with will not hold cheap the lives of poor men. Yet I do fear we may not avoid a battle with yon fellows."

On the far bank the fires of the French danced in the dusk.

"Nor have I ever thought we would avoid a battle," I said.

"What?"

"I would not say such a thing to the others. Give me your word you shall be silent about it until I am ready."

"I give you my word, yet in all truth how can you have sought battle with so few of us?"

"Rhys, Rhys. You are a Welshman, an archer. You have seen what the longbow may do to a man on horseback."

"A lone man, aye. In Wales the terrain suits ill for a pitched battle. Yet when the numbers are so great—"

"Then is our advantage multiplied. You shall see."

"It was not so at Shrewsbury. Percy had archers there and he lost."

"So did we have archers. And Percy did not use his properly. As for these Frenchmen, they have but crossbowmen, and only a few at that. Worse than useless they are. We shall have them ere they have time to wind a bolt."

I did not worry over my strategy, but rather the lack of food. If we were weak with hunger and our ranks riddled with disease, how could we stand? Already some were stricken with the bloody bowels of Harfleur and must be borne on litters by their fellows. Nourishment we all would need. The years of cruel war had stripped bare the surrounding countryside, even had I allowed plunder. And what of the spirits of the men? If they believed themselves lost, if they had no confidence in me, then would we all be dead men. God I might trust to bring us safely home again, but it would be to me that the men looked for guidance. I studied them at their tasks of setting up camp. They were subdued, talking quietly in small clusters, pausing to look fearfully into the darkness. Theirs were plain, bearded faces, faces etched with the care of disease and famine. Many bony children they would have fathered, and stringy-haired women would wait for their return, hopeful of the wages that might buy a cow for fresh milk or keep the eldest girl from the brothels of Hereford or Shrewsbury. Shame welled up in me that I had brought them to such a place to lie at night in mortal fear. No, I thought then, it is for good cause. It is so that none after them must be here. It is so that their French fellows may know some peace as well. And afore God, they shall not be here for naught. I shall bring them out of this if I must die for it.

I took my meal standing, my dried meat and hunk of cheese, and then set out on my charger. From camp to camp I rode, from vanguard to rear. Patiently I explained our situation, why we had turned aside and what lay before us. I shared what little I knew of the location of the French army somewhere to the south. I told them if it came to a fight, I would not abandon them for a ransom, nor would any of my lords. I held their frightened eyes to mine.

"We stand together," I said to them. "We have a hard march ahead, but we march together. Those who sicken and tire shall be carried or taken up on the horses, even my own horse. I swear to you before God and all His angels, not one of you shall be left behind. Not one, even if he is too weak to fight. God as my help, I shall bring you all to Calais."

In Welsh I spoke to my countrymen, and in the plain good English tongue to the others. I clasped their hands, spoke to them of their homes, and saw hope raise their heads, tauten the muscles of their thick necks.

"No plundering," I reminded them. "No raping. Whores enough there are in Calais." Laughter then. "Already have I sent to the Calais madams to expect you." They moaned their appreciation. On to the next troop, and so on the next day as we marched, and into that night, until all had word of my purpose.

"They are yours," said Rhys. "I swear, they would follow you into Hell."

"God forbid I should lead any there, or that they be so foolish as to follow."

Though it led not to Hell, it was a hard enough path we had taken. At Rémy the bridge was found destroyed, and the fords along our way as well. The French knights rode proudly beyond the glittering expanse of water upon their gaily caparisoned horses, at times drawing near enough to call over insults. My archers had not the French tongue, but they guessed well enough what was said to them.

"I knew not there were so many gentlemen in the world," John Wotten grumbled as we walked, "nor that they could be so boisterous. Where be all the plain men?"

"Starving to death, from what I have seen," said Lloyd.

"They'll not fight alongside common men, the French knights," I said. "It would mar their honor to share the feats of war with the baseborn."

Dafydd hooted loudly. "Is it so? What do they think then of our king?"

"Little enough," I said.

"Do ye mind?" asked Wotten.

"No," I said. "It only shows their foolishness. Indeed, I would stand in fear of them had they fellows such as you about them. As it is, I say let them come on."

"So say I," cried Dafydd. "I'll not be taunted by a dandy dripping in perfume."

"Yet soon their horses shall eat better than we do," Lloyd complained. "I finish my rations this night."

"As do I," I said.

"Did ye not set extra aside?" Wotten asked.

"Would I eat before men who have none?"

They fell silent.

"What of my lord of Suffolk?" Lloyd asked after a time.

"He no doubt is rubbing his belly and cursing me this very moment," I replied.

"Do him good." Dafydd sniffed. "Give him a taste of what it is to be a poor man. Maybe he shall be easy on his tenants when he's back in England."

"No," Lloyd scoffed, "it never works that way."

It was a damp country we passed through that day and the next. Mid-October it was and, as often happens at that time of year, the sultry heat of summer returned to bedevil us. Nor could we refresh ourselves easily at the riverbank, for we were forced some yards away from it by a dense marsh in which a man might sink up to his waist. The earth was dying around us. The trees sagged mournfully, their leaves rotting brown in the muck. I shall never forget the stink of the place.

We were as bedraggled as the landscape. Noblemen and yeomen alike sported beards. My own was thick and brown. Never before had I allowed it to grow, and for a time it itched me near to distraction. No sooner was I used to it than the itch started again, this time from lice which I also had in my scalp and groin. My tunic and breeches, damp with sweat and with lying upon the sodden ground, grew moldy upon my body. We all of us smelled like the fish market at Billingsgate.

Twice as much ground did I cover as any man in the army. Back and forth I rode, stopping here and there to dismount and walk alongside the men. Calais, I promised them, over and over again. They hung upon my every word, their eyes pleading for some sign of hope. Each step took us further into the heart of France. More men fell sick and must be carried. Our pace slowed and on occasion nearly halted. The French horsemen knew it, and their taunts grew more frequent.

"Sluggards!" they cried. "Our horses want exercise."

"Be content with our pace," I reassured the men. "We need not race with them. Conserve your strength for when we reach the bend in the river."

Then we ran out of food.

"How shall we outdistance the French at the bend if we have no food, no strength?" Humphrey complained.

"I shall find food, brother," I replied.

"And even with food, how shall you urge these poor, stumbling wretches to greater speed?"

I wondered myself.

We came that evening, our bellies griped and limbs trembling, to the castle of Boves. I sent heralds to the garrison in search of food, and they returned to say that there was none.

"Tell them this," I said. "Thus far, I have held back my men from plunder. Yet if they do not help us, I shall set fire to every building and field within three miles of this place. I want food and I want wine. Tell them I shall pay them for all we take."

There was a small town clustered about the castle, and the people were in no mood to be burned from their homes. After an hour of stalling the gates were opened to us and a store of bread and wine made available.

"If anyone is harmed in this town, I would hear of it," I said to the captain of Boves.

None of his people came to pour out any grievance against my soldiers, who to a man settled quietly in the lanes and fields to eat their ration of bread.

"It is amazing to me," Oxford said as he gnawed a black crust, "how they listen to you. They are docile as nuns."

It was not so for long. Boves, it seems, was a center of winemaking, and there was a greater store there than I had anticipated. I gave my permission for the men to drink of it, and to fill their bottles to carry with them on the morrow. But of course no man feels drink more than a hungry one. I watched in alarm from the castle gate as more casks were seized and broken open. The din grew louder, and many were soon quite drunk.

"Perhaps it is best," said Humphrey. "Poor devils, they should have been in Calais by now. This shall give them some vent for their frustrations."

"No. They shall be in no shape to march on the morrow," I said. "Even more do I fear what damage they shall do while drunk. They may loot the town."

Just then a hue and cry was raised from a knot of men in a nearby meadow.

"It starts already," I said with a sigh. I mounted my horse and rode toward the fight, passing many on foot who were running to see the specta-

cle. A large crowd of screaming men surrounded two in the middle who
circled one another warily with knives drawn.

"Enough of this!" I cried. No one heard me. I slid to the ground and
forced my way into the crowd, shoving men this way and that as I went.
Then I stepped quickly between the two antagonists. One raised his blade
on a sudden, and I feared he would not recognize me in time, but he froze
then and ducked his head in fear.

"What are you doing?" I screamed.

The crowd pushed and shoved against me, the smell of sour wine
stronger than the odor of unwashed bodies.

"Fools!" I drew my sword and held it out before me so that they must
back up and leave a clear space. A sullen silence descended upon them.
"Have you not enough enemies about? Must you then fight one another?"

"Who prates to us of enemies?" someone called from the rear. "Do we
not have a bellyful of the enemy?"

"Hush!" said another. "It is the King!"

Still I held the sword out, and turned slowly round and round.

"You were not so full of fight today," I taunted. "You moped along like
whipped curs."

They stared back at me in frustration. I turned then to the two who had
drawn their knives.

"Why this fight?" I asked.

"He stole my bread, filthy Welshman," one said.

"Did you see him take it?"

"No, but who else? They are all thieves and liars, the Welsh."

There were outcries of anger from the crowd.

"Pig!" spat the accused Welshman in a broken English. "I know naught
of your bread."

"Enough!" I cried. I dropped the sword at my feet and turned to the
Englishman.

"Throw down your knife," I commanded. When he had done so I
looked him up and down. He had three inches in height over me, I judged,
and thirty pounds.

"You insult my countryman," I said.

His jaw fell slack. "Your grace is not Welsh," he said feebly.

"But I am," I snapped, "and I shall not be called a liar or thief by any
Englishman."

He fell to his knees. "I beg your pardon."

"It is not enough," I said. "You must fight me."

A murmur of excitement ran through the crowd, and I knew that I had
them.

"Clear a space," I ordered, "that we may have at each other."

The poor Englishman was in tears. "It is death to come armed against the King," he blubbered.

"We do not fight to the death," I said. "We wrestle. Have you never wrestled?"

"Aye, at home in Banbury."

"Were you good?"

"Aye, one of the best in the town."

"Then are you fit to uphold the honor of England," I said, and smiled.

I stripped off my tunic and boots and faced him.

"I shall pin you upon your back," I said, "and then shall you repent of your slander of the Welsh."

I waited for him to strip and then I crouched low and approached him, seeking how he would fight. He backed away from me uncertainly, still in awe to find himself ranged against the King.

"Do you run from me?" I mocked. "Come after me, you whoreson English bastard! Coward!"

He charged like a bull, then, and wrapped his arms about my trunk. I slithered sideways and down, catching the back of his leg with my knee as I went. He fell heavily on his side. I could have pinned him then, but chose to let him rise as a delighted roar went up from the crowd. I extended my hands to him, palms up, and waved my fingers teasingly. He blundered in again and the weight of him toppled me over backwards. I winced, as my back and head struck the ground, and heaved with all my might, twisting my torso so that his own momentum carried him over into the dirt. I was on him in an instant, one arm wrapped beneath his armpit, the other under his knee, turning him on his back. He struggled ferociously and I feared I might lose him, for he was a powerful man. But I held on gamely, and soon his shoulders were down and his chin poking his own chest.

The men cheered wildly as I rose, the din so loud it would have roused the dead. I extended my hand to the befuddled archer and helped him to his feet.

"Apologize to Wales," I said, laughing.

"I beg pardon of all Welshmen," he replied sheepishly.

"You are pardoned," I said. "As for yon Frenchmen, if they wish to tangle with me, I say let them come."

They hurrahed, clapped me upon the back, reached eagerly for my hand. I joked easily with them, called many by their Christian name, and then sent them to their beds with a warning of the rigors of the day ahead.

When I returned to the cottage I would share with a smith and his family, I found my captains still in disbelief of what they had seen. I stifled a smile at the look upon their faces.

"Never fear, my lords," I said. "They shall march on the morrow."

Old Erpyngham was the first to chuckle. "If you fight the French so cannily, they are in peril," he said.

"Jesu, when they hear of it in London," chortled Humphrey.

"But your grace," asked Umfraville, "what if he had beaten you?"

"My dear Umfraville, I was trained in wrestling when I was young and no one could take my measure. Never would I have provoked him if I thought I would lose."

We were up and away well before dawn and quit Boves before the French had awakened. The Somme curved away in the dark to our left, and we were none of us sorry to leave it for a time. We carried with us a supply of bread and wine, and while it was not meat, it filled the belly and set the blood to flowing. We followed a track cut straight through a dense wood, and we went at a right brisk pace.

We passed by the walled town of Corbie that afternoon. The garrison rode out to harass us, as at Fécamp, and just as before the sting of our shafts sent them flying back for cover. Several prisoners we took when they were thrown by their horses, and one of these captives caused an uproar among the archers.

"He claims he has been in Rouen with the French army," said Rhys when we halted for the night. "The archers in the Earl of Oxford's company are full of his stories. He says the French will not be harmed by our archers as at Crécy. They have formed two companies of knights whose task it shall be to charge our archers and cut them down as soon as a battle should begin."

"At least they have learned half a lesson."

Rhys was not amused. "This tale frights the men," he said. "It frights me."

"Will they catch us then?" Lloyd asked. "Shall we never cross this river?"

"We may yet cross the Somme," I said, "but aye, I think they shall catch us ere we reach Calais."

They moaned.

"Then you think us lost," said Lloyd.

"That I did not say. Have I not pledged to bring you to Calais?"

"You say it to make us march."

"You are bold so to challenge me, young Lloyd," I said. "Do you doubt my word? If you do, I have no use for you here."

"No," he mumbled. "I did not mean that."

I sat down and wrapped my cloak tight, for the air had turned chill.

"They are chivalry's fools, the French," I said. "The times have changed, weapons have changed, but their minds have not. They think that courage still wins battles. It does not. They think battles are won by knights in armor, honorable gentlemen. Well, they lost all they knew of honor long ago. Even so, battles are not won by knights. Battles are won by archers, which I have, and by wits, which I have as well."

"But if we are run down ere the battle begins, we cannot serve your grace," said Dafydd.

"Whoosht! Can ye not see our King 'as a plan?" John Wotten croaked. "Let 'im tell us of it."

I pulled a stick from a pile of kindling and set to whittling on it with my knife while they watched me impatiently. I scraped the bark from it and honed it to a fine point at either end.

"Imagine that this is six feet long," I said, "and thick as my wrist. Imagine a row of these stakes thrust into the earth at an angle as high as a man's waist, their points facing outward." I thrust the stick into the ground. "So. Now suppose you are a horse, and the fool of a man riding you is spurring you straight onto this barrier—"

"Hoo—oo!" Dafydd leaped up and danced around. "It is beautiful!"

"Already you are stung and frightened by these screaming arrows. What do you do if you are a reasonably intelligent horse?"

"Ye bolt!" cried Wotten. "Ye rear into the air!"

"What if there are hundreds of horses behind you and in front of you, and beside you?"

"Chaos," said Rhys.

"What if archers are pouring round after round into your ranks?" I began to sicken then at the thought of it. I closed my eyes. "The fools. They shall ride blithely upon us as though to a joust. Only I do not joust."

"If we did not kill them, they would kill us," Dafydd declared. "They count our lives not for this." He snapped his fingers.

"Each man shall have a stake?" asked Rhys.

"That is my plan."

"They should cut them soon. It will put heart in them if they know of this," he said.

"Aye. With the Frenchman spreading his stories, it is time."

I called together my captains to give the order. Suffolk could not contain himself when he heard of it.

"I must risk the anger of my King to say it. Never have I heard of anything so outrageous."

"Do you doubt it will work?" I asked.

"That is not the point. It may work too well. It is beneath the dignity of a knight, it violates all codes of honor. Totally unfair it is. Why not just sneak up on them at night and slit their throats? It would be no worse."

"What do you suggest, that I wait with open arms while they run down my archers?"

"I suggest the only honorable course left open to us in these perilous straits. Surrender and pay our ransoms."

"They would slay the archers anyway. That is five thousand dead men."

"So? They are but baseborn."

"I will not have it, Suffolk." I turned away.

"You care not for them," he cried. "You fear the French shall put you in prison, as we did to their King John after Poitiers."

I whirled around and thrust my face into his. "You forget yourself, my lord. I know what you think. You think Richard of York spoke truly of me. Well, you may think what you like, but you shall do as I say. Is . . . it . . . clear?"

He looked helplessly at the others.

"The King is right," said Erpyngham. "You are insubordinate, Suffolk. You shall be fortunate if he does not punish you."

Oxford rubbed his beard. "Our situation is desperate," he said. "It calls for desperate measures."

"If there be any blame in this," I said, "let it rest with me."

Humphrey said nothing, but his eyes glittered with amusement. I have ever suspected he has no conscience.

The archers cut their stakes the next day, sharpened them as they trudged along, and slung them across their shoulders. Some grumbled, deeming it a frivolous idea, but most were heartened that their King looked toward their safety.

Once more we drew nigh the Somme. I was able to buy small amounts of food from villages along the way. They seemed glad enough to be rid of such ragged, desperate-looking fellows, and surprised as well to receive some coin for their troubles.

It was on our leaving one such place—Caix, as I recall—that Oxford came up from the rear, bearing upon his horse a skinny little priest. Like a crow this clerk was, his black robe pulled above his bony knees that he might ride more easily, and his bare white legs flailing wildly as he sought to keep his seat.

"Would he ride a woman so awkwardly?" Dafydd said. We all did laugh, but my own mirth died when I learned the man's errand.

"Forgive me that I trouble your grace," he said, "but you harbor a thief among you, one who defiles the holy places of France with his greed. A pyx containing the Host has been stolen from my church. A woman praying in the shadows saw the thief and swears he was attired as one of the English soldiers. A red cross he bore upon his tunic, so she says."

I regarded his balding head with hatred.

"What sort of pyx?" I asked.

"It is but copper gilt. The thief may have thought it to be gold."

"Search them all," I said to Oxford. "We go no farther until the thief is found."

"God shall bless the King of England that he does take such care for the protection of the Church," said the priest. "It is marked by all in our village how gently we have been used by your army. Not even a woman of Caix bears any grievance."

"I thank you, father," I muttered. "I fear I am now brought to a distasteful undertaking so that all may remain as you say."

It took more than an hour to find him, a Cheshire archer of Umfraville's retinue, with the pyx stuffed in his bedroll. I thanked God that I did not know him. A rough, dull fellow he looked, who had thought his copper pyx to be a prize of great worth. He stood before me with bowed head and kicked up the dust with his feet.

"You took the pyx?" I asked.

"Aye. I thought no harm."

"You know the punishment I have set for looting?"

His face was pasty white beneath its layer of grime. "You'll not hang me?"

"You knew the penalty beforehand."

He began to weep. "Jesu have mercy," he wailed.

"I cannot keep faith with God if I lose control of my men." I spoke as though to beg his pardon. I looked at Umfraville. "He is of your muster. Have your archers hang him from yon elm."

The poor wretch was hauled screaming to the tree and hoisted into the air. His tongue came out, his eyes bulged—

I looked away.

The priest beamed toothlessly upon me. "God bless you, my son, that you punish the sinner in your midst."

I waved him away irritably. Once more I proclaimed throughout the army my edicts on pillage and rape.

Late that night I sought out Umfraville.

"Your man," I said, casting about for the proper words. "I was sorry to deal with him so."

He shrugged. "What is one archer, your grace? If you must have such discipline . . ."

"You thought the hanging unnecessary?" My face grew hot at the tone of his voice.

He studied his fingernails. "How can I say? I am no king."

I knew what he would have been saying to Oxford and young Suffolk, that the hanging had cost us valuable time on the march. Now he would go to them and laugh. "First he delays us over a petty theft and now he frets over the hanging of the archer. Of all things! We are in the hands of a fool."

I took myself away and prayed that night for God's pardon.

We came the next day to Nesle. Again I sought food, but here was no Boves. The gates of Nesle were all shut and the walls draped in scarlet cloth in defiance of us. The citizenry gathered upon the walls to jeer as we made our painful way toward the river.

Beyond the town were some smaller villages, but these had been stripped bare of food, even for the inhabitants. This I learned when I threatened to set the torch to the area if we were not sold food. A wizened old man named Guillaume had come reluctantly forward to plead for his people.

"You must believe we have nothing to give," he implored. "The soldiers of the King have taken it all."

"The French king?" I asked.

He nodded. "They crossed the Somme north of here two days ago. Thousands there were, and they spread like locusts, devouring the grain and stealing livestock for miles around. We have nothing left ourselves, and we know not how we shall live out the winter."

"Why would they cross the river?" Humphrey asked. "If they were so close to us, why did they not come against us?"

"They toy with us," said Erpyngham. "They think we shall never cross the Somme, so they march along the opposite bank as Boucicaut did, until we have not the strength to set one foot in front of the other. Then they shall take us."

I looked around the village. Nothing moved, for the people were all hid at the sight of my men. Nowhere did a scrawny chicken pick its way through the dust and offal, nor did any cow low.

"You speak truly, and your situation is indeed desperate," I said to Guillaume. "I have coin with me. Coin for food for the winter, and seed for the summer. I need to cross the river. Tell me where the French crossed."

"Those who came here were on their way to Audemer. But you are too late, for they have destroyed the bridge behind them."

"You know this country well, Guillaume?"

"Have I not lived in it these fifty years?"

"My gold shall buy food in Nesle."

"English gold would do us no good."

"I have French gold taken at Harfleur from those who refused to swear me allegiance."

"You shall burn the village," he said. "We shall have no shelter against the winter."

"No, I will not."

He licked his lips. "One ford they have not destroyed. I know, for my son has crossed it now that the bridge at Audemer is down."

"Jesu be praised!" Erpyngham exclaimed.

"Where?" I asked.

"At Bethancourt, but two miles to the east."

"Why was it not destroyed?"

"It is not given to me to know such things. It lies in a great marsh. Perhaps they thought you would never find it. The ford cannot be reached save by a wooden causeway through the swale, and this has been broken up, but it is not impassable."

"Is this place guarded?"

"My son said nothing of guards."

The old man's directions were sound, and it was not difficult for Umfraville and a party of lances to locate the ford.

"The causeway is indeed damaged," Umfraville reported, "but a day's work would make it passable. Even in its present condition we were able to reach the ford. It is a fine one and has not been destroyed."

"How deep the current?" asked Erpyngham.

"To our chest, but not strong. We should cross it easily."

Hope made our breadcrusts as sweet as any cake that night. We shared a little of what we had with the poor folk of Guillaume's village, where we rested for the night. I lodged with Humphrey and Erpyngham in Guillaume's tiny hut, while my archers took a turn at standing guard to see that no harm was done to me. There were six in Guillaume's family: a son, Alain, his wife, and four children. They sat on their pallets and stared at us, their eyes dark smudges in the flickering firelight. When the woman rose to tend the fire, she was followed by the youngest child, a girl of about four, who halted uncertainly where I sat cross-legged. She swayed back and forth and smiled. I smiled back.

The woman turned and saw her. "Colette!" she said sharply. "Come here."

"No," I said in French, "she does not bother me." I held out my finger to the child, and she took it in one tiny fist. "Will you sit next to me?"

She plopped down beside me and grinned, showing the blackened stumps of her teeth.

"What is your name?" she asked.

"I am called Harry."

From the corner of my eye I saw her father squirm uncomfortably.

"Is that your brother?" I asked and pointed to a little fellow of about six. "What is his name?"

"He is Raoul," she answered. The boy ducked his head shyly.

"Raoul, would you like to hear a story ere you sleep?"

Soon I had all four children about me. I told them of Arthur and his
Round Table, of Galahad and his search for the Grail. Their eyes widened as
I described the wonders of Camelot, the beauty of Guinevere. The old ones
listened as well, Guillaume now and then murmuring at some knightly
adventure. I held them enthralled until the fire burned low and then shooed
them off to bed.

"Grandpère says you are a king," said Raoul.

"So I am."

"Are you like Arthur?" Colette asked.

I shook my head. "No, not like Arthur, I fear."

"Of course not," said Raoul. "He is as ragged as we are."

"*Merci*," the woman said when the children had clambered into the loft
to sleep.

"I enjoyed it as much as they did," I said.

"Such a tale," said Guillaume. "To think there could be such a place as
Camelot."

I stretched out on the hard earthen floor next to Humphrey.

"Is it not funny," he said in English. "Poor wretches such as these could
know nothing of knightly quests and Holy Grails. Yet they were held by your
storytelling."

"Why not? Was it not for them that Arthur ruled in Camelot?"

We set out the next morning to repair the causeway, a mile-long path of
wooden planks. The French had hacked it down the middle so that splin-
tered boards stood jagged in the air, and the marshland oozed an invitation
to any unlucky enough to lose his footing. It would be a slow and precarious
crossing for a man, impossible for the horses. But as Umfraville said, it could
be repaired, so we set to work. The men groaned at the thought of such toil,
for they had grown weaker by the day. The bloody flux plagued many of
them—some could walk, others could not. They were heartened, though, to
learn that none would be exempted from hard labor because of his station.
Knights, earls, aye, even the King would scour the region for branches and
wood and then bear debris to fill in the gaps. Two lines snaked across the
causeway, one bearing our scavengings, another returning empty-handed to
search for more. Erpyngham I set because of his age to supervise the place-
ment of the debris. Those who were too ill to work I sent to the woods to set
traps for hares and shoot at squirrels, or on to the ford to fish.

We took turns at midday in sitting to eat. It was the last of our bread
from Boves, and we knew not when we should see more. I sat beneath a
spreading willow with Dafydd and ate of some walnuts he found in the wood.

"Oh, for an egg," he lamented. "My left arm I would give for an egg."

I sighed and lay back on the grass.

"What would you eat if you were in London this very moment?" he asked.

I moaned. "You torment me, Dafydd!"

"What would you eat?" he insisted.

"A haunch of venison," I said. "Some sweetmeats, perhaps. And I would have a flagon of Burgundy. No, not Burgundy, but good London ale."

"Ale!" he cried. "Ale! I had forgotten such joy exists. I would have mine with mutton, Welsh mutton. Cold I would have it, that I may chew the fat better."

"We must go back to work ere we die of longing," I said.

He looked sidelong at me. "Shall we truly come to Calais?" he asked.

"We shall come to Calais."

"I would believe none other if he said it. Why then do I believe you? Is it that you starve with us?"

"More fool I that I starve with you."

Foot by foot the causeway grew. Besides limbs and other debris we piled on doors and shutters from houses, ladders, and parts of wagons and barns. Guillaume's cottage lost its door and the stall where the cow had been quartered.

"The door can easily be replaced," he said. "As for the stall, we have no cow anyway." He spat. "*Mon dieu,* may the Frenchman who stole our cow rot in Hell!"

The longer we worked, the harder was our task. Soon we must bear our burdens half a mile, then three quarters of a mile, only to turn and trudge back the way we had come over the rude thoroughfare. We wasted not our strength for speech but only puffed for breath and sucked in our bellies and pushed ahead. Once on my way to the woods I met young Suffolk. None would have known him for the gay young chevalier who set out from Harfleur. His once golden hair was matted and plastered to his skull, his face was gaunt and his tunic torn. He struggled with a long trough which he had taken from a mill, perhaps, or a barn. Poor boy, I thought. It was not this he bargained for when he rode blithely away to war with his lover's favor stuck in his bonnet. He did not see me, so intent he was on dragging his burden to the causeway. No plowman could have labored harder.

We finished well after darkness had fallen and dragged ourselves back to the village. Had we possessed food, we would have been too weary for it. A small quantity of fish and game had been caught, but there was not nearly enough for all. I ordered it distributed to the sickest men and to the children. Humphrey, Erpyngham, and I sprawled against the wall of Guillaume's cottage and watched blearily as the old man's grandchildren gobbled a hare cooked with a mess of wild onions. I nodded and slept even as I sat, and woke only to the insistent shaking of little Colette.

"Maman says you should lie down. Your neck shall hurt you."

"Your mama speaks truly." I slid to the floor next to my brother. In my dreams I saw the causeway stretching endlessly into a darkening horizon.

Colette wept when we took our leave. "I want the King to stay," she cried.

I swung her up over my head, kissed her cheek, and set her down again. *"Au revoir, ma petite,"* I said.

"We shall pray for you," said Guillaume.

"I thank you," I answered.

I saw in his eyes that he thought himself to be looking at a doomed man.

We were slow in starting that morning, for the men had slept past sunrise and I had not the heart to rouse them. When at last we reached the causeway, the sun was high above our heads. Gilbert Umfraville I sent first to the other shore with a contingent of two hundred archers and lances to secure our passage lest the French catch us at our crossing. Then we could but wait. I paced anxiously, straining to hear any outcry Umfraville's men might make, but of course they were too far away. An hour passed. Then a man appeared on the causeway. He waved and I saw the red cross upon his chest.

"High and dry on the other side," he called. "Come ahead."

A thin cheer greeted his words. The men pushed forward, anxious to be out of the hated marsh. I called Rhys to me.

"I must stand guard at the end of the causeway to see there is no crowding and jostling," I said. "Will you stand with me?"

"Gladly shall I stand," he said. "But why must you? You look in no shape for it."

"Neither do you. We are all of us worn out."

"You were up before dawn. I woke once and saw you speaking with the sentries."

"I feared they would sleep at their posts. Yesterday they worked as hard as any."

"As did you. If you fall ill, we are indeed lost."

"If I do not use the last ounce of strength I have to bring us to Calais, then are we lost."

We set ourselves at the entrance of the causeway, Rhys at one side, I the other, so that none could pass save between us. We sent them across in single file lest they dislodge our fragile bridge with too much tramping or topple one of their fellows into the mire. They were a somber lot who passed through our gate. Man after man, I was confronted with the sorry state of my army. Dull of eye and pale of face they were, and they walked in that hunched way which is brought on by a painful belly. Many limped. The sick came sprawled on rough stretchers of saplings. Ten I judged to be near death with the flux. The stink of their clothes was distinctive even in that malodorous throng.

Not a man passed who did not seek my eyes with his own. Like children they were, imploring their father to keep from them the evils of the night. A reassuring smile hovered upon my face. I nodded to this one, spoke to that one. It was not long ere there came the archer I had wrestled at Boves. I winked at him.

"How goes the champion of Banbury?" I asked.

He shrugged sheepishly.

"He is a new man, your grace," said his fellow behind him. "He wrangles with no one for fear the King shall come throw him again."

I shared a laugh with them, but there were few other signs of cheer.

An hour had passed when the line halted. Back through the terror-stricken ranks came the word, "The French are on the other shore." Everywhere men signed themselves.

The Earl of Oxford came to me. "Shall we withdraw these?" he cried. "We yet have most of the men with us."

"No," I said, "we stay and we wait."

"Fight them off," went the message back to Umfraville. "We wait in confidence for you."

I used the time to walk up and down, that the blood might flow more freely to my legs. I had sunk into the soft earth up to my ankles. With every attempt to shift my weight the marsh had sucked at me, held me like a fly in honey.

"You should retire," Rhys said.

"So should you," I replied.

A cheer took wing from the far wooded reaches of the marsh and fell hopefully upon our waiting ears.

"The French are driven off!" soon followed.

"Then forward we go," I cried.

"They know our position," Rhys said. "Still they may set on us ere we are all across and destroy us."

"They shall not," I said. "There is no honor in it."

After five hours of toil, none remained save my own company of archers. They were in a finer fettle than the others had been.

"How long until Calais?" Dafydd sang out.

"No more than eight days' marching," I said.

"'Tis what he said when we left Harfleur," Lloyd said and poked Rhys in the ribs as he went by.

"Young pup," said John Wotten. "The King 'as you across the Somme, does he not?" He paused and looked me up and down. "Shall your grace not cross?"

"Presently," I answered. "Now on with you ere the line falters."

Then there remained but Rhys and I. I slogged wearily to him and threw my arm about his shoulder. He smiled thinly.

"We have done it," he said.

"So we have."

"For the good name of Monmouth."

"Aye."

"The fight is still ahead, but we shall come out of it."

"Aye, we shall."

Slowly we moved onto the causeway and labored our way among the branches and planks. The passage of six thousand men with horses and baggage had rendered it as broken as when we found it. My limbs, once numbed by the hours and hours of immobility, now screamed in anguish as we scrabbled along, sometimes on hands and knees. Once I slipped and would have fallen headlong into the swamp had Rhys not grasped my wrist.

"Have a care," he said. "They shall hang me if I lose you."

At last we reached the ford and plunged into the icy waters up to our chests. The current was deceptively strong and we fought with each step that we might not be carried over the edge of the ford. On the far bank, the waiting archers shouted their encouragement.

"It is a miracle if none were lost here," I gasped.

Rhys, in front, did not answer but held his bow and quiver high above his head and pressed on. The gap between us widened. I longed to halt, to sink beneath the green waters and sleep. To forget my hunger. Forget the illness of my soldiers. Forget the French I would slay. I stopped. The current buffeted my loins, seduced me. Merryn came to me unbidden. Her arms were opened wide for me.

"Come and rest," she whispered.

But it was Rhys's eyes I saw, hard and green. He grasped my arm.

"They wait for you on the bank, Harry. You must come. You are right; they shall perish without you. Come."

I took an uncertain step forward.

"Do you recall when we were boys in Gwent," he said, "and we went off to hunt in the Forest of Dean? Tom was with us, and Gwyllym. We lost our way and night found us in mortal fear of wolves and of demons. You it was who calmed us and set us to build a fire and huddle together beneath a tree."

"And I it was who was beaten by Joan the next day when we were found."

I came abreast of him. The river rippled before us and fell away in soft sighs. Then a hand grasped my shoulder and hoisted me from the water.

"The French," I gasped. "What of them?"

"There were but a few," said Humphrey, "though I daresay they have warned their fellows by now. I know not how we may avoid them. But say it not to the archers. They think we are saved, and their spirits soar."

"We must find food," I said.

"Already I have sent out foragers," said Humphrey. "The French have not yet stripped this side of the river of its provender."

"They shall not rob poor villagers?" I asked.

"They shall find food," he said.

I lay back, too weak to argue. Nor did I hesitate to swallow hunks of the cheese and bread which Humphrey's men brought in.

My army marched the next morning with full bellies and hearts brimful of hope. As a weary horse quickens its pace when it nears its own stable, so the men set out with renewed strength. Calais seemed before their very eyes. For the first time in many days laughter rang through the ranks. There were many jibes about the whores of Calais, and wagers were placed on whether Englishmen or Welshmen would be more welcome. John Wotten, who like many a good border man spoke a halting Welsh as well as English, served as interpreter, but the good-natured insults flew faster than he could put his tongue around them.

"Balls!" he would cry in mock despair. "How say you 'balls' in Welsh?"

"Ask the King then," another of the Englishmen said. "He be a better man than you, and so he shall know of such things."

"Shall you seek a whore in Calais?" Rhys spoke softly so that none other might hear.

"No," I answered. "I have taken an oath to touch no woman until that I am wed. I do it in memory of my Merryn."

He whistled. "It is a hard oath. Even priests do not keep it."

"Hard indeed. It torments me. Each day I pray forgiveness for my lust. Yet I shall not break my vow. Now is England my only lover."

It rained steadily. We were on the Calais road, which ran straight before us through a dense forest. Like the nave of a cathedral it was, the trees arched to meet over our heads, save that there was no end to it.

"I care not for such a country as this," said Lloyd. "It is too flat and the forest affrights me. I see a Frenchman behind every tree."

"We need not look for the French here," I said. "They shall seek the open country to come upon us."

"And shall they come upon us?" Dafydd demanded.

"Aye. They shall come."

They came indeed, and sooner than I had expected. We had halted in a clearing to eat our meager dinner and take some rest. There was no escape from the rain, and we ate our soggy bread while the water dripped from our noses and beards. We sat huddled together, our heads down, and so we did not see them until they were quite close. Lloyd stood to piss, and then he cried out, "Jesu defend us! It is the French!"

I started up. They rode out of the mist, three heralds with the fleur-de-lys borne before them by a page. A gloomy Gilbert Umfraville was with them.

I sloshed through the mud toward them. Dandies they were, all attired in velvets of blue and gold, their cloaks lined with fur. The fleur-de-lys was everywhere, even embossed in gold upon their leather gloves. One rode toward me, halted, and looked about, his face a study of haughty puzzlement.

"You, fellow," he said to me, "where is your king?" He turned impatiently to Umfraville before I could reply. "You said the King was just this side of the road."

"I am the King," I snapped. "State your business, herald."

His jaw fell slack as he took in my filthy jerkin and tattered cloak. He and his fellows slipped from their horses and knelt before me.

"Forgive me, your grace," he said. "I am Jean de Graville. I did not think to find the King of England dressed so rudely." A note of mockery had slipped into his voice.

"Do not name my dress rude, de Graville," I said. "I am better suited for this weather than you. The feathers in your cap droop most unbecomingly, and the fur of your cloak this moment trails in the mud."

I turned to the archers and translated the exchange. Behind me the men tittered, and the herald's face flushed crimson.

"No doubt your grace speaks truly," he answered with false courtesy.

"No doubt. You may rise."

They stood, and the mud clung to the knees of their parti-colored hose.

"As you see, my archers gather eagerly to hear your tidings," I said. "Therefore you will not mind if I converse with you in English and rely upon a translator."

"Such tidings as I bear shall quench whatever spirit is left in these poor wretches. Do you really wish them to hear?"

The men stood sodden and subdued and leaned heavily on the stakes they had cut but a few days earlier.

"I would have nothing hidden from them," I said. "Speak on. Sir Gilbert Umfraville shall translate for you."

"Very well. I am sent by my masters the Duke of Orléans, the Duke of Bourbon, the dukes of Bar, Brabant, and Alençon, the Constable d'Albret, the Marshal Boucicaut, the counts of Nevers, Richmond, and Vaudémont, Marle, Blamont, Grandpré, Roucy, and Vaucourt. These all stand arrayed against you, along with many other brave chevaliers. Our gracious King Charles finds your presence in his realm offensive. He sends thirty thousand of his most loyal subjects to stand against you, that his honor, and the honor of his son the Dauphin, might be restored."

There were gasps when Umfraville translated their numbers.

"Thirty thousand knights is a goodly number," I said agreeably. "There are not so many in all of England, and I have but a thousand with me here. Still, you have not mentioned your archers. How many archers have you?"

"Perhaps the Marshal Boucicaut has a few Genoese crossbowmen. Is it of consequence?"

"No." I smiled. "No consequence. Tell me how near this great host of chivalry lies to us."

"Quite near. Do not trouble over our position. We shall make ourselves known soon enough. In the meantime we seek a field for the battle. My masters wish me to assure you we shall fight chivalrously. The site we choose shall be a fair one. The lay of the land shall favor neither side."

"I am sure it shall not," I replied. "As for me, I care not which field you choose. I seek only the Calais road, as I ever have. If the lords of France wish to find me, that is where I shall be. I do not hasten for fear of them. And tell them if God wishes to set me upon the throne of France, all their power shall not keep me from it."

"Bold words from one in your position."

"In truth, herald, I would not trade my army for yours."

He smiled indulgently. "I have nothing but admiration for your courage. I shall tell my lords that the King of England shall be an honorable opponent, bedraggled though he be."

"Not too honorable, I hope," I muttered as they cantered away. I turned to my men and threw up my hands. "A few crossbowmen they have! A few crossbowmen! And I with five thousand of the finest longbowmen in Christendom. It is not fair."

They laughed uneasily.

"Did it affright you, that glorious list of the French nobility?" I called. "They are fools, all of them. Did you hear? They choose a field which gives them no advantage. Such courtesy! Well, by the mass, I pledge you this: I shall take every advantage of the field I may. We are a filthy rabble, are we not? Yet shall we fight with our wits, and we shall have them."

They cheered and set themselves with grim determination to renew the march. Our departure from that place was delayed until my knights and I might don our coat armor. This was so we might be delayed as little as possible if the French should come upon us. An unhappy necessity it was, for none of us was in a condition to bear easily the extra weight.

"I swear by Our Lady," Humphrey groaned, "this armor is twice as heavy as when I wore it last at Harfleur."

"Indeed, I rattle about in my armor like a sack of bones," said Oxford. "How the French lords shall mock at us when they learn from Graville our sorry state. So sure should they be of victory, I am surprised they do not have their King with them."

"What good would come of it?" I said. "He is a feeble old man with but half his wits."

"The Dauphin, then," said Humphrey. "He at least should be with them."

"It is said he has no stomach for war," said Oxford with a curl of his lip.

"No, cousin," I said, "do not chide him for that. Yet I am told that though he cares not to risk his own safety, he does not turn from cruelty."

We came out of the forest and into an open country, as strange as any I have seen. Perfectly flat it was, the monotony of it broken here and there by patches of woodland. In one place a lone tree stood twisted on the plain.

"Where are they?" Lloyd said. "Do they yet toy with us?" He looked round as though the French might magically swoop down upon us from the fog which was moving in on either side. The Calais road melted into the mist. Impossible it was to tell if anything moved upon it.

"They may seek to exhaust our food supply," I admitted. And that was my greatest concern.

Three men died that day. We carried their bodies until we halted for the night and then laid them in water-filled graves and tried as best we could to cover them. I had been expecting such deaths, but it came as a blow nonetheless. I had pledged to bring them to Calais, and I could not keep faith with them all. More would die of disease, others in the battle. I slept little that night.

On the morrow we came across a sight which caused alarm throughout the army. A wide swath of the earth across our path had been churned into a sea of mud, as only could have been done by a great host. Men crossed themselves and cast their eyes fearfully about. I watched them slosh into the quagmire. The archers slipped and slid and waved their arms wildly to balance themselves. A few fell, to the derision of their fellows. The knights had the most difficulty of all. Though they wore but coat armor, they were so weighted that they moved as though walking underwater, and they fell more often than the archers. The horses proved troublesome as well, for the mud sucked at their heavy-shod hooves.

"Have a care," said Oxford at my side. "It is no easy task to bear armor in this quagmire."

I smiled. "You speak truly, cousin. Pray that the rain may continue."

*   *   *

Rain it did, with no end in sight. It was a chill rain with the promise of winter in it. One uneventful day passed, then a second and a third. Still there was no sign of the French, and still it rained. Our food supply was again exhausted, and there seemed little hope of obtaining more. We were yet three days' march from Calais. Ten men died, and many more took sick. One of these last was young Lloyd, who was afflicted with fever of the lungs. He could not rest for coughing, and his cheeks beneath his soft boy's beard were unnaturally flushed.

"Never fear," he said weakly. "I have taken this before, in the mountains. It is nothing. I shall yet draw bow for you."

"Do not concern yourself with that," I answered. "Only husband your strength."

"You need every man of us."

"You shall serve me best if you live."

We made a bed for him in the cart which bore my armor, trying as best we could to shield him from the rain but it proved impossible. He huddled beneath wet blankets and shivered, and we could not even warm him at night, for the rain would have quenched any fire.

The land now had some slight slope to it, so slight we might not have noted it did we not strain our eyes so hard to seek what lay before us. We were searching one such obscure horizon when a messenger came splashing back from the van.

"The French!" he cried. "The French block our way!"

I took horse at once and galloped past a blur of upturned faces toward where Umfraville had halted at the crest of the rise. The French were emerging from a wood half a mile to the east of us. Thousands there were, all brightly clad despite the rain, and they swarmed into the brown plain, across the Calais road.

"So it is come at last," I said. "God be praised, for our strength is nearly spent."

They saw us then. Scarecrows we must have looked to them with our tattered cloaks flapping against the ashen sky. They jeered, a skirling sound to set the teeth on edge.

"The falcon screeches, for now it has its prey," said Humphrey, who had ridden up behind me. "The herald spoke truly of their numbers. Now shall you surrender, Harry?"

I stared straight ahead. "Have I come so far for that? The advantage is yet with me."

"So you say. But you have been wrong, brother. You have erred before this. Forgive me, but I speak now for all your captains. We have followed you faithfully thus far, and still shall. But think, now that you see the enemy face to face, how dread is their strength. You misjudged the crossing of the Somme, and we were not sufficiently provisioned for so long a journey. One in four of our men is ill, all are hungry. You have brought but a few lances."

The jeering across the way had turned to singing, but I could not make out the words.

"I know you fear surrender," Humphrey said. "So do I. We are likely never to see England again, we two. Yet we would live and be treated chivalrously according to our rank. It would be a most genteel captivity. And who knows, perhaps Tom and John may raise a ransom."

"I shall not betray my men," I said. "I promised them Calais, and I shall take them there. Now send word to my captains that the army is to be arrayed in battle formation where we now stand. The French may have in mind to attack us ere darkness falls."

The men stood silent in the rain, a thin line stretched across the plain. Soon it became clear that the French would not engage us that day, for they busied themselves with the setting of tents and the pounding of their armor. I sent my men to seek shelter in the woods and orchards to our west and to rest as best they might.

I stood by with my captains to study the field.

"I see no benefit in any particular part of it," said Umfraville. "It is flat as any table save for the slope where we stand, and that is not great enough to aid in defense."

"The French have not played false with us," said Suffolk. "In truth, neither army shall be set at disadvantage here."

"No," I said, "it is foolishly chosen. The advantage is ours, if we move forward but a few hundred yards."

"How so?" Humphrey asked.

"See where we now stand? The woods are far to our left and right. Even had we twice as many men here, we would be lost in so vast a field. It is the same where the French now stand. But see just ahead of us. The woods are extended inward and the field narrows considerably. It is like the neck of an hourglass. If we position ourselves there on the morrow, we can easily fill the gap, even with our small numbers. The trees, my lords, shall stand for the English."

"Can a tree swing a sword?" Suffolk scoffed.

"Fool!" said Erpyngham. "Can you not see the King is right?"

"So he is," said Oxford. The hope rang in his voice. "Something else I see now. Even with all their great numbers, the French would not be able to come upon us all at once, for there would be no room. The narrowing of the field shall force them in upon each other."

"Exactly," I said. "Exactly. You begin to think."

"Yet the sheer weight of numbers—" said Humphrey.

"How judge you the condition of the field?" I asked him. I ground my boot into the mud for emphasis.

"It is a veritable lake," he said.

I lifted my leg and the boot came away with a loud scrooshing sound. Brown water filled the depression.

Erpyngham chuckled. "The stakes shall go easily into it as well. We shall be a prickly bottleneck."

"And the French would do well to come at us in boats," Oxford said. "If only we had a few of those healthy men who languish now in England, I would begin to think we had a chance."

"No," I said, "do not speak so. In truth, I would not have one man more. Are these few not enough to suffer as we have suffered? Our numbers lull the French into complacency. Yet I deem our strength sufficient. If God means us to have the victory, these few are enough. We have enough to fill yon gap, and more to draw bow than they. No, I do not wish for one man more."

I spoke strongly, and they seemed to take courage from it.

"Go then, encourage your men and prepare yourselves," I said. They went away, but not before I had seen a strange light burning in their eyes. They were desperate men, they were facing death, and never had they relished life so fiercely. They would fight like men possessed. I stared moodily across the vast field. The distant Frenchmen floated on its sodden surface in the twilight, their merry shouts bespeaking their vitality. I pictured their mad, gallant charge across the muddy field, the hail of arrows, the thousands of heavily armored men forced in on one another, the stakes awaiting them. I squeezed my eyes shut, but the vision would not fade. Deep within me a still voice said, Stop now, Harry, else it shall be too late.

I turned on my heel and sought out old Sir Thomas Erpyngham as he saw to the billeting of his troops.

"Erpyngham!" I cried. "I cannot do it."

He stared at me in astonishment. "What do you mean?"

I pulled him aside and lowered my voice. "I cannot fight this battle," I said urgently. "I know how it shall be. They shall die by the thousands, the French. I cannot go through with it."

His face was stern. "This is unbecoming, your grace. Have you not established that your cause is just? Do the French not oppose you of their own free will?"

"I cannot do it."

"What then do you propose? Shall you desert your men as you have sworn you would not?"

"I shall treat with the French."

"And what shall you offer them?"

"Myself. I shall offer myself, my head."

"My gray hairs give me the courage to say to my sovereign that this is foolishness. Yet you are King. You must decide."

I sent my herald to the French leaders. I wished to see no blood spilled, I said. Harfleur would be restored to them, and restitution paid. I would surrender my person to them for execution or imprisonment, as they willed. I asked in return only that my army be given safe passage to Calais.

I retired to a nearby village to wait the reply. Maisoncelles the place was called, and it stood deserted, for its inhabitants had fled at the approach of the two armies. No doubt they huddled soaked to the skin beneath some hedgerow. Their goods they had left behind in their haste, but there was little enough food. Rhys came to me bearing two eggs he had found.

"The hen was nowhere to be seen," he said. "I hope some of our poor fellows found her."

"The eggs should go to Lloyd," I said. "He is ill."

"No, he says the fever robs him of his appetite. He craves only water. Dafydd boils him some with roots he found."

"Neither have you eaten."

"Take them. You must wear full armor on the morrow, and swing a sword. I daresay you shall be up all the night, if I know you. If you do not eat you shall have no strength, and if you are slain we shall all be lost, for our hearts shall be robbed from us."

I had not the will to refuse him, and he boiled the eggs at the hearth of the cottage where I lodged. I ate them slowly, savoring their creamy golden yolks.

"These are noble eggs," I said.

Rhys was still with me when the herald returned, and I did not send him away.

"The terms?" I asked.

"They were refused."

"On what grounds?"

"Forgive me, your grace, for I must speak baldly their insults. They care not for your terms, for they think you already achieved, and with far more glory than a surrender would offer. They name you a libertine and a wastrel and long for the morning that they may prove their knighthood against you. They have already painted a cart with gay colors. They mean to bear you in it disgraced through the streets of Rouen and Paris. As for your men, they say the nobles shall be ransomed if not slain in battle. The archers they shall execute, and their fingers shall be sold in Paris for five sous apiece."

"The fools," I said. "Their mocks shall die in their throats."

"You have sued for terms!" Rhys said. "Why? Is our cause so hopeless?"

"I only wished to spare the lives of the French from the slaughter that shall come."

"And what did you offer? Yourself?"

"Aye."

"God's blood, Harry, did you think these fellows would stand by and see you give yourself up to yon Frenchmen? They would not have abided it, I tell you. They guard you as fiercely as you guard them."

"Do they indeed?"

"As for the painted cart, I shall see they hear of it. It shall fire their blood."

The French knights were up nearly all the night at their merrymaking. I know, for I was sleepless as well, and the sound of their revelings followed me on my rounds through the camp. My own men were too weary and fearful for such antics. Yet everywhere that I went, they assured me they would fight bravely and well. From watch to watch I went, speaking with as many as I could. They crowded about me and plied me with questions.

"The stakes, shall they really work?"

"Be it true that the field lies in our favor?"

"We heard of the cart," they would say. "By the mass, we shall not let them lay a hand upon you."

My heart filled to bursting with care for them. They were men as good and plain as Piers Plowman himself, and none better than my own archers. I was longest in their company, Rhys, Dafydd, Wotten, and Lloyd, and I could have wept at the leaving of them.

"The lad says he shall fight," Wotten said. Lloyd lay nearby, asleep under one of the supply wagons to escape the downpour.

"You must prevent him," I said. "I shall not be able to see to it."

"Likewise shall we be engaged," said Dafydd. "He has been headstrong as long as I have known him. He shall fight for the love of his King."

"His King does not deserve such love," I said, "for see where he has brought him."

"Is it not the duty of kings to fight their wars? I understand little of it. This I do know, never have I heard of a king to look to his poor men, as you do us. If I live, all Wales shall hear from me what a man King Harry is."

"Even if I lead you to folly?"

"Yet you say you have not. But if folly it be, I care not. These are fine fellows to die with. Far better than to die old and alone. We are the ones for whom the songs are sung. We are like Llewellyn and Hywel Dda of old."

I told Humphrey of these words when I returned to our cottage.

"Crazy Celt!" he said. "They are sated with such notions. When the worms have a man, what shall he care how he came to the grave? What shall he care of anything?"

"I know something of what he means. If I am to die young, I would as soon it be tomorrow. We have striven so hard, all of us, there seems little left to do save to die together."

"You begin to sound like Suffolk."

"No. I would not willingly die for honor, nor kill for it. But to belong to something other, truly belong—aye, I would die for that. I would die for the love of those fellows who sit soaked in yon rain. But is it reason enough to kill? That is what torments me."

"If you die it shall be from your conscience. Take no thought of the French, they bring this on themselves. And have you not taken an army across the north of France without one rape or murder? When else has it happened?"

"It does comfort me," I said. "I must remind myself why I am here. I am here to put an end to Christendom's warrings. That is why I can face tomorrow."

I had my men up before the dawning that they might prepare themselves. For those of us who would fight as knights, this meant being bolted into our armor. This I detested nearly as much as the battle. It was not only the boredom of standing motionless while being encased in confining metal. It was the sensation of smothering that nearly overwhelmed me whenever I donned breastplate and helmet. It had been this way with me since Shrewsbury. I was put in mind of the effigies of knights which mark the tombs in our churches. It is not the man one sees, but his armor. The man in the tomb has long since rotted, like a mollusk cast upon the beach. Only the shell remains. I longed to be an archer, to wear but a leather jerkin and to care only that my bowstring was kept waxed and dry.

My captains and I readied ourselves together in a spacious barn in Maisoncelles. They protested when they saw my armor, for a ruby shone like a drop of blood in the center of the basinet.

"I had thought to offer to wear your colors, to confuse the French," said Oxford. "It would do no good if you wear such a basinet."

"No one shall impersonate me," I said.

"Father had it done at Shrewsbury," Humphrey said. "It saved his life."

"I care not what Father did. I'll have none die in my place. Nor would I have my men think that I hide. I wish them to see me, to know I stand with them. If that puts me in jeopardy, well, so be it. That is my duty." I paused and looked at Suffolk with a smile. "Besides, it would not be chivalrous to hide, would it, my lord?"

"It would not," he agreed solemnly.

Sir Thomas Erpyngham had already marshaled the archers in the field when we arrived. The heavy rain had continued throughout the night and still fell upon us intermittently. In some places those in armor sank to their ankles in the mud and walked only with the greatest difficulty. The priests moved among us with the Host, their robes hoisted to their thighs and tucked in their cinctures. They slipped from one man to the next, placed the Host upon waiting tongues, blessed each recipient, and then moved on. I sucked upon the morsel in my mouth until the last particle had melted away.

When the mass was distributed and the priests retired to our rear with the sick and the baggage, I called the men to me. They crowded close, smelling foully of wet rotting leather and fear, to where I stood perched upon the bed of a cart.

"Look at yon French," I said. "See how already they are drawn up in their battles."

The French stood still across the way, as though patiently awaiting the laggard English. Their center was a dense sea of armored knights, some fifteen thousand, I guessed, all on foot. Their spears stood up from their shoulders like a forest of metal trees. To their left and right, thousands more knights sat poised upon their chargers, ready to ride down our archers. Behind all these was another line on horse, which was larger by itself than our entire army. These I guessed were knights of a lower degree who were set to ride down our last pitiful stragglers and butcher them ere they could flee.

"Indeed, they are awesome," I cried. "Yet look carefully. Where are their archers? They have none, it seems. They have only knights who must lumber across this swamp in heavy armor. Nor should you fear those on horseback. Aim low, hit their mounts. If your shafts do not stop them, the stakes shall."

Their heads bobbed up and down, their eyes pleaded.

"You see that I wear no spurs, nor is my horse near me. I have no means to flee, because I intend to stand and fight with you. Nor shall I endanger your lives by seeking my own ransom. We shall face this peril together, you and I. And if I be slain, you must fight on. Fight on, and you shall prevail."

They seemed an army of old men, hunched and bent with their bows clutched before them.

"Today is the feast day of saints Crispin and Crispinian. Cobblers they were, common men like you. They were martyred for their faith many years ago in the town of Soissons, in Burgundy. This same town of Soissons saw a dreadful massacre at the hands of yon French knights only a year ago. Hundreds were slaughtered, good common men, and their wives and children with them. When I came to France, I promised her poor people I would guard their lives. I have kept my word. Likewise I pledge to you, I shall bring you out of this. I shall bring you to Calais. I do not believe God shall turn his back on any who have struggled together as we have.

"I know you are hungry today, and weary. So am I. We have suffered, have we not? Together we have suffered! Together! Yeomen and peer and, aye, King together. We have faced hunger and illness, we have slogged through swamps and toiled at hard labor. Together, we have reached this place and all the haughty knights in Christendom shall not keep us from reaching Calais!"

They cheered loudly and waved their arms. When the shouts had died down I continued.

"One thing more I would have you know. These French noblemen count your lives for naught. You are of no more importance to them than a cow or a pig; indeed, they value their chargers over you. It is not so with me. I love you all. French lords may call you a rabble, but the King of England names you his brothers. God in heaven has died for us all, and does that not make us so? If it does not, then have we bonded ourselves by our travail. Aye, brothers I name you. Kinship you may claim with your King because you have served so faithfully."

Many wept as I was helped from the cart and made my way among them.

"God save your grace," they murmured as they reached to touch my hand. "God save King Harry."

"And you," I answered, my heart full. "And you."

I drew them in a single thin line with the narrowest part of the field just to the front of us. The archers were set at intervals in wedge-shaped clusters, and before them were the stakes, plunged deep in the soggy earth. I held for myself personal command of the center of the line. With me were Humphrey, Erpyngham, and Suffolk and my own company of archers. I would be the main target, and we were sure to bear the brunt of any charge.

The rains came again and beat a hollow cadence upon my armor. I licked my lips and stared across at the French host. They gave no sign of attacking. Again I went over my plans, and I began to doubt. There were so many of them! How could we few stem such a tide? Suppose I were slain and the men panicked? My stomach churned and a fire burned deep in my bowels.

Jesu, I prayed, *if I am to be the bearer of your peace, I know you shall save*.

"Why do they wait?" Suffolk asked. "Why do they not come on?"

One hour dragged by, then another. The French seemed more menacing with each passing moment. Sometimes they jeered at us.

"Come to us, English fools," they cried in their tongue. "We have food for you."

"Were our prisoners released last night?" Humphrey asked.

"They were," I replied. "It seemed just to me."

"It was a mistake," he said. "Doubtless they will have told the French of our hunger."

"It is why they delay," said Erpyngham. "They think to take advantage of our weakness, to drive us to despair. No doubt they could stand a fortnight in the field."

"Perhaps they await reinforcements," Suffolk said. "I do not yet see the banners of the Duke of Brabant."

My head was swimming from the weight of my armor. "We cannot bear this long," I said. "We must play upon their pride and sting them into an attack. We must go forward."

"If we advance too far we shall lose our advantage between these woods," Erpyngham warned.

"I count upon their pride to spur them on ere we have gone so far."

I sent orders down the line that the archers pull up their stakes, and I walked out into the field.

"Avaunt banners!" I cried. "Saint George, help us this day! Forward!"

The lances struggled out into the mud behind me. The archers, not so encumbered, knelt thrice, as is their custom, kissed the earth, and took a morsel of dirt beneath their tongues as a sign of their mortality. Then they clambered nimbly on to join in the attack. We had gone no more than fifty yards when the French line rippled and advanced. I turned and flung up my arm. The line wavered and halted, the archers worked frantically to set their stakes into the earth, then leaped behind the barricade and pulled each an arrow from his quiver.

The French center was coming on foot, but already these had been passed by the mounted knights, now nearly within bowshot. I saw them in a blur through the slit of my visor. My arm was yet above my head, I had only to drop it. . . . They came slowly, tight pressed together, each hoping for the honor of being the first into our line. The massive coursers threw up great clods with their hooves, rolled their heads at the exertion. I pressed my lips together. Some horses had fallen already, tripping on furrows or jolted by their fellows. Through the rain drifted screams, and the clang of hooves on armor.

"Bend your bows!" I cried.

Erpyngham flung his warder into the air. Bowstrings were drawn back to ears, held taut. Along the line captains stood with arms upraised. The thunder grew. The foremost riders drew their swords and held them out like lances at a tournament. The white-faced archers rolled their eyes toward me. I admired the graceful curve of the bows falling away from me down the line. Then my hand dropped. A hissing cloud leaped and fled faster than thought to fall

among the French. The horsemen were as toys flung about by the invisible
hand of a petulant child. Their mounts reared and bellowed in pain at the
shafts protruding from their bloodied flanks. So large were the beasts that the
arrows only wounded them, and maddened them as well. They tossed their
riders about, crushing them or leaving them to wallow broken and helpless in
their armor. Many horses were thrown to the ground by the fallen bodies of
those who had gone before. Still others veered crazily toward the stakes, then
away again at the sight of the barrier, their riders reduced to clinging for dear
life. They floundered back the way they had come and crashed into the ranks
of the knights advancing on foot. The densely packed press of men had no
place to run in the mud. The crazed horses cut great swaths through their
ranks and left a trail of crumpled bodies in their wake.

"Jesu!" Humphrey cried in awe. "Shall we not have to lift a finger?"

The Frenchmen on foot closed their ranks quickly. Here were the
cream of French chivalry, their brightly colored banners borne proudly with
them. They staggered with difficulty through the quagmire churned up by
the horsemen. But they did not stop. They could not, for their fellows
behind them, eager to get to the fight, pressed them onward. Some went
down and promptly disappeared in a forest of mailed legs.

"They shall suffocate," Suffolk said, his voice filled with horror.

The archers loosed arrows into their ranks, but they were yet too far
away to do more than bounce the shafts harmlessly from shining breast-
plates. I raised my hand into the air once more.

They were but thirty yards from us when I brought my hand down
again. The shafts took them from the sides, penetrated their armor, drove
them in on one another. The mass gathered itself, lurched ahead with inex-
orable momentum. All at me they seemed to come, all at me. Tentatively I
drew my sword as though facing accusers. A cacophony of screams swelled.
A Frenchman fell at my feet, his basinet riven to his temple by an archer's
shaft. Then the surge was upon us, not attacking us but coming to rest
against us. Their journey was done, the long desperate effort to keep on
one's feet, to avoid being trodden. For one eternal moment our line sagged,
threatened to break under the weight of these weary chevaliers. Then we
pushed them back, thrusting mindlessly with our swords. Under the arm,
ever under the arm. Try not to see the spurt of red blood on wet metal.

Most of the French were so tightly pressed they could not even draw
their swords ere they reached us. Behind them came thousands and more
thousands, hearing the cries, eager for honor, not knowing that they pressed
the faces of the wounded into the mud, that they thrust their comrades
helpless onto our sword points. They fell in wallowing heaps, and the archers
flung down their bows and waded among them, thrusting with their long
knives.

One small band of the French, perhaps a score of them, managed to break clear of the growing heaps of the dead and wounded.

"*Le roi!*" they shouted. "*Mort pour le roi!*"

I turned clumsily in the mud to meet their challenge. Humphrey and Suffolk proved the more nimble and placed themselves in the way of the onslaught. A dozen swords flailed at shields and armor. One thrust caught Suffolk full in the visor. The point must have taken him in the eye, and he was dead ere he fell. Humphrey cried out as a sword bit into the soft flesh of his underarm. Little curly-headed Humphrey. I slashed out in fury and felled his attacker, then bestrode the prone body of my brother and fended off two others with some deft swordplay. Several more loomed into my vision and I thought myself dead. A blade flashed before my eyes, the blow caught my basinet with stunning force, and I nearly blacked out. Yet somehow I kept my senses and my feet. One more blow I fended off desperately with my shield, when a slim brown figure flung itself onto the armored back of my nearest attacker. A knife was plunged into the knight's face. It was Lloyd. The others now joined the melee, Rhys and Dafydd among them. They danced nimbly around the clumsy knights, parried and slashed, while Wotten and I dragged Humphrey away from the fighting. We stretched him upon a piece of sodden turf and set back his visor. His face was contorted with pain, but he breathed freely. The cold rain washed the stream of blood from the side of his armor.

"You have affrighted me, brother," I said. "And you saved my life as well."

"And you mine," he gasped.

"That is the way of brothers," I said. I turned to Wotten. "Will you stay with him, John?"

"Aye, if you wish."

"Make him comfortable. Get that armor off him and stanch the bleeding."

"Aye, your grace. And have a care yourself."

When I returned to our line, the archers were picking their way methodically ahead among the heaps of armored men, clubbing as they went. From beneath these piles came the muffled cries of those trapped or wounded. Several thousand of the French were struggling back across the field whence they came. The remainder, who had waited on horseback, were melting away into the misty forest. I sought out Erpyngham.

"Call a halt," I said. "The field looks to be ours. There has been enough death."

He sounded his horn and the archers wearily put away their weapons. I rocked back and forth on my heels, head ringing, and surveyed the nightmarish scene. The moans of the wounded lodged in the pit of my stomach.

The English knights were pulling bodies from heaps of the fallen, searching for those who yet lived. They did so not to render them aid, but to seek prisoners they might hold for large ransoms. Several thousand they pulled living from the piles; many, unscathed by any blade, had fallen and been unable to rise. The dead were strewn heedless about, their mud-smeared armor clattering. I blinked my eyes against the pain in my head.

"You should remove your basinet. I see through your visor that your head bleeds."

It was old Erpyngham. He sent for an armorer and soon had the battered basinet off. Proudly he held it out before him.

"Every one of your subjects should see this," he said. "A testimony to your valor." He studied the wound on my scalp. "It does not appear serious. The rain shall soon have it clean."

The rain coursed in refreshing rivulets down my cheeks and chin.

"How does Humphrey?" I asked.

"Well. They have his armor off. The wound is deep but he breathes easily and does not lose consciousness, so I doubt it has pierced a lung."

"Suffolk is dead."

"Aye."

"In truth, I repent me my harshness toward him. He placed himself between harm and his King."

"As a knight is supposed to do."

I dropped my eyes. "You chide me, Erpyngham."

"No," he protested. "How should I chide the King who has led us to such a victory as this? It is not to be believed, yet it is just as you said it would be."

"I feel no victory."

"Look at the field," he urged me. "There must be ten thousand of the French slain, and but a few hundred of our English."

"If we are saved, give thanks to God for it," I said. "As for the dead, aye, that credit do I accept, and with no joy."

"Of course not," he said. "No one rejoices at death."

I walked haltingly toward the milling crowd of men. "How many of my archers have I lost?"

"It is too early to say," said Erpyngham, "but I do not think many. You have kept your promise to them. And soon they shall have nourishment, for the French have abandoned great stores of food."

I saw Dafydd then, waving his arms at me. He stood with the others by a body. When I drew nigh, I saw it was young Lloyd. His throat had been slashed so deeply as to near decapitate him. Yet there was no blood. Indeed it seemed that his veins poured forth icy rainwater from the gaping white wound.

"He died soon after you were struck," Dafydd said, weeping freely. "He was too weak; he was not quick enough on his feet to escape their swords."

I stared at the body. "I promised him," I whispered.

"You did all you could do," Rhys said. "Lloyd would have said so himself."

"It was not enough."

A horn sounded then far in the distance, and we all froze. On the edge of the forest Frenchmen reappeared on their horses. They gathered in small groups and conferred as though expecting reinforcements. Again the horn sounded.

"Jesu preserve us!" Dafydd cried.

I cast about for my captains. "Umfraville!" I cried. He stood nearby, three French prisoners in hand. "We are yet under attack," I said. "Call your men together."

He looked at me in bewilderment. "What of these prisoners?" He asked. "Who shall tend to them?"

The prisoners exchanged glances. They understood none of our frantic English, but I knew they must guess what was happening. One looked about as if seeking a weapon. I realized with horror the full danger of our position. Our ranks had been swollen by the taking of as many captives as there were Englishmen. Unarmed they were, yet if we came under attack . . .

More horsemen had appeared at the edge of the wood, and a banner. I turned to Umfraville and said with an ease which startled me, "Kill them."

"What?"

"Kill them," I repeated. "We must kill the prisoners ere we are overwhelmed."

"It cannot be," he protested. "These here have pledged me a ransom."

The horn sounded again, closer. Now I could hear the sharp cries of men riding as though to a hunt.

"Fool!" I screamed. "Think you I shall see my archers die because you wish to save your ransom? Kill them!"

He blanched. "No," he said. "I shall not. They are unarmed."

I stalked away in a blind rage.

"Rhys!" I called. "We soon shall be set upon again. Take a detail of archers and slay the prisoners ere they do us harm." When he hesitated, I grasped his arm. "The blood be upon me. We must reach Calais. Now go!"

I turned away as the stabbing and clubbing began and tried to whip my disorganized archers in line. Behind me the screams of protest mounted.

"Have mercy!" they cried. "Mercy!"

A troop of several thousand horsemen burst from the woods bearing with them the banner of the Duke of Brabant. They were just within bowshot, and I ordered the archers to loose their shafts upon the new-

comers. The horses reared and plunged, the men of Brabant took in the
lacerated field, the thousands of bodies, and melted away into the woods
whence they had come. Yet they did not leave ere over three hundred
prisoners had been slain.

The field was named Agincourt, at the Earl of Oxford's suggestion, after
a nearby village. My soldiers feasted that night on the French stores, but I
ate nothing, for I could keep no food on my stomach.

I came ill to Calais. My head yet throbbed from the blow I had taken, but it
was my belly which griped me most, the pain sucking what little remained of
my strength so that I could scarcely sit my horse the remaining forty-five
miles to the city. Rhys noted my weakness and stayed by my side.

"Is it the flux?" he said.

"I don't know. There is fever, and my belly burns with fire. I cannot
keep down my food."

"It would be strange if you were not ill. You have driven yourself too
hard. Shall we bear you on a litter?"

"No. I would make nothing of this."

We came to Calais amid much rejoicing. The bells could be heard
pealing their welcome when the spires of the town were no more than dark
points upon the horizon. The citizens jammed the streets to call out their
greeting. She was an English town, Calais, the last of what had once been
the vast holdings of the English kings in France. The lion of England had
flown over her battlements for over sixty years.

Somewhere I found the strength to make the procession of thanksgiving
through the crowded streets to St. Nicholas' Church. Afterward we retired
to the castle, where I took to my bed for a night and a day. I woke feeling
somewhat better and received a visit from the Earl of Warwick, who was
serving as Captain of Calais.

"I pray I find your grace resting more easily," he said.

"Aye, I am better. I think I shall be able to leave my bed and join you
this evening, and hear mass upon All Hallows."

"These are good tidings. It was grievous to think of you brought low by
illness after so glorious a victory."

"Glorious?" Here was the same young fool with the face of a cherub I
had clashed with during the siege of Aberystwyth. "Is it named glorious?"

"So men say. Already Agincourt is spoken of as the greatest victory ever
achieved by English arms. The odds so great, the perilous journey—"

"Made more perilous by your failure to hold the ford at Blanche-
Taque," I said.

He flushed crimson. "Indeed, I know it. The shame is almost more than
I can bear. We went out bravely enough to meet the French but we were

driven back by Boucicaut's men. There were so many of them. We were sure you would be lost because of our defeat. The victory is to you, not to us."

"How many archers had you?"

"Archers? Why, none. I left them in Calais, and we went all on horse that we might travel more swiftly."

"There it is, then. Archers would have held Blanche-Taque. And archers defeated the French at Agincourt. With God's help, of course, and without that we all would have perished. Archers, Warwick, and so much for chivalry. I have seen in France what chivalry has done, how the powerful have despoiled their own people, devastated the land. I have seen those same knights who perpetrated these crimes cut down before a ragged handful of archers. It is God's judgment upon this chivalry which has claimed for itself the good. As for glory, well, I have seen knights impaled upon stakes and butchered while wallowing helpless in the mud. And I have learned for myself what evil is possible when one is fighting for one's life. Chivalry is dead, Warwick, smothered in its own gore on a bloody field. And if that is glorious, the word means not what I think it does."

I expected a blustering response such as Suffolk would have given me, but it did not come. He was a long time in answering, and when he did, his voice was measured and tinged with sorrow.

"You think me a fool," he said. "I know it. I recall Aberystwyth, how you mocked me and my fellows for our endeavors there. Yet I pray you mock me no longer, for I have only sought to follow the good as I have been taught it."

"I mock no one save myself," I muttered, and turned my face to the wall. "Leave me. I would husband my strength if I am to sup with you this night."

"Forgive me if I beg your patience a moment more. You have spoken of the death of chivalry, and your words are dreadful to me. If chivalry be dead what is left?"

"I know not. I am no seer."

"Then I must hazard a guess. Ever had I thought the world to make sense. If you speak truly, then it does no longer. If knights do not protect the weak, but harry them, and if the weak pick up their bows and slay the knights, what then? Are the weak better off? Or shall they be tyrannized by a new master, who wields power but speaks not of love and honor?"

"What good to speak of love and honor if they are not practiced?"

"Little enough, perhaps. Yet is it not good to hear them spoken of? The speaking of them can conjure them from time to time. When shall we hear of them again, if chivalry be dead?"

He seemed to tower over my bed from a great height.

"You slew prisoners at Agincourt," he said.

A lump of pain caught in my throat. "Aye. Along with ten thousand others. What difference is it, one or ten thousand, prisoners or not?"

"It is a terrible thing to slay defenseless men. Do you fear for your soul because of it?"

"I despair of my soul for many reasons."

"Yet you also refused ransom in the face of great danger. Was that not worthy of Galahad? I think you are more chivalrous than us all." He spoke as though chanting a tale of long ago. "You believe deeply in honor, despite your mocks. You long to be Arthur. And so, when you slip, the fall is very far. I hear you go to war to unite Christendom. It is the Grail you seek. If you achieve it, your name will be revered. If you fail . . ." His voice trailed away. Then he resumed in a burst of passion. "Chivalry dead? Perhaps not! Perhaps it is the last battle to purify it. To rid it of hypocrisies ere this new age you speak of overtakes us."

He knelt and grasped my hand.

"I leave you to rest. But first I pledge anew my service, my life. All true knights shall pledge themselves, and so shall Holy Church. We shall fight the demons which assail the soul, and we shall speak of the good. Aye, we shall speak boldly of it. And if we fail—well, at least we shall have joy in the fight."

I lay awake and stared at the ceiling long after he had gone, sighing for his foolishness and yet enraptured by it. The late-afternoon sun poured through a casement at the foot of the bed. It was that sort of congealed light which captures objects as though preserving them in amber. The shadows crouched in the far corner, awaiting their time. What would be, would be. Still, there is a sweetness in lost causes, and a joy, as Warwick said, in the fighting for them. I closed my eyes and wended my way past the bodies of French knights, ever seeking the road that runs straight and true toward the city.

V

1416-1422

He ne'er lift up his hand but conquered.

—*Henry VI, Part 1*, act I, scene i

14

"To think that I missed it!" Tom cried. "England's greatest victory, and I was abed at Portchester. Abed! I shall die of the shame."

I heard with a cynical amusement his moanings. "You would not have liked it," I said.

"Not have liked it! What a thing to say! It is a matter of honor, not of liking it. All my life I have waited for such a moment, to follow in Father's footsteps as a valiant warrior. Now I have missed my chance unless you go back, Harry. You shall go back?"

I frowned and swished the claret in my cup. "I know not. It depends upon how the Armagnacs react to their defeat. I prefer to negotiate with them. I pray there need be no more battles such as Agincourt."

"I for one am glad Tom was not there," said Humphrey. "It was bad enough to tolerate Harry's wrangling with Oxford and Suffolk. Tom should have been insufferably pigheaded."

"What mean you?" Tom demanded.

"He means you would have disagreed with all that I did," I said. "Nor would you have starved very well. It is something poor men are more practiced at than the brothers of kings."

John spoke for the first time. "Still, it is a wonder to me how rude archers would bring so low the fabled chivalry of France."

Uncle Beaufort chuckled. "However it was done, it has not been lost on our own peers. They grumbled all the while you were away, Harry. Had you lost, John and I feared for our own heads. Now they are silenced for good. There shall be no more rebellions while you are King."

"What matters but success?" Humphrey said and grinned.

For a time England had despaired of my success, I learned upon my return. It was known that we were long overdue at Calais, and then that we were weakened by hunger and beset by a massive French army. London had gone into mourning, John said, and many were seen weeping in the streets. But sorrow had turned to joy when word of Agincourt leaped across the Channel. To the Londoners I was their own King Harry, well known by sight to most, a bonny tavern brawler who had played a fine trick upon the haughty French knights.

London gave me such a welcome as had never been seen before, and it both affrighted and delighted me. I was met at Blackheath by the Lord Mayor and aldermen and scores of other citizens, all clad in scarlet and white robes with fur tippets. We rode together across London Bridge to find the city a tumult of decoration and celebration. Every building, no matter how humble, was festooned with swaths of bright cloth, of scarlet, azure, and jasper. At every turning of the way, mock castles and towers had been ingeniously constructed. Upon these turrets and false battlements were perched boys and young maidens all clad in white, singing Deo Gratias and Alleluia. They showered me with sprigs of laurel and gold leaf which settled in clouds upon my head and purple-clad shoulders. In Chepeside there were many fine houses, and here the noble lords and ladies had gathered in all their velvet finery to view the procession apart from the mob. Below them were the people, my people. They filled the streets to overflowing, waving and screaming my name as loudly as they could. Many times I could not go forward for them, but must keep tight rein on my skittish horse until my escort could clear a path. Everywhere arms were thrust out seeking to touch me, as though in some strange angular salute. The women wept and blew kisses from gnarled hands.

"God save the King," they cried. "God save our lovely Harry."

What can I say of such adoration? I sought to receive it humbly, and kept my face grave and composed, my head slightly bent as though to deflect all honor from me. Yet it warmed me, thrilled me, I cannot deny it. These were such ones as I had striven for on the way to Agincourt, and their acclaim went far to erase the scenes of blood and death that lingered in my mind. I tingled with pride and thought how I should serve them better than had any other king. Aye, and the French as well. Someday I would hear such grateful cheers in the streets of Paris.

The great conduit of the Chepeside ran red with Gascon wine, and many ragged fellows were lined up, tankards in hand, to drink from it. To a man, they raised their cups to me as I passed by.

"Harry Monmouth," one bellowed above the crowd, "I drank with you once in East Chepe."

I raised my cap to him and rode on to St. Paul's.

England was not yet done with pomp and ceremony. The Holy Roman Emperor, Sigismund, came to visit after first inflicting himself upon the court of France.

"He is not easily borne," Beaufort warned. "The French were glad to see the back of him."

"Easy or no, we must bear him," I said. "I shall want his support."

Humphrey laughed. "You shall want his crown."

I silenced him with a look.

"What did Sigismund to discomfit the French?" Tom asked.

"He has in mind that the French should treat with us," said Beaufort, "while they, in turn, burn for revenge. They are in no mood to speak of peace. They want your brother's head."

"There is more," I said. "It seems Sigismund is a blustering fool with no manners. He on his own raised a Frenchman to knighthood, not realizing this to be the prerogative of King Charles. And he insisted upon presiding over the French council."

"Shall he try such a thing here?" John asked.

"He shall not," I replied. "I shall have none of it."

"There is more to Sigismund's offense," said Beaufort. "It seems he is overly fond of drink and of women. At a banquet held in his honor he became quite intoxicated and proceeded to fondle the breasts of several noble ladies, including the Duchesses of Berry and Bourbon."

Humphrey snickered. "Even the French court could not stomach that. How shall you handle such a jackanapes, Harry?"

"I shall feed him well, ply him with wine, and see that every whore in London visits him."

His grand title belied his condition, for he was poor, Sigismund. Charlemagne had once been Holy Roman Emperor, but those days were no more. The eastern half of Christendom was a hodgepodge of petty duchies and princedoms, and Sigismund was no more powerful than the others. Still, he bore the title which could yet stir the blood with its splendor and call to mind a time when Christendom was one. I took him in, fresh from French insults, and soothed his wounded pride with lavish attention. The luxury-loving French had mocked his clothing, plain like my own, and surprisingly tattered. Quickly I gave him fine gowns to wear and set the whole of the

palace of Westminster at his disposal. No expense was spared for his enjoyment, and he soon was loud in his praise of English hospitality.

"A stiff-necked people, the French," he proclaimed to me as we supped
together. "Most cold, most cold. I have little hope now that I shall succeed
in getting them to sit and treat with you. Still I must try, for I have pledged
upon my honor to seek this peace."

His speech was jumbled, for his mouth was ever filled with his food. Yet
he was a handsome man, about fifty years old, with flowing white hair and a
long pointed beard flecked with brown.

"And how are they disposed toward me?" I asked.

"They detest you. They clamor for your blood. And despite your victory, they have no respect for you. They blame the rain and the treachery of
the Duke of Burgundy for their defeat." He leaned forward and grinned.
"Tell me, are they right?"

"I should have beaten them even had Burgundy fought for them."

"And the rain?"

"I would have lost more men. But still I would have won."

He chuckled softly. "How old are you?"

"Twenty-eight."

"It is young to be so self-assured. You must have very great plans for
yourself. I wonder what they are."

I knew he would not appreciate subtlety, so I was plain with him. "I
believe I am called to unite Christendom."

He looked at me long and hard. "I suppose I should tremble at such an
ambition," he said at last.

"Why? You have no need to fear me."

"And what happens to the rest of us when you have achieved this
unity?"

"I do not seek to set you from your place. You shall live in peace. And
you shall be secure from the designs of the Turks. You above all men should
care for that."

Sigismund had nearly lost his life at Nicopolis, a disastrous battle in the
days of my father's youth when the Turks had slaughtered a host of Christian
knights. Now the infidel had overrun many Christian lands and threatened
Sigismund's empire.

"The Turks," he said solemnly. "That is why I seek peace between
England and France."

"You fought them foolishly at Nicopolis," I said. "You went at them with
armored knights and they cut you to pieces. You fought like Frenchmen. I
tell you, I am the only prince in Christendom who can turn them back. And I
am the only one who can win the affection of the people."

"You are more arrogant even than the French," he grumbled.

I smiled and called for more wine.

"Why do you want him so badly?" John asked. John was my apprentice, the most capable of my brothers at governing.

"Why? Because empty though his title be, he is the Holy Roman Emperor. And he has no sons."

I spoke to Sigismund of unity as often as I could, in between feasting and roistering. We moaned over the corruption of the Church, with her rival popes. A council had been called at Constance to set aside the two debauched men who claimed the Holy See and select an honorable heir to St. Peter. I knew that my dreams would be smashed if the division of the Church could not be healed, and so I had sent my ablest churchmen to the council. Sigismund spoke highly of their efforts.

"Nothing is more dear to my heart than to restore the unity of the Church," he said.

"Nor mine," I replied, "unless it be to see all Christians living together in harmony and justice."

He would only grunt, then, and turn to some ribald story. Fortunately I could match him there, my tavern years standing me in good stead. Sigismund's coarse manners, which had so revolted the French, I began to find refreshing. Here we were kindred spirits in our love of earthy pleasures.

"You know well how to raise a cup with your fellows," he said approvingly as we sat late one night over great mugs of ale. "It is a rare quality in a prince. It was said in France you are a great wencher as well. Is it true?"

"It was once," I acknowledged, "but no more."

"What! And why not? Are you not healthy?"

Reluctantly I spoke of Merryn.

"I have known some fine women," Sigismund said, "but none whose loss would make me a eunuch."

I flushed angrily. "I'll not be spoken of so," I said. "You shall apologize."

He looked startled, as though unaware of the offensiveness of his words. "Very well," he said at last, "I beg your pardon. Yet tell me, do you not burn with desire?"

"Of course," I said.

"Then how do you bear it?"

"I ignore it. I busy myself with other tasks, other thoughts. I work late into the night, until I am too exhausted for anything but sleep."

Had I not drunk such a quantity of ale, I would not have admitted such things to him.

"Bah!" he cried. "It is no good. You shall die of such chastity ere you have one gray hair. I slept with a whore last night who remembers you well. She says you are still spoken of fondly in the London Stews for your lovemaking. Shall you not have her tonight? I can find another."

I lingered on the exquisite edge of my desire and wondered if he were not right. It had been so long, and Merryn's face had faded past memory. Yet I was constrained. When my lust had been assuaged, I knew I would rest no easier. It was love I craved, love that eluded me. All I had known of it moldered in a Monnow grave—or, perhaps, interceded for me in Heaven. This last hope I could not bear to turn from.

"No," I said. "I cannot. I have taken a vow. I must be faithful to it."

He urged me at other times, did Sigismund, yet I stood firm, and at last he gave up.

Toward the end of his stay, I presented him with a gold Lancastrian collar of linked S's, embossed with fine jewels. In addition he was made a Knight of the Garter, and of this honor he was so proud he later boasted of it wherever he went.

"It would be impossible to exceed the kindness you have shown me," he said to my brothers and me.

I smiled. "We would have you know of our affection for you."

"I am touched," he said. "And because of this affection, I am sure you shall be pleased at my decision."

"Decision?" I asked hopefully.

"Aye," he said. "I have decided to remain with you for three more months."

My smile froze. "Three more months? You honor us indeed."

"I thought you would be pleased," he said. "Now we may continue to discuss the future of Christendom, may we not?"

"Three months!" John exploded when Sigismund had retired. "Harry, do you know what expense it is to house that fool and his entourage in this fashion? Three months!"

Humphrey roared with laughter. "Still, it is a fine trick, is it not? I would swear he has done it on purpose."

I kicked a bench and sent it flying. "May he burn in Hell! Does he think I have no better use of my time than to drink with him?"

"He uses us because of his own poverty," John said. "You should turn him out."

"No," I muttered. "I must be patient. I have much to lose here."

My patience was soon to be tried on other counts as well. Through Sigismund's urgings I had offered once more to treat with the Armagnacs. Their reply was to raid the south coast of England and set siege to Harfleur. While Sigismund dallied at Westminster and Windsor, the fair Isle of Wight was burned and sacked, the garrison and townspeople of Harfleur saw their supplies dwindle away, and English merchants grumbled at the harassment of their shipping. Quietly I ordered a fleet of ships assembled to clear the Channel of French vessels and to relieve Harfleur. But I hesitated to act, hoping that Sigismund would at last show some sign of his favor and fearful that another attack upon the French might increase his fear of me. Only when it seemed Harfleur would fall did I send to her aid. The command was John's, for much to my chagrin I must stay behind to deal with Sigismund.

The Emperor was moody when he heard of this expedition, grumbling that I might have warned him. He was ready, he said, to depart at last for the continent and had hoped to leave as my ally.

"You have only to say the word," I said, barely controlling my impatience. "I have told you all along I welcome your support."

"But you have not consulted me," he complained. "When you send to fight the French, do I not have a right to know it?"

"No. You do not. You have signed no treaty. You have given me no pledge. You have enjoyed my hospitality these months past, but it gives you no right to interfere in my affairs."

"Hospitality! You dare speak of hospitality? It is true you have lavished attention upon me. But do you think me so great a fool that I do not know why?"

"Nevertheless, you cannot complain."

"I shall not make you my heir," he blustered.

"I have not asked it."

"Have you not?" he scoffed.

"I ask you to side with me against the Armagnacs. That is all I ask that you put your name to."

"To stand idly by while you snatch the French crown from the Dauphin's head. And what then? When you are King of England and France, and the Duke of Burgundy is either destroyed or pledged to you, what then? Shall you look to sit upon my throne as well?"

"Not while you live."

He laughed. "So, we have it at last. I am told your father despaired of you while he lived. Should I be anxious to suffer his fate?"

This touched me sore, but I hoped I did not show it.

"You bear a glorious title," I persisted, "but an empty one. I can restore the Empire to greatness."

"It is a fantastic claim for one who has not even achieved France. I have observed you carefully these months, and there is something that troubles me. You seem to expect I shall disapprove of your aggression against the French, that I shall throw up my hands in horror at your ambitions. Why? Why, I have asked myself, do you think me so squeamish? I am an emperor. I have no illusions about power and the wielding of it. I know what I must do to survive. You need not explain your motives to me, or fall back on high-minded ideals." He winked at me. "Perhaps I must acquiesce while Henry Monmouth disinherits the Dauphin. It is not hard. If I must agree to it to get ahead, so be it. That is my philosophy. It is not yours. And so, you shall fail. Shall I cast my lot with one whose cause is lost?"

The blood rushed to my cheeks. "You make the same mistake as the French. You underestimate me. How can you, after Agincourt? How can you, after you have seen how well my England is governed?"

He raised his hand and smiled. "I do not question your ability. I say it to you plainly, you are a genius. You are a splendid commander and administrator, and the affection your people bear you is remarkable. Yet I am a student of more than women and wine. I am a student of history. I have read of Alexander the Great, as you have, I am sure. Do you think he cared that men were used justly? Of course not. Or Julius Caesar: did he agonize over the well-being of the people of Gaul? Faugh! He wished to rule them, that is all. Pious sentiments make clumsy baggage for a would-be conqueror."

I answered him through clenched teeth. "I have sought to know God's will for my life. Everything points to this. Someone must rescue God's people, and to no other has He given the gifts you name for me. If I place myself in God's hands, He shall use me."

He shook his head. "Those whom God uses know little enough of success, it seems to me. More familiar with madness, they are."

"You should confine your ruminations to your whores," I said bitterly. "You are ill equipped to spout theology. If you shall not support my cause, then that is an end of it."

"Do not spurn me so quickly," he said. "I shall indeed sign a pact with you against the Armagnacs. You are the ablest man in Christendom, that I grant you, and I would not be at odds with you. But as to the other matter, I promise nothing yet. Achieve France first; then we shall see."

"Indeed you shall see," I answered him. "Give me but five years, and I shall send to treat with you."

We journeyed together to Canterbury, that we might pray for a good outcome at Harfleur. True to his word, Sigismund signed a treaty, proclaiming his support for me in my just quarrel with the Armagnacs. On the very day, our small English vessels destroyed and dispersed the bulky French carracks and lifted the siege of Harfleur.

One year after Sigismund's departure, I sailed for France. Again my destination was secret and my landing on the south shore of the Seine estuary unopposed. With me were Tom and Humphrey. John again remained to govern England, Beaufort I had dispatched to the council at Constance, to press for the continued reform of the Church. To my great joy, Rhys, Dafydd, and John Wotten were once more in my company. I had greeted them in Southampton.

"Fools you are to go this way again," I said to them.

Rhys grinned. "We but follow our King," he said.

Dafydd spat in the dust. "Know you what I have done these two years past? I have toiled at a smithy, sweating and cursing all the time. I was the happiest man alive when I heard you would go again to France."

"Dafydd would even starve again to escape the smithy," said Rhys.

"No," I said, "none shall starve this time. I have learned that lesson well."

Indeed I had learned many lessons. My strategy for the invasion was even more meticulously planned than before, my diplomacy more painstaking. I met in secret with the Duke of Burgundy and secured his pledge that he would not join the Armagnacs. It was a hard meeting, that encounter with the Duke. Ambition and cruelty had etched deep lines on his face, and I shuddered to look upon him. I knew that, if he could, he would crush me with no more compunction than swatting a fly. I could easily guess at his plan. He coveted the French crown for himself. What better way to achieve it than to stand by and let the King of England invade? Even if successful, which was unlikely, my effort would weaken me. Then would Burgundy step in and place the crown upon his own head. So he thought, and I would let him think it for as long as he remained neutral.

With equal care I chose my first target. Caen was the leading city in upper Normandy, and there I would set my siege. At first glance she seemed impregnable, Caen. But I believed that every city had its weakness, and Caen's was soon obvious. Just without the city walls, on both east and west, loomed two majestic abbeys that had been founded by William the Conqueror. Their walls towered well above those of the city. At our approach, the garrison of Caen ordered the abbeys razed, for they feared what use we might make of them. They reckoned not with the monks, who would not stand to see their beloved sanctuaries destroyed. They came to us, as we lay yet a day's march away, and led an advance force commanded by Tom into the abbey precincts under cover of darkness. The startled residents of Caen woke next morning to find the standard of St. George fluttering from just beyond their walls.

Tom was jubilant at this little adventure, for now he had some small success to boast of. He had driven me near to distraction with his chatter those last weeks. He had shown himself upon the quay of Southampton wearing a red eye patch with the golden lion rampant of England embossed upon it.

"What in the name of all the saints!" I said when I saw it.

"I have taken an oath," he had explained. "I shall not remove this patch from my eye until I have achieved some glorious deed in France."

"That is ridiculous! What purpose is there in blinding yourself?"

He puffed his chest with wounded dignity. "Do not berate me because

of your own lack of chivalry. Besides, I am not alone in this. The Earl of
Warwick wears a patch as well, one that bears the device of his house."

"He would," I muttered as Tom strolled jauntily away.

I knew Tom would expect to be my second-in-command. I was reluctant
to give him such responsibility, for he was truly untested and his head was
filled with chivalric fancy. Still, I noted, he exerted a charismatic hold over
his men, much as I did, and his courage I did not doubt. If he kept his head,
he could soon become my most able lieutenant. I set him in the abbey of the
Trinity on the eastern side of Caen, in charge of half of my troops.

We placed our guns high upon the abbey walls and rained balls into the
city. This caused little harm to the inhabitants but opened wide breaches in
the walls and knocked down many buildings. One ingenious gunner, Henry
Fermer by name, devised a hollow ball packed with straw, sulfur, and
powder. This strange missile blew apart upon impact and spewed fire upon
the thatched roofs of the city. Many buildings were burned in this manner.

The citizens, I am told, urged the garrison to surrender, but they would
not hear of it. As for me, I wanted no repeat of the lengthy siege of Harfleur
with its rampaging disease. After a fortnight of waiting, I ordered an assault.

I swear by the Host that my orders were explicit. Noncombatants were
to be spared, and the fight taken to those who bore the sword against us. We
poured into the breaches simultaneously from east and west, but most of the
defenders rushed to the western walls, for there fought the King. They did
not know that I had anticipated this and sent the bulk of the attackers to Tom
and Warwick. For a time my own outnumbered men were stymied, and a
score died in a barrage of stones and boiling oil dropped from high up on the
battered walls. Then Warwick and his men appeared inside the city, and the
French fled in a panic through the crooked streets toward the castle.

"Tom is in!" Warwick screamed above the tumult when I had met him.
"Already he drives for the castle."

"Then should we join him," I replied.

My men gathered calmly about me in an open space of rubble, as they
had been taught. Then we advanced, street by street, swords drawn, driving
the now frantic defenders before us. The castle loomed closer. A loud din
seemed to rise from its vicinity, pierced by shrill screams.

Then I saw her.

The babe still nursed at her breast, clutching in its tiny fist a swath of
bloodied cloth from her dress. She was sprawled on her back across a doorstep. Where her head had been there was but a stump.

I halted our march and called for Warwick.

"What is this?" I was trembling violently. "Has Tom come this way?"

Warwick blanched. "Indeed he would have. His charge was fierce and impetuous, and he led his men headlong into the city, in this direction, it seemed to me."

"I fear this slaughter continues yonder," I said.

I was right. The inhabitants of Caen had fled to the castle, seeking entrance, but were turned away by the garrison. There, packed in the courtyard before the castle gate, they were set upon by English soldiers already loaded with booty. Women and children, old and young, they were being put to the sword when I arrived. The cobbled stones were slick with bright red blood and the bodies of the slain lay in heaps. Over and over the buglers blew a halt. My own men risked their lives to pull their crazed comrades from the shrieking mass of humanity. Several hundred more innocents fell ere order could be restored.

I wandered the streets of Caen until nightfall, my archers for bodyguard, to see for myself that the looting was at an end.

"It could not be helped," Rhys said. "Such things happen in an assault. When men screw their courage to the point of braving boiling oil to go over a wall, why then, they are indeed more than a little mad."

"You do not comfort me," I said. I saw the corpse of an old woman, her belly ripped open, and was put in mind of the slaughter I had seen long ago in a tiny Welsh village. "I promised death to any man who did this," I said. "What shall I do now? Shall I hang half of my army?"

At nightfall I returned to the abbey of St. Stephen, and there Tom came to me as I stood alone before a fire. He had not time to speak ere I was on him and struck him a blow across the mouth which sent him crashing to the floor. I stood over him.

"I should kill you," I cried.

He staggered to his feet and backed away. "Do not blame me," he protested. "It is your own fault."

"My fault! I ordered no slaughter!"

"You ordered the siege! You ordered the assault! Afore God, they were uncontrollable." He began to sob. "I'll not be blamed for it. When Father was alive, you ever blamed him for your predicaments. You'll not blame me now!"

I stared speechless at him for a moment and then turned away toward the fire. Pain shot through my midsection so that I moaned softly and hunched my shoulders.

"What is it?" Tom asked.

"Nothing," I managed to say. "A bellyache, that is all. I see you have removed your eye patch. Are you then proud of yourself?"

"Indeed I am," he said defiantly. "You may take on about it, but I shall not be ashamed of this day's work. When we went over the wall, it was a thing of beauty. I cared not for my life, I tell you, but only for glory. I missed Agincourt. I swore I would make up for it, and I have. As for the dead, I am sorry for it. But they were none of them people of note, and the city did resist. By all the rules of war, what happened is acceptable. You shall find none to condemn it, not the Church, no, nor even the French. The garrison knew they invited retaliation when they did not surrender. They shall not blame you."

When I did not answer, he said, "We took much plunder, enough to reward the men handsomely."

"If the owners are alive, return it," I said. "If they are dead, keep it yourself. I want none of it."

"So you will not acknowledge what I have done for you. I suppose I shall be relieved of my command as well."

"I shall seriously consider it."

"Then I say this. If you treat me so, you are a very great hypocrite unless you also give up this city I have got for you and get yourself back to England."

When he had gone, I sent for my confessor, Thomas Netter. This was a slender, scholarly man who had served me for a year upon the recommenda-·tion of Archbishop Chichele.

"Forgive me, Father, for I have sinned," I said to him.

"I see illness in your face," he said. "What is this sin?"

"The blood of hundreds of innocents stains my hands. I crave pardon, though it may not be possible."

"Pardon?" He raised his thin eyebrows. "Do you speak of Caen, my son?"

"Of course I speak of Caen."

"There is no need for pardon. There is no sin. You gave the city fair warning, which was not heeded. You have come here for a just cause, a holy mission. The sin is upon the heads of those who stand in your way."

"You shall not absolve me?"

"Please, your grace, I pray you put your mind to rest. I shall absolve you, but only for that fallen state into which each of us is born. As for Caen, there is no sin."

Tom I kept with me after exacting a pledge that he would keep tight control of his men in future. To this end I enlisted the aid of the Earl of Warwick. Warwick had been much chastened by the Caen massacre, confiding in me that he believed it contravened the ideals of chivalry. He would, he said, bring his influence to bear on Tom, who saw in him a kindred spirit.

For all my grief over Caen, I had to admit that it made my way easier. Town after town opened its gates to me, anxious to avoid an assault. Everywhere I was recognized as duke and rightful ruler of Normandy. Many seemed glad of my coming, for where my rule held sway the roads were once more safe for commerce and the fields for planting. The hateful taxes with which the rich had oppressed the poor were revoked. Churchmen praised me as well that they were able once more to conduct their affairs in peace. Lower Normandy seemed a blessed land delivered from the disturbances which afflicted the rest of France, and my confidence in my cause grew once more. Tidings from home buoyed my spirits as well. Richard Whittington wrote on behalf of London's merchants that the city had never been more prosperous nor her people more content.

"We lack only your presence," he wrote, "and pray daily for your safety and your return to us."

I passed the winter of 1418 at Falaise, where a messenger came to me from Archbishop Chichele.

"The Church in England salutes your grace," said the travel-worn clerk.

"How does my lord of Canterbury?"

"Well, your grace. He is yet at Constance but prepares for his return to England. He rejoices at the happy events I report to you. The schism in Holy Church is healed, thanks in large part to the efforts of your uncle of Beaufort. Christendom has but one pope now, and he a man removed from the sordid dealings of the past."

"Good news indeed!" I exclaimed. "And who might he be?"

"He is Cardinal Colonna, who has taken the name Martin the Fifth. He is deemed a holy man. Beaufort claims to have gained his confidence. A most able man, Bishop Beaufort."

"I shall commend my uncle for this good work."

"One thing more the Archbishop would have you know. Oldcastle has been taken."

"When?" I gasped.

"Two months past."

I sprang to my feet. "I must send to my brother John! He must take no action until I think on this."

"Forgive me, your grace," the clerk said uncertainly, "but there is nothing to be done. Oldcastle has been executed. He was condemned by his treason against you, and by heresies out of his own mouth. He was hanged in chains and burned at Smithfield."

I recall little of what followed, only that I fell into such a rage as I had never known. The clerk was driven in a panic from my presence. Then I took to my bed for two days.

It was a fortnight ere any dared speak to me of Jack. It was Humphrey, ever rash, who at last approached me.

"The man was mad at the last, Harry. John writes that he proclaimed to one and all that he would himself rise from the dead on the third day after his execution."

"John had no right to do it."

"Have you not given him authority in your absence?"

I only stared at my fingernails.

"John also writes that Oldcastle's wife remains in custody with her son in the Tower. He seeks your advice."

"It is late for my advice, is it not? I shall tell him this. He has no right to hold her. She is to be set free at once and restored to her property."

Poor Joan. Jack had treasured her well.

"Did you say she has a son?" I asked. "I knew not of it."

"Only a child. It seems he was born about the time you were struggling toward Agincourt." He watched me closely. "The boy's name is Henry."

"Is it so?" I whispered.

"Will you not weep for what was? You may find it a comfort to mourn him."

"Long ago I forgot how to weep," I said. "Alexander the Great slew his best friend, did he not? Cleitus was his name. Alexander was in a drunken rage, I believe."

"It is not the same thing," Humphrey said.

"Of course not. Sigismund says I am not at all like Alexander."

For years the French nobility had mocked at me, scoffed at me, but no more. Now they trembled, for it seemed none could stand against me. And not only the French held me in awe, for Sigismund wrote that all Christendom spoke of the deeds of King Henry of England. In the east, men looked fearfully over their shoulders at the advancing Turks and wondered if an Englishman might be their savior. My newfound respect was not without its price, for it brought me the enmity of the Duke of Burgundy. I had known that if I met with success, Burgundy could not afford to ignore me. By the time I held most of Normandy, he had declared himself my enemy and sworn he would drive me from France.

Men inclined to wager might have placed their coin upon Burgundy. He was considered the most powerful man on the continent, and his court was more glittering even than that of the French king. Outwardly chivalrous, in reality he was vicious as a wild boar. Most vital of all, he had with him the Queen of France, Isabeau.

Even now I cannot think of her without a shudder. The She-wolf of Bavaria. So she was known by rich and poor alike, after the place of her birth. At first she was aligned with no party but sought only her own pleasure. Her appetite for lovemaking was legendary, and it was said there was not a man at the French court who had not enjoyed her favors. When King

Charles had been afflicted with his madness, more and more power fell to Isabeau. She proved capricious and cruel in government as in love, and soon the court was clamoring against her. She had been recently driven out by her own son, the Dauphin. King Charles, in one of his few lucid moments, agreed to her going, having suffered her long enough. Still it was a foolish thing to do, for she went straightway to Burgundy and sold him her body and many other services he would find valuable. Together they fomented a rebellion in Paris which ended in the massacre of several thousand Arma-gnacs. The terror-stricken Dauphin fled under cover of night to Melun. Burgundy and Isabeau rode in triumph to Paris, where they took charge of the King, once more sunk into a drooling fit. Then they turned their atten-tion to me. France, Burgundy claimed, had been troubled long enough by this son of a usurper.

In answer I set siege to Rouen. It was the most important city in France, save Paris. It was called impregnable. And Rouen belonged to the Duke of Burgundy.

"Come see, Harry!" Tom called. "They shall soon be ready to charge."

He waved at me from a group of knights who stood with arms folded and stared across the brown plain toward the city. I joined him, curious in spite of myself.

"It is foolishness," I said.

"Fie! It is a diversion. If you must set us at such a boring siege, do not deny us some pleasure."

"You may be bored, but I have plenty to do. Not only must I govern Normandy, I must watch Rouen like a hawk to see that none bring relief to her. If you are bored I can busy you with some task."

"You know my meaning. For months we sit idle. We do not use our guns or dig mines. And of course we launch no assault. The only excitement comes when the garrison sallies forth to attack us, and that is not often enough. I pray daily that Burgundy shall come upon us, that we may settle this once and for all."

A trumpet drew his attention back to the plain. Two knights sat motion-less upon their horses, lances couched. Again the horn sounded and they charged, nearly invisible to us in a swirl of dust. Because of the distance, the noise of the crash came late, after one mailed figure sprawled helpless in the dust.

"Who—?" Warwick cried, then, "Jesu, it is Blount who is down."

The second knight dismounted, walked deliberately to the fallen man, drew his sword, and plunged it in under the armpit.

We stood in stunned silence. From the walls of the city came a triumphant cheer. It seemed the entire populace had clambered up to view their champion's victory. I flung up my hands in disgust.

"That is the end of the jousts. I lose a good man, a valuable man, and for what? So that the people of Rouen are heartened by some meaningless victory!"

"We were challenged," a crestfallen Tom said. "Someone had to answer. Poor Blount. He was not our best jouster. Warwick should have gone."

"He should not have! And if he does, and returns alive, I shall send him in chains to England."

I stalked back to my tent. A stack of documents awaited my signature. Then I must make my rounds, hear each captain's report, speak with my men, assure myself that my orders were followed. There could be no mistakes, for each error meant prolonging the siege. Hunger was the weapon I would use against Rouen, and the vise I had drawn around her must not be loosened.

I believed Rouen would be of two minds. The garrison was a strong one, some six thousand men, I judged, many of them knights. Burgundy's men, they were. Never had they faced me, and they would be passing proud, anxious to prove themselves and in no hurry to surrender. But the people—ah, the people would have other concerns. They would have heard of Falaise, of Louviers, how they prospered under my rule. They would think, too, unfortunately, of Caen, and fear to resist me. They would have no great love for the rapacious Burgundy. No, they would care not for loyalty. They would look to their goods, to the ancient privileges of their town. And they would look to their bellies. I counted upon the people of Rouen to oppose the garrison far better than any army might.

I could only guess what happened behind the thick stone walls of the town, but after three months' siege I thought the food supply must be dwindling. I knew I was right when sallies by the garrison grew more frequent and more daring. Rouen was surrounded by a massive dry moat some forty feet in depth. Six gates studded the wall, their drawbridges providing the only access to and from the city. At any time these were apt to open and spew out a churning mass of horsemen. It was a ploy born of desperation. They were outnumbered, my men were alert, and ever we beat them back. But each time the gates opened, Englishmen died. I heard no more complaints of boredom, and men's eyes were ever turned toward the city.

At the same time that the winter's chill set in, Rouen's food ran out. I heard it from a boy who had slipped out of the city and ventured to beg food from my soldiers. I watched him gnaw upon a hunk of bread, the bones of his face sliding back and forth beneath the skin. When he was done, I questioned him.

"The horses are gone," he said, "save those the soldiers ride. We cannot get at those, for they guard them night and day. The dogs are gone as well. Cats and mice are sold in the marketplace, but you must be rich to buy one. Soon there shall be no more of them. A city without mice! Is such a thing possible?"

"What of the garrison?" I asked. "They have strength enough to fight, it seems."

He spat his contempt. "They yet have food hidden away in the castle. We all know it, though they do deny it. Our women have seen it. They go to the castle to sell their bodies that they may feed their babes. Aye, there is food in the castle."

"Do the people want surrender?"

"Of course! Yet the garrison will not hear of it. It is death to speak aloud of surrender."

"Why think you the garrison is so stubborn?"

"They wait for their master, Duke John. They have word that he seeks to raise an army for our relief."

"Is it so?" I mused. "We shall see."

He was but a lad. I let him stay on with my troops to look after the horses for his food. I wondered what I would do with the others who were sure to follow.

For four days the garrison did not show itself, and my captains wondered at it.

"It is some trick," said Humphrey. "They are plotting something to catch us off guard."

"Perhaps not," said Warwick. "Likely they see the futility of such sallies and husband their strength. What think you, your grace?"

"I think they expect the Duke of Burgundy momentarily," I said. "I have just learned from my spies that Burgundy assembles an army at Pontoise."

"Jesu be praised!" Tom cried. "We shall have a battle at last!"

"We shall prepare for one," I said. "Every man shall sleep with his weapon at his side. Yet truly I do not expect a fight. I doubt we shall see the Duke of Burgundy."

"Why not?" Tom demanded. "He is no coward."

"No," I said. "But he is prudent. He dare not oppose me if the Dauphin is my ally."

I enjoyed their astonished stares.

"How got you the Dauphin's support?" Humphrey asked.

"Quite easily. Burgundy is now in power, the Dauphin is not. The Dauphin is desperate to gain any advantage over his uncle. He is glad to treat with me."

"What shall you promise him?" Humphrey asked.

"Nothing that I intend to give him. I doubt this alliance shall be long-lived, my lords. Still, it may keep Burgundy safe away from us."

That day the bells of Rouen pealed madly for hours on end, their defiance puncturing the thick white-gray winter sky.

"Burgundy comes," Tom said hopefully.

"Perhaps," I said. "Yet I hear of no movement from Pontoise."

The bells were rung the next day, and the next, and three days hence. The walls were crowded with antlike men ever searching the empty horizon, and at night a thicket of torches glowed like cats' eyes in the dark. They watched in vain, for Burgundy did not come.

"He could not raise a large enough army," I explained to my archers. "Many of the great lords yet back the Dauphin and would not send troops. Of those he did gather, many prefer the Dauphin to the good Duke John. There was much quarreling, and Burgundy fears his contentious captains more than he does me, no doubt."

"Then does this city have no hope," Dafydd proclaimed. "We shall be in within a fortnight, I shall wager."

"I worry for the people who are hungry there," I said. "I pray you are right."

He was not.

Once more the gates of Rouen were opened, but no horsemen issued forth. Instead came women, children, and old men, the poorest and weakest of the city forced out at the point of a sword. Rouen, the garrison had decided, had too many mouths to feed.

"Jesu, what shall I do?" I cried in dismay.

"You cannot feed them, that is certain," said Humphrey. "We have the bulk of the winter to face out and must think of ourselves. I have no desire to relive the march to Agincourt."

"It shall do no good to let them pass through the lines," Tom observed. "There is no food to be had in the countryside now. They would but wander and starve."

They huddled together not a hundred paces from our camp. Their ragged clothing hung loose upon bony frames, and they walked as through deep water. Bright eyes stared from skulls. Many of the women were with child, and their bellies sagged as though to pull loose from the slender frames which held them.

In a wild state of mind I consulted Netter.

"The garrison's resistance is foolish, is it not, with no hope of aid from Burgundy?" he asked.

I licked my lips, which were cracked from the cold. "Aye. They are foolish."

"The garrison put these people out of Rouen, not you."

"Aye. The garrison wishes to hoard its food."

"You have ever sought God's will, and He has blessed you with success."

"Aye. I knew it would be hard. I knew I must make harsh decisions that a greater good might come, that God's people might be united. If God wills it . . ."

I sent everyone from me that I might spend the night in prayer. At last I sank exhausted onto my pallet and lay upon my back, rubbing my belly and staring at the roof of my tent. Outside the poor people of Rouen were huddled in a trench which had been dug for the city's defense and which surrounded the city wall at its base. There they were at least sheltered from the worst buffets of the wind.

"They shall not hold out much longer," I said aloud to myself. "They shall hear the cries of their people and they shall surrender. They cannot bear it long, to see the people in the ditch. They shall not let them starve."

They lowered baskets from the walls, baskets at the end of long ropes. At first I hoped the baskets to be full of food, but I saw there were not enough of them. Then I learned the baskets were for the babes born in the cold mud of the ditch. They were hoisted up from the ditch to be baptized by the priests, then sent back to their mothers to die.

"Now they shall surrender," I said. "They cannot look upon such misery and remain obstinate."

I saw little of my archers now, of Rhys, Dafydd, and John Wotten. I held myself aloof, knowing I could not laugh with them as before. I feared to face them, feared to learn what they felt for the wretches in the ditch. I knew that the women sometimes clambered out and made their way to my men to beg food or to sell themselves for it. I feared to meet one of them. I kept to my tent or rode straightway to the Charterhouse, about a mile from the city, where I conducted affairs of government. I slept little, and then fitfully, for I often dreamed of a wolf, snarling and ridden with mange, which pursued me, nipping at my heels while an invisible choir of monks chanted solemnly. I would wake just as the yellow teeth sank into my flesh.

One by one the people in the ditch died, and Christmas was fast approaching.

"A merry holiday this shall be," Warwick said. "I cannot bear much longer the sight of those people, and I know not how they can inside the city."

"Conditions there are probably nearly as bad," said Tom.

"Save with the garrison," said Humphrey. "They still eat, I'll wager."

"This siege is nearly six months old," Warwick said. "It cannot last much longer. It cannot."

It was nearly midnight, and they soon took their leave of me. All, that is, save Warwick, who lingered like a shade in the flickering candlelight.

"You were very quiet this night," he said.

"I am ever quiet."

"This is different. You brood, and there is a pale look about you that I like not. Are you ill?"

"Ill? My belly gripes me now and then. Food does not set well with me. A fitting ailment, is it not, for a man who starves a city?"

He turned his gaze from me.

"Come, my lord of Warwick," I coaxed him, "what would Galahad say of this? What would Arthur say?"

"It is a complicated situation. I know not the answer."

"Of course not. I do not ask for answers. I only wondered how a knight of your sensibilities lives with Rouen, that is all."

"I trust you, my liege. I have heard you speak many times of the holy cause of Christian unity which you pursue. I too believe our cause to be just, and so I serve you wholeheartedly. On the day of your hallowing, I took an oath, as a knight, to serve you. Knowing your good motives, I render you that service with a willing heart."

"Ah, my motives. They are good, are they not? Can any ill come of such motives?"

"You should not speak so bitterly," he said. "When you seek so to follow God, He shall not withdraw His guidance."

I sent to the captain of the garrison with an offer to feed the people of Rouen upon Christmas Day. He refused, for fear the sight of English food would incline the people even more toward surrender. He did permit a truce with terms which allowed my soldiers to approach the ditch in safety and bear food to the people there. Humphrey's men were given this responsibility, and my brother was subdued when he returned to the Charterhouse from overseeing it.

"Nearly a third of them are dead," he said, "and many others too weak to eat. They huddle together for warmth, the living and dead alike. From a distance they seem a great heap of rags, nothing more. And the stink— Mother of God, it is indescribable!"

"Enough!" Tom said. "You shall spoil our Christmas goose."

I tried to eat, but I could not for the pain. That night one of my attendants held a silver bowl before me and I vomited. There was blood in it, ruby-red blood.

"Shall I send for a physician, your grace?"

"No. There is no physician's trick for such a thing. Get you gone and leave me to rest. And I charge you, tell no one of this. I have much to do and I would not be interrupted."

The screams at first seemed a part of my dreams, and I rolled over with a grunt. Then a hand clutched at me from the dark and a voice cried, "The French are upon us, your grace! The French are upon us!"

I ran from the tent clad only in hose and nightshirt. Someone thrust a sword hilt into my hand, another dragged me behind the cover of some barrels. A bolt from a crossbow hissed by and rent the canvas of my tent.

"That might have struck you," said one of my companions. It was Warwick.

To our right I heard the braying of horses, the brittle clash of arms.

"Now they come on us at night," I said.

"Aye, and from one gate only, the Porte St. Hilaire."

"Then it would seem their purpose is not to engage us, but to break through our ranks and escape."

"My guess as well. They must then be low on food at last."

Two armorers came breathlessly bearing my coat armor, and I struggled into it.

"Sound my horn," I called to Warwick. "The men must know I am in the field."

I was too late to be of any help, for the French turned back to Rouen even as I arrived. They left behind them the dead and dying, and as I walked among them for a closer look, it seemed most wore the cross of St. George. Men of my own guard they were, and I pressed my lips tight in bitterness.

"It was a fine watch," said Warwick, "a brave watch. They must have seen the French at once and set themselves as they should between the charge and your tent."

Still I walked silently and counted the bodies sprawled in the torchlight. Twenty. Twenty-five.

I found Dafydd first. He was dead of a thrust to the heart. Rhys lay nearby, his coiled entrails shining from a gash in his belly. I placed my hand beneath his red curly head and lifted gently. His eyes fluttered at me.

"Rhys?"

"Harry. Kill me. Kill me."

"In God's name," I cried to Warwick, "bring a priest!"

"They come even now," he answered.

"Harry," Rhys gasped. "We just did say how little we see of you. Jesu! The pain!"

A black robe loomed behind him and the familiar chant commenced.

"Harry, my da thanks you for the coneys."

I wiped the blood from his lips.

"There is the river," he said. "I shall beat you in. . . ."

The eyes rolled back in his head, and I shut them quickly.

The French prisoners were brought to me at dawn, and I hanged three of them in full view of the walls ere one agreed to talk. He was brought in chains to my tent.

"They will try again two nights hence," he said.

"If you speak not the truth," I said, "you shall die."

"It is the truth," he said.

"What is their object? Do they seek to force a way out?"

"Aye. They would ride to Burgundy and seek to persuade him to come to Rouen's aid. And they sought your life as well. Yet for the sake of surprise they will come not from Porte St. Hilaire next time."

"Where from then?"

"From Castle Gate."

When he was gone from me I turned to my captains.

"I shall double my forces at Porte St. Hilaire," I said. "It shall seem to them I am setting a guard about myself."

"And I must guard Castle Gate with a reduced force?" Tom protested. "It may be they shall break through."

"No," I said. "That I promise they shall not do."

The sky on the appointed night was overcast, so I knew they would come. I had moved in secret to Castle Gate to join Tom. With me I had John Wotten, grim and silent. For endless hours we watched the gate. It was a black rectangle set in the wall above the equally black chasm of the dry moat. Often I thought the gate moved, but it was some trick of my eyes, a playing of clouds upon the wall. Then there was a distant creaking and the blackness deepened as the bridge came down.

"There they are!" Tom cried.

They rode quickly across, the first of the horsemen, their armor rippling like black velvet.

"Now!" I said. "Now!" Tom looked at me quizzically.

Still they came, more than three score fanning out across the field.

"They shall send out a thousand," Tom muttered. "They may break through."

They crowded across the drawbridge some fifty at a time, and the hooves of their horses drummed upon the wood. Then there was a tearing sound like the scream of a banshee. The horses seemed to dance for an instant, to leap into the air. The bridge plummeted into the chasm. A gray cloud of dust rose from the pit with the screams. Still the knights poured through the gate, the exuberance of their charge carrying them headlong into thin air.

"Holy Mother of God!" Tom crossed himself. "It is not to be believed."

"Send your men and gather up those few who crossed over first," I said.

"You knew this would happen."

"Of course. I sent Wotten last night to cut the stanchions of the draw-bridge."

The garrison sued for terms the next day.

So I came to Rouen and entered her in mourning, clad all in black and riding upon a black charger while the living cheered me weakly and the dead lay all unburied in the streets.

15

Evreux. Vernon. Mantes. They fell to me one by one and in short order, without the suffering of Rouen. Still it was a wearisome business, and I sought once more to treat with the Duke of Burgundy. He would not meet with me unless I renounced my claim to the French crown.

"Perhaps it is enough without the crown," I said to Warwick. "Soon I shall rule nearly half of France. It may be I can wed the daughter of the French King. I would then be the most powerful man in Christendom, without doubt."

"What of the Dauphin?" he asked.

"He is a weakling, an incompetent. Even if he be King of France, I could rule him. And there is always Sigismund. There is always the Empire."

"It is true. This way may be quicker."

It was arranged that I would meet with King Charles and Queen Isabeau at Meulan. The Duke of Burgundy would accompany them, along with the Princess Katherine. A splendid pavilion was erected, all of silks and cloth-of-gold, embroidered with leopards and lilies. Within these were thrones of finely carved oak with velvet cushions and hangings depicting the chivalry of England and France. The balmy breezes of late May wafted through the entrance and teased the shimmering walls of the tent. In all it was one of the pleasantest things I have ever seen.

I walked to the pavilion with my entourage, each one clad in scarlet and azure. Minstrels strolled behind us, playing upon their rebecs and lutes. The French came likewise from the opposite direction, and we halted together before the pavilion. King Charles had fallen into one of his fits, I was told, and was not present. Burgundy I had met before. It was Queen Isabeau who arrested my attention.

Clearly she had once been a great beauty, but there was now an aura of rot about her. It was not only the sagging skin and the sallow complexion, for these are common enough in women of her age. No, it was the feel of her hand given to me in greeting, cold and plump as an overripe peach, which most discomfited me. And there was the look of her as she stared at me, the lickerish widening of her pupils, the flaring of the nostrils.

"Welcome, cousin," she crooned. "I had been told that the King of England is a handsome man, yet I had not dreamed you would cut so splendid a figure."

Behind her the Duke of Burgundy stood stiffly, his smile frozen.

"I thank you for your kind words," I replied.

She took my arm, and there was nothing for it but to escort her into the pavilion.

We did little that day but pass vapid pleasantries and sip the sparkling wines of Burgundy's vineyards while the minstrels plucked their lutes. Isabeau's eyes were ever upon me, clinging as fiercely as leeches. Her attention brought a hot glow unbidden to my cheeks.

"I look forward to meeting the Princess Katherine on the morrow," I said. "I knew your eldest daughter when she was in England as King Richard's bride. A sweet girl, Isabel; we were great friends. My memories are fond ones."

"Aye, Isabel," she said. "She has been dead these ten years."

"I know it. I mourned to hear of it."

"Still, I trust you shall approve of Katherine," she said. "She is a beauty and has learned well the ways of a court."

I inclined my head politely. "It would seem that she takes after her mother," I said.

"You are very kind," she said.

Burgundy for the most part sat and glowered. He was a bald, squat man, this latest lover of the Queen. I tried to imagine the two of them in bed, she raking her swollen fingers in a frenzy across his bare pate.

We did speak of weighty matters the next day, but my mind was much unsettled, for Katherine was present. She was fair indeed, and she knew it.

Her face beneath the high coif was delicate, her mouth full and red, her eyes rich brown and long-lashed, her skin white. She was full-breasted, as her low-cut gown made amply clear. I could not keep my eyes from her, and she was likewise attentive to me. If all went well, she would share my bed, and the thought of it quickened my loins with a desire such as I had not known in years. I urged myself to caution, for this was potent bait with which to lure a king. I must be clear of head and stick to my terms.

"Touraine, Anjou, Maine, Brittany, Flanders, plus the lands I have already conquered." I pressed again and again. It was a comfortingly long litany of places with which to calm the beating of my heart.

"It is too much," Burgundy would say. "My followers will never hear of it."

"I have already given up my claim to the crown which is rightfully mine," I would reply, "and that is a very great sacrifice."

Katherine would look anxiously from one to another, our eyes would meet, and a smile would play at the corner of my mouth. Once she pursed her lips as though to blow a kiss, and I raised my eyebrows teasingly.

When we had done with our talk, Isabeau dug her fingers into my arm and smiled. "Your grace has been flirting with my daughter. I have watched you." She clicked her tongue in mock severity. "As a mother I should be concerned. The King of England has a reputation as a seducer of maidens."

I masked my irritation and said, "I would like to speak in private with the Princess Katherine."

"In private! It is most unusual. You are not yet wed, though I trust you soon shall be."

"I would speak with her but a moment. I would not wed her and we two total strangers. I would hear her voice and know of her how this match suits her."

"You are strong-willed, cousin of England."

"That you should have learned long ago," I said.

I had my way and faced Katherine in the center of the pavilion. For a moment we stood without words, two slender figures clad in flowing robes of purple and white. Katherine broke the silence.

"Ste. Genevieve has answered my prayers," she said. "When Maman said I might be wed to the King of England, I feared you would be ugly or that you would be fat. It is not so. You are the most desirable man I have ever seen. Such good fortune is beyond belief. I shall love to kiss that dimple upon your chin."

"You seem very sure this match is to be. Burgundy grows more stubborn. He yet opposes our union."

"Him! That swine! He tries to fondle my breasts when he thinks no one watches." She took a step closer. "You shall not allow that, I know. Do you find me beautiful? Do you want me? That is all I care about."

"You are passing beautiful," I said. "I want you badly. And so I shall have you."

She smiled and her eyes glittered. "I knew it. I knew when you looked at me today that you would be such a man. Now my brother the Dauphin cannot wed me to some repulsive old man. I shall belong to the King of England."

I drew her to me and kissed her, and she thrust her tongue impertinently into my mouth.

When we parted, she said, "This was but a promise of things to come. I know well how to please a man." She looked me up and down one final time and giggled. "Maman shall be so jealous."

I returned to my quarters at Mantes and sat before the fire late into the night, nursing my desire. Humphrey joined me there.

"We are deceived," he said. "Word comes from Meulan that envoys of the Dauphin are with the Duke of Burgundy and that even now they convince him to pull back from these negotiations. They fear the power you shall gain from this match."

"In truth," I muttered, "it is not the power I think on right now. I am sick with the wanting of her."

"What? After all these years of iron chastity, you are lovesick? I would have thought you at last beyond such a state."

"Do not mock me so soon after you have brought me bad news. It is the nearness of the thing which has overwhelmed me. Marriage would release me from the vow of continence I have taken, and marriage has seemed so close. Nor am I the cold man of iron you name me."

"I know it, and I crave your pardon. It is only that it has been easy to think of you so, these last few years."

"I long for love again, yet I do not know about this match. I am nearly thirty-two and she is but eighteen. Is the difference too great?"

"It is not her age which worries me," Humphrey said. "It is whether she is her mother's daughter. And remember, her father is mad. With such a bloodline, what sort of heir would she give to England?"

"I would not judge her so harshly," I said. "Sweet Isabel was their daughter, and I see much of her in this Katherine."

"Harry, I know how it was with the Welsh lass. Do not think to find that again."

"No," I said. "I would not dare ask for it. Yet I could have been content with Isabel. Perhaps it could be so with this Katherine as well."

"Perhaps. I pray for your sake it shall be so. Yet beware the Dauphin, for he shall use every wile to keep his sister from your bed."

"I have given her my word. Katherine shall be my queen, and neither Dauphin nor Duke shall thwart us."

Burgundy glowered at me across a table. The Queen and Princess Katherine were gone, as were the minstrels and the fine wines. The Duke's advisers stood frozen, arms folded across their chests, like a row of chess pieces. Behind me, Tom, Humphrey, and Warwick were likewise grim.

"I fear I cannot trust you," Burgundy said. "You say you have given up your claim to the French crown, yet you give no surety of it. Why then should we believe it?"

"Do not play games with me, Burgundy. I have no time for them. You pretend to provoke me, to impugn my honor, when in fact you have already come to terms with the Dauphin, have you not?" I leaned forward. "You are not a master of deception, my lord."

His face reddened. "Is it not meet that I should inform my sovereign King and his heir of your aggressions?"

"My lord, I shall chase you, and your sovereign, and his son the Dauphin, out of this kingdom."

"Indeed?" his voice rose. "Indeed? Sir, you shall be very tired from the effort." He stood and addressed his advisers. "Come, my lords, let us be gone from this place. We shall no more treat with this son of a usurper. We have suffered his impudence long enough. Now we shall see who is the better man, the Duke of Burgundy or this tavern crawler."

Tom came forward, but I set my hand to his shoulder as Burgundy swept from the pavilion.

"I should have challenged him," Tom said.

"Poor Harry," said Humphrey. "You have lost your princess."

"Not lost," I said. "It is only delayed. And afore God, now I shall take the crown as well."

Only Burgundy's city of Pontoise lay before Paris. We marched at once to Pontoise, and she surrendered within a week. In the meantime, Burgundy sought a meeting with the Dauphin, that they might make common cause against the English invader. Alas for Burgundy, the quarrels that had bled France for twenty years past were not so easily laid to rest. The foolish Dauphin saw his chance to be rid once and for all of his powerful uncle. They came together at Montereau, and the Duke had knelt to pledge his fealty when his skull was cleft in twain by one of the Dauphin's captains, wielding an ax from behind.

"They do say his brains spattered the Dauphin's velvet gown," Humphrey said with relish.

I shuddered. "I know not why you dwell on such things."

"But is it not fitting? They destroy each other even as they have destroyed France."

"Now France shall be yours," Warwick said, "to rule justly as you have desired. Burgundy's heir and Isabeau shall come crying to you for vengeance against the Dauphin. I see God's hand in this, that it happens so expediently."

"Perhaps you are right," I said. "However it may be, I think that I may dream once more of a wedding."

France was plagued by wolves during the winter of 1420, countless packs of fierce, lean wolves which roamed the countryside and terrorized villages, even slipping through the gates of Paris in the shadows of the night. The beasts were starving, even as the people were. Ragged beggars were attacked upon the roads, and peasants in their fields. The ravenous animals tore down the bodies of thieves hanging upon the gibbet and despoiled newly dug graves to gnaw upon the bodies of the poor who had died of hunger and cold. The winter itself was unusually long and harsh, and the previous summer so wet that the crops had rotted in the field. What could be done? I tormented myself with questions. Something there must be which displeased God, for why else would He visit such evil upon His people? My Normandy fared better than most places, for I administered my new lands with care. Yet even there the suffering was great. Bands of brigands, mostly poor men desperate for food, spilled blood as they robbed rich and poor alike. Then reports came to me that English soldiers were among the pillagers, and I nearly wept with fury. My troops were now scattered about the north of France, and the captains who commanded them not so careful of discipline as I. Once more I issued regulations for the behavior of my soldiers, but I feared in my heart that the situation had got beyond my control and that the people would come to hate me.

Is it any wonder then that the murder of the Duke of Burgundy gave me hope? That foul deed sent Burgundy's son and heir, Philip, clamoring to me for vengeance. It left the Queen of France bereft of lover and protection. To whom could she turn save the King of England? With Isabeau came Katherine, and with them both the crown of France. What could I think but that God yet smiled upon my venture and that He would yet vouchsafe me to deliver France from her distress?

My ministers scurried back and forth from the Burgundian court, and a treaty was drawn up which provided for my marriage to Katherine and named me heir to the French king. Until the death of Charles, I was to be styled Regent of France, with all power of government in my hands due to the incapacity of the King. Nor did I expect it would be long ere the crown rested upon my head, for Charles, it was said, grew feebler in body as well as mind. His condition I was able to judge for myself, for he was brought to meet me at Troyes, where the treaty would be signed and the marriage blessed.

Charles sat in state at the royal palace, and I waited nervously in the anteroom to be presented to him. He was doing well that day, I was told first, but then, no, a fit was upon him, a particularly severe one, and he had bloodied the nose of one of his courtiers who strayed too close to his flailing arms. Perhaps I should come another time, but the Queen was with him, and Katherine, and if I was patient he might be calmed.

"I shall be patient," I said. "If I am to rule for him and take him for father-in-law, then I must honor him whatever his condition."

The retainer nodded. "I beg your grace, do not take offense at him if he be rude with you. It has been a long time since he has truly understood what takes place around him. He may take you for his valet or for a Turk. One never knows what to expect."

"Of course," I replied, and I was left to pace once more. The longer the delay, the more unwelcome thoughts crowded in upon me. Suppose in his madman's ravings there was a burst of perception unhindered by the reasonable fears of a sane man? Would he then berate me, name me usurper, murderer? My stomach knotted with dread, though I named myself foolish. I had nothing to fear from a madman even if he did rave at me. I was master of France, and the words of this pathetic old man could do me no harm. I started when the doors to the hall were thrown open and I was announced to those assembled. There was a swishing of many robes as the company knelt in unison. I took a deep breath, raised my chin, and entered.

Charles was seated upon the dais, his throne draped with the gold fleur-de-lys. He was a scrawny little man with thin gray hair plastered to his skull. His face was smooth and round, the face of an innocent, a cherub. He slumped back upon his seat, his hands splayed in his lap and his head thrown back so that he gazed open-mouthed and rapt at the hammered-beam ceiling. What he saw there I do not know, but his attention was fully upon it and he did not acknowledge my entrance.

"Henry Lancaster, King of England and Regent of France," the herald cried.

Charles smiled sweetly, like a babe who sees a rattle, and began to whisper, still studying the ceiling. Slowly but firmly I walked toward the dais. He saw me then. The whispering ceased and the smile vanished. He still had not moved his head, but his eyes were turned toward me so that the whites showed. With an effort I held his gaze and then knelt before him.

He leaned forward so suddenly I thought he meant to spring upon me, but he only peered. His eyes darted here and there, studying every inch of me. Then, apparently satisfied, he sank back onto the throne. He seemed to shrink, to draw himself up; or rather the throne did swallow him, the armrests clutching at him to hold him fast forever.

"So," he said, "it is only you. I suppose you are welcome, since it is so. Greet the ladies."

He shut his eyes and seemed to sleep.

The court breathed a collective sigh of relief, and I with them. I rose hastily and went to Isabeau and Katherine, where I knelt once more. Isabeau raised me and kissed my cheek, and her fingernails dug into the flesh of my hands.

"Welcome, cousin of England," she said. "Already your presence quickens the pulse of the court with excitement. Your power clings to you like a fine perfume, and we thank God it is turned now toward the preservation of France."

"That has ever been my goal," I said.

Katherine was subdued. I kissed her full upon the mouth and the courtiers murmured pleasantly. Her brown eyes flashed, and I knew she still wanted me. I would have spoken with her, but Charles was not done.

"A king?" he cried tremulously. "Did you say he is a king? I have much to tell him then. He must beware of bathing, for the water burns. It burns, I say, and will eat the skin off a man, though none believe me. Of course they do not believe. Only kings know such things."

I stared at him in spite of myself.

"Never mind," Katherine whispered. "When all this ceremony is finished, we shall lock him away and be done with him."

Upon the signing of the treaty, Katherine and I were betrothed, with the wedding set to follow twelve days later. The interim was taken up with round after round of the most boring festivities, banquets and dances and pageants. It was my first experience of the French court, and I was not impressed. All was aimless frivolity, men and women floating about like so many gaudy butterflies drunk with nectar. They conversed of clothes, of jewels, and who could be found in whose bed. When some serious subject did make an appearance, they grabbed it up greedily, like children after sweets, devoured it whole, and then chattered passionately as though they had savored of its fullness.

At the center of this court sat Isabeau like a spider in her web. Pleasant afternoons found her in the palace gardens, surrounded by fawning servants and a bizarre assortment of animals. Isabeau had a passion for animals and they wandered the gardens freely, save for the leopard, which was held on a leash of gold chain by two attendants. Whippets and cats lounged together at Isabeau's feet, awaiting her attention. Rabbits hopped from the hedges, and imperious swans floated upon a little lake which flowed from a cascading fountain. Each creature bore about its neck a red velvet collar with Isabeau's emblem embroidered with silver thread. The Queen's favorite was a monkey, Jacquette she named it, who wore a little fur coat with a red collar. Jacquette perched upon Isabeau's shoulder and ate grapes which were patiently peeled by a sleepy-eyed retainer.

"You do not care for my little ones." Isabeau pouted. "You show them no attention."

"Indeed, I do not care for them," I said.

"You are rude! I suppose I must bear it as you have us all under your thumb."

She did not seem so displeased at the prospect, I noted irritably. Her eyes continued to roam over me in a frankly lustful manner. I would not have borne her, but I must if I wished to be with Katherine, who sat by my side, her hands folded in her lap.

"What sort of husband shall you make my Katherine?" Isabeau pretended to fret. "You hardly ever laugh, and you seem to care little for court life."

"I have found that the responsibilities of a king leave little room for frivolity," I said stiffly.

"But why do you have ministers, if not to bear such burdens for you? After all, Charles has been mad all these years, yet France is still governed."

"And governed very badly."

"Certainly we have had our little quarrels, and these we may thank for your presence, may we not? But such things as taxes are best left to dull clerks scribbling at their desks."

"When such matters are left to clerks and greedy noblemen, then poor people suffer most grievously, as they do in France every day."

"Poor people!" Isabeau scoffed. "And is it meet that the King should bend his labors toward such an insignificant rabble?"

"That rabble feeds your monkey while its own children starve."

"Nonsense! You sound like a wandering friar, not a king. A king need have no care for such matters. I find your scruples tedious and unseemly, and I fear for my Katherine's happiness at your hands."

I gritted my teeth and sought to control my rising temper. After all, she was a queen and as used as I to speaking plainly. She would be a force to be reckoned with for some time to come, and I must learn to live with her. I answered her calmly enough.

"I pray that Katherine shares my concern for the welfare of the French people," I said, turning to her.

She dropped her eyes in confusion. "I know little of affairs of state," she murmured.

"Perhaps then you may learn," I said. "As Queen you may do much good, if you so desire. There are many matters which could benefit from your attention."

"I do not know what such matters might be."

"Why, you could be patroness of many houses of mercy, or of schools. Jesu knows France needs more of both." I tried to draw enthusiasm from her, but there was no answering spark in her eyes.

"I know nothing of schools," she said.

"Of course not," Isabeau said. "She has been at court all her life. What does she care for schools?"

At long last, Katherine and I were wed and I brought her to my bed. This marriage was my moment of triumph, for after years of struggle France was truly mine. Yet I swear before God it was not this I thought upon, but only of Katherine and my dreams for our life together. My small time with her thus far had not been satisfying, but I put it down to the odious presence of Isabeau. Katherine seemed to shrink before her mother, and little wonder. It would be better, though, when we were truly husband and wife. I would see to it that Isabeau did not intrude upon us.

The wedding banquet was lavish but I ate sparingly, for I would not have surfeit hinder our lovemaking. I contented myself with watching Katherine, admiring the way her slender fingers caressed her wineglass and the confident tilt of her head as she surveyed the feasting courtiers. The long years of lying lonely in my bed were done, vanquished by this vital maid. My desire for her was so strong that I nearly swooned when we rose to leave the table.

The minstrels struck up a merry rondel and the laughing throng pressed in upon us as we shared the wine cup, our arms linked and fingers entwined about the stem. Katherine's eyes teased me above the rim. We were swept away in the midst of a great hubbub to our bedchamber, where Thomas Netter blessed the wedding bed, sprinkling the fine silk sheets with holy water that our love might be likewise holy and pure. Then they were gone, the whole boisterous crowd, though not far away, for they carried on with their drinking and shouting outside, sometimes banging upon the door and jiggling it as though they might force an entry. I turned the key in its latch and sighed in anticipation.

Katherine was already pulling off her dress. "I should send for my woman," she said. "This dress is so clumsy. But I cannot wait to have you." The lacy white dress fell in a heap. She snatched away her headdress and let down her tightly coiled hair. I gaped as though I had never seen a woman's hair before. Indeed I had not seen Katherine's hair. It was the rich brown color of a winter field, and it hung in thick tresses below her waist.

Her fingers paused in the unlacing of her shift. "Hurry!" she urged. "You are still in your clothes. Do you not want me?"

"Of course," I answered, and blushed like a boy. "I was caught up in watching you. You are so beautiful." I took a step toward her. "May I help you with your shift?"

She tossed her head. "*Mon dieu!* You would likely tear it. It is very dear, this shift, it comes from Cathay. Now hurry! I want to see what you look like."

When I stood naked before her, she nodded with satisfaction. "You did not lie," she said. "You do want me." She set aside the shift then and came to me, pressed her full breasts against my chest, and ran one hand down my back to my buttocks. "I am so glad," she said. "I am so glad you are young and handsome, and that you want me."

I took her rather too quickly, too roughly. It was so long, so many years. . . . She reproached me as we lay together afterward.

"You make love like a boy," she said.

"Forgive me. I have so long looked forward to this night. I was too eager, I know it. I did not hurt you?"

"Of course not!" She laughed. "You are too abrupt, too clumsy, that is all. You make love as I would expect an Englishman to do. There are ways to please a woman, and you would do well to learn them."

My mouth was very dry and tasted of metal. "You speak as one experienced in lovemaking," I said.

"Of course. I am no girl of twelve, but a woman. What do you expect? For years I have been a pawn. My father's pawn, my brother's pawn, Burgundy's pawn. Shall I not have some say in what I do? What do you expect, that I should save myself all these years, that I should have no pleasure while I wait for you men to decide my fate?"

"I meant you no reproach," I said miserably. "I know it has been difficult for you. It is only—" Then, "It is no matter."

"*Bon.* Enough of talk. It was a wearying day, *non?* I think I could sleep until the middle of the day."

The courtiers of King Charles would have reveled for weeks had I allowed it. My own followers were unused to such profligacy, and I saw them drawn to it like moths to a candle. It was not, I decided, a healthy example, for much remained to be done. When Warwick came to me all bedazzled by the chivalry of the French, I was stirred to action.

"The Burgundians propose a tournament," Warwick said, and his eyes grew misty. "The champions of King Charles and the finest of the Burgundians to break their lances with us. I myself am reckoned the most skillful jouster in England. Would it not be a fine thing—"

"You know my view of jousts."

"Aye, your grace, but is it not a special occasion? It is your marriage we mark, your great achievement."

"An achievement not yet fully realized," I said. "The Dauphin still holds part of France, and the people there suffer grievously. There is no time for sloth. Leave such to the Dauphin, but I shall be at my work."

"Surely you must rest awhile," Warwick protested. "Have you not earned it?"

"I have not! I earn nothing save more responsibility. As for the tournament, you and your champions of France shall prove your courage in a fight which has some meaning. There is no finer act of courage than to punish evildoers so that poor people may live."

I prepared to march, not without much grumbling from the gentlemen. Nor was Katherine pleased, and when we lay together she charged that already I did neglect her.

"You have heard me speak of my duties," I said.

"Endlessly," she answered. "I tire of your duties."

"You must learn patience, then. You have not wed some idle fool."

"It is funny, is it not? That is what you were called at one time. A fool, a simpleton, and a drunkard. I heard them say it when I was a child."

"They were wrong. And much to their chagrin, I should think."

"Would you not miss me in your bed at night, if you go off upon some siege?"

"Of course I would miss you."

"It was good tonight. It was very good, the best it has been. You do please me after all."

"I am glad," I mumbled. "I want to please you."

"Do you? Then how can you bear to leave me all forlorn?" She ran her fingers through the hair of my chest.

"I do not want to, but what can I do?"

"Take me with you," she cried on a sudden. She raised up on one elbow. "Oh, Harry, take me with you. Then you may fight your silly battles of a day and come to me at night. Would you not like that?"

It was indeed an intriguing plan, for it would make my way much easier to have her companionship. "Would you not be bored during the day?" I asked. "I would have no time for you there, and you would have none of the court around you."

"I shall take Maman," she said. "She is amusing enough."

My heart sank. Still, it would be enticing to have Katherine so near, enough so to bear Isabeau's presence. After all, I need not see her often.

"Please, Harry. Please." She nibbled my earlobe.

"Very well. We shall try it. Perhaps it shall not be a strenuous campaign. After all, I am now your father's heir. It is done. I shall be accepted easily enough, I think."

We went first to Sens, then Bray, then Montereau. Each town opened its gates to me and swore allegiance. My spirits rose. It would go quickly, easily. Soon the way would be open to treat with Sigismund. Then could I set aside the armor which yet bore so heavily upon me and go about ruling. It was all I wanted now, to rule in peace. From the Danube to the Channel I would establish justice. The fields would yield their abundance once more, the milkmaid and the shepherd would go secure about their tasks. Katherine would bear me children, and they, along with my brothers, my good and faithful brothers, would realize the dream with me.

Then we came to Melun.

The gates were shut fast against us. I sought to quell the panic that welled in me and sent for King Charles. He stood in his robes and crown, the spittle trickling from a corner of his mouth, and read in a singsong voice an order for the garrison to surrender. The reply enraged me.

"We would gladly obey our sovereign King Charles were he free. But he is a captive of the usurper Henry of England, the enemy of France. This Henry we shall never obey."

The pains came upon me that night, and I would not go to Katherine in such a state. I lay moaning in my bed with Tom for companion.

"It is but a temporary setback," he said soothingly.

"And if it is not?"

"Well then, see what you have accomplished in these few years. You can do as much in the years to come."

"I know not if I have the strength for much more."

"Is it so bad then?"

"Aye. I bleed from time to time, and the physicians know not why."

Tom's forehead was creased with worry. "You should rest."

"Rest! It seems Melun will not let me rest!"

"I am here. Will you not trust me to take Melun?"

"Of course I trust you. You have served me well since Caen. But I must answer this defiance myself. If I do not, it may encourage others to oppose me."

"Surely it would do no harm to return to England for a time. The good folk there long for a sight of you, I am sure. Take Katherine with you to London and crown her there, then go on to Kenilworth to rest. I would be honored to stand for you here. I shall do well. You shall see, and be proud of me."

I shut my eyes, and the bed seemed to roll beneath me as though it were a raft upon a lake.

"It would be good," I admitted. "I have not seen England these three years. Perhaps, when I am done with Melun. . . ."

The leaves turned to gold and russet, then drifted into sodden heaps or were borne away by the langorous waters of the Seine. Still Melun held out. As the wind turned chill my soldiers grew restless, and for the first time my hold over them weakened. Several hundred deserted, some to make their way home to England, others to join outlaw bands and pillage the countryside. Many rapes and murders in the neighborhood of Melun were laid at the door of Englishmen. I blamed myself for this lawlessness, for I had not been so attentive to my men as in years past. In part it was the illness which sapped my strength, but even more telling was my preoccupation with Katherine. She was housed with Isabeau in a small manor two miles from the city. If I spent more than one night from her she complained bitterly, and so I came to her more often than I should. No, I must not blame her. I would have gone to her with little urging, for my need of her drove me to our bed. Each morning at my prayers I implored Our Lady to open Katherine's heart and fill it with love for me. At night I went with longing to her and was convinced by our ardent coupling that my prayers were answered. Nothing gave me more peace than to fall asleep to the rhythm of her gentle breathing against my chest.

I had even managed to tolerate the presence of Isabeau. She brought her menagerie, save for the leopard (I had been firm upon that point), and had in tow a new lover as well, a minstrel named Roger. Isabeau adjusted quickly to her new situation and was as well tempered as I deemed it possible for her to be. All was altered when I announced I must spend all my time at Melun.

Katherine wept and shouted. "How dare you desert me? I have made such sacrifices for you. I have come to live in this dreadful little hovel with but a few members of my household to attend me. How dare you leave me here alone?"

"I will come when I can," I pleaded, "only it shall not be so often. I pray that you understand."

"How shall she understand?" Isabeau said. "You have brothers. You have captains. You have the young Duke of Burgundy. Why must you spend your nights away from us?"

"Apparently all those you name have not sufficient control of my army," I said. "I must do it myself."

"Why do I care for that?" Katherine said. "So your soldiers slay a few peasants. Is it such a great matter that I must sleep alone for it? You do not love me!"

"I swear that I love you, Katherine. But by all the saints I also swear you shall not come between me and my duty to God. You must understand that."

"I understand nothing except that you leave me in this awful place."

"If you hate it so, you may return to Troyes," I said. "But I hope you shall not. I shall seek to come to you once a week if only you will stay."

"It is not enough, my lord husband. And I tell you this. If you leave my bed, I shall fill it. Ah, *oui*, do not look at me so. I know how to do it. I have lovers at my father's court who shall be glad of my company once more. I shall not live as a nun for you."

She left me alone with Isabeau.

"Where has she learned to say such things, to wound so deeply?" I asked. "Has she learned it from you?"

"Why do you accuse? This is of your own making. She is strong-willed, my daughter. She will not have you neglect her as Charles neglected me. And that is that."

She picked up her skirt and swept out the way Katherine had gone. I stood for a time and stared at the fire. Then I called for my horse and rode for Melun.

Winter was full upon us ere Melun surrendered. When the gates were opened at last, I ordered twenty men of the garrison hanged. A worried Warwick came to me where I sat brooding in my tent.

"You are more harsh than usual," he said.

"Still not so harsh as most," I replied defensively.

"Will you not spare them? I have heard you say yourself the men of Melun fought bravely."

"I cannot long bear this opposition. It is the ruler of France they deny now, and they shall not do it lightly. If there is to be peace, I must be obeyed. Now go from me. Your pleadings move me not."

When Melun was mine I followed Tom's advice and set my mind toward England. There were practical reasons. Katherine must be formally crowned as Queen of England. And, for the first time since I set foot in France, I was in need of money. John wrote that I must come soon.

"The people forget what you look like," his letter read. "They thrill at your accomplishments and yet do not quite believe in them, for you have become for them a phantom, a shade. Harry, they have need of flesh and blood. I recall well what a way you have with the people. Tom writes that you are often ill and need rest. Come home to England, good brother."

Home. The word filled me with sweet longing. Tom could manage in France. I would take Katherine to England, see her crowned, and perhaps gain some small measure of reconciliation and peace.

I went first to Paris to observe the Yuletide, for I had not yet been in that city. King Charles was somewhat in his right mind and met me in the rue St. Denis with a great host of men of the town, all clad in red. A swaying procession of black-robed clergy bore the most sacred relics of the city for me to kiss, but I insisted Charles must first be so honored, for he was yet King of France. I searched his eyes for some sign of resentment at his position, but saw only the pale innocence of a babe.

"It is good to see you." He had nodded pleasantly when we met. "Good to see you. Where is Isabeau? Have you slain her yet?"

I explained that Isabeau was well and that she would arrive the next day from Troyes with Katherine.

"Very good. Very good. Now, my boy, there are many people here. You are a king, you know how you must behave. Tell your beads quietly and they shall leave you be. They will wave at you, but the beads shall protect you."

"Of course," I said.

"Very good. You are a wise young man."

The crowd was a large one, not so boisterous as the London throngs but welcoming none the less. They stretched before me, an unending row of open mouths raising a flat din not unlike the cawing of crows, an impenetrable mass with no mark save that shrill shared voice. We must have been to them equally formidable. Rank upon rank of armed knights thundering by on thickly muscled coursers, all plumes, velvets, cloth-of-gold. Kings, unreachable, not men, powerful, both wise and foolishly cruel, anointed of God. See the young one from England, they would say, how handsome, how grand, but cold. He controls our fate, that one, surveys proudly his conquest. What knows he of our fears, our hunger pangs?

What knew they of my humanity?

I rode on and wondered which of us had wounded the other more.

Paris is a pretty place, much like London, with her river flowing beneath the towers and spires. The churches of Paris are unmatched. Notre Dame floats majestically upon her island in the Seine, a fit offering for the Blessed Virgin. Most exquisite of all is Sainte-Chapelle, for her windows seem a very wall of glass and the light splashes rainbows of red and green and blue onto the pale faces of men so that they glow like many-hued angels. I fell in love with Sainte-Chapelle, but in the end I cared not a whit for Paris, so like London yet not London. It is a haughty, affected place, Paris, without London's earthy humor. Perhaps I am unfair. Perhaps it seemed so because I knew only of Paris' decaying royal court and not of her taverns. I longed to venture from the cavernous palace of the Louvre and seek some warm hearth, but of course it was impossible. I closed my heart to Paris and dreamed of my England.

Isabeau and Katherine soon arrived from Troyes, and this new taste of

life with the French royal family did little to cheer me. Katherine greeted
me with a cold kiss and refused to allow me into her bed that night.

"You have ignored me these months," she said at my protest. "Now it is
you who must wait."

She spent her days closeted away with her ladies and, I suspected,
visitors from her father's court. I was left in the company of Charles and
Isabeau. Charles was sometimes lucid, sometimes not. On his good days he
would chat amiably about the most trivial of subjects and toss in peculiar
observations which we all must smile and nod at. At other times his head
would loll back and his spittle run and he would stare at nothing for hours on
end. Then he would be tended by a little woman named Odette, who was
reputed to share the King's bed. Charles in his trances would shiver uncontrollably, and this Odette would cover him with furs, pat his hand, and wipe
his mouth. I marveled at her, a chinless, mousy woman, but kind and
patient. When Charles had roused himself she would step again into the
background, self-conscious in her plain dress amid Isabeau's ladies. Once I
came upon her alone and asked her why she waited upon the King.

"Your grace, he is kind to me."

"I see by your manner you are lowborn."

"Aye, your grace. My father was a tailor."

"And do you love the King?"

"I suppose I do," she said after some hesitation. "He is kind to me."

I watched her afterward, dull Odette, as she sat by the drooling king,
and I pitied Charles no more.

Isabeau did not mind the presence of her husband's companion, for she
cared little enough for Charles herself. Indeed, Isabeau bore no affection for
any one of her family. Katherine she used, it seemed to me, but did not love.
Her absent son, the Dauphin, she named a "scrawny worm."

"He is like his fool of a father," she complained. "He even has fits,
though they do not last long."

"You speak with contempt of him," I said. "Do you not bear him some
measure of a mother's love?"

"Ha! And why should I? He has been nothing but trouble for me. I
nearly died in the birthing of him, and so it has been ever since. Do you
know, he once had a lover of mine sewn into a sack and thrown into the
Seine? And he drove me from the court. Is that a son? Why should I love
him? Besides, he is a coward. No, he is no match for you." She simpered and
patted my cheek. "You are my son now, are you not? Upon you I bestow my
motherly affection."

It was a gift I wanted no part of.

With Isabeau's return to Paris, the banquets and dances resumed. Isabeau had her own minstrels, her own fools, her own actors to put on plays for

the court, and she would be entertained by no others. She had now a new sport as well, a company of dwarves given to her by the young Duke of Burgundy. One night they came toddling out, all clad in nut-brown jerkins with tiny pointed hoods. They wore shoes with points nearly as long as their own stubby bodies. Isabeau cackled at the sight of them.

"Here they are, my newest little pets. What have you for us, my little loves?"

It was a joust they played at, complete with tiny wooden lances. Two of the larger men among them acted as horses and whinnied and pawed the earth. There were dwarf squires as well, and dwarf trumpeters, and dwarf ladies with tall headdresses perched upon round little heads. The audience shrieked with delight at this parody of knightly antics. The "knights" charged. One was caught square in the throat by the flattened lance of his opponent and fell with a surprised grunt, flinging his lance nearly the length of the tile floor. The onlookers cheered while the poor fellow clutched his throat and gasped for breath. He was swarthy, with wild tufts of black hair and thick eyebrows which met above a flat nose. His beady black eyes rolled in panic and then rested upon me. I watched in fascination as he regained his breath. The other dwarves were bowing mechanically and bending over to collect gold nobles thrown to them by Isabeau and her courtiers. At last the fallen knight gained his feet, but the coins were all gathered up and he could but limp away on his bowed legs.

I went sickened to my bedchamber with a dwarf fantasy teasing my thoughts. I would renounce the throne of France, renounce the throne of England, my marriage to Katherine, everything. Then I would rescue the dwarves from Isabeau's clutches and take them—where? To some faraway mountains where they need not joust or be laughed at but might live in peace, live as anyone else. This reverie was strangely compelling, comforting, and I sat before the fire and nursed it with a cup of wine. The flames were a blur when there came a knocking at the door.

"The Queen of France to see your grace," said my attendant, and Isabeau burst in before I could say aye or no.

"I wish to speak with you. Alone," she said.

I sighed and nodded to the attendant, who bowed and left us.

"You did not enjoy the evening," she said. "I saw it in your face."

"You are very observant. Why are you here?"

"To say I am sorry."

"Sorry?"

"I want you to be happy but you are not. Who can blame you? That selfish Katherine, silly child, denies you her bed. You must be mad with desire by now, unless you have taken a lover. Of course you mistreated her, but it should not come to this. I tried to shake some sense into her but it does no good. Then you were so sad tonight. So I have come to console you."

She stepped closer. Her eyes were larger and darker than usual. She wore a gown of green velvet with a thick collar of white fur.

"Sometimes you are so strong, so masterful, and other times you are like a lost little boy. Let me hold you. Let me love you."

I opened my mouth but no words would come. She stood against me now, the gown opened, and she wore nothing underneath it. Her heavy breasts sagged nearly to her waist, like the pointed tits of a sow.

"Come to Isabeau," she moaned, and reached for my groin.

I roused myself and pushed her away roughly, so that she staggered and nearly fell.

"Queen you may be," I said, "but I name you a harlot. Do you think I could love one such as you? Go from me."

Her face contorted into a mask of hatred. "Bastard!" she screamed. "Whoreson, dung-eating English bastard! How dare you use me so?" She began to pant. "Who do you think you are? Usurper's son, Devil's son! I see you watching us, so haughty, so full of judgment. It is you who shall burn in Hell!"

"Get out!"

She rushed at me, the long fingernails seeking to rake my skin. I caught her arms and she screamed again. "I shall laugh to see you burn in Hell! I shall laugh when the Devil has you!"

I dragged her through the doorway and threw her into the arms of the startled attendant.

"Get her from my sight!" I said. "I want her out of here this very night. Send her to the Hotel St. Pol, and her husband the King as well. I shall not have them under the same roof with me."

Her screams echoed the length of the hallway. I sank upon the bed and lay trembling all the night, nor did I sleep for one moment.

The next morning I sent for Katherine and told her of what had passed. She flushed with anger.

"How dare she? Oh, I do hate her for it!"

"Can you not see it, Katherine? She has sought to turn you against me only to satisfy her own lust. It is because of Isabeau that you left my bed."

"It was your neglect of me as well."

"Katherine, if only you could learn to love me. Then it would not matter so much, our separations. I want to care for you. I do not ever mean to neglect you."

I searched her face hopefully, desperately. Her hesitation heartened me.

"Perhaps," she said.

"You have threatened to take lovers," I said. "It may be that I am already a cuckold. But I am willing to forget that, and the harsh words which have passed between us. Please, Katherine, can we not start anew? Your mother's poison has blighted our marriage from the beginning, but I have sent her away for good. I beg your forgiveness if that gives you pain, but it shall be best for us in the end." I squeezed her hands in mine. "I need you so badly. Say that you shall try to love me once more."

She nodded. "I shall try."

I kissed her. When I looked once again into her eyes, they were black with passion.

"Do not wait for the night," she whispered. "Take me now."

When a Queen of England is crowned, the King by tradition stays away from both hallowing and banquet, that he may not divert attention to himself. While Katherine was feted in splendor at Westminster Hall, I supped in my chamber with my brother John, my uncle of Beaufort, and the London merchant Richard Whittington.

"Your Queen is lovely," Whittington said genially over his claret.

"Indeed she is," John agreed. "You are fortunate that mad Charles did not produce a horse-faced daughter."

"How did she at the hallowing?" I asked Beaufort.

"Splendidly. She looked radiant. Everyone was enchanted with her. As the others have said, she is handsome."

"Aye," I said. "She is."

"She gives you some contentment, I hope," said John.

"Aye, she does."

"One would not know it to look at you," Beaufort said. "You are thin, and your face full of care and weariness. You are not the same Harry Monmouth who left England more than three years ago."

"It would be strange if I had not changed," I said.

"True. But men die of such changes as you show."

I glared at him and did not answer.

"Gloomy sentiments, these," Whittington said with false joviality. "The King is weary, of course, but all shall be set right when he has breathed enough good English air."

"Indeed, it is good to be home," I said. "I cannot describe my feelings when the Dover cliffs loomed before us. I wanted to reach out from the ship and embrace them."

"I trust you have been likewise pleased to come home to our governance," John said.

"Aye, you have served me well, brother and uncle. And you, Whittington. The support of your London merchants has made my achievements abroad possible. That is why I invite you here to sup, that I may thank you."

He bowed his head modestly, knowing full well that I was again in need of money.

"We are pleased to be your loyal servants," he replied. "Nor should your grace hesitate to call upon us. Our merchants have found this French venture to their liking. Many of them prosper handsomely."

"But that is not the purpose, of course," I said, pained at his words. "To prosper, I mean. You are fulfilling God's will, to bring peace and justice to His people. That is what is important."

Whittington seemed taken aback for a moment, but recovered quickly. "Of course. We ever seek the will of God."

We spoke for another hour of matters pertaining to France, and then Whittington took his leave.

"It was a pretty speech you made," Beaufort said when the merchant had gone.

"What do you mean?"

"I mean that pious claptrap about the merchants of England serving God. Jesu, Harry, you still speak like the fool of a boy you once were. Whittington shall be snickering all the way home."

"Do you demean the justice of my cause?"

"What matters your cause? What is a cause? You are Regent of France, and shall be King when that idiot Charles is dead. That is what matters." He raised his cup. "To the merchant his coin, and well he deserves it. And to Harry his conquest, and that is well earned as well."

"You sound no man of God to me," I said furiously.

"Faith," he answered. "I seek to praise you, and enrage you instead. No wonder you look ill. You know not how to accept your success."

"Peace!" cried John. "What good is there to such wrangling? You are both stubborn, that I know well, nor do I expect either of you to change. So, then, let us have peace. Good uncle, will you not tell Harry the news you have from Rome?"

Beaufort stroked the point of his black beard, obviously pleased with himself.

"I have been offered the cardinal's hat," he said.

"You shall not take it," I said at once.

For a moment I was affrighted, for I had never seen my uncle so shaken.

"Why shall I not?" His voice quivered. "There are no English cardinals. Think of the honor—"

"I have need of you here. I will not have you running off to Rome upon the Pope's business. Nor will I have you paying the Pope such allegiance. You are to serve me."

"Afore God, Harry, you shall not keep this thing from me! It has been my dream."

"I knew not that men such as you dreamed."

He stood rigid, clenching and opening his fists. "I see now what you have become. You prate of your ideals, as you have ever done. You accuse me of heartless machinations, of using you for my own ends. So have you ever accused me. Yet it is you who use others, Harry. It is you. It is a fine joke, is it not? Poor little Harry, so put upon by his usurping father and conniving uncle and all the others. Yet here he sits, the Regent of France. And who has he devoured along the way? Who has he destroyed? Oldcastle and Percy and Glyndwr—"

"Get out!"

"Courtenay, the innocent—"

"In Jesu's name, I'll not bear such charges from you!"

"—both English and French, all the while posturing and praying, fretting over his soul—"

I reached for the decanter of wine and flung it at his head. He ducked, and it crashed against the hearth, its contents exploding purple in the flames.

"Good night, Nephew," Beaufort said, and left.

I sank onto a bench and buried my face in my trembling hands. "It is not fair," I whispered. "He lies. I have ever tried to do what is right. Why did he seek to wound me so?"

"He spoke from anger," John said. The rustle of his robe as he sat next to me was somehow reassuring. "He is himself wounded. He wants very badly to be cardinal."

"I will not have it." I was more determined than ever. "A cardinal should be devout, saintly. You know as well as I that our uncle is no such man."

"That is not the reason you gave him."

"There is the other as well. I do have need of him. Afore God, how does he think I gained France? It was not by allowing my captains to do as they please. I have kept strict discipline over my men, and I'll not tolerate such independence from him, uncle or no."

"Harry, have a care. You need him, as you say, to govern England. Do not press him too far, or he shall withdraw his services."

"I think not. He has threatened it before, to no avail. He has no one else to turn to, and he would rather be chancellor of England than nothing at all."

It happened that my uncle did not resign, just as I had thought, but he was ever cold with me from that day on.

Despite the counsel of my physicians to rest, I resolved upon a tour of the leading towns of the realm, from Bristol to Shrewsbury, Coventry, and York. I was to show myself to the citizenry, allow myself to be wined and dined, and so encourage the people in their support of my continental venture. Katherine I left in London, for she balked at so much travel.

"Do you not wish to see England?" I cajoled.

"I have seen too much of it. London is backward enough, so that I fear to think what the provinces are like. Besides, it is too cold to bounce around in a carriage."

I left her then and set out with my household upon my journey. The brown and muddy land awaited spring, and the green countryside I loved might never have been. We rode first into the west, and though we stopped short of Wales my heart was weighted with dread at each passing mile. I slept little at Bristol, for I knew that just beyond the Severn estuary lay the little hills of Gwent and the rushing waters of the Wye.

Everywhere I was met by cheering, gaping crowds and petty officials puffed up at this encounter with royalty. Praise, ever praise, and unquestioning adulation were showered upon me. Rebellion and unquiet times were things of the past, it seemed, and fervid protestations of loyalty were the order of the day. Good King Harry, the conquering hero, could do no wrong. I went to my bed each night cursing that demon which curdled the enjoyment of this adulation. And despite my growing recognition of what she was, I longed for Katherine.

She joined me at Kenilworth, at my insistence. Disquieting rumors reached me that she had taken into her bed a squire of her household. She came to me so sullenly that I could but accuse her.

"And if it is true?" she said. "You neglect me as before. I did warn you."

I laughed bitterly. "And if you get a son, whose heir shall he be? It would be a fine joke, would it not? The son of a squire crowned King of England and France all unknowing."

"A fine joke indeed," she flung back at me. "Think well upon it. I am not without my own power, as you are learning."

I sent her from me in anger, but to my surprise she called me to her chamber that night. My desire overcame my pride, and I went. I found her most prettily contrite.

"Forgive my harsh words," she said. "It is only that I want you so, and I am so unhappy when you leave me." She encircled my waist with her arms and laid her head penitently upon my chest.

"If you care so, why do you cuckold me?"

"'Twas you who accused. I did not admit to it, though I did not deny it. I was angry with you today and would give you no easy answer."

"Then you have been faithful?"

"I have. Those who say otherwise speak falsely. Now, will you not love me?"

I studied her doubtfully for a moment, then lifted her in my arms and bore her to the bed.

I sat my mount as the messenger's horse splattered through the April mud of the York road. The news would be bad, for why else seek me out in a lonely high way and stare pale of face while I slit the seal with my dagger? Still I was not prepared for the words Humphrey had written.

> We have engaged the Dauphin's army at Beaugé, and the field belongs to the enemy. Tom is slain. Sir Gilbert Umfraville died as well, and many other knights. No archers died, for Tom took none with him. They say he fought bravely but was outnumbered from the start and sacrificed a strong position in a foolish charge. May God save him. Think not too harshly upon him, Harry. He loved you well and sought to please you with this venture. I shall send to you when I know more. God forgive me that I must bear such news, brother. Come at once, ere all is lost, for the Dauphin's followers are much heartened.
>
> Humphrey.

Doughty, foolish Tom! I ached for him with a childish yearning, to throw my arms about him as when we were boys and he had injured himself in some wild escapade, to chastise and comfort him. Jesu! To seek battle when there was no need, to leave his archers behind, that knightly honor might not be tarnished. I crossed myself and gazed over a freshly plowed field tinted blood red by the setting sun. Soon, across the land, cows and sheep would be driven home, and smoky fires lit upon the hearths. Darkness would cloak the combes and wild moors of that England where Tom had sent me to seek my solace. Scenes of tranquillity were but a mock to me. It was a relief to return to my task in France.

Within four months I put the Dauphinists to rout and recovered all that had been lost by Tom's folly, then set out to capture the town of Meaux. I especially wished to have this place, for it was the seat of a notorious band of ruffians who had terrorized the poor folk of the surrounding countryside. Their leader was called the Bastard of Vaurus, and I had long wished to bring this villain to justice. None in France had more evil reputation than this Bastard. His favorite trick was to murder poor yeomen while they lay abed at night and seize all their goods. The unfortunate man's children would be turned out to face the terrors of the night. The worst fate of all was reserved for the poor wife, who would be ravished repeatedly, then hung in chains from some tree to be finished by the wolves. This was the Dauphin's trusted captain, and I vowed to rid France of him.

It was a long, harsh siege, like Rouen, for the garrison knew they would be given no quarter should they surrender. Time and again they would sally forth, only to be driven back by my ever-vigilant soldiers. Along with these forays a different sort of war commenced. Each morning at sunrise a trumpet would sound and English prisoners were hanged from the walls. When no Englishmen were available, a terrified townsman was dragged from his house and sent to the gallows. My men were much unnerved at this and lived in mortal fear of capture. With chill determination I set up a gallows of my own, and for each Englishman who died upon the walls a Frenchman perished below.

Again I vomited blood and sent for my physician in Paris.

"You should not be here," he chided. "You get little rest and you are too much out in the winter chill. You should go to Paris, at least until spring."

"I cannot leave until Meaux falls. It is my responsibility."

"There is little I know to prescribe for you save rest."

"I swear I shall spend more time abed."

My only joy was in tidings from England, where Katherine had unhappily remained. By the summer it was known that she was with child, and in December she gave birth to a son.

A handsome, healthy son, John wrote. *We name him Henry, for Katherine insists upon it. The bells of London town do ring for him.*

Wings of hope fluttered in my heart. My son. I lay upon my back, squeezed my eyes shut, and sought to conjure him: wee babe with red skin and tightly clenched fists. Poor little one, for he would be a king, if he lived. I prayed for him fervently, that God might sustain him, that I might see him soon, that he would not grow to hate me for his fate. I wrote urgently to John that the child must be loved.

"I fear Katherine may neglect him. She has known little enough of maternal love herself, poor girl. Send for Joan Waryn, for I know she shall love the babe."

But Joan Waryn was ill and feeble and still would not leave her Monmouth. The child did not lack for nurses or attention, John wrote, and I must be content with that.

It is a frightening thing, the birth of a child, for it calls one's life into question. To become a father is to meet mortality and to ask what shall be handed down at death. Likewise the tenderness of a father's love opposes the cruelty of war. I fought the pains that seemed to rip my belly asunder, and the clinging weariness, and wondered how much of real good I had accomplished. True, I had brought some stability to Normandy, but how much more might I do if I were freed of fighting? Must I in truth defeat the Dauphin, from town to battered town, year after year? Why not treat with him, now that the crown would be mine, leave him the south of France, let him be king of it? Then treat with Sigismund as well and rule in peace, establish justice, watch the fields bloom with their bounty.

I sent to the Dauphin at the Yuletide. Would he but discipline the Bastard of Vaurus and recognize my claim to the crown and those lands I held, I would retire from Meaux and leave him to rule his present territories.

My envoys were insulted by the Dauphin and turned away. Twelfth Night passed, and the hangings resumed.

The garrison of Meaux held out until May, when starvation forced their surrender. The Bastard of Vaurus was seized and beheaded, to the delight of the peasantry, and his body I left unburied for the wolves. The severed head was set upon a pike at the gate to the city, its face set in the grotesque leer imposed by sudden death. I passed beneath it as I made my entry and saw it that night in my dreams. The head would not rot upon its stake, and the grin was one of triumph.

Katherine came to me at Paris and gasped when she saw me.

"You are so thin! What has become of you?"

I perched uncomfortably upon a bench and sought to hide the effort I made to sit up.

"I have the bloody flux," I said, "yet I recover."

"Men die of the bloody flux!"

"I recover!" I said. "Did I not just say so? Tom had it before Agincourt, and he lived. Most do."

She sat next to me. "I did not bring the babe. The physician says he is yet too young."

"I know it."

"Are you disappointed?"

"Of course. I want nothing so much as to hold him."

"Nothing?"

"Nothing."

She looked away. "If you wish to see him so badly, you may go to England."

"Of course I cannot."

"Is it so bad to be there? You did not mind to leave me there, though I did protest it."

"I left in a hurry, as you well know. I had much to attend to. And then I heard you were with child. I wished the babe to be born in England."

"Why is that so important? It may be the babe has no drop of English blood in him."

I stared at her in horror. "What mean you?"

She smiled with her lips pressed tightly together.

"What mean you?" I cried again. "You told me you were faithful."

"Perhaps I lied. And perhaps I did not lie. Perhaps I have been faithful and the babe is yours. Yet I like it not that you think more of a babe than me. It is a scrawny, whining babe and not to be set above me. It is bad enough that you make yourself ill with work so that you cannot love me."

I stood to flee from her presence but collapsed in a black whirl of senselessness.

Too weak to sit a horse, I was borne on a litter to Vincennes, a pretty castle set in a green and pleasant wood where I thought to rest. I was lodged in the largest chamber of the keep but soon moved to a tiny turret where I might look out the window from my bed. Humphrey came to me there from his post in Normandy, and Warwick as well.

"You were better occupied in your duties than in this visit," I pretended to grumble, but smiled to show I was indeed glad of their company.

They returned my smile but avoided my eyes.

"It is cool here," Humphrey remarked. "The day is fiercely hot, yet it does not touch you here. It must be the trees and the river nearby. . . ." His voice trailed off.

"Why do you come?" I asked. "Is it the babe? Is he ill?"

Humphrey shook his head. "It is not the babe," he said. "It is you, Harry. We have been summoned by your physicians and your confessor, Netter. Harry. Jesu, Harry, they say you are dying."

My heart skipped, fluttered. "No, I am not. I have not finished this work. If it is God's work, He would not take me ere I am done. I am young. I am but thirty-four."

"Harry, they say you are dying. They say you have but a few weeks. You must begin to make arrangements for the governing of your lands."

"No. Many recover from the bloody flux."

"Courtenay did not recover," Warwick said. His eyes were full of pain.

"There is more than the flux," Humphrey said. "You have long had bleeding in your belly which the physicians cannot stanch. God would that it be not so, but you are dying, and you must think on England and France, on your son. You must make arrangements."

I stared at the stone ceiling.

"Go from me," I whispered. "I must consider this."

"Forgive us," Humphrey said, and they left me.

"It is God's work I have been doing," I said aloud, and even as I spoke I knew what the grinning head of the Bastard of Vaurus had told me, what the dead of Wales, of Agincourt, Rouen, and Caen, what my own bleeding body had revealed to me, that it was sin, that it was ever sin and the same sin from time immemorial. Nothing had come from it save the death of everyone and everything I had loved, and the everlasting fires of Hell would be gentle compared to the knowledge of it.

EPILOGUE

I am awaiting a visit from a nun. A sister of the Poor Clares claims she has received a vision of the Virgin Mary and been commanded by Our Lady to go to the King of England. It is the very thing to cheer my dying days, this anticipation of a pronouncement of damnation from that very Lady to whom I have prayed with special fervor all of my life. My confessor, Netter, makes light of my fears. When has Christendom known a more godly or obedient king? he asks. He absolves me repeatedly and sees to the establishment of chantries where devout men shall pray for my soul day and night. None of this brings me peace.

My condition has made me prey to a bitter humor. I take a particular delight in tormenting Warwick.

"Good my lord," I say, "it is a very long way to Westminster, and the heat is very great. How then shall you deal with my body?"

He turns red, wrings his hands, and mutters, "Your grace should not think on such things."

"Why not? What else have I to think on? Come, my lord, what shall be done with me?"

"I believe that the flesh will be separated from the bones by boiling." His voice is thin and strained. "The flesh will be buried here and the bones interred at Westminster."

"The flesh? The bones? You mean *my* flesh, *my* bones. Let us be precise."

"Aye, your grace."

"So I am to be boiled like a haunch of beef until the flesh does fall away all tender. A fitting end to a wasted life, is it not?" I hold a thin arm up to the sunlight. "Think on it. 'Twill not be long now; but a fortnight, the physicians say."

Poor Warwick. It is not fair to discomfit him so, for he has a good heart. But it gives me a perverse pleasure to dig at him, to accost his innocent gallantry with my rotting limbs. He flees my presence as soon as he may.

Never mind Warwick. The nun has come, and I cannot so easily defend myself against her. Netter brings her to me.

"Your grace, this is the woman from the Poor Clares."

The slight figure kneels beside my bed, and Netter stands stolidly behind her.

"Leave us, Netter."

He hesitates, for he opposed this visit.

"Your grace, this woman, I have only just learned, does not belong to the Poor Clares, but is a woman of common parentage. She lives among the sisters and serves their needs, nothing more."

The woman's eyes are cast down. The face beneath the kerchief is round and plain, the nose large, the brows thick, the skin rough.

"What is your name?"

"I am called Marie, your grace."

"Leave us, Netter."

"Is it wise, your grace? I would not have you upset. It is strange to me that Our Lady would present herself to a peasant woman such as this."

"Was not Our Lady a peasant woman? Leave us."

I bid the woman rise and be seated beside my bed.

"So, Marie, you have seen Our Lady?"

"Ah, *oui!*" When her eyes glisten, they are almost lovely.

"Was she very beautiful?"

"I could scarcely bear to look on her. She shone with a light which is not of this world, in truth."

"I fear to ask you but I must know. What message has Our Lady entrusted you to bring to me?"

"Oh, your grace, no message. She said I should come to you, and that is all."

"No message?"

It is perplexing, and somehow more unsettling than the words of doom which I had expected. Marie's cheeks are mottled with red.

"Forgive me if I have disappointed the King," she says.

I shake my head and stare at the crucifix that hangs upon the wall at the foot of my bed.

"I know fear more than disappointment," I say to her. "I despair of my soul. Yet am I resigned to my fate, for it is not important. Nor do I think the torments of Hell could exceed those I now suffer. I have made all the wrong choices, Marie. It is the dead I think upon now. If my damnation might bring them to life again, then would my burden be lifted."

"God shall bring the dead to life again," she says softly. "I long for the day."

"In heaven they shall live again. But that gives me no comfort. I have robbed them of their earthly time. I have sought power to preserve the good, and even so I have destroyed it. I think now there is no good unless it also be weakness. I have lacked the courage to be weak. But then I think, how could I have walked away from my crown? Must not the powerful seek to do good? What shall we do, Marie? Have you no message at all?"

Marie is weeping. "The Virgin would wish me to comfort you, yet I know not what to say. I am but a poor woman with no learning."

We do not speak for a very long time.

"You are dying." I start at the sound of her voice. "I did not know it before I came here."

I pass a hand over my eyes.

"I am sorry," she continues. "I recall how you were long ago. You were weary and ragged, yet a light did shine in your eyes."

I stare at her. "You knew me long ago?"

"*Mais oui*. Do you not recall? You came to our village with your soldiers. You slept before my hearth. You told stories to my little ones."

It comes to me again: the long road to Agincourt. Old Guillaume and his grandchildren, Colette and Raoul.

"How are they, the little ones?" I ask their mother, for I know her now.

"Dead these two years," she whispers, "all four of my babes, and their father and old Guillaume as well. Killed by English soldiers who came to our village."

"Jesu!"

"They ravished me and left me for dead. I could not bury my babes, for the wolves came. When I was brought to the sisters, I knew not who I was, and only their prayers restored my mind. That is why I stay with them. When the Virgin appeared to me, I did not wish to obey her, for I feared I would go mad again at the sight of you."

I cover my face with my hands, for I wish to hear no more.

"How you must hate me!" I cry. "I brought this upon you."

"So you did," she says. "And I have tried to hate you, but now that I see you here, I cannot. I yet recall the stories you told us, of Arthur your king and the young Galahad. They were lovely, those stories. And you were so gentle with my babes. Never did they forget you. How then may I hate you?"

She kneels suddenly, and her lips are like the brush of a butterfly's wings upon my forehead.

"I shall light a candle for you every day of my life, but I shall not mourn for you. You die because you must, and I have been healed at last."

And she is gone.

How then may I hate you?

I do not think I hate you, and when my da comes I shall tell him so.

I have not wept since Merryn's death, but the tears are upon me now, blinding me. My thin chest is racked with sobs. I weep for Jack and Courtenay, for Rhys and Tom, for my father, for all the nameless ones, for us all. I bury my face in the softness of my pillow and give myself over to my grief.

The dead yet crowd my dreams, but they accuse no more. Their faces are pale and sad, and touched with wisdom.

"Harry," they say.

Only that.

"Harry."

I am shriven. It is night. The voices float out of the darkness, hover above my head.

"It is not long now. He drifts from us."

Netter holds me in his arms, my head cradled against his chest. I listen to the rise and fall of his breathing.

My fingers wander along the smooth edges of the crucifix. "I have meant no one harm."

"*Pacem.*" Netter says. His hand tightens upon my arm.

Someone is chanting, far away.

"Jesu, mercy."

They hold guttering candles and peer at me, their faces afire.

"He is yet with us."

The faces swim, the fire recedes. Chanting.

Hissing.

"Come, you are mine."

He rises up and beckons, his hand grasps for me, clutches.

"You lie! You lie! My portion is in the Lord Jesus Christ!"

"*Pacem! Pacem!*"

"*In manus tuas, domine . . .*"

I see her. She stands beside the green river, and the wind catches her hair. How ever did I forget?

I long to call her but I am so weak.

"Mer-"

A voice weeps faintly.

"He has seen Our Lady."

"Merryn! I love you!"

She waves and calls to me.

"Harry! See, I have kept my promise. It is not yet over."

The wide river flows between us. The water is clear as glass, and passing cold when I enter it.

If only I may cross.